Reviews of
QUICKSILVER: a greyhound at sea

Overall Rating: ★★★ **Three Stars: Recommended. A solid effort.** Commander Wells writes with authority which makes this fictional account of a destroyer's action during the Viet Nam war very readable... The characters come alive and most readers will find themselves putting names and faces to each from their own experiences... The day to day life at sea is familiar to any who has been there...and one can almost feel the sea beneath them as they read. The detail on every page will keep the reader attached. The author's credibility is established early on and continues to the end... Two or three story lines are too important to reveal in a review and the readers will have to find them for themselves. They add personal and tragic dimensions to this well written novel about a time that many might like to forget.

Bernie Ditter
Reviewer, Tin Can Sailors
The National Association of Destroyer Veterans

Thoroughly enjoyed <u>**QUICKSILVER: A Greyhound At Sea**</u>, and I've asked our manager to order copies to sell in our gift shop. Our ship, the USS TURNER JOY (DD-951), now a museum ship in Bremerton, Washington, was one of the two ships that took part in the Gulf of Tonkin Incident, and as such, has a close connection with the Vietnam War. It seems only natural that this book should be available in our book selection. I was "downstairs" – and had little appreciation for the doings of the folks "upstairs" – the guys that got us there, and back, in one piece. We were young then, and I'd forgotten how exhausted we were most of the time...

William Metcalf
Executive Director
Bremerton Historic Ships Association

QUICKSILVER

a greyhound at Sea

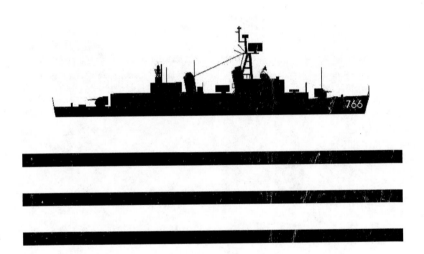

CDR Jack L. Wells,
United States Navy (RC),
Retired

Copyright © 2007 by Jack L. Wells

ISBN 0-7414-4059-8

Published by:

INFIN∪ITY
PUBLISHING.COM

1094 New DeHaven Street, Suite 100
West Conshohocken, PA 19428-2713
Info@buybooksontheweb.com
www.buybooksontheweb.com
Toll-free (877) BUY BOOK
Local Phone (610) 941-9999
Fax (610) 941-9959

∞

Printed in the United States of America

Printed on Recycled Paper

Published December 2007

Dedication

To the brave men and women of the U.S. Armed Forces who served in the combat zone during the Vietnam War.

Preface

This is an historical novel and is based roughly on the experiences of the officers and enlisted men who served their country on destroyers during the Vietnam War. It is not an action adventure as such, although there are multiple action sequences. It is my attempt at a realistic chronicle of a real war and the action sequences are interspersed with human interaction and normal at-sea evolutions.

If someone who was there at the time sees themselves or someone they think they know in this book, please ignore it. It is not intentional. The characters are a compilation of many people I met or made up. I did use some of my own experiences, along with others, using different people and locations. Please forgive the wrong dates, wrong ships, wrong aircraft, wrong call signs, and wrong details. Some of the ships in this book never existed. They are figments of my imagination, although the class types and capabilities are, to the best of my knowledge, historically correct. A novel allows an author to be creative. It is as technically accurate as any remembrance 40 years later can be. Today's Navy is significantly different and ultimately more capable.

USS LARTER (DD-766), herein a Gearing class destroyer which fictionally underwent Fleet Rehabilitation and Modernization, never existed. Hull number 766 was originally laid down as LANDSDALE, but was never completed. But, LARTER is representative of the multiple FRAM I destroyers who served their country in the waters off Vietnam. Over the intervening years, all FRAM I destroyers have been scrapped or transferred to allied governments. Now most of the transferred units have also been scrapped. Two have been preserved in museums: USS J.P. KENNEDY (DD-850) rests at Battleship Cove, in Fall River, MA. USS ORLECK (DD-886) rests at the Southwest Texas War Memorial and Heritage Foundation, in Orange, TX. Many historic ship museums have also restored or maintained other ships that you may tour. They are worth a visit.

I hope this accurately depicts the day to day life of those young men who spent deployments on destroyers away from home and loved ones during this period. It was not a fun time for them. For most, it was a time of limited sleep and frustration. A time of loneliness missing loved ones, and a time of tension under fire. But also a time of community with the others in the same boat, literally and figuratively.

I have tried to limit the jargon, or at least translate it as much as possible. However, some jargon is essential for conveying real life situations, especially the combat sequences. For those who desire more information, please consult the extensive end notes, which amplify the brief descriptions in the main text, and which will help those without some knowledge of the US Navy of the sixties, place situations in context. The end notes are for the purist, and are not essential for enjoying the story. Just prior to the end notes are the credits which list where the photos, maps and drawings came from, along with permission to publish. The web site, **www.JackWellsAuthor.com**, has some additional interior and exterior photos of FRAM I destroyers.

Some passages, including some in the end notes, are my opinions formed while aboard ship or in the war zone. Agree or disagree as you wish. I have tried to build in attitudes towards social situations and the Vietnam War that were prevalent in the US Navy at the time. Many are far different today.

I have also tried to explain some of the odd Navy traditions. When a sea service develops over hundreds of years, some words and even actions that made real sense over 200 years ago remain, even if no longer relevant. They become part of the mystique.

This was written from the viewpoint of a mustang officer, or an officer with prior enlisted service; something I experienced, and a different perspective from those who were enlisted or were commissioned alone. Prior enlisted service gives an officer insight.

And my respect and gratitude goes out to all those who served and the few who did not come home or who came home irreparably damaged. War is hell for all, but it is a special hell for those who grieve or are left maimed.

Jack Wells, November, 2007

Watch for a follow on novel
Paper Dragon, Wooden Ship
Which traces Patrick Dillan's career through
1969, and 1970, to be published mid 2008

ii

USS LARTER (DD 766)

Mount 51   Bridge   Director   ASROC   Hanger   Mount 52

USS LARTER (DD 766)

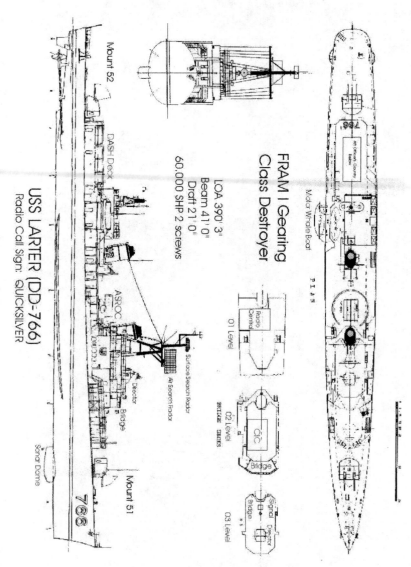

Mount 52

DASH Deck

USS LARTER (DD-766)
Radio Call Sign: QUICKSILVER

Sonar Dome

766

Mount 51

Bridge

Director

ASROC

Air Search Radar

Surface Search Radar

Motor Whale Boat

**FRAM I Gearing
Class Destroyer**

LOA 390' 3"
Beam 41' 0"
Draft 21' 0"
60,000 SHP 2 screws

PLAN

01 Level — Radio Central

02 Level — CIC / Bridge

03 Level — Signal Bridge / Director

Fleet Rehabilitation and Modernization program

FRAM I Group B Tall Mast

Twin Gun Mount

As installed (2) on USS LARTER (DD 766)

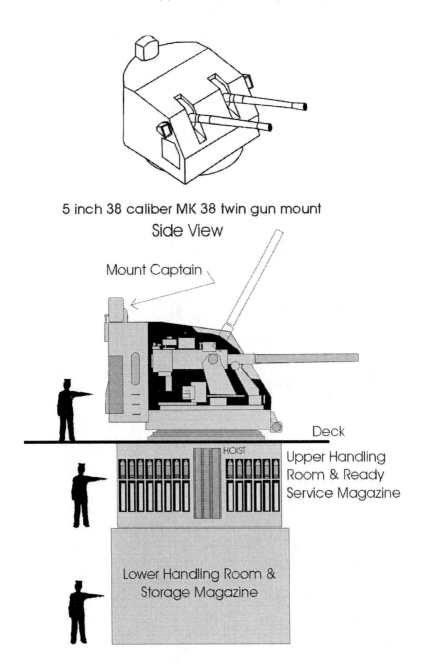

5 inch 38 caliber MK 38 twin gun mount
Side View

Mount Captain

Deck

Upper Handling Room & Ready Service Magazine

HOIST

Lower Handling Room & Storage Magazine

USS LARTER (DD 766) Officers

Billet	Rank / Name / Service
	Source Home
Commanding Officer (CO)	CDR Mike Norcourt, USN
	USNA 51 CA
Executive Officer (XO)	LCDR Chuck Peterson, USN
	USNA 53 MN
	LCDR Jim Henderson, USN
	USNA 53 ND
Chief Engineer (ENG)	LT Eric (Red) Redmond, USN
	NROTC 56 WI
Weapons Officer (WEAP)	LT Chris Harcourt, USN
	USNA 61 IL
Operations Officer (OPS)	LT Fred Finistry III, USN
	USNA 62 MA
Supply Officer (SUP)	LTJG Tony Carpiceso, USNR
	OCS 65 NY

***Engineering*:**

Main Prop. Assistant (MPA)	LTJG Eric Ebersol, USNR
	NROTC 65 PA
Damage Control Assist. (DCA)	ENS/LTJG Sam Blongerinski,USN
	USNA 66 MI

Weapons:

Assistant Weapons (W)	LTJG Len Ottaway, USNR
	OCS 65 NY
ASW (WA)	ENS/LTJG Jim Kirpatrick, USNR
	OCS 66 RI
Gunnery (WG)	ENS Billy Hoffman, USN
	NROTC 67 TN
First Lieutenant (WD)	ENS/LTJG Joe Rederman, USN
	USNA 66 VA

Operations:

Combat Info. Center (OI)	LTJG Ted Brunshall, USNR
	OCS 65 TX
Communications (OC)	**ENS/LTJG Patrick Dillan, USN**
	OCS/NESEP 66 OH
Electronics Material (OE)	ENS/LTJG Pete Donovan, USNR
	OCS 67 PA

THEATER MAP
Naval Operating Areas SE Asia

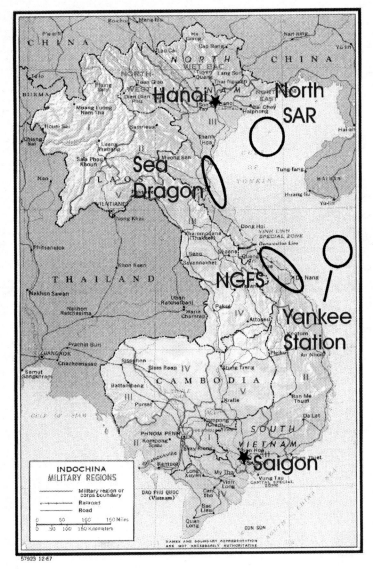

Theater Map - East Asia

Theater Map - PUEBLO Incident

Combat Information Center (CIC)

Note two air scopes in background, surface scope on right, NC-2 plotter on left, sound powered phone and radio hand set above plot table.

Bridge

Note helm on right, lee helm in center, pelorus in background under window.

> **Above all, Vietnam was a war that asked everything of a few and nothing of most in America.**
>
> --Myra MacPherson, 1984
> Journalist at the Washington Post
> Author of the Vietnam War classic,
> *Long Time Passing*

1

Haze gray. Everything was haze gray...the ocean, the sky, the ship. Just like steaming around inside a big gray ball. Water almost like glass with a few undulating swells. Outside the temperature was 92 with 98% humidity, a steam bath. On the weather decks one's uniform turned to mush in 10 minutes. But the bridge was air conditioned, at least somewhat. Early November, 1967, and a month into what was supposed to be a six month war zone deployment.

Ahead was the aircraft carrier, about 1100 yards, moving directly away, a dark grey monster in the haze. You are supposed to be 1000 yards astern, but the carrier was going 30 knots trying to get some wind across the deck, and the old destroyer could only do 27 knots on 2 boilers, so slowly it fell behind.

The F-4 Phantoms came swooping overhead, gear and flaps down, wings drooping, like great blue herons making a landing. They dumped JP-5 jet fuel all over as they dropped toward that elusive "meatball" light that showed them they at least had a chance of catching a wire and landing on what looked like a moving postage stamp from the pilot's view. As they cut back on their throttles, they made a puff of dark grey smoke. They dumped fuel to minimize the amount they were carrying in case of an "awh shit." It came down in a mist. Smelled like kerosene. Messy. And the ship's topsides all had a dirty sheen. Soot, salt, and jet fuel mixed. The bridge windows needed washing often.

As the Junior Officer of the Deck (JOOD), 12-16 watch, ENS Patrick Dillan, USN, was bored to death, tired, and his knees and feet hurt. Over the past 24 hours he had been standing on the steel bridge deck for almost 16 hours and had about 3 hours sleep. A bit punchy, he had to fight to keep his eyes open. So much for the glory of naval combat operations in the crummy little war called Vietnam.

Dillan was a 25 year old, who graduated from Officer Candidate School (OCS) in Newport, Rhode Island, a year prior. He got his regular USN commission through the Navy Enlisted Scientific Education Program. Most USN officers were graduates of the United States Naval Academy at Annapolis, Maryland. Dillan was previously enlisted, was lucky enough to get selected, and in June of 1966, got a degree in Electrical Engineering from Ohio State. Then, OCS, some other schools, and orders to this ship, USS LARTER (DD-766).

He stood there in his starched washed khakis, binoculars hanging from their neck strap resting on his chest, dark blue ball cap with the ship's name embroidered on it, one little gold bar on each of the collar points of his short sleeve shirt. Almost 5 feet 9 inches tall, moderately thin, short blond hair, blue eyes, a small moustache he had just started. With his blond hair he took a lot of heat from his peers for trying to grow an invisible moustache.

ENS Patrick E. Dillan, USN: 702189/1100, his service number and designator. Unrestricted Line, Regular Navy.[i]

USS LARTER was a Gearing class destroyer, initially commissioned in June, 1945. She was 22 years old and showed it in many ways, almost as old as Dillan. A close look at her side plating, especially near the bow, and one could see the oil canned plates and the outline of the frames and stringers underneath, since the plating was thin; like looking at an under cooked waffle.

Full load displacement 3200 tons, 390 feet long, 41 feet wide, 21 foot draft with the big under the bow mounted sonar dome, 2 shafts, 60,000 shaft horsepower from two steam turbine sets: a bit of steel and aluminum wrapped around a big engine. In April, 1965, LARTER had completed the Fleet Rehabilitation and Modernization program (FRAM) and was extensively changed.

Now she carried 2 each twin 5 inch 38 caliber gun mounts, 2 triple tube MK 32 ASW (Anti-submarine Warfare) torpedo tubes, and one Anti Submarine Rocket (ASROC) 8 cell launcher canister. A small helicopter deck and hanger was installed for the Drone Anti-submarine Helicopter (DASH). She also got lots of new electronics. Living and working spaces were rehabilitated, the bridge was enclosed, and she was air conditioned. This was a big habitability issue. There was nothing hotter than a steel ship in the tropics.

She was home to 278 men – 14 officers normally (she had 15 now) and 260 enlisted normally (she had 263 now): staffed up to wartime complement. She had 4 boilers, and with all 4 on the line, she could do 34 knots. But with 4 boilers on line, she burned fuel at an alarming rate. So with 2 boilers on line, using full superheat, she could manage 27 knots and burned almost 30,000 gallons a day.

Painted a light or 'haze' grey on her vertical surfaces and a darker 'deck' grey on her horizontal surfaces, she blended well with her surroundings. The top of the mast, stacks, and antenna platforms were painted black. The only color was the red and blue squadron shield on her side and the small battle ribbons on her bridge, some for World War II, some for Korea, some for Vietnam.

She had black shadowed white numbers on her bow and helo deck. LARTER was painted across her stern in block black letters. Black rubber life raft blobs in grey racks were lined up just aft of the bridge wings and along the DASH hanger roof. She carried one motor whale boat, on a davit on the starboard (right) side of the DASH hanger, complete with a white half shell over its bow.

Small metal pipe cages protruded from her stern on each side. These were to protect things from the props submerged immediately below. There were two Navy stockless anchors mounted on each side of her bow.

When back in the states or in port, she had white canvas stretched over her life rails on the front of the signal bridge, and the top of ASROC launcher control. But at sea, in a war zone, these were removed.

Her primary mission: to hunt and sink submarines.

A directional flashing light signal from the carrier:

C (Charlie) 230 (two three zero), S (Sierra) 12 (one two) then a pause and E (Echo).

Called 'BrevTac', this was sent in Morse code by flashing light and although Dillan couldn't read code he had learned to read Charlie, Sierra, Echo and the numbers. Self preservation was the motivator. A few seconds advance notice. Almost instantly the carrier's shape started to change. She was turning right and slowing down. And things happened quickly.

Dillan thought,

We now have something like 15 knots of relative speed difference and will close the 1100 yards in just over 2 minutes. Wake up boy, time to earn your nickels.

"Bridge, signal bridge, signal in the air from the OTC[ii], corpen[iii] 230, speed 12, standby, execute," came over the 21 MC intercom speaker under the window and waist high in front of

3

Dillan. Courses and bearings were always stated as "two-three-zero" never two hundred thirty. Courses less than 100 were always preceded with a zero: 090 or zero nine zero.

"Bridge, Aye," Dillan said as he pushed the transmit button. The carrier was turning down wind and slowing to 12 knots.

Conventional wisdom said that one should turn in the carrier's wake, continuing to follow.

So much for conventional wisdom; LARTER couldn't slow from 27 knots to 12 knots instantly. If the steam flow to the turbines was cut back before superheat temperature was lowered in the boilers, the steam pressure safety valves would blow – shooting all that hard to get boiler feed water into the air by the ship's smoke stacks and making an awful racket. And the skipper would be pissed, and so also the chief engineer and a whole lot of other folks.

So, as the officer with the "conn" or the one designated to give orders to the helmsman and lee helm (engine order telegraph), he said, "Main control, bridge, drop superheat, we're coming to 12 knots. Do not lift safeties," and the bridge-main control sound powered telephone talker standing behind him pressed the talk button on his head set and repeated what Dillan said into his microphone.

A moment later the talker repeated what he heard in his earphones, "Main control, Aye."

Meanwhile another talker, the one connected to the combat information center said, "Combat recommends turning right to 230 and slowing to 12 knots."

"Aye," from Dillan. Then he gave the order,

"All ahead standard, indicate turns for 12 knots."

The lee helm operator repeated exactly what he said, with an "Aye, aye, sir," at the end, pulled the levers on the engine order telegraph back from full to two thirds, then up to standard, and dialed in 3 numbers on the gray box corresponding to shaft revolutions for 12 knots as shown on the engraved placard in front of him.

Pulling the levers caused the device to emit a ding as each position was passed. Engine orders were based on speed ranges. When maneuvering turns (888) were set 1/3, 2/3, standard, and full were 5, 10, 15, and 20 knots respectively. Flank was 25 knots.

There was some overlap in actual speed ranges and incremental speeds were set by setting turns (shaft RPMs).[IV]

Ding, ding, ding and the engine room answered with matching positions and numbers. "Engine room answers up, all ahead standard, turns for 12 knots, sir."

"Very well."

The distance to the carrier was closing rapidly. When the carrier put her rudders over, she slowed and her stern kicked out to the left as her bow started right. Ships turned around their center of gravity, not their rudder. The carrier was over 1000 feet long so 500 feet was now sticking out to the left.

And a big rudder angle acted like a brake. So LARTER had to turn left and then make a slow turn to the right outside the carrier's wake to keep out of her way and to allow superheat to be lowered.

"Left 10 degrees rudder, steady 030," Dillan ordered. The helmsman repeated and moved the ship's rudders to left 10 degrees.

"My rudder is left 10 degrees," said the helmsman, "Coming to new course 030." Slowly the carrier started to drift right.

"Steady 030, checking 033, sir."

"Very well."

Dillan had been taught that the checking comment was to insure that that the helmsman was steering by the ship's gyrocompass and then checking that course against the ship's magnetic compass. A gyro compass theoretically pointed to true north and a magnetic compass to magnetic north. And they were different. If the ship's gyro ever went out, one could still steer by magnetic compass[V].

The Navy had long since given up on the cardinal points of a compass to tell course directions. Now courses and bearings from the ship were all done in three digit 360 degree format: 000 was true north, 045 North East, 180 dead South, 270 due West, etc. So 359 was one degree short of being back to true North again.

The Navy also used nautical miles and yards for distance. A nautical mile was 2,025 yards. One minute of latitude. The Navy used 2,000 yards. Close enough for government work. A nautical mile was about 15% longer than a statute mile.

This created a unique correlation between speed and distance. If one added two zeros to one's speed in knots (1 knot = one nautical mile per hour), that was the distance the ship would go in 3 minutes, expressed in yards. Called the 'three minute rule', and something every young officer had to be able to apply in his head quickly.

Over the next few minutes as the speed dropped, Dillan made a wide slow turn to the right, and slipped into the carrier's wake, 1000 yards astern and at 12 knots. The Officer of the Deck (OOD) and his boss on the bridge, Lieutenant Junior Grade (LTJG) Len Ottaway, about a year senior, coached him to insure he got on station as soon as possible with no overshoot. Len also picked up the sound powered hand set, and buzzed the captain who was in his sea cabin behind the bridge.

"Carrier went to downwind and we followed, Captain[vi], course now 230 speed 12," he said.

Then to Dillan, "OK, good, right on station."

Leaning against the pelorus[vii], "Happens now and then, Len, just passing through."

The truth was that one was almost never perfectly on station. One was always trying to get there. The carrier wandered a little. LARTER wandered a little. Wind and seas affected the ships differently. Sensors had some inaccuracy so one was always trying to get back to perfection.

USS RANGER (CVA 61) didn't worry as much about superheat. So she could slow from 30 knots to 12 without difficulty. But it kept the old FRAM tin cans on their toes.

The excitement over, it was back to boring. Get a range to the carrier from the surface search radar repeater on the bridge, and cross check it with the hand held statimeter – an optical device for measuring, inaccurately, the range to a known height object like the carrier's mast. It was left over from World War I, pre-radar.

Check to see if the carrier was wandering to the right or left of the given course like it sometimes did by taking a bearing from the pelorus, sighting on the "G" in RANGER on her stern.

Dillan had been told by a World War II Navy veteran that war was 95% boredom, 4 % excitement, and 1% pure fear. So far it was living up to its reputation, very little excitement and no fear.

Follow along like a puppy dog on a leash after the carrier as it made the 30 mile run down wind for the next two and a half hours more or less. Then the carrier would turn back into the wind, crank up the speed and start flight operations again. By then Dillan would no longer be on watch and some one else could worry. Anyway, down wind legs were always easier. The carrier mostly stayed on the same course.

On up wind legs the carrier searched for maximum wind across the deck to make it easier to launch and recover aircraft and if the true wind direction changed the carrier would chase the wind – and in most cases not notify the plane guard destroyer. One had to be aware up wind sometimes. Destroyers had been hit by carriers: bad news for the destroyers.

Dillan also had the mid watch, the 00-04. The Navy, like all military units, used the 24 hour clock. The 00-04 was the mid watch, midnight to 4AM.[viii]

The plane guard destroyer was there to pick up an airplane's crew if it ended up in the drink. After all the days of plane guard, LARTER only picked up two this cruise: pilot and radar intercept officer (RIO) off an F-4 Phantom while doing the workup off Hawaii on the way to Westpac. Dillan never knew exactly why the F-4 didn't get enough airspeed off the catapult, but the plane did not have enough to fly, and as it started down into the sea just off the carrier's deck, the pilot and RIO punched out.

Their ejection seats shot them up to about 1,000 feet, and then their chutes deployed and the seats fell away. A few moments later they were bobbing in the sea. LARTER picked them up with the motor whaleboat about 20 minutes later, wet, cold, but mostly in one piece. The plane made one nose up splash and sank like a brick.

2

Quarter to four (1545). Pete Donavan, another Ensign like Dillan, but about 8 months junior, came on the bridge and over to him.

Dressed just like Dillan he smiled. "Ready to relieve you, sir," he said. Tradition required this be done by the book and watches were relieved 15 minutes early.

"Hey Pete, more than ready to be relieved," Dillan said with joy in his voice. He then helped Pete understand the current situation, what was supposed to happen in the future, and any new standing orders from the captain and the navigator. He filled him in on any major equipment that was inoperative and on the ship's course and speed.

"I relieve you," Pete said. Dillan pulled the strap over his head and handed him the binoculars.

"I stand relieved," was Dillan's reply. "On the bridge this is Mr. Dillan, Mr. Donavan has the conn."

"This is Mr. Donavan, I have the conn," throwing the strap over his head, letting the binoculars rest on his chest and then sequentially turning the focus ring on each eye piece to his personal setting.

The helmsman and lee helm stated what they were doing:

"Helm, aye, steering 230 checking 233, sir."

"Lee Helm aye, all engines ahead standard, indicating turns for 12 knots, sir."

"Very well," Pete answered.

The quartermaster of the watch wrote the change of JOOD and who had the conn in the quartermaster's notebook in pencil.[ix]

Dillan went over to the officer of the deck, saluted and said, "I have been properly relieved by ENS Donavan, sir."

Pete saluted and said, "I have assumed the watch, sir."

The OOD returned the salutes and said, "Very well."

All very formal, there never could be any doubt about who had the watch and who, alone, had the authority to give orders to the helm or engines: the officer with the conn.

Dillan was looking forward to getting his feet above his butt to get some feeling back into them. Then Pete walked over to

Dillan and said, quietly so the rest of the bridge watch could not hear,

"I have a problem. And I hate to bother you with it, but I don't know what to do."

Turning to Pete as he scooped up his empty coffee cup from where he had jammed it in a corner, "OK, what's up?"

"Well, Fred (LT Fred Finistry III, the Operations Officer and Dillan's and Pete's boss) is being a pain in the ass."

"That's not new news; it's in his genes, his life's work."

"But now he's even being a roadblock about ET1 (Electronic Technician First Class Petty Officer)^x Renaldo's recommendation for chief."

"Renaldo is a super ET," Dillan said, "Maybe a few pounds overweight. Fred thinks all enlisted are his slaves. Beat them regularly like gongs. He's a couple of cards short of a full deck in relating to people, but why would he do that?"

"Don't know, but he has decided to withhold my recommendation, which means Renaldo can't take the test this next cycle. He said Renaldo isn't ship shape enough for a chief. Should I go to the XO?"

"Only if you want to be on Fred's shit list. But in your shoes I would."

"OK, I'll go to the XO tomorrow."

As Dillan was leaving the bridge he thought about this a bit. Formulating a strategy, he turned and walked back to Pete's side.

Quietly, "Pete, I intend to talk to Fred on this myself."

"Yeah, right, you're going to talk to Fred. You'll just get your tit in a wringer. You don't need to do that. All that'll happen is that Fred will be on your ass more than he already is. And be pissed at me for telling you."

Dillan answered, "Renaldo worked for me, and he did a super job. His knowledge base is very good, very capable. Good at fixing things. He's a bit on the plump side but a real knowledgeable worker."

Leaning over to Pete, again quietly, "He was one of the major reasons the yard communications suite worked. I have a right to my input as his former division officer. And Fred has no way to know that you blabbed – hell the ship's office could have told me. The PNC (Personnelman Chief Petty Officer) watches Fred."

"I wouldn't have involved you if it meant another confrontation," Pete said. "But I'm pretty much fresh out of options. I'll go to the XO but careful like. You don't have to talk to Fred."

"I love confrontations with that stuffed shirt. Let me have a go at him. I love tilting at windmills."

"OK, Don Q, but be careful. His windmill has whacked many jousters. You'll just get knocked on your ass. He dislikes you now. Don't want to be a part of making that worse."

"Don't think it could get much worse, and I've got an angle than might just work," with a wave.

Dillan left the bridge and immediately, without thinking it over as long as he should have, went to Fred's stateroom. Down the ladders two decks then aft, ship vibrating slightly and men to sidestep in the passageways. And he allowed himself to get wound up tighter as he walked.

Fred was in his stateroom desk chair, feet on his desk, back to the doorway, some folder in his lap. He knew someone was there. But he just ignored him.

Quietly and carefully, "Excuse me, Fred, I heard that you refused to recommend Renaldo for chief?"

Without turning around, "That is none of your concern Dillan; you are no longer involved with OE division; this is between me and Mr. Donovan."

"Renaldo worked for me for almost a year. He did a super job. Our new communications suite was a success because of his actions. I have an interest in his future."

A bit firmer, "You do not have an interest in any enlisted man's future. You would be a lot better served if you worried about your own."

Again, carefully, "I'm asking you to reconsider withholding his recommendation. He's a good Sailor[xi] and deserves a recommendation."

"Go away, you are getting on my nerves," with irritation.

OK mister. You want to play hard ball.

Firmly now, "Fred, I will write a letter of recommendation, with specifics, to Bupers (Bureau of Naval Personnel in

Washington) via the chain of command, and submit it to you and the XO (Executive Officer = 2nd in Command)."

Dillan knew that the XO was obliged to forward such a letter to Bupers via the captain. Not something anyone wanted to have happen counter to his recommendations. Dillan was skating on the edge, the thin edge, but within Navy regulations. Dillan had been the man's division officer for a year, which ended just 3 months ago.

Fred pulled his feet off of the desk, and turned to Dillan.

"That would be very unfortunate Mr. Dillan," Fred said with a dark look, "very unfortunate. I have very good reasons for refusing to recommend Renaldo for chief. Reasons you, as a former enlisted man, are too inexperienced to understand. Are you sure you wish to do this?"

"I will if I have to, sir. And I'll accept the consequences as they may be. But I feel very strongly that you're not seeing Renaldo as he really is, not seeing his capabilities and contributions to this ship, and may be misinformed as to his ability. I have first hand knowledge. I feel that he'll make an outstanding chief petty officer and will both be a technical expert and develop his people into fine petty officers and competent ETs. Again, it was in large part through Renaldo's efforts that we got the new communications equipment up and running and the CO (Commanding Officer, the captain) knows that."

Fred's face tightened up. He just looked at Dillan for a moment. Then in a very stilted and precise voice, "I will take your input into advisement, Mr. Dillan. But do not think that questioning my decision making is something that I will put up with. This discussion has concluded. Dismissed," with a wave of his arm.

Fred turned back around, feet up again, and picked up his folder. The back of his neck was red.

Fred will pull his reservation on Renaldo's recommendation for chief. He has little choice unless he wants to cope with my letter being read by the XO and then CO. It will not be a glowing recommendation, but not disapproval. Let the exam result determine selection.

Dillan stood there a moment. Maybe Fred would say something else. Fred was ignoring him again.

Fred knows he'll lose major face if I write that letter. The XO will not be crazy about it, and even the skipper might not like it. In fact the XO might well try to get me to pull the letter. But if I insist, they are both obligated to forward such a letter to the Bureau, with endorsements. And they both will have little justification for adding anything but "Forwarded, recommending consideration," as the endorsement. Ha. Fred's ace has been trumped.

Dillan started back forward, zig zagging up the main passageway, then up the two ladders; basically narrow steep stairways with chrome hand rails and shiny steel steps.

I have just shot myself in the foot again. Not that my feet are not full of holes already. Like swiss cheese.

3

Dillan was a mustang officer, one with 6 years of prior enlisted service, and took a strong stand against anyone trying to screw over the enlisted men. Once, the previous year, he had served on a Court Martial. And he had been at odds with Fred over dealing with enlisted men then also.

During the shipyard overhaul Dillan was selected to serve on a Special Court Martial. A Special Court Martial was a unique form of court. Not to be confused with the fancy stuff on TV. There were 'trial counsel' or the prosecutor, 'defense counsel', and the court, all appointed by the convening authority – some senior officer. None were lawyers. The court had a president, and 4 other members who all sat at a table in the front.

The accused could have a civilian attorney, at his expense, but few could afford one. The court was essentially the judge and the jury. Witnesses were called and testified and were cross examined. The court members could also ask questions. A 1960s military court martial was for finding out the truth, not protecting the accused rights.

No defense lawyer stage shows. The accused was innocent until proven guilty, but complicated rules of evidence and fancy footwork by attorneys were not part of the game. All evidence was "in" regardless of the source. It was up to the court to determine relevance.

All the ships in the yard had to provide one officer every so often to sit on a court martial. The court was for a Sailor from the base charged with being absent with out leave (AWOL), resisting arrest, and striking the shore patrol petty officer who apprehended him. These were serious charges and multiple violations of the Uniform Code of Military Justice. Found guilty the Sailor would have been looking at some hard time.

Service dress khaki, the uniform with a single breasted coat and black tie, shoulder boards on the coat, collar devices on the shirt, and the court: one LT as court president, 3 each LTJG, and Dillan, junior man, all sitting at the long green table when the trial began. Dillan was the only man from LARTER. He could smell the mothballs that the green wool table cloth had been stored in.

It was a big room in an older building, some sort of conference room, white walls and ceiling, light grey tile floor waxed shiny, folding chairs and tables, and no spectators. A base Master at Arms guarded the only door left unlocked, and was there to bring witnesses in and out.

Seaman David Kaperski, USN, 5452895, was the accused and sat, in his service dress blue jumper uniform, hands folded in his lap, looking down at the defense table, next to defense counsel, a LTJG. Kaperski was about 5 foot 10 inches, thin, and looked to be about 16 although he was just 18. His head had been shaved like a boot camp haircut. He had a couple of nasty red marks on his scalp.

Trial counsel stood and read the charges and specifications, "Violation of the UCMJ (Uniform Code of Military Justice) Article 86 Absent without Leave: to whit, Seaman David Kaperski, USN did, on or about 3 February, 1967, fail to report to his duty station at Naval Supply Center, Long Beach, California, at the required time. He then absented himself from his command until apprehended at 1620, on 8 February, 1967, being AWOL for a period of 5 days and 9 hours more or less."

Then it went on from there. Article 91: Insubordination, Article 92: Failure to Obey a Lawful Order, Article 95: Resisting Arrest, Article 105: Misconduct of a Prisoner, Article 117: Provoking Speeches and Gestures, and Article 134: The General Article - bringing discredit upon the Armed Forces of the United States.

In simple terms, he was subject to court martial for going AWOL and then fighting back when the shore patrol picked him up. However, with all the charges and specifications, the base commander, a US Navy Captain by rank, or someone on his staff, upon convening the court and establishing all the charges was throwing the book at seaman Kaperski.

Trial counsel looked all spit and polish – right off a recruiting poster. He had one tiny red and yellow National Defense ribbon over his left pocket: sometimes called a "gedunk metal" – short for obtainable at a snack bar or "gedunk". Everyone in the service over 3 months got one: obviously, no real sea time.

Dillan thought, probably a shore duty puke. He even pointed at Kaperski at each charge.

Theatrical: This is set up for a railroad.

Seaman Kaperski was in deep shit. Convicted on all counts, he was headed for at least a year at hard labor in Leavenworth Federal Prison, probably along with being busted to Seaman Recruit and forfeiture of pay for the duration. Maybe a bad conduct discharge. The AWOL charge was not a small one. But the others were more serious. Striking a petty officer in the performance of his duty / resisting arrest was a much bigger deal.

When it was time to take seaman Kaperski's plea he pled guilty to being AWOL and not guilty to all the other charges and specifications.

Then the prosecution witnesses started. First their were witnesses from the supply department stating that Kaperski was supposed to report at 0730 on 3 February, and that he did not so report, followed by testimony that he was not present the following consecutive 5 days. No cross.

But in a court martial one still had to attempt to prove a charge even if the accused pled guilty; a fact finding trial.

Then the case got more interesting. Trial counsel called one BM2 (Boatswain's or Bosun's Mate 2nd Class Petty Officer) Patrick O'Malley, USN. O'Malley was about 6 feet tall, big, burley, had 4 hash marks (4 years service each) on his sleeve and looked like a bouncer at a local topless bar. He had a Navy Unit Commendation ribbon, gedunk medal, and Vietnam Service medal.

Over 16 year's service and still only a second class. Not one of the US Navy's brighter lights. Blue uniform jumper stretched tight across a big belly, red face probably from the intake of a significant and daily ration of grog. One row of ribbons, no personal awards and conspicuously missing the Navy Enlisted Good Conduct Medal maroon ribbon most enlisted with over 4 years of service wore.

Hell I've got one and all it really stands for is 4 years of undetected crime. Bet he has been 2nd more than once.

Walking up to the stand the bosun had a definitive swagger. And during the testimony, O'Malley pretty much proved Dillan's initial impression. He spoke with pride about capturing 'deserters' as he called them. Desertion was a big deal and was very hard to prove. One had to make it more than obvious that one never intended to return to the military, burning one's uniforms, and telling others.

O'Malley bragged about all his previous apprehensions and how, if the Sailor resisted, he had ways to bring them back in line. He said he identified Kaperski from a photo his boss had provided. He said that Kaperski had tried to run and then had swung at him. He said that Kaperski had swore at him and told him he was never coming back.

Under cross, O'Malley squirmed in his chair a bit when asked who threw the first punch although he said Kaperski did. Then under more cross he was asked if he beat Kaperski with his billy club. He said he had to get him to stop fighting and get the cuffs on him.

"That seaman," pointing at Kaperski, "swore at me and tried to get away. I had no choice. I had to defend myself," he said.

The court president dug deeper, asking if O'Malley had ever been accused of excessive force. O'Malley's answer, "Once, sir, but that was awhile ago and I cleaned up my act, sir."

There were three other prosecution witnesses. One was a man, a 3rd class, that had been in the paddy wagon when the arrest was made and who did not see much but who could testify that O'Malley had told him that, "This piece of shit tried to get away." This was hearsay evidence generally not admissible in a civilian trial but admissible in a court martial.

The other two prosecution witnesses were Marine guards at the base brig that testified about Kaperski's condition and general demeanor after being brought to them. Angry and hurt was the opinion, but a cooperative prisoner. A corpsman[xii] had been called to administer to Kaperski's wounds.

Finally the prosecution rested and trial counsel sat down with a pleased look

Defense counsel was another LTJG, neat and clean, but not a recruiting poster child. Two ribbons, gedunk and Armed Forces Expeditionary, at least some sea time, probably east coast, Dillan thought.

The defense called two witnesses. The first was a civilian and reportedly Kaperski's girl friend, a small mousey looking woman in a granny dress. She said that she and her 2 year old daughter were very sick and that Kaperski had stayed to help them get well. She indicated that he knew he had to go back to the base soon and that he would be in trouble for not coming back on time. She said she was in the house and did not come out until she heard

Kaperski screaming and then she saw O'Malley sitting on his back pulling his arms into hand cuffs, and that Kaperski was bleeding from his head.

In cross, the trial counsel fooled around trying to get her to admit that she heard Kaperski swear at O'Malley unsuccessfully. Then he asked if the child was Kaperski's.

"No, the child is another Sailor's who was transferred."

Trial counsel was not as happy walking back to his chair this time, concern on his face.

Then it was Kaperski's turn. He slowly walked up and sat in the witness chair when defense counsel called him, and looked down at his hands for awhile until sworn in. He admitted that he had gone AWOL to help his girlfriend and intended to come back. He said he was wearing civilian clothing but had his uniforms in the house.

He said he did not resist arrest and that O'Malley had started in on him with the club even when he was on the ground covering his head with his hands. He said he screamed in pain and told O'Malley to stop. He showed a left hand with an oversized band-aid.

On cross, and sensing that he was loosing it, the trial counsel tried to get Kaperski to admit that he took a swing at O'Malley. "No sir, never took a swing at him," was all Kaperski would say.

Dillan asked, "Seaman, at any time did you resist arrest or do anything to make O'Malley think you were resisting?" Kaperski said he had just lain face down and had put his hands on the back of his head when O'Malley yelled, "Stop, hit the deck, you f'ing deserter."

Summations were as expected. The court went into closed session and quickly and unanimously came to a verdict.

And Dillan, along with the four other officers including the LT court president, found the Sailor innocent of all but AWOL. It was somewhat obvious that the shore patrol man had decided to teach the Sailor a lesson and started in on him with a billy club. All the Sailor was doing was defending himself.

Prior to sentencing it was time for matters in extenuation and mitigation. Basically a chance for the court to find out what kind of Sailor Kaperski was and whether he had been in trouble before. Also a chance for the trial counsel, now not so well off, to ask for the harshest sentence he could.

Kaperski had not been in trouble before but he was not a star Sailor either – being a bit lax with his duties. Trial counsel asked for 6 months in the brig and a bad conduct discharge – penalties that were not in keeping with the first offence guilty verdict.

The court met again in closed session. The court president proposed a sentence and all concurred. They sentenced Kaperski to reduction in rate to Seaman Apprentice, and 30 days in the base brig, time served to count. The sentence was lenient, but Kaperski had already been beaten and in the brig for two weeks of pre trial restraint.

Navy brigs ashore, operated by US Marines, were pure hell. Far worse than civilian prisons in many respects. Like a chain gang. Men were worked hard 16 hours a day, doing grunt work with no meaning. Like hauling telephone poles from one side of the yard to the next, and the following day hauling them back. They were caged the rest of the time, and utter silence prevailed.

No books but a Bible and Navy Regulations, no TV, no conversation, and no feeling of self worth. Sunday morning enforced church, Sunday afternoon locked up. It was the ultimate form of regimentation. Prisoners even had to call their enlisted Marine guards, "Sir." This was unique. Enlisted were never called "Sir" except in boot camp for drill instructors.

The court also recommended that O'Malley be brought up on charges for the use of excessive force in apprehending a prisoner. Dillan figured that the chances of that happening were nil. O'Malley would probably get transferred to some ship headed west.

When Fred found out the results he thought the verdict was a travesty even though he was not present for the trial. And he blamed Dillan's attitude toward enlisted men as one of the reasons the Sailor got off easy. Fred believed strongly that firm discipline and making appropriate examples of transgressors was the only way to deal with ruffian enlisted men.

Dillan got a lecture which went something like,

"You can not coddle these people. They need to know their place. They need to be kept in line. You can't have them think they can run off or strike a petty officer and get away with it.

I'm sure you swayed the court Dillan. You talked them out of guilty verdicts on the other charges. That is unconscionable. You are an officer now and you damn well better act like one."

When Fred was in one of these moods, Dillan generally did not talk back since it only incited Fred.

This is a bit much. Fred is being a hard ass. Careful now, a little of your seldom used diplomacy might be appropriate.

So Dillan said, "Being an officer doesn't mean that I gave up being interested in facts verses conjecture. You judged this case and you weren't even at the trial. You have no right! The man was acquitted of all but the AWOL charge because he was innocent of all but the AWOL charge. The shore patrol was a bully and just getting his kicks from beating the crap out of a defenseless man. The accused may have made some dumb assed decisions and for that he'll be punished – appropriately."

Fred flipped, "Listen Mr. Dillan, as long as you work for me you will not address me in such a manner. Do not tell me what is or is not my right. And you better get over your bleeding heart enlisted loving liberalism in a hurry. It's totally unacceptable. Now get the hell out of here and get back to work."

Oh God, I've got to put up with this dip shit for over a year yet.

Dillan was in 'split tour' mode. He would put 18 to 24 months on this ship, be transferred to another probably larger destroyer or cruiser for another 18 or so, and then be sent off to Destroyer School.

In the cruiser and destroyer force, regular Navy officers usually were assigned to one ship for their initial division officer's tour. After that they were transferred to another ship, or sometimes to an afloat staff for a second division officer's tour to round out their experience. Following this, and roughly at the 4 year point, the good ones went to destroyer school for a year and then back to the fleet for a department head's tour. Unless, of course, they got sent off to the 'Brown Water Navy,' the riverine forces in Vietnam after their first division officer's tour.

4

After his discussion with Fred over Renaldo, Dillan did the long walk back to the bridge to tell Pete about his conversation with Fred.

Pete was still on watch and when Dillan came up to him he said quietly, "Shouldn't have told you about Renaldo."

Leaning over to Pete's ear, "If you hadn't and I found out later, I would've been ticked. Fixing things like that is why I have all the years as enlisted. Keeping officers from screwing over the troops is my job. No. Not a job, an avocation. It's one of the reasons I'm here. Maybe score one for the white hats this time."

He added, "You don't have to go to the XO. Fred will give the man an average report or not say anything about a recommendation one way or the other. The Bureau will assume that your comments on his test application constitute a recommendation and will order a test for him."

Continuing, "He'll have to do well on the test and may or may not get picked up for CPO, but at least he'll have the opportunity to try. Give Fred a day and then check Renaldo's file in the ship's office. Bet ya a beer that Fred's comments are gone."

"Fred'll make you pay. And I owe you that beer even if Fred doesn't pull his comments."

"So what's new? Fred always makes me pay. He'll pull his comments; otherwise he loses face with the XO. Fred'll do anything to keep face. I have to get to radio."

"Thanks."

"Thanks yourself - enjoyed it."

Dillan figured that Fred was discriminatory. Since Renaldo did not look like something on an academy recruiting poster, and was not a white face, Fred had let his background screw with his head. Dillan's wife Patty (Patricia) said that people with Portuguese backgrounds were looked down on in the Boston area. They called them "Portagee." Renaldo was from Fall River, Mass, and probably had relatives working in some grubby mill for Fred's family.

Fred is a fourteen year old private school kid trapped in a 26 year old body. He probably doesn't even know he is being discriminatory – just doing what feels natural.

Dillan turned and walked off the bridge. Each officer except the Commanding Officer, Executive Officer, and Supply Officer had a "day job" and also had to stand watches. Dillan's day job was as Communications Officer – responsible for the ship's external communications links to the outside world. This included the signalmen up on the deck above the bridge called the signal bridge, and the radiomen. The Navy broke enlisted jobs down by specialty, called a rate, and then relative rank within that specialty.

So down the ladder one deck to radio central Dillan went, punching the code into the keypad on the door for entrance. Radio was a SECRET space and only those with a SECRET security clearance or above could go in. Radio was noisy, crowded and hot. The air-conditioning could not cope with all the heat generated by 12 radios, 4 teletypes, and 5 radiomen in a small space. Three teletypes were banging away, one non-stop.

The majority of the ship's communications was by teletype, and encrypted. One wall was just racks of radio equipment, floor to ceiling and 12 feet long. Radio smelled of cigarette smoke, sweat and carbon paper. A lingering note of mimeograph fluid mixed with the smell of hot electronics.

"Richards, anything new?" Dillan asked his 1st class radioman and the radio watch leader. Petty officers were ranked as 3rd, 2nd, 1st class and then chief petty officers. Chiefs were the highest. Under 3rd class were 'non-rated' men, or 'strikers.'

"There is some new intel on the board, and we missed 6 numbers last hour," he said. "Mr. Finistry was in earlier checking the skeds for an unrep. Oh, and there are message orders for the XO, and he has a copy."

"What're we doing about the numbers?"

"We asked the carrier and they said they weren't for us."

"OK, thanks. Let's keep after the frequencies. Always have a back-up ready. [xiii]"

LARTER, administratively, was assigned to Destroyer Division 152, and then to Destroyer Squadron 15, Cruiser Destroyer Flotilla Eleven, a part of Cruisers and Destroyers, Pacific Fleet. These commands were all on the west coast of the USA.

But in the Western Pacific, on deployment, she was also assigned for operations to Task Unit 77.3.1 with two other destroyers, Task Group 77.3 with RANGER, and as part of Task Force 77, the Yankee Station and theater force, and finally 7th fleet – the fleet assigned to the Western Pacific. The task designations were fleet, force, group, unit, and element: a very effective way to organize operational ships.

Dillan was lucky; he had a tiny office called the crypto room tucked into the back of secure teletype. Few officers had real offices. There was just enough space in crypto for the safes, a tiny desk, one chair and the off line encryption equipment. Not much bigger than a restroom stall. He grabbed the message boards, punched the code into the key pad, unlocked the crypto door, and went in; shoes off and feet immediately on the desk. He leaned back in the chair as far as possible with the back of his head against the big safe.

Oh, God, that feels good.

He read through the message boards, usually less than riveting. There were lots of messages, most administrative – like supply codes recalled, dates for the next advancement exams, a daily news compilation which was about the only way a ship got news from the real world, a message operation order for an upcoming task group communications exercise, etc. And on the Secret board there were intelligence summaries, situation reports, and other operational stuff.

Message orders for the XO (Executive Officer, second in command and responsible for all administration and navigation). He was being transferred and was going to the Naval Post Graduate School in Monterey, California. Lieutenant Commander (LCDR) Chuck Peterson, an Academy grad from Minnesota had been on LARTER for 24 months. This was his 2nd Westpac cruise on this ship.

Dillan figured that the XO, and his wife and new daughter, would enjoy a year ashore – together. There should be orders on the XO's relief soon, and then do the swap the next time LARTER got to Subic.

Unless we get stuck out here longer than anticipated. We have been out here forever already. At least it seems like it.

Dillan figured that if that happened they would fly his relief from Cubi Point to the carrier on the daily COD (COD =

Carrier Onboard Delivery - a logistics flight from the air station to the carrier, a 2 engine propeller driven aircraft) and helo him over.

Another message: the carrier skipper wanted to do some cross deck training for his JOs (Junior Officers, on LARTER Ensigns and Lieutenants Junior Grade, on large ships also Lieutenants). Other ships in the task group – basically LARTER and two other destroyers out in forward zone picket screening positions 4000 yards either side of the carrier, got to nominate 2 officers each. Dillan wondered who the skipper would pick.

It was 1650, and time to drop down to the main deck to the wardroom for dinner. The wardroom had a big 5 foot wide by 14 foot long table, and a small lounge off to the side with a couch and a couple of chairs, built in TV, and a book rack. The TV was inoperative – no station signal strong enough to reach Yankee Station.

The lounge area had fake wood paneling and a few plaques from other ships along with a black and white photo of Staff Sergeant James P. Larter, USMC, who had received the Navy Cross (posthumously) in World War I and for whom LARTER was named. There was also a painting of LARTER in her Korean War configuration, on the wall.

Back in the 50's LARTER had 4 single 5 inch gun mounts, some 40 millimeter anti-aircraft guns aft, some 20 millimeter anti-aircraft guns, and used depth charges against submarines. The bridge was open. She looked a lot different after FRAM, and was a lot heavier. In the 50's she only displaced 2250 tons. FRAM added over 40% to bring her up to 3200. This made her a little top heavy and she rolled with a snap in beam seas.

The officers waited in the lounge for the captain.

"Hey there, Mr. D. You hoarding the AP ranking?" from Billy Hoffman.

Most of the junior officers had nicknames based on some characteristic. Usually these were a bit derogatory. Dillan's was "Mr. D." a shorthand reference to what Festus Parker called Marshall Matt Dillan in the old Gunsmoke TV show, sometimes accompanied with a stiff leg limp on the part of the pronouncer.

"You don't want to know Rocky Top," from Dillan. "Gators beat the crap out of you last week. UT is headed for the cellar. No SEC for the Volunteers this year. Who'd you play this week?

Besides, it's only Sunday in the real world; AP's aren't out till tomorrow PM."

"Don't count the Vols out yet. And we played Kentucky and won. Still a chance if the dogs beat the Gators. Your horse chestnuts got beat again I see."

"Buckeyes, ignorant hillbilly, Buckeyes."

LARTER officers took their college football serious. The Navy transmitted scores and Associated Press rankings over the broadcast and it generated quite an interest. Money quietly changed hands on rankings and games.

"Attention on deck." The skipper had arrived. Everyone stood.

"Carry on," from the captain.

They all filed into the table.

Dinner was a relatively formal affair and those who were not on watch sat around the table with the captain at the head, XO to his right, next senior to his left, etc. down the table. The junior officer unlucky enough to be the appointed "mess president" sat at the other end from the captain.

Officers had their own mess and their own cooks and servers. One junior officer was assigned as mess president and had to do the books and make up the menus with the captain's agreement. The officers got a mess bill monthly for the food consumed. And if the skipper, who fancied himself as a bit of a connoisseur, insisted on fancy food, the bill got a lot higher.

White linen and heavy china with a blue ring and anchor, Filipino stewards served, 3 courses, soup first, starting with the captain. They served from behind, placing food on each plate with heavy silver serving ware. The wardroom cooks and servers were Philippine nationals allowed to join the US Navy. They had their own small table in the wardroom galley and made their own food, paid for as part of the officer's mess bill.[xiv]

No one got to eat until all had been served. The food was generally quality and well prepared. Although it was warm once, it became cold quickly. Being hungry and smelling the warm food on your plate as it cooled while one waited was torture.

There were 9 for dinner. Given the Condition III (wartime steaming) watch requirements, 5 to 6 officers were on watch at any one time. Watches were 4 hours on and 8 hours off, 24/7.

The captain, Commander (CDR) Mike Norcourt, USN, was an Academy graduate 16 years out. He was 39 years old, and the "old man" by tradition and literally. He had been a Commander for just over 2 years. Some of the chief petty officers may have been older, and the chief engineer, LT Red Redmond, who was out of the Navy for 3 years after his first tour, was 32, just a bit younger than the XO who was 35.

But the wardroom was for all practical purposes boy's town. Most of the other officers were between 22 and 26. The skipper was short, stocky, had dark hair, penetrating gray eyes, and was a traditionalist and perfectionist.

The junior officer that had the "buck" in front of him got to say grace. A "buck" was a large brass chess pawn, and the stewards moved it counterclockwise around the table before each meal to put it in front of a plate. Grace said, and when the captain picked up his spoon, the rest could also.

The captain loved small talk at the wardroom table and usually selected one junior officer to start a conversation on some subject the captain thought was challenging. Lots of times it was naval history. This was tough for OCS and NROTC (Naval Reserve Officer Training Corps) officers since they had not had naval history drilled into them for 4 years like the Naval Academy graduates had. Most of the junior officers dreaded getting selected for this. Dillan sure did.

Recently the skipper had chosen weekly sayings of important naval officers that the junior officers were to memorize. This week's was one from John Paul Jones.

ENS Billy Hoffman, USN, 'Ridge Runner' or 'Rocky Top', almost 23, a 1967 regular NROTC grad from Tennessee, got the short straw and had to recite it for the captain. Billy was the gunnery officer, responsible for the ship's 5 inch 38 caliber guns and their associated handling rooms and magazines. He also was the WG (weapons, gunnery) division officer and had 12 gunner's mates or nonrated seamen reporting to him. Billy got the quotation right.

"Yes, sir, Captain," Billy said. "In a letter from Captain John Paul Jones to the war department, 1782: It is by no means enough that an officer in the Navy be a capable mariner. He must be that of course. But also a great deal more. He should be a gentleman of liberal education, refined manners, and the nicest sense of personal courtesy. He should be the soul of tact, patience, justice, firmness and charity."

"Very good, Mr. Hoffman, very good," from the skipper.

This stuff is like plebe year at the academy. Nice to know but not essential by any means.

Halfway through the main course a buzzer rang. The captain picked up the sound powered handset from its holder on the table leg to his right.

"Captain," he said. All quiet for awhile.

"Very well, proceed as ordered."

The captain hung up the handset and announced, "The carrier is turning into the wind for flight operations. It looks like only a CAP launch."

CAP, or Combat Air Patrol, was a group, sometimes two, sometimes four fighter aircraft that were launched to take up positions around the carrier to protect against incoming enemy aircraft or surface vessels. Although there were no enemy aircraft expected – the North Vietnamese air force wouldn't dare try to reach Yankee Station – and no enemy surface vessels expected - the carrier usually kept CAP up 24/7.[xv]

Back to the meal.

Once dessert had been served and eaten, one could be excused, providing that the captain was not lecturing. If one had to go relieve a watch so they could eat, you were expected to skip dessert and would be excused early. Out here on station, dessert was not a big deal, usually fruit cocktail.

Dillan figured there must be a 55 gallon drum of this stuff aboard – it went on forever. And it never fermented. Sigh.

That would at least be a welcome change. For someone who loves desserts, I could easily pass them by if this crap continues much longer. Ah, for a nice warm apple pie – a la mode. Maybe a hot fudge sundae. Stop it you dip shit. You are going to start drooling. Explain that to the skipper.

5

Dillan got excused after dessert and went back to radio. A quick scan of the message boards again, and then he sat in the tiny crypto office and wrote a short letter home to his wife, Patty. By 1930, he headed for his bunk. One tried to take advantage of every moment for sleep. Since the messenger of the watch would be waking him up at 2315 to get ready for his mid watch, this was an opportunity for almost 4 hours of sleep.

Dillan went down two ladders to after officer's country on the main deck. Although the practice was discouraged, many men would place their hands on the polished chrome hand rails and just lift their legs and rapidly slide down the rails. Dillan did this often.

Most internal spaces on the ship were painted a pastel green, beige, and a few light blue. The overhead was covered in braided cables on racks and spray painted an off white. The deck was covered in a beige or light grey 8x8 asbestos tile, and waxed and buffed shiny. Slippery when wet. Passageways were narrow and had a small diameter chrome handrail about waist high, essential for moving around the ship when it was rough.

All furniture was a medium grey, darker than the external haze grey. All the furniture, except chairs, were fixed in place. Bolted to clips welded to the deck or bulkhead.

Dillan's stateroom was shared with LTJG Eric Ebersole, the main propulsion assistant (MPA) who worked for Red, the chief engineer, one of the few without a nickname. Or at least Dillan didn't know it. He was responsible for the operation and maintenance of the ship's main engines. Tall, dark, lanky and a reserve officer who was "short", he had maybe 10 months to go before he got to rejoin civilian life. He planed to go home, to Mechanicsburg, PA, and get married, working for his future father in law's construction business.

Eric's degree was in Business Management from the University of Pittsburg. Eric had been on LARTER since the summer of 1965, and was aboard for the previous Westpac cruise. Eric and Dillan were not really friends as such although they got along fine.

The stateroom was painted pale green, smelled a little like gym socks, and had two bunk beds; some closets and two fold down desks all painted medium grey, and bolted along one wall. It had a tiny sink with a mirror and light above it. Green and brown woven curtain for a door, light coral colored bed spreads on the narrow stacked bunks, head (toilets and showers) down the passageway. Just enough room to squeeze between the closets and bunks.

If Eric was using his fold down desk, Dillan had to crawl over the end of his lower bunk to get in. For some reason Eric had selected the top bunk even though, being senior to Dillan, he could have his choice. Aft officer's country was right over the turbines. At speed in a seaway[xvi] it was like sleeping on top of a writhing serpent.

And there was always noise and always a little vibration. The turbine whine if the ship was at speed, but also the rumble of ventilation fans, a buzzing florescent fixture, men talking. In a seaway, a squeak from the curtain hangers on the door curtain, as it swung back and forth. If it ever got quiet Dillan would wake immediately. A totally quiet ship was weird.

A destroyer was basically a big engine with a long bow and weapons stuck on it. From the main deck down, halfway back, it was mostly all boilers, turbines, reduction gears, auxiliary equipment, and miles of thick, asbestos bat insulated pipes and armored cables. Scuttles, little cat walks and ladders let the engineers have access to Main Engine Control (main control), the engine rooms and the boiler rooms. This allowed them to operate the equipment and maintain it. Major work required the ship to be placed in dry dock and hull plates cut off to get at equipment.

Officer, and especially crew, berthing compartments were stuck wherever a bit of space remained – over the shafts aft, in the bow, main deck forward, etc. The bow also had storerooms. And there were fuel tanks along both sides, outboard below the water line. The main deck itself was where most work spaces, offices, and the wardroom were located. The crew's mess, or Mess Deck, was one deck down, roughly under the wardroom and over some store rooms.

Only the CO had a cabin above the main deck. The CO had a large "in port" cabin on the 01 deck forward, which was also used for a Squadron or Division Commander when embarked, and his tiny sea cabin just aft of the bridge on the 03 level. The XO had a small cabin on the main deck to starboard. Only the CO and XO had heads in their cabins. The rest used community heads.

The crew slept 3 high in canvas covered two foot wide pipe racks with thin mattresses. Each man had a small locker to call his own. Some crew compartments had a tiny table, with a couple of bench seats. There was essentially no privacy.

Chief petty officers had a small compartment of their own in the bow, euphemistically called the 'goat locker.' Larger 3 high racks and more space. There was even a tiny forward officer's stateroom ('boy's town') across from the chief's quarters. It was an overflow stateroom, and the most junior, shared it. Quarters in the bow were a bit like having a room in a small express elevator.

Driving into heavy seas, the area went up and down 40 feet every 2 minutes. The joke was that the junior officers and chiefs berthed up there should be drawing half submarine pay since they spent at least one half of their time submerged when steaming into rough seas.

Officers were sourced from the Naval Academy, Naval Reserve Officer Training Corps at civilian colleges, and Officer Candidate School after college.[xvii] The officer group on LARTER had migrated into what could have been called cliques. The department heads and XO tended to go ashore, together although Fred was left out on occasion.

The primary department heads were LT Eric (Red) Redmond, USN, the chief engineer, regular NROTC, 56, from Green Bay; LT Chris Harcourt, Academy 61, and the weapons officer, from Peoria; and LT Fred Finistry III, Academy 62, from Boston as the operations officer. Department heads may have had nicknames among themselves, and Fred was referred to as "Fred Cubed" or just "Cubed" by the troops out of officer ear shot, but Dillan didn't know Chris' nickname.

Fred Finistry was Dillan's main boss. As a department head, he had Dillan as the communications officer (COMM), LTJG Ted Brunshall as the combat information center officer (CIC), and ENS Pete Donavan as the electronics material officer (EMO), Dillan's old job. Dillan had worked for Fred since he reported to LARTER almost a year ago.

Fred was a U.S. Naval Academy graduate and very proud of it. He had played lacrosse for USNA and had a pair of lacrosse sticks with NAVY painted on the handles mounted in X fashion on his stateroom bulkhead. He was about 5 feet 8 inches tall, well built, dark brown hair which he kept in a crew cut, grey eyes and was bound and determined to make a name for himself with this assignment.

After 3 years on a destroyer on the east coast, he had attended 'DesTec.' Destroyer department head school, or 'DesTec', was a very intense, almost year long school in Newport, Rhode Island, that taught everything there was to know about cruisers and destroyers. Fred was a relatively new LT. His DOR (date of rank) was 6/1/66 and he had reported to LARTER about 3 months prior to Dillan.

Fred came from a well-wired Boston family and had attended private boarding school. He was the youngest of 3 boys. His father had been a Naval Reserve Officer in World War II, and had served on commandeered civilian yachts for anti-submarine patrols off the east coast of New England. Fred was the first in the family to attend the Naval Academy. All gleaned by Dillan from the Naval Academy yearbook on Fred's desk.

Dillan found out from Chris that Fred's family was loaded and 'summered' in Edgartown, on the 'Vineyard': Martha's Vineyard, a large island off the south coast of Massachusetts where the wealthy played. Dillan 'summered' cutting grass for the neighbors and working as a caddy at the local golf course. Dillan was raised on tuna fish casseroles and deer burger meatloaf, Fred on lobster and steak. Dillan and Fred could have not been from two more diverse backgrounds and still both be white Anglo Saxons.

Fred, as did most of the unmarried officers, lived aboard. He had a stateroom in aft officer's country of his own next to Eric's and Dillan's. Bigger than theirs it also had a big desk. Fred could be found at his desk day and night. Even on weekends. With no active female interest, Fred was all Navy, all the time.

From day one, Fred and Dillan were at odds. It probably started over the prior enlisted status of Dillan verses the 'elite professional' status of Naval Academy graduates – at least in Fred's mind, Dillan surmised.

Dillan thought Fred was a pompous ass with a silver spoon still jammed up there. Fred accused Dillan of lacking in social graces and implied that he did not give proper respect to the traditions of the naval service.

To help Dillan understand traditions more, Fred assigned Dillan to numerous "Shitty Little Jobs Officer" or SLJO jobs.

These jobs should have been parceled out more equitably among all the junior officers aboard. Jobs like inventory the ship's store, page check all the tactical publications, inventory the controlled drugs in sick bay, and audit the crew's mess journals. This was on top of his regular job, a real pain in the ass.

The junior Ensign aboard, called 'George' by tradition, usually got most of the SLJO crap. Dillan had never been 'George.' Seniority was based on date of rank. Time in service was the tie breaker for officers with the same date of rank.

Although ENS Jim Kirpatrick, USNR, and Dillan had graduated from OCS at the same time, and Jim had even reported to LARTER a couple of weeks prior to Dillan, Jim was 'George' for awhile. Later in the summer of 1967 two new Ensigns had to compete for the un-coveted title of 'George.' ENS Billy Hoffman currently had that distinction. DOR 6/3/67.

There was also another tradition: that of 'Bull' Ensign – the most senior Ensign aboard. Dillan always thought that seniority among Ensigns was like virtue among whores, but tradition persisted. A 'Bull' Ensign wore a single extra large Ensign 'raincoat' bar on his left collar point that had 'BULL' engraved upon it, only aboard, never ashore.

ENS Sam Blongerinski, USN was the current 'Bull.' He wore the big bar with pride. Traditionally the 'Bull' would assign SLJO work to all the Ensigns and consequently did not have to do any himself.

6

For the JO's, first there were the old timers, reserve officers who had been aboard approaching three years, all class of 65 LTJG types. Eric Ebersole, Len Ottaway, and Ted Brunshall made up this group. Len was the assistant weapons officer from Albany, NY, and had attended SUNY prior to OCS. His nickname was "Porcupine" even though he was not fat. It came from his perpetual crew cut which, because of his coarse hair, stood out like small porcupine quills.

Competent and a bit of the clown, Ted was a dyed in the wool Texan from outside Waco and was a Baylor grad, nickname "Tex" or "Cowboy". Short, and stocky, blond hair, blue eyes, Ted was the CIC officer, and was damn good at it, Dillan thought.

The supply officer, although technically a department head, Tony Carpiceso, was only a LTJG and tended to pal around with the old timers since he had also been aboard for a couple of years and was a reserve officer like them. He was out of OCS after CCNY in business administration. Supply officers were restricted to supply duties only, wore crossed pouch like emblems on one collar and on their shoulder boards as opposed to stars, and were generally called "Pork Chop" for the appearance of the emblems, like crossed gold pork chops.

Sam Blongerinski, tall, thin, dark hair, brown eyes, large nose, was the damage control assistant (DCA), a 1966 academy type from Lawton, Michigan, nickname "Green Egg" or 'Greeny' for a children's book. He was mostly a quiet guy who spent what time he had off the ship with Jim Kirpatrick, an Annapolis JO and the anti-submarine warfare (ASW) officer, responsible for sonar and the ASROC and DASH. Jim was big, almost six three, light complexion and jet black hair. Nickname "Pinger" for his sonar, and his tendency to ping on officers who had not graduated from 'boat school' (Naval Academy). Jim was originally from Tiverton, RI.

Joe Rederman and Billy Hoffman were a team, two southerners, and a year apart. Rederman was the first lieutenant, a title that went back to the days of sail, and deck division (WD) officer, Academy 66, "General Joe" or "Rebel", and from Richmond, Virginia. About six feet, stocky, brown hair and eyes, and wore a size twelve. Many also called him "Beaver Tail" for the size of his feet.

And Dillan and Pete Donavan were a team. This was not to say that these cliques didn't go to the club or such on their own and with out others. With the 3 section in port duty, and the 4 or even 5 sections in effect back in the states, there were no hard and fast rules. But the ENS/LTJG types seldom got invited to join the XO and LT types.

Pete was Dillan's friend. Behind his back he got called "Chocolate Drop", but not by Dillan. His other nickname was 'Panther' for the Pitt Panthers but maybe also for the Black Panthers. He was from just outside Pittsburg, PA, and had an industrial engineering degree from Pitt.

He was black. He was small and dark, curly black hair and brown eyes. Pete was married, one of only a few other junior officers who were. Dillan and his wife Patty were the 'host' couple when Pete and Rita, Pete's wife, arrived. They got along well.

Having been raised in a little northeast Ohio town, Dillan had not known blacks growing up. His enlisted Navy days were not much different. His first ship had a few black enlisted men aboard but they tended to keep together exclusively. At college he really met them for the first time and considered them to be struggling students just like he was.

Dillan did not understand, and did not agree with discrimination. He felt that each person should be judged on results, not skin color or religion, so sometimes Dillan did not like Billy's or even Joe Rederman's less than generous attitude towards Pete, or the enlisted blacks aboard: 5 in supply, 2 in engineering, and 6 in weapons.

The US Navy took a very dim view of discrimination based on race or creed. Even a southerner's remarks were carefully tempered. Get a reputation for being discriminatory and get in deep trouble. Reality was that the US Navy was way ahead of the civilian world in equality for blacks.

Sexual preference was another matter. The official position was that homosexuals were not permitted in the US Navy. Even the slightest indication of homosexual tendencies elicited persecution bordering on paranoia, and was cause for immediate transfer ashore to a mental hospital or brig followed by a general discharge, sometimes under less than honorable conditions.

But usually the men handled this stuff themselves, and someone who approached another man would have an unfortunate and painful accident, like falling down a ladder or such. This was assault under the UCMJ but was not investigated or prosecuted – senior enlisted just looked the other way. When two 'queers' were caught together they were both transferred ashore, sometimes after accidents. Navy enlisted men were a macho group and most had zero tolerance for homosexuals. If someone really was gay, he had better keep it well hidden, especially aboard ship.

The Vietnam War was fought on the ground, especially in the Army, by draftees. One could get a draft deferment if one was in college, or married with a child. Otherwise one was subject to the lottery system. Naturally, enlisting in a service other than the Army or Marine Corps would generally keep one out of the rice paddies. But draftees only served 2 years while signing up for another service usually meant 4 years.[xviii]

As was always true, there was a form of loneliness for the captain: the loneliness of command. He may have had dinner at the club in port with the XO, but it was mostly working dinners. Being with his peers, the skippers of other ships, was the norm.

At sea, standing Condition III watches, there was essentially zero free time. One could go days and not see, except maybe at lunch or dinner; officers who were not in one's watch section. Since the supply officer did not stand watches, his after officer's stateroom, shared with LTJG Ted Brunshall, was the JO's gathering place.

Tony Carpiceso had decorated his space as far as regulations allowed, and then some. It was as he called it, a 'snake ranch.' He had Playboy centerfolds. Nudie pictures were not officially allowed, so most were on the inside of locker doors, viewable only with the doors open. Tony had a nice collection, augmented monthly.

There was a Vargas print of a blond in a negligee on one wall that Tony called "art" although he would take it down if there was to be a zone inspection. And there was a big tool calendar, naturally with scantily clad women for each month holding a pipe wrench or such, with days numbered and crossed off.

This was his short timer's calendar, marking the days until he was to be released from active duty. Days were numbered backwards from that important date and Tony held a small ceremony each evening as he crossed another off. This had to come down for inspections also.

He had a stereo and usually has some form of protest rock or folk spinning on his Teac reel to reel tape recorder. Bob Dylan, Joplin, etc. But he had to keep the volume low. Protest music was frowned upon. Red Redmond and Chris Harcourt just let it go mostly and Tony's stateroom was a way away from Fred's. But if Fred could hear Tony's stereo he would jump him about, "inappropriate music for naval officers."

Dillan would stop in at Tony's now and then. Tony knew all the rumors and liked being the den mother for the JOs. He was good at it. He kept his fingers on the pulse and would know who was getting along and who was not, what the skipper's pet peeve of the day was, and what enlisted man was in trouble with his chief. Also being in the good graces of the supply officer had its advantages. Not only could one get the repair parts so essential for running his division, but supply had the market cornered on coffee.

And the Navy ran on coffee: the second most necessary fuel after fuel oil for the boilers. Most divisions had a coffee pot in their work spaces. Strapped to the bulkhead so it didn't wander off in heavy seas, it was perpetually half full of a hot black liquid about the consistency of tar that could be used for removing rust in a pinch.

There was always a big urn of coffee going in the crew's mess. Not as thick, but nicely burnt and jet black. Would dissolve a spoon left in it for more than a minute. The enlisted said that coffee wasn't any good unless it had a pint of Navy Standard Fuel Oil in every pot for taste. Just a joke, but real Navy coffee would put hair on your chest. Sometimes the stewards would fill a pot on the mess decks and have it in the wardroom.

Pete popped his head into Dillan's stateroom. Dillan was in a chair, leaning over and removing his shoes and socks. Shirt over the chair back and pants around his legs.

Pete said, "I owe you that beer, checked with the ship's office on my way down after watch. There's no comment on Renaldo's application for the chief's exam except mine, recommending approval. Fred just pulled his comments. The PNC is routing it to the XO and skipper tomorrow. He said that they would assume that Fred agreed with my recommendation, since he had not commented."

Looking up, "Good, and I'll sure collect if we ever get close to a watering hole. Tell Renaldo that he better really hit the books. He needs to do well on the test, very well. Without a big gee-whiz recommendation, his multiple will not be very high."

"This is his first attempt and he has no delusions. Just wants a chance to pass."

"Good," Dillan said, yawning, and with a bit of snap in his voice, "Go away. My rack is calling me."

"What language is it calling in? Bitchey, I think. Maybe pig bitchey, later you grumpy old coot." Pete was all of 2 years younger than Dillan.

"Only grumpy when harassed by an insensitive whipper snapper. Beat feet Mister – your senior needs some zzzs. Oh rack, oh rack, come to Daddy."

With a wave, Pete left, headed for boy's town and some rack time also.

Dillan turned off the overhead light and crawled into his bunk. Eric was sitting at his desk writing something, his back shadowed by the small light over the desk. No communication. Eric was always a quiet type. Dillan turned his bunk light out. He could hear a couple of men talking down the passageway and the always muffled rumble of the air handler. He was exhausted and wanted to sleep. But his mind kept spinning.

Dillan laid there, right arm under his head, staring at the wire mesh springs of Eric's bunk above, feeling the ever present vibration of the shafts deep under him.

What is Patty doing now? Will I get a letter tomorrow? The next day? Six weeks into what is supposed to be a 6 month cruise. God, homecoming is such a long way off.

Then his mind slipped back to his parents and his short history, kind of an edge of sleep daydream.

7

Dillan was the only child of a carpenter and a key punch operator. His mother died when he was 10. His dad remarried and moved taking him along. Home was Warren, Ohio. Smack in the snow belt. Childhood was not very good. A stint in the boy scouts. No money, a demanding step mother, lots of after school jobs.

His dad worked when there were jobs. Not many in the winter. Dillan wanted to go to college, got moderate grades in high school, and had been accepted at Ohio State, but again no money.

Dillan was always a bit of a rebel. School grades were A's and B's in core subjects and D's in deportment. He was basically unmotivated by what he thought was the slow pace of public school and was always getting crossways of the system for being creative with the rules. Dillan was small, but wiry and with an attitude. Like a feisty little dog snapping at the butt of larger dogs. He dated a little in high school, but work ate up most of his time.

He enlisted in the US Navy a few days after high school graduation, mostly, to get away from the stepmother. Boot camp in San Diego: his first trip outside Ohio. Boot camp was tough, but San Diego with its palm trees, cold dark Pacific Ocean, beaches, and zoo was wonderful. He tried to meet girls, but as a Seaman Recruit, he was well at the bottom of their selection list.

He flew home after boot camp – bad move. Parents were fighting over his father's unique ability to alleviate all his relationship frustrations with promiscuity. Most of his high school friends were on with their own lives. Back to San Diego early with a big loan to the Navy Federal Credit Union to pay off the airplane tickets. With a crappy home life the Navy had become his home.

Dillan was assigned to attend Electrician Mate's class "A" school – a 16 week intensive course. He graduated at the top of his class, and even spent Christmas on base, since he did not have the money or desire to attempt another trip back to cold frozen Ohio. There were 22 men in his class and they had a lot of fun playing pool or drinking pitchers of 3.2% beer at the enlisted club. One guy wanted to go into submarines – and did, going down with USS THRESHER (SSN 593) about a year later.

One guy from Stone Mountain, Georgia, used to say, "The reason the south lost the Civil War was that they figured one southerner could whip any five yankees, and they was wrong, he could only whip four." He had gotten busted for running moonshine and the judge gave him a choice, enlist or chain gang – pick one. He picked.

Dillan took a trip south over the border to Tijuana, Mexico, and his first fully nude strip show ever at 18 years and 2 months old: eye opening. Tijuana was a wild place, and service men were discouraged from going there. That made it all the more enticing. Only a few streets were paved. Mostly old cars with their required small plastic statue glued to the dash.

There were stalls selling multicolored blankets, plaster of Paris statues, tooled leather handbags, paintings on black velvet, and all prices negotiable. A few restaurants, but mostly bars with their usual cat house upstairs. Taking gringo's money was the primary source of income. They did it with any kind of perversion one was willing to pay for.

But Dillan was afraid of collecting social diseases, so he did not succumb to the number one Tijuana temptation, even if he desperately wanted to. The Navy made a big deal out of VD, and insisted on monthly 'short arm' inspections. Infection guaranteed an automatic restriction to base and multiple injections in the butt.

After school Dillan had orders to a repair ship in Norfolk, Virginia: USS VULCAN (AR-5), a big ship. Assigned to the electrical division, Dillan was immediately sent mess cooking. In the Navy, all of the grunt work preparing, serving, and cleaning up after the crew's meals fell to the junior enlisted men sent for 3 months at a time to work for the cooks (Mess Service Men) in the galley, an awful job.

Up at 5AM, help prepare, and then clean up for 3 meals, off at 7PM, repeat. Dillan worked at the deep sink, scrubbing pots and pans, one weekend day a week off. Three months seemed like three years.

Once mess cooking was over, Dillan had an opportunity to learn his trade. Assigned to work with a 3rd class petty officer who the crew called "Spider" due to his dark complexion and long arms, Dillan went to work running cable, repairing motors, fixing lights, and standing watches in the engine room on the ship's generators, or "cold iron" watch when the ship was on shore power. A repair ship spent most of its time in port, with different ships tied up along side, executing repairs that did not require a trip to the shipyard.

Duty was one in four which meant that every 4th day, one had to stay on the ship for 24 hours and stand watches since one was in the duty section. The rest of the time after working 7AM to 4PM, one could go ashore. But being mostly broke, Dillan spent his off evenings aboard reading, watching the crew's movie, playing cards, and catching up on sleep lost from duty days or a long night bar hopping. He acquired an old junker and at least had wheels.

The ship did get underway twice that year for exercises. Then Dillan was standing 4 on and 8 off on the main switchboard. Being at sea was a new experience. The clear air, blue sky and deep blue rolling surface were invigorating. But, when it got rough, ugh! Once, when a hurricane threatened Norfolk, the fleet was sortied. Large ships were less subject to damage at sea than they were in port where they got slammed together or bounced off piers.

Out to sea VULCAN went and it got rough as hell. Sea sickness was no fun. The old Navy joke was that first you think you are going to die; then you know you are going to die, and finally you are afraid you are **not** going to die. Dillan got at least through stage two. And if you were sea sick, tough, your duties did not change. You were expected to stand your watches and do your work. Thank God the rough seas only lasted a week.

The ship had a helicopter deck aft, generally used for transferring repair parts. And for awhile, Dillan was assigned as part of the flight deck crew. "Flight quarters, flight quarters – man your flight quarters stations" would boom over the 1MC, the ship's general announcing system. And back to the flight deck the detail would go.

Dillan got hurt. His job was to connect the fat auxiliary power cable to the bottom of the helicopter once it had landed, and while the rotors were still spinning, so the helicopter could have electrical power once the engine was shut down. Usually he had to do this while other flight deck crew members were attaching the tie down straps.

On this occasion, it was rough as hell and the helo was bouncing around a bit. Dillan's left arm was under a strut when the helicopter took a deep bounce. Crack. Finish up the tie down and power connection, but the arm hurt like hell.

Dillan went down to sick bay and the chief hospital corpsman felt it and said, "Yep, it's broken. Grab on to that stanchion over there with your right hand and do not let go."

A quick jerk on the left arm and it was set. Dillan sank to his knees. Then a plaster cast, 3 APCs (aspirin), and a chit to take the rest of the day off and hit the rack. Dillan wore the cast for 2 months and had fun getting the bar maids on Granby Street to sign it, his badge of courage. One was supposed to be 21 to drink in Virginia. But like so many others, he had concocted a fake ID card.

In the early fall of 1961, Dillan passed the Navy wide examination for advancement in rate and was promoted to Electrician's Mate Third Class. He was just 19. Now as a petty officer, he did not have to go mess cooking again, and had a junior enlisted man assigned to him for work on ships' electrical systems. His boss was an older 1st class and the division had a Chief Petty Officer Electrician's Mate (EMC).

Reality was that the chief petty officers ran the Navy. Usually enlisted men with 12 or more year's service, chiefs were the technical experts, were very knowledgeable about almost everything, and could keep the systems humming and the rest of the enlisted ranks in line. Screwing up and getting the chief on your case was a good way to have a very unhappy life. In the late fall of 1961 Dillan applied for the Navy Enlisted Scientific Education Program (NESEP).

The NESEP application process was brutal. One had to be 3rd class (E-4), have super evaluations, and pass a grueling all day test in math, science, and English. Then a major physical examination and physical fitness test. Then go before a board of officers for a 2 hour grilling, then before the ship's captain for another grilling. By the end of 1961 there were 18,000 applications forwarded Navy wide with recommendations to Washington.

In May, 1962, they announced the 1,800 selected for the 1962 program. Dillan was on the list, one in ten. He had to say goodbye to his not so committed girlfriend, a secretary at the Navy Exchange. They had dated off and on since shortly after he arrived in Norfolk, and he spent what weekends he could at her apartment. She had at least eliminated his awful virginal affliction. But it was more of an arrangement of convenience than a long term thing. So Dillan departed for the Naval Training Center, Bainbridge, Maryland for a 10 week prep school, promising to write. Neither did.

Then Dillan was off to Columbus, Ohio for a 4 year degree in electrical engineering at Ohio State University, paid for totally by the US Navy. He had to re-enlist for 6 years and then extend after his sophomore year for two more to insure that he had a minimum 4 year commitment once he graduated from college. For Dillan, this was probably the only way he would ever have been able to afford to go to college, and it was a super opportunity.

The Navy paid him his regular salary, gave him a subsistence and quarter's allowance, and even bought his books. As a student, he had more money than most. He had to go to school, and get good grades. When school was not in session he had to work at the Naval ROTC center inventorying uniforms and books and doing other grunt work, including teaching a NROTC course in ship's electrical systems his senior year, or take leave.

One day a week he had to wear his uniform to class and report in. He went to school year around and had to carry a big class load. There were no electives for NESEP's. The Navy picked all the classes and there were no cake courses. There was all the engineering stuff and lots of management, psychology, social studies, and history courses. Flag a course or get two "Ds" and you were out - back to the fleet to finish your enlistment. The US Navy played hard ball.

8

Four years later, Dillan graduated, having advanced to petty officer first class (E-6) during the interim. Only 6 NESEPs graduated out of the 18 that started Ohio State. The other 12 had screwed up and were sent back to the fleet. Not that they were not smart enough, but having money and being in a target rich environment (girls) did them in.

Spending time on wine, women, and song at the expense of studies did not work very well. And Dillan partook big time – but he was just a little bit more careful: skating on the edge; his life philosophy. He graduated with a 2.3. Not stellar.

Off for Officer Candidate School in Newport, Rhode Island. A 16 week glorified boot camp. Most NESEP's got to be company officers. Dillan was company commander for Bravo Company. In the fall of 1966 he was commissioned Ensign, USN. An officer and a gentleman by act of Congress.

During his time at OCS Dillan met and fell in love. Patty: a local girl, going to college there. He met her at a Saturday night dance club in the Viking Hotel his first weekend liberty. She was 20. Dillan was 24. Twelve weeks later they decided to get married.

They planned the wedding for spring 1967. They had some great parties at the officer's club, and Patty gave him the big tour of Newport. Ocean Drive, mansions, the Cliff Walk, and lots of super restaurants specializing in lobsters and sea food that Dillan had never tasted.

A dinner with Patty Saturday night, maybe their 2nd date, and the first one alone, at Christies, a very expensive but very good sea food restaurant on the water front.

Patty was 20, almost 21 from a Scot & Irish family, and had been born in south Boston but raised since she was 4 in Middletown, Rhode Island. She had one brother, a bit older. She had attended Middletown High School and then got a scholarship to Salve Regina College, an expensive Catholic college for girls in Newport.

Although she was not Catholic, her father worked in maintenance at the school and there was a program for scholarships, including room and board, to be given out to deserving employee's children.

She lived with a three other girls in a dorm room, and she worked part time at Cherry & Webb's department store to make ends meet. Pretty, about 5'3", long brown hair, blue grey eyes, and a good figure. Dillan thought she was super.

Dillan, in his service dress khaki, with Navy blue shoulder boards with one embroidered gold star on each, his tiny section leader bars on his collar tips, was a bit stricken with Patty, especially that night in her light grey dress which matched her eyes.

"So, Patrick, soon to be a Naval Officer, tell me again where are you going with your life?" Patty asked.

"Well, you know I've been in the Navy since I was 3 days out of high school. Over six years now. It's like home. The plan is to make the Navy a career. Although it's a long way off, maybe work my way up to Admiral."

"Admiral Dillan. I can see the headlines now. Admiral Dillan appointed Fleet Commander."

"Not really, that kind of stuff's for the Academy graduates. Maybe I can make Rear Admiral, a bit junior to fleet commanders. How 'bout you," as he drained his wine glass.

"Well, you know I've got 2 years to go at Salve to get my teaching degree, then maybe a job teaching. Kindergarten would be fun if I can cope with the little demons 6 hours every day. I'll do my student teaching my last year and can choose then. But I'd like to travel some. I've never been very far – once to Washington, DC, for a senior class trip, a few trips to Boston to see relatives, and one New York trip for 4 days last year."

"I want to go to Europe and Japan some day," Dillan said.

"That'd be fun. Being in the Navy you'll get to go lots of places. I had a friend in high school whose dad was in the Navy, a Commander I think, and she got to live in Italy for 3 years once. Didn't you tell me that once you finished OCS you were going to a ship?"

"Yeah, a can. Sorry, a destroyer, out of San Diego. I loved San Diego when I was there years ago, warm and nice year around. No snow except in the mountains to the east. Coral colored houses with red tile roofs, palm trees, flowers, and so clean – the dirt of winter never affects them there. But we have a war on, and I've a lot better chance of seeing Southeast Asia from a haze grey cruise ship than I do of actually exploring Japan."

"This damn war scares me," she said, munching on salad. "One of my high school class mates got killed a month ago in Vietnam. He was in the Army. I didn't know him much. And my brother is stationed in Thailand in the air forces. The news is always talking about how much progress we're making, but then there are all the protests and causalities. Will it end soon?"

"I sure don't know. I guess we're doing the best we can. I've never been much of a political person. I do buy into the domino theory – we have to stop the damn communists some-where. But Vietnam seems like an awful place to do it. I've heard that our troops have a hell of a time sorting the good ones from the bad ones. They say you can only tell the bad ones when they shoot at you."

Refilling his wine glass from the carafe, he continued, "I still wish Kennedy was President. I went to his funeral in Wash-ington. The ROTC group sent a bus, a long overnight ride, and then one of the thousands of Sailors lining the street for the parade. Cold."

"I think he was a good president, but I'm a New Eng-lander. I felt bad when he was killed. I was in high school. I think most people will always remember where they were when they found out he was shot. Good for you to get to go. I watched it on TV."

It was quiet for a bit as she showed him how to crack a lobster shell. Messy, but the meat was good dipped in butter. But that green thing called the 'tomalley' was ugly. Patty, a born and bred New Englander liked it. Dillan took one little bite and decided that the taste was the weirdest thing he ever had in his mouth.

"So how many girls have you left behind in the ports you have visited, Sailor?"

"Few, very few," Dillan said with a smile. "You know, a French girl in Marseilles, a German in Berlin, a Chinese one in Hong Kong, a Polynesian girl in Hawaii, just like Ricky Nelson. Ha. Not really, wishful thinking. Maybe soon I should consider sticking to one and taking her with me."

Silence, she took a long pull on her wine glass. She looked 21 – and besides, Christie's was not about to ask for ID when a couple was spending the big bucks for dinner.

"A girl would be lucky to be the one you take with you, I think. You seem to be a nice guy soon to be Ensign Dillan, a nice guy."

And that was the beginning of a real romance. And it blossomed. When Dillan got engaged, the troops gave him a fully clothed trip into the shower.

Then time for OCS graduation, in working blue with white leggings on the lawn in front of the main building. Cool but clear day, Narraganset Bay sparkling in the sun. A light breeze made the color guard's flags flutter and company guide-ons, with their achievement ribbons streaming, stand out from their shafts. Drum beats and the bugle corps playing Anchors Aweigh. Dillan with his wrist up, cutlass tip tucked against his right shoulder, marching in front of his company for pass in review, proud as a peacock. Patty there in bleachers to watch.

After the parade, shift to service dress blue with its one gold band around the sleeve, officers cap with its gold chin strap, and his first salute by the company chief, acknowledged with a $5 bill – traditional.

After OCS he took a week's leave and he and Patty spent it together with time out for her classes. They went to Boston, walked the Freedom Trail and had raw clams from a cart in the Haymarket. They visited the USS CONSTITUTION in Charlestown. They visited Patty's aging aunt in Dorchester.

Finally, her parents drove them to T.F. Green Airport in Providence, and Dillan boarded a DC-9 for the hop to LaGuardia. Changing planes for a 707, Dillan was headed west again.

9

Once back in San Diego, Dillan was sent to Combat Information Center School and Air Intercept Controller School. San Diego was totally different this time. It was a military town in a war time environment. Ships were coming and going all the time. Service members were coming and going all the time, crowded, intense, expensive, and all military.

After the schools, and Christmas in the bachelor officer quarters at the Fleet Anti Air Warfare Center, Point Loma, Dillan went to USS LARTER (DD 766), which was getting an overhaul at the US Naval Shipyard, Long Beach, California. A shipyard was an awful noisy, dirty place. The ship was sitting at the bottom of a dry dock, big holes cut in the side, hull being sandblasted for new antifouling bottom paint. The electrical power was on and off.

LARTER was a construction project and verged on being uninhabitable. This was the first overhaul since FRAM, and there was a lot of work going on, mostly new electronics.

Although not really liking the idea, the captain finally agreed that the officers and enlisted could take up temporary quarters ashore. If the crew lived ashore, the ship was almost impossible to keep clean. But in the yards it was impossible anyway. They were moved to crummy old quarters. Two story wooden barracks left over from World War II.

Officers and chiefs were 8 to a room in bunk beds, communal head, and ate in a closed mess. The rooms had thin walls that ended 4 feet short of the high ceiling. Enlisted, 80 in a big open room, communal head, and ate in the base chow hall. It was better than living with the dirt and noise of a shipyard, but not much.

One was stuck on the ship 24 hours every 4th day for duty, and all day every day for work. It was almost impossible to sleep on duty nights and cold food brought over from the chow hall was typical. When the Navy Exchange Mobile Canteen, or 'roach coach', came down the pier, most grabbed something to eat there.

Dillan's job then was as electronic material officer, or EMO. The ship was getting a new communications electronic suite, a major upgrade. All the radios were changed out, new antennas installed, and radio central and radio II were totally rewired. New electronic countermeasures equipment was installed. The cabling design was badly screwed up and it took a lot of effort to sort out. Dillan had been well educated in the workings of communications and radar equipment, and worked hand in hand with his electronic technicians. And the result was a successful installation and the skipper was pleased.

Dillan got along well with his troops. Some Academy graduates were aloof and treated the enlisted people more like robots than humans. Having been there and done that, Dillan treated them like real people, and looked out for them. He worked them hard, but he respected them and they respected him in return. Dillan thought, "One day I was a 1st class petty officer, the next day an Ensign. I didn't change who I really was over that 24 hours."

Dillan and Patty talked often on the telephone, and wrote letters. There were the wedding plans: a small wedding with her family and friends at the local Episcopal Church. Dillan's dad was planning on coming. Dillan had arranged for the reception to be at the Datum Club, a smaller officer's club on the hill above the destroyer piers at Naval Station Newport.

They shared ideas about how to set up a home. Dillan was saving money but soon would need to buy another car, being wheel less then. Patty had never owned a car. And he needed to buy airplane tickets, two ways for himself and one way for her. She was finishing up her junior year.

Dillan had to tell her about a six months Westpac cruise starting in the fall of 1967. This did not go over really well with Patty. But then she said maybe she would go back to Newport and work at Cherry & Webb's again and be around her friends during the cruise. She wanted to finish her degree and would try to do that, maybe part time, in San Diego later.

There were twelve weeks in the yard, then weeks of sea trials and exercises. There was an old Navy adage which said USS stood for 'underway Saturday and Sunday' instead of 'United States Ship.' LARTER followed this adage.

In the spring of 1967, Dillan went back east and got married. He wore his dress whites; a small wedding and reception. Patrick and Patricia: the 'two Pats' as her friends called them. No honeymoon since he had to rush back. He was being sent to a 10 week Communication Officer course. They moved into a little apartment off Rachael Avenue in east National City, a suburb of San Diego, got crummy old blond oak furniture from the Navy's housing office ('early motel' Dillan called it), and tried to learn how to be man and wife.

The ten weeks were wonderful, since he had no duty, did not have to go to the ship, and had every weekend off. School was 8 AM to 4 PM each day. He and Patty saw San Diego, went to Disneyland, went to Sequoia National Park and Las Vegas, and enjoyed.

They started talking about the up coming separation.

Patty said, "Six months is a long time, and it'll be over the holidays. Maybe I should go home then?"

"I don't know, Honey; we had to scramble to get this little apartment way out here. And we had to sign a year's lease. We'll still have to pay. The only way to break a lease is with official transfer orders."

"Maybe I'll just stay here and get a job."

"That would be great. We sure could use the money. Ensigns don't get paid much. Being broke sucks."

"Maybe we really didn't need a new car, although I like the one you bought. A used car would have made more sense."

"Yea, probably, but I fell in love. The Lemans is super and with its 215 six, goes like the wind."

"You, Mr. Dillan, are a certifiable car nut. I'm sure the sales person was some cute woman who wiggled her tush at you, and you never had a chance."

"The sales person was an ugly old man, no tush at all, but I felt sorry for him: ears like Dumbo and more hair growing out of them than on his head. And anyway, if I fell in love, it was for the car."

"Only a man would fall in love with a machine. Sometimes I think you love it more than me," with a playful pout.

"No way, Beautiful Woman, no way. Besides, sleeping with a car is cold and oily. It doesn't have curves in the right places," giving her a big hug.

"What'm I going to do when I get lonely?"

"Well, a lot of the ship's officer's wives are staying here. You can go to dinner at the club with them now and then."

"That drill last week (required attendance for officer's wives at 'tea' at the CO's with the CO's wife) was not fun. Besides, tea wasn't the beverage of choice. And only three of us are married to JO's, all the rest were wives of Lieutenants or above; older, kids, nothing in common. Tammy Norstrand's nice and we pretty much sat together and listened, trying not to get totally lit on the never empty wine glasses. They even had stewards in white coats serving." ·

"Rank has its privileges. I'm sure all the wives left their card in the silver tray. Have to follow protocol. Not allowed to slip one in that says 'Bull Shit.' I'd like to see the CO's wife's reaction if someone did."

"We all did our naval officer's wifely duty. It's too stuffy. Wish there were more JO's wives."

You'll find more wives that are staying here. You guys can get together."

"I'll try. After this cruise how long before you have to leave me again?"

"Not a clue, Honey. We'll be getting orders summer 68. Could go east and I'll request that. But I sure can't tell."

"East would be good, maybe Florida? I love you. But I think your job really sucks."

"Sure does whenever it takes me away from you," with a peck on the cheek.

Dillan dreaded the thought of going off on a 6 month deployment. But he knew it came with the territory, and he would not be the first or the last to do so. And Patty knew that also. It was just a part of reality that civilians did not understand.

Deployment schedules for destroyers were usually 6 months in Westpac, 12 months back in Eastpac. But that changed. An overhaul would extend the time in Eastpac. Heavy operations requirements reduce it. So the 6 over, 12 back rule wasn't a rule at all, just a guide.

10

The time together for Dillan and his wife was not to last. It was summer 1967. Back on the ship and Dillan relieved the communications officer, a LTJG who, unhappily had orders to an 'incountry' tour in Vietnam. Those assignments were for 1 year, naturally unaccompanied by spouses, and were risky. Most were to the riverine forces running boats up and down the extensive river system to patrol or provide fire support for the ground forces. Frank sure had not volunteered. But he had "refused" one set of preliminary orders to a DLG (destroyer leader guided missile) out of Long Beach. He had requested Norfolk. Refusing one set was allowed, but seldom done since the second set usually was worse.

LTJG Frank Norstrand, USN, a regular NROTC graduate, social science, from North Carolina State in 1965, had been on LARTER for 2 years. He had been assigned as Dillan's 'host' when he arrived, and later he and Patty had had dinner at their (wife's name Tammy) apartment in Chula Vista. Frank was a nice guy, and he helped Dillan get his act together with the communications officer's job before he went off to a short Vietnamese language school enroute to Vietnam.

Then Refresher Training started for LARTER. Reftra was a 6 week workup to get a ship ready for deployment. Designed to be exhausting and stressful, it easily met its goals. They were underway almost every day for a week at a time. There were drills, drills, and more drills as they exercised all the weapons, day and night.

Critical evaluators were aboard grading everything. When in port, LARTER hung on a mooring buoy off Shelter Island, a 45 minute boat trip to fleet landing. This was undoubtedly to discourage the crew from going ashore, and it worked, mostly. Dillan went ashore every chance he got, but it usually meant home at 10PM, gone again by 5AM. Maybe two days a week maximum, mostly one, sometimes a weekend day off.

Once he had to go to the ship for a meeting on a Saturday, late afternoon. He decided to have Patty come and have dinner in the wardroom. They went down to the fleet landing to catch a boat to the ship. And the CO was there with his Captain's Gig. This was the ship's one and only motor whale boat, and only called the

Gig when the skipper was aboard it. He asked if Dillan and Patty wanted to ride with him. The Gig had a white plastic cover over the bow section like a cabin.

Once in the Gig and headed for the ship, Patty said, "Captain, I have no understanding why, on a weekend, the ship is hanging way out there on a buoy instead of being at a perfectly good pier?"

'Well, Mrs. Dillan, the Navy decided that is where we're to be now."

"But it makes no sense. The men leaving the ship have to ride the boats, and it takes time away from their families, and burns up extra gas." Dillan was getting nervous.

Patty is getting into challenging the skipper!

"It keeps the crew ready for training," the skipper said.

"Well, Captain, I think it's stupid. You should have the ship at a pier on the weekends at least. Then all the men could go home and see their families, and have time before the ship goes running off for 6 months. You should think about your men and their family's more."

No answer from the captain. Dillan was mortified. But that was Patty: tell it like she saw it. He loved that in her, but not with the skipper!

Quiet for awhile, just the boat's engine noise and ripple sounds from the hull. Smell of salt air and diesel fumes. Coxswain standing on his platform driving, bow hook man standing beside him, both in undress whites, looking ahead over the top.

"Thanks for your opinion, Patricia," was the final reply from the skipper, said quite distinctly. She looked a little mortified at that. Bit her lip.

The rest of the boat ride was uneventful. The skipper made small talk about Newport. And Patty made small talk back.

Dillan went to his meeting and Patty sat in his stateroom to read. Dinner in the wardroom was uneventful, only a few officers aboard and the captain gone again. Patty was a hit and got lots of attention. Then they rode a 40 ft utility boat provided by the Naval Station back to the fleet landing. Dillan had Sunday off, thank God. But Monday at 5AM, back to the ship.

All ships had certain exercises they had to complete every year. Although they did these exercises on their own for training, finally they were done again for a grade with evaluators, normally from Fleet Training Group or the squadron staff. The grade a ship got on these counted towards the coveted Battle Efficiency "E."

LARTER did well enough, getting top honors in engineering and anti submarine warfare, but not well enough to win the overall "E" in competition with the other 9 ships in the squadron. The captain was not pleased. Dillan's division came in 2nd place for the communications "C", but as far as Fred was concerned 2nd place was totally unacceptable. Close only counts in horse shoes and hand grenades.

"If you had ridden your troops harder we could have made the "C," Fred said. "You just don't demand enough of them. You let'm slack off. And if we had made the "C," and one other first place, we would have gotten the "E". You don't try hard enough. Coddling'm again, I see."

"I worked their buns off, but we had a tough old master chief for our evaluator, and he nitpicked everything. Some of the other ships had better evaluators," from Dillan.

Reality was that he had worked his troops hard, but had not insisted that they spend their liberty time aboard working also. They were departing soon for 6 months and needed to be with their families or friends. Dillan was not into image. He wanted his group competent and capable. But winning wasn't everything. And the evaluator they had was known for being very tough – a lot tougher than the other evaluators: the luck of the draw.

"Don't blame things on the grader, blame it on yourself. There is no excuse for not winning, no excuse. Better get your act together, Mister."

Slowly the crew learned and started functioning as a team. General quarters (battle stations) could be manned and ready in less than 4 minutes. Guns fired quickly and accurately, generally at tug towed sleds or aircraft towed sleeves. They did Naval Gunfire Support training, shooting at San Clemente Island trying to miss the goats, who were its only inhabitants.

Damage control parties could make temporary repairs or fight simulated fires. The ship could come along side an oiler or stores ship and execute underway replenishment. Aircraft could be controlled through voice radio while tracking them on the air search radar. Imaginary night PT boat attacks could be repulsed, and a solid week of playing hide and seek with a US Navy submarine. LARTER had become a fighting ship.

The skipper arranged a command performance dinner at the North Island officer's club. It was nice and a chance for all the wives to meet each other, if they had not already. But a bit stuffy, Dillan thought.

Many of the officers wore a burgundy blazer with the ship's patch on the left pocket, purchased last cruise in Hong Kong. Most of the new officers just wore regular blazers and khaki slacks. Wives wore cocktail dresses. And there was a lot of booze and wine consumed.

During the preliminary cocktail hour, Fred even came over to Pete, Dillan and their wives. Fred was wearing a white shirt, Navy blue suit, blue and gold striped Naval Academy tie, and even a Naval Academy tie tack. Suit looked expensive.

"Nice chance for the officers to meet the wives," he said, looking at Patty and then Dillan.

"Patty, this is Fred Finistry, my boss."

Fred said, taking her hand, "Nice to meet you Patty. Dillan here got lucky to marry such a beautiful woman."

"Thank you," pulling her hand back. "But I'm the lucky one." Oh, thank you Patty, Dillan thought. Patty was more than aware of what Dillan thought about Fred.

Then a look at Pete, "And Mr. Donovan, introduce me to your wife."

"Rita, this is my boss, LT Finistry."

He did not take her hand. "Pleased to meet you, Rita, hope you're enjoying San Diego."

"Yes I am, especially when my husband is not on that damn ship." Good for you Rita, Dillan thought.

"Well, getting the ship ready takes time. We want to be 100% prepared for our cruise. Rest assured that the Operations Department will be 110% ready. Make sure the wives get to talk to the skipper and XO. I have some other people to meet, enjoy yourselves," and Fred was gone.

"He's a true Boston blue blood, the pompous ass," Patty said quietly watching Fred's back as he walked away. "And Fred needed nailed, Rita, he needed to hear that."

"He strikes me as one of those who hears only what he wants to. And he's way too quick at making Pete do some stupid job before he can come home. Pete says he does that to you, too Dillan?"

"Sure does, all the time. Fred's one of those who thinks his polish is his personality. I think he dreams in blue and gold, sees himself as CNO. Too much time hobnobbing with the jet set. He looks down his nose at everyone who doesn't own a company or have lots of rank."

Dillan went on, "Suit probably cost two month's pay. And did you see the tie? Naval Academy, figures, a real ring knocker. Fred doesn't give a crap about others unless he can use them to make himself look good."

"OK, Pat, enough already," from Patty. "Let's talk about something a whole lot more fun than Fred. Let's talk about going to the beach next Sunday."

When the dinner was over, they were glad. The girls thought the CO, XO and Chris and Red were nice. And they thought Ted was funny – always the clown. Telling knock knock jokes and doing a fair impression of Sergeant Bilko. They thought Billy looked like he was 12.

Getting home from North Island was a long trip. Instead of waiting for the ferry, Dillan drove all the way around through Coronado.

Dillan and Patty saw Pete and Rita seldom socially. They lived quite away apart, Dillan and Pete were in opposing duty sections, and there just wasn't time. Patty and Rita would meet to shop and grab a bite now and then when the ship was at sea. They got some funny looks sometimes – a young black woman and a young white woman together.

11

After a few short weeks in port, standing 4 section duty, it was time for a two week fleet exercise. LARTER was out there with a bunch of destroyers chasing submarines and doing endless maneuvering to tactical signals. One night they were all charging around changing stations when a couple of ships almost had a collision. The skipper had LARTER haul out to starboard and wait until the dust had settled. No need to dent the metal.

Then there was an issue that popped up during one of Dillan's Saturday duties. About 2:30 in the afternoon one of the enlisted men in the duty section, a machinist mate 3rd class, came to Dillan's stateroom.

"Mr. Dillan, I have a problem. I need to get off the ship right now."

No crow on the sleeve, but a darker place where one had been, small enough to be just a 3rd. Dungaree crows were iron on and didn't stand up to the ship's laundry unless also stitched in place. Looking at the man's name stenciled over his dungaree shirt pocket, "You're in engineering, Bigsby, aren't you? Did you talk with your duty engineer?"

"Yes, sir, Senior Chief Smallson is the duty engineer, he said I needed to talk to you, and that you would help me talk to the CDO."

Dillan thought, get me to run interference, since I am a mustang. Get me to help him convince the Command Duty Officer (CDO) to let him go. *Careful.*

"OK, Bigsby, what's the problem?"

"My wife's having a miscarriage and I have to go help her."

"Where is she?"

"In a motel just outside the base gate."

"Did she call for medical assistance? We can call the Naval Hospital and have them send an ambulance and EMT."

"No, she just called me. And she don't need no hospital."

"How long ago?"

"About 20 minutes. I really need to go right now, Mr. Dillan."

"Just a moment, come with me. Give me the name of the motel. Do you have a phone number?"

"No number," a long pause while Dillan gave him a questioning look, "It's the Baseside Inn, on Pacific Highway, sir."

Dillan went into Fred's stateroom. Fred was ashore. Fred had a shore connected telephone and Dillan called information, got the number, and called the motel. Bigsby stood there, nervously.

When he got the motel on the line, he asked Bigsby for the room number. Bigsby told him. But Bigsby was getting real agitated.

Dillan had the motel ring the room.

"Hello."

"Mrs. Bigsby?" from Dillan.

Silence, then, "I'm not Mrs. Bigsby."

"May I speak to Mrs. Bigsby; this is the duty officer on her husband's ship calling."

"I'm, I'm his girlfriend."

"This is Ensign Dillan. He tells me his wife - or you - are sick. Having a miscarriage he said."

"I'm not sick. I just told him that to get him to come see me."

"Well, if you're sick, get the motel to call an ambulance from San Diego General. And this game won't work. Bigsby is not coming to see you, he has the duty. He will be off at 8 AM tomorrow and can come then if he wishes. Any questions?"

"No, goodbye," and she hung up.

Dillan turned to the Sailor, "Bigsby, either you have been had or we both have. She said she was not your wife. Do you have a wife? Why would your girl friend pull a stunt like that?"

"I have a wife sir, back in Iowa. I don't know what came over Elsa to call like that. I thought for sure it was real."

Dillan wasn't sure he bought it. But there was a remote possibility that Bigsby had not been in on the scam himself.

Standing, "Well, Bigsby, get your story right the next time you come to me. Telling me she was your wife was a lie. And if your girl friend is pregnant, and you know you are the father, you have a bigger problem to deal with – especially when your wife finds out. Now get back to your duties. And, you have to tell Smallson, now, dismissed."

"Yes, sir," with a sad look, and he turned and walked towards the officer's country door.

The enlisted were quite good at trying to figure ways to get away from a duty day, mostly on a Saturday. Some of the stories got quite creative. Especially from those who thought of themselves as sea lawyers. But "my wife is having a miscarriage" was one of the best excuses yet.

LARTER was judged ready for deployment by Fleet Training Group after passing the Operational Readiness Evaluation, and by COMCRUDESPAC (Commander Cruiser Destroyer Force, Pacific Fleet) inspectors. The CO posted the letter on the board outside the ship's office.

Dillan bought up all the teletype paper he could find and stuffed it into every corner of the operations department's spaces, remembering Frank's tales of shortages. As the Registered Publications System (RPS) custodian, Dillan made a registered publications run.

Crypto material was all considered registered publications and had to be very carefully controlled, kept under an officer's custody, and every page and all the associated equipment accounted for. Screwing up as a registered publication system custodian guaranteed you an all expense paid tour to Portsmouth Naval Prison for an extended stay. It was an administrative nightmare, but came with the territory for a communications officer.

Once, Dillan lost a cover page for a tactical publication. There was a system of periodic page changes, and somehow one of the old pages had gotten lost. And he had made the page changes. It was only a cover page but still from an RPS publication listed as confidential. Knowing that this was going to be a major awh shit for him personally, he went into a frantic search.

He went through every safe, every publication, and every file cabinet. No luck. It looked alarming. Like there was going to have to be a formal report to the entire chain of command of the ship, and all the way to Washington.

If lucky, all he would get was a letter of reprimand in his service record. And his Navy career would be over, although he would have to stick it out, probably as a permanent Ensign, until at least June 1970.

Reluctantly he told Fred. All Fred would say is, "You better find it Mister. Find it or die."

Finally, the panic culminated with dumpster diving with a flash light at night. He found it, in the ship's trash, a bit stained from coffee grounds, but there. He came out of the dumpster looking like a khaki hobo and smelling worse.

Fred had fun with that one.

"You got lucky there, Dillan. Thought you were going to really get in over your head: in garbage. Was it fun in the dumpster? Maybe we should get you some coveralls for your next dumpster diving trip. Maybe a wet suit."

"There'll be no next trip."

"Better not be. You dodged a bullet this time."

"Yes, sir."

You probably already had the gun loaded and an itchy trigger finger.

12

Fall 1967: the day of departure rushed at Dillan and Patty like an oncoming thunder storm. It was always there, closer and closer, and it overshadowed their life. They tried to be normal, to think normal, but the dark cloud spread over them, ever encroaching, ever darker. Finally, it was their last sleepless night holding each other, then into the early morning.

Patty decided not to come down to the ship to see Dillan off. They talked about it. Getting underway would be a total zoo. They decided that they would say goodbye at home. It was 6:30 AM: Dillan in service dress blue, bag packed by the door.

"You will write me every day, every day just like you promised," she said. They were standing by the door, in each other's arms, her still in her nighty.

"I will. I will. Every day," from Dillan. His eyes were misting over.

Damn, brace up, Mister. Grown men don't get weepy.

"Hold me tighter. This really sucks. I ... I want you here. Tell'm to go to hell, your wife won't let you come," in his arms looking up at him.

"I don't want any part of it, but six months'll go quick."

"Crap. Double crap. When will you call me?"

"I'll try from Hawaii, but can't be sure. We have to do a carrier work up there, and I don't even know if I'll get ashore or for how long. But if I can, I will."

Another long hug as she trembled in his arms. He pulled her back and looked at her face. Tears, tears were running down both cheeks.

"Honey, I really have to go. Sam came over to pick me up you know. He's waiting. Traffic will be a bitch, and we're supposed to be there by 7:30."

"I think I'll tie you to the bed. Then you'll be right where I want you," in his ear as she hugged him. She tilted her head back, "Give me a kiss, a good one, enough to last six months."

A long kiss, then Dillan pulled away. He turned, not daring to look back, and out the door he went grabbing his bag. He went down the stairs and into Sam's waiting car. Bag tossed in the back seat. Silence, as Sam pulled out.

"Leaving a wife must be a bitch," Sam said.

"A real bitch, Greeny, a real bitch."

"Some one told me once that if the Navy had wanted you to have a wife or family, they would have issued you one."

"No shit, I've heard that one. Seems like that, especially right now," from Dillan. He felt like his heart had been ripped out.

They drove to the ship in silence. Sam turned his car keys over to the storage representative at the pier parking lot. They would store his car until LARTER returned: inside storage in an old warehouse on the waterfront. They would put it up on blocks and run the engine every 2 weeks for $80 per month. It was expensive, but the only way to keep a car in good shape.

If one left a car for 6 months in the head of the pier parking lot one could expect to come home to a car with most of the paint rotted off from the acid generated by all the ships blowing boiler tubes, mixed with rust spots from the salt air. Just parking there on a daily basis required weekly washes and monthly wax jobs to keep the yellow spots off a white top.

They walked to the brow together. Ted had the watch. Even though it was still early, there were families on the pier. Dillan went aboard and tossed his bag into his bunk.

At 0730, "Now all hands muster on station; make muster reports to the ship's office. Now make all preparations for getting underway, make readiness reports to the officer of the deck on the quarterdeck," came over the 1MC.

Then up to the wardroom for coffee. Not a good idea. There were wives and a couple of who knows kids there. He saw Pete's wife who waved at him. She knew Patty wasn't coming. The CO's wife was there.

"Where's Patty, Dillan?" she asked.

"Decided to say good bye at home, Maam. She thought the ship would be a zoo."

"A zoo it is Dillan, usually a zoo at departure and again at return," from Chris' wife.

Dillan knew that she had been through these cruises multiple times. Like this was her third in 5 years. It took a special woman to do it, Dillan thought. She must have come to terms with spending six months alone, with a kid, and running her own life.

Then the husband comes home and the situation changes. He also knew that the divorce rate in the Navy was twice what it was in civilian life. And that there were lots of alcohol and anti depressant drug problems for wives. The US Navy's chaplains were always trying to sort out marriages on the rocks because of the separations.

Dillan went by radio. All calm. All present. Then he went up to the bridge. About half way up the ladder,

"Now station the special sea and anchor detail," from the 1MC preceded with a shrill 2 note whistle on a bosun's pipe.[xix]

Glad Patty didn't come. We would've had a few more moments, and then I would be up here on the bridge, and she would be stuck in the wardroom until the wives and children were herded ashore. It's nice to remember her in our little apartment.

"The officer of the deck is shifting his watch from the quarterdeck to the bridge." On the bridge Dillan assumed the JOOD watch. The OOD had the Conn.

The captain and XO came on the bridge and the CO was announced.

Fred ordered, "Main control, bridge, stand by to test main engines."

"Main control, aye," from the JA phone talker.

"All stations, testing main engines," was passed by the multitude of sound powered phone talkers standing behind the helmsman.

"All ahead one third." Then, "All stop." LARTER surged against her lines as each engine spun up a bit then stopped.

Dillan watched from the bridge wing. They were all alone at the end of the pier, port side to. The going and coming spot as it was called. Civilians and the squadron commander were ashore. Families were waving. Brow moved off to the pier. He knew that on the other side two pusher boats were standing by. But he figured they would not be needed. It was a nice day, little wind, and besides destroyer skippers prided themselves on handling their ships without tugs.

"Main control reports ready to answer all bells."

"Captain, we're ready when you are," Fred said.

"Very well, let's single up."

Fred turned and said to the 1JV phone talker, "Single up."

Single up meant take in the double line loops leaving only one strand of the 6 lines still connected. Usually the ship was moored with a bow and stern line, and two sets of crossed forward and aft facing spring lines – one set forward, one set aft. Then an extra loop was passed to the pier for each line, making three strands of each. Mooring lines were numbered 1 through 6 starting at the bow.

The captain said, "OK, XO, let's get this show on the road."

"Yes, sir. On the bridge, this is the XO, I have the conn."

"This is Mr. Finestry, the XO has the conn."

The helm and lee helm answered up.

Then from the XO, "Hold two, take in one, three, four, five and six."

The line handlers scrambled pulling up the remaining single strands for all but line number 2.

"Left full rudder, starboard ahead one third."

"Starboard stop."

LARTER twisted left, bow in, stern out, held from going forward by the number two or aft running spring line.

"Rudder amidships."

"Take in two."

"Underway, shift colors," as the last line was lifted off the pier bollard and pulled back to the ship. The ensign (flag) at the stern and the union jack on the bow were lowered and another ensign was raised at the truck on the back of the forward mast.

"All back one third."

"One long blast, three short blasts." The ship's whistle moaned one long wail and then three short toots: Inland rules of the nautical road. One long blast meant I am underway, e.g. I am no longer moored or attached to a pier. Three short meant my engines are in reverse.

LARTER backed into the fairway, turbulence and a flat spot in the water from the screws moving up each side. Once clear of the pier, engines were put to all ahead 1/3 and left standard rudder was ordered. She slowed to a stop and then started forward, swinging left.

"All hands to quarters for leaving port."

The troops who did not have stations for controlling the ship or handling the lines formed up in ranks on the weather decks, self generated wind lifting their blue collars up against the back of their heads and white hats. Line handlers were rolling mooring lines up on big grey drums for storage. Bow men standing by to let go an anchor if an engine or rudder problem occurred.

Down through San Diego harbor LARTER went, leaving the naval station behind. Crowd on the pier dwindling in the distance, while some still waved, and others walked back to their cars.

Down town moving by on the right, then Point Loma rising out of the sea on the left behind the hangers at NAS North Island on the left. A long sweeping left turn into the outer channel, past the Marine base, Naval Recruit Training Center, and speed increased to 10 knots. Soon a freshening breeze and the clean smell of the sea.

"Secure from quarters." The crew scrambled back inside. LARTER ran south well past the tip of Point Loma and the Cabrillo National Monument and light house, past 1SD, the outer red channel buoy bobbing on the left, its bell just audible over the ship's noise. Then a right turn to the West, pointed at the open sea. The ship started to rise and fall to the long low Pacific swell. Wind increased.

A glance astern and the tan and green of the land capped with the brown haze of smog making the distant mountains only shadows. Gone: off for a six months Westpac cruise to the Western Pacific and Vietnam.

13

The ship went north and met another destroyer. Off San Francisco they rendezvoused with a carrier and headed west for Hawaii. During the transit there were exercises and some 'tic-tacs' where ships were ordered to different stations around the carrier to practice signal book work and maneuvering.

The Task Unit, 10.2.3, stopped in Pearl Harbor for a few short days. Dillan did get an opportunity to spend most of an entire day ashore with Pete and some of the other junior officers. They went to the USS ARIZONA memorial, and rented a car and drove up through the hills to the north side to see the famous Bonsai Pipeline, and the Punch Bowl. They had drinks at the Royal Hawaiian, expensive as hell, then dinner at Fort Derussy, the Army's recreation club near the Royal Hawaiian and Waikiki beach.

Dillan talked to Patty for a few moments on the telephone. She was looking for a job and lonely. Conversation strained and kept to small talk.

"Some day you must promise to take me to Hawaii," she said.

"I sure will, Honey. It's a very pretty place, all the palm trees and flowers, big flowers that I've never seen before. But crowded and lots of oriental looking people. Expensive."

"You didn't spend a lot of money, did you? You know we're tight as hell. Will you call me again?"

"Didn't spend much, I'm the resident cheap skate. I'll try from Japan, maybe in a couple of weeks."

Finally the, "Love you, bye."

"Love you, bye."

Then there was a 3 day carrier work up where the pilots made bombing runs on a deserted target island. There was one plane guard incident.

Upon completion, they were off for Yokosuka, Japan, a US Navy base on a peninsula south of Tokyo. It was a very rough trip across the northern pacific. Sometimes the ship's bow was totally buried in a wave right up to the bridge. Dillan was sick again. As they crossed the International Date Line there was an initiation ceremony for entering the "Realm of the Golden Dragon."

Like the initiations for crossing the Equator (shellback) or crossing the Artic Circle (bluenose), complete with a chief dressed up as King Neptune and lots of degrading for the uninitiated, including Dillan: traditions that went back 100's of years.

Also, as the task group crossed the date line, it "chopped" or changed operational commanders to COMSEVENTHFLT from COMFIRSTFLT. Now they were officially in "Westpac", but still under CINCPACFLT. And one day of their lives disappeared, regainable when they crossed again on their way back to the states.

About half way across the north western Pacific they had their obligatory fly over by a Soviet bomber. The bomber was expected and fighters were launched. As the bomber came low over the carrier, there were two US F-4 Phantom jets tucked in under and behind his wings.[xx]

Yokosuka was a World War II Japanese navy base turned over to the US at the end of the war. It stuck out into Tokyo Bay. It was big and mountainous with caves and tunnels everywhere. There were dry docks and a shipyard. Some US ships were even home ported there. Yokosuka was about 50 miles south of Tokyo.

Pete and Dillan took the train from Yokosuka to Tokyo for half a day.

"This place is a multi-level ant hill," from Pete as they walked through Tokyo station.

"The world's largest train station, but a least some of the signs have English subtitles."

As they exited the station, it was cold with snow flurries. They walked around the Imperial Palace huddled in their jackets, then a walk through the Ginza or shopping district. At a store front restaurant they ate tempura, a light battered fried thing.

"Hell, Pete", Dillan said as they ate, "even the vegetables are fried. And this hot sake is semi-sweet and oily -- different from any wine I've had before, but warming from the stomach upward. Yum."

"I sure can do with warm. That wind off Tokyo Wan is like an Alberta clipper in Pittsburg. Freeze the balls off a brass monkey. This sake isn't bad. But these tiny cups should keep us from getting crocked. There's only one swallow in each," as he popped one down.

"I think you are supposed to sip it, not gulp it down like beer, you heathen. Interesting that they have their own scotch – I've heard the only country outside Scotland that makes scotch, tastes different."

"You go ahead and drink that Suntory stuff. I'll stick to hot sake, even if I have to pour it out of these little jugs all the time. If you're not going to drink yours, hand it over. Probably shouldn't be drinking both at the same time anyway; mixing hard liquor and wine. You'll get looped twice as fast."

"Yeah, OK, you drink the sake – I'll drink the Suntory," from Dillan passing his jug over while waving his arm at the waiter.

"Kompai," from Pete as he popped another down.

"Domo arigato," from Dillan to the waiter as a fresh Suntory scotch and water was delivered.

"God, we're turning into Japs."

"It'll take more than sake or booze to make that change. Just practicing from the wonderful military phrase book."

"A few more pops and we'll both be speaking Japanese like natives."

"Yeah, but we won't understand it – hell, we won't understand English," from Dillan.

When they got back to the train station, they promptly got on the wrong train and headed north instead of south. The scotch and sake probably had something to do with the mistake. Had to get off at a small station and catch another train back south to Tokyo station again. It took hours.

Tokyo was not a vacation spot, in Dillan's mind. It was very expensive and very crowded. Taxis had white seat covers. And the joke was that all the World War II Kamikaze pilots who didn't have airplanes took up as cab drivers in Tokyo: the divine wind of the roadways. Crazy drivers, but one had to be to zip in and out of traffic like they did.

Dillan tried to telephone Patty again. But after 3 attempts and 5 hours total wait time, he gave up. A few more cold and rainy days in Yokosuka to fix what the rough seas broke, drinks one night in the club's Black Ship bar, then off, via the Taiwan Straits, with a carrier task group, for Subic Bay in the Philippines.[xxi]

Subic was the main base for ships involved in the Vietnam War. A large bay northwest of Manila, on the west coast of Luzon, it had a major US Naval Base and a Naval Air Station. Built by the Spanish in the 1890s, it was a good location with a great harbor. It had been used by the occupying Japanese during World War II.[xxii] The air station, across the bay, was called Cubi Point, and the carriers tied up there.

The rest of the ships tied up, usually 3 or 4 deep, to the main base piers. Sunny and warm, Subic had a great officers club, and even a telephone exchange where for a fortune one could make phone calls to the states.

Dillan went to the telephone exchange as soon as he could after arrival in Subic. One went in, signed up, and waited for the operators to connect your call, like Yokosuka. Used under ocean cables. Maybe an hour or two later, sometimes a lot longer, you were notified and went into one of a bank of phone booths.

It was mostly very crowded in the morning since morning in Subic was evening the day before on the west coast of the USA. Subic was 16 hours ahead of San Diego. Dillan talked to Patty for 23 minutes. She was lonely, depressed, and generally miserable.

"You didn't call me like you promised. It's been weeks. I'm all alone in this damn place and there you are with hundreds of other guys."

"Not all it's cracked up to be Honey, and being stuck on the same ship with Fred is no fun."

"Screw Fred. Screw the Navy," said with an edge to her voice.

"How is your job search going?"

"I got a job at the Chula Vista branch of Bank of America as a teller, but it doesn't pay much. I'm thinking about getting Karen (another Navy wife whose husband was deployed on another destroyer and who lived in the apartment complex) to move in with me. Then we can share expenses," she said.

Dillan knew things were tight. Ensigns did not make much and San Diego was expensive. In a military town, demand for everything was high and supply was low. Patty had decided to wait until he left to get a job, so she could be available for the few times he got off the ship. She had taken a couple of summer courses at San Diego Community College.

Dillan said, "I got the china and stuff that was on your list at A-33, the special NEX (Navy Exchange) in Yoko they told us about, not much selection here in Subic."

"You get the Mikasa pattern I wanted? But to hell with things, I am married 7 months and abandoned by my husband." Then, in her little girl's voice, "I miss you."

"Yeah, I got the pattern, service for 8. Cost $48. I miss you too, Honey. But 5 months from now we'll forget all this."

"Maybe, I think I'll remember it forever. This Navy wife stuff sucks."

"I haven't received all your letters, you wrote every day like we said right?"

"Most days, unless I was too upset, and sometimes I'd write, but they would pile up on the dresser till I could get to the post office. And your letters come in batches and are weird with all that Navy jargon. Talk about us, not some damn air craft carrier."

"Are you going to use the tape recorder and make me a tape?"

"The damn thing intimidates me…maybe sometime."

They made small talk: stilted small talk. Like the miles separating them were a thick fog that they could just barely hear through. And the connection had an echo which made it seem, oh so far. The reality of the separation had come home to roost.

"Well, I've got to go, Honey. Phone calls from here cost a fortune."

"When will you call me again, and why can't you call earlier." Dillan had to wait until 2PM to get through – and it was 10PM for Patty. "It's late and I have to go to work in the morning."

"Sorry, it was the only time I could get a connection. Bye, and I love and miss you."

"I love you, too."

Cost $63, so much for a morale boost. Being a Navy wife was not setting too well with Patty.

Four days later, underway with the carrier task group for Yankee Station, that circle in the ocean, roughly 60 miles south of

Communist China's Hainan Island, where the carriers operated. Sometimes there was just one carrier on station, generally launching strikes to help the ground forces in South Vietnam. When a big attack on North Vietnam was on, there could be 2 or even more carriers all launching or retrieving strikes 24/7. Then Yankee Station would move a little north to shorten flight times[xxiii].

LARTER was assigned to USS RANGER (CVA 61) (CVA=Carrier, Aircraft, Attack) as one of three destroyers. USS KITTYHAWK (CVA 63) was due on station soon bringing the current total to 2. The first week was picket duty 4000 yards away from the carrier. It was an easy, if boring, job. Then take plane guard station off the carrier's stern.

All part of the glory of the Tonkin Gulf Yacht Club.[xxiv]

14

Back to reality in Westpac, chasing a carrier on Yankee Station, and Dillan was up for a boring mid watch, then off watch and back to the rack. The watch was uneventful. A few loops to recover CAP and launch new ones. When Dillan was relieved after the mid at 0345, he tumbled into his rack and slept like a log. Since he had the mid, he could sleep till 0700. Everyone else was expected to be up at 0600.

After a quick shower, he got into fresh wash khakis. One had to pull the pressed like cardboard pant legs apart to get one's foot in. Dillan had requested no starch. But by what he could see from the other officers and chiefs – one starch level fit all: heavy. It took a little time, with fresh khakis, to be able to walk like a man instead of a robot.

And the laundry was hell on uniforms. Fraying after 3 months was the norm. Since officers had to buy their own, Dillan was always getting new ones at the uniform shop when the ship was in port.

Dillan got a cup of coffee from the crew's mess where one could get coffee in steaming heavy white ceramic mugs, one sugar, and no cream. There wasn't anything but powdered milk, or filled milk which was reconstituted powdered milk with coconut fat added for cream. It had a light brown tint and tasted funny. One wasn't supposed to take the mugs off the mess decks, so he used his own mug with the ship's patch on it and his name, picked up in Yoko for $4. Then up to radio.

He had heard that some enterprising Sailor had his wife send him a case of the tiny cans of evaporated milk and then sold them for $5 each. But Dillan had learned to drink his coffee black with sugar only aboard VULCAN, so he was not lining up to pay $5. Dillan seldom ate breakfast and was late for the wardroom seating anyway.

He ran into Joe.

"Hey there, Mr. D. Heard that the FTs and TM's (Fire Control Technicians and Torpedomen) are running a black jack game in the hanger. They wanted someone to pass the word around. Need fresh money."

"The skipper and XO will take a dim view of that. And if an officer buys in – slit," said Dillan making the throat cutting gesture.

"Not advocating khaki involvement – just a heads up."

"They better keep it below the XO's or Fred's radar or they will have some serious incoming to deal with. The hanger isn't a real creative location. How'd they pull it off without the MAA getting on them? One of the MAAs is a first class FT."

"Strickland's in on the game, but yeah, I'll tell'em."

Dillan knew that the master at arms force (MAA) was a collateral duty assigned to one 1st class and three 2nd class petty officers. Men of the MAA force were supposed to keep order on the mess decks and keep gambling, liquor stills, and other unauthorized diversions in check. They also helped with captain's mast and managed the tiny brig.

And floating craps, poker, and black jack games were the norm aboard ship at sea for the enlisted.

Hell, I financed my first used car with winnings in 62.

But most officers would stop it if they become aware. Young enlisted could get into real financial difficulty. The usual follow up to the games was loan sharking to cover losses above cash on hand at exorbitant rates. This was racketeering and would be dealt with harshly. Joe knew better. And Strickland, if caught, was in for a crowectamy.[xxv]

I better let on I know about the game to my chief. That might be enough to make it go away quietly. God, Joe. This is real stupid.

Every 4th day the destroyer had to come alongside the carrier for underway replenishment. Destroyers had small tanks and all the running around ate fuel like crazy. So every 4th morning set the underway replenishment detail. Dillan was lucky. His unrep station was as CIC watch officer in combat. Not much to do and a chance to sit. But it kept him from doing his normal work for the 3 hours it took. LARTER would top off from the carrier's massive tanks, and then go back to station.

Each US Navy ship had what was called the Watch, Quarter and Station Bill. This chart listed every man's job for every evolution the ship engaged in. Not that everyone had a different job for each. And some only had one job for all. However, most men had to get to their station when an evolution was called away.[xxvi]

Dillan had different assignments on the Watch Quarter and Station Bill for most evolutions and for watches. And these would be changed periodically as the captain attempted to broaden the knowledge base and impart skills to his young officers. The captain also had to insure that his most competent officers were on their best station for critical evolutions, like general quarters.

Dillan noticed a message on the board, outgoing from the captain to the carrier skipper. Nominate ENS Patrick Dillan, USN, Top Secret Clearance certified and ENS William (Billy) Hoffman, USN, Secret Clearance certified for cross deck training.

Oh boy, a chance to spend some time on the bird farm Wonder why he didn't pick boat school types?

Also an intel message indicating that the Soviet AGI, (Auxiliary, General, Intelligence) a small trawler like ship, was headed for Yankee Station. During flight operations the Soviet Union usually kept a small intelligence ship within eye shot of the carriers operating on Yankee Station. These looked like fishing trawlers, and had probably been converted from one. They bristled with antennas, and flew the white and light blue stripe on the bottom Soviet navy flag, with a red star and hammer & sickle, if they flew any flag at all.[xxvii]

For the past two weeks there had been no AGI on station. That was about to end. Since they were in international waters there was not much that the US Navy could do besides play shadow and keep between the AGI and the carriers. Maybe have the destroyer play "rules of the nautical road" with them by keeping on their right side in crossing situations and making the AGI turn away.

An offline encrypted message was waiting. Dillan took it to crypto, set up the equipment and started the laborious task of typing one character at a time in. Clunk, clunk, clunk. Once it was broken, Dillan put it on the Top Secret board and took it to the captain. The captain was in his chair on the starboard inside corner of the bridge, where he spent most waking hours. He took the board, read and initialed the message, and said,

"Thank you, Mr. Dillan. Make sure the XO, Ops and Weapons read this."

Off Dillan went to find these officers. The message was about an upcoming exercise, just administrative.

Most FRAM destroyers carried small nuclear depth charges which could be launched using the ASROC. But it required a special coded message from the President for authorization to launch. It was a very strict system, requiring 4 different officer's involvement. It was tested every so often on a random basis. This message was to be another test. No launch, just administration and procedures.[xxviii]

LARTER got relieved from plane guard and went out to picket station. The ship had been having a lot of problems with the Drone Anti Submarine Helicopter (DASH). LARTER carried two. They were about the size of a Volkswagen, unmanned, had counter rotating rotors, were jet turbine powered, and theoretically could be flown under radio control out to 10 miles from the ship. They could carry the MK 44 or new MK 46 homing torpedoes. The idea was a stand off weapon delivery system.[xxix]

The DASH idea was one that was great in concept and awful in execution. DASH was a major maintenance headache and very difficult to fly. Flight control consoles were on the helo deck and in combat. But DASH had a tendency to just go flying over the horizon, ignoring radio commands, never to be seen again. LARTER had lost one during Reftra in the SoCal (Southern California) operations area, big flap. Later all ships had been limited to flying DASH no more than 5 miles from the ship.

The captain called the screen commander and then the OTC using the encrypted voice radio in combat. It was the only encrypted voice radio on the ship and was generally only used CO to CO, XO to XO, or OPS to OPS. Sounded funny but one could understand if the sender spoke slowly.

When you keyed the handset you had to wait a moment while it emitted a honk like a Canadian goose in heat as it synced with other units. After the honk, you could talk. When someone on another ship was transmitting, it honked again, so everyone knew which handset and speaker was encrypted voice. If it didn't sync, it just emitted a loud hiss. Then one would have to try to sync again.

It was a great idea, but LARTER only had one, picked up in Subic first stop. They belonged to 7th fleet, were scarce as hen's teeth, and had to be turned in when a ship left Westpac. Dillan or

Ted had to set the day's code in every day. It was a box with maybe a hundred little wires, like a tiny telephone operator's patch panel. Once the wires were set to the day's code, the little box plugged into the unit. Get one wire wrong and you couldn't talk to anyone.

The skipper asked if LARTER could exercise DASH and got permission. So the ship went charging off 10 miles away and set flight quarters. Four hours of trying and LARTER got one DASH off the deck for 10 minutes, but then had to get it back since it was acting erratic. Secure flight quarters and back to picket station.

By the time flight quarters had been secured, Dillan was back on the bridge on watch again. Skipper in his chair buried in a paperback. LARTER was steaming around keeping roughly 4000 to 6000 yards from the carrier and its attendant plane guard destroyer.

Dillan thought that this is more boring than plane guard.

Stand here for 4 hours and try to keep your mind on a job with zero excitement. And show interest so the captain doesn't think I don't give a damn – which sometimes I don't. I bet this is how those factory workers on an assembly line feel. Adding a right headlight to a Ford all day, every week, ad nauseum. But, adding a head light pays a hell of a lot more than being an Ensign does!

Looking down from the bridge windows to the 01 level he could see that Billy was exercising his gun mount crew on the 5 inch loading machine, mounted on the deck there. Men in "T" shirts handling dummy cartridge cases and projectiles, practicing loading while sweating profusely in the humidity. Usually the loading machine had a grey canvas cover and was just a blob. But gun crews were expected to drill on it every other day, weather permitting.

15

One of the radiomen came up to the captain.

"Sir, we have an operational immediate message from Commander Task Group 77.7." He handed the captain the board.

Total quiet on the bridge.

"Officer of the deck, we have been directed to detach and take up shadowing of the AGI. Come to course 085 at 27 and we should have him on radar in a couple of hours."

"Take this message to combat." Then on the 21 MC, "Combat, bridge, plot the location in this message the radioman is bringing in and give us a vector to intercept."

"Combat, Aye."

Then, Dillan, who had the conn, was directed to comply with the captain's orders by the OOD. Not verbal, just a wave meaning "get on with it."

OK, now time for some fun. "Right standard rudder, come to new course 085. All engines ahead full, indicate turns for 27 knots."

"My rudder is right standard, coming to new course 085, sir." "Engine room answers up all ahead full turns for 27 knots."

And away...y we go. Picture Ralph Cramden shaking his arms up and down and shuffling.

LARTER started to gain speed and heeled sharply to starboard.

Dillan thought destroyers were fun and getting to do something on watch was a hell of a lot better than just steaming around in circles. Something longer than a football field charging along at 30 miles an hour must be a sight. Big bow wave rolling over as LARTER cut through the sea.

Dillan went out the open hatch to the starboard bridge wing, strong wind, and he had to hold on to his hat. A glance astern from the bridge wing platform, leaning against the waist high wind brake: a big boiling pale turquoise hump in the water and bright white wake behind.

"Bridge, combat, the AGI range is 34 miles at 088. Course 273 at 12 knots, per the message. Recommend 089 at 27 knots to intercept," said the JA phone talker.

Stepping back through the hatch Dillan said, "Bridge, aye, come right steer 089."

"Come right, steer 089, aye, sir. Steady 089, checking 091, sir."

"Very well."

The OOD plotted the range and bearing on the maneuvering board. A maneuvering board was a round paper compass rose with range rings.[xxx] Most naval maneuvering was done considering relative motion. One could think of the center of the maneuvering board as moving with your ship. Then one could use graphics to plot other ship's relative courses and speeds and figure out what to do to intercept them. And the ship's surface search radar was a relative motion device so it all fit together.

The OOD then plotted LARTER's course and speed and the reported AGI's course and speed with arrows sized to the speeds. A bit of work with the parallel rules and pencil, and he announced,

"Time to intercept about 50 minutes, course 089 looks good Captain. We will refine this when we get him on radar estimated in less than half an hour."

"Very well," from the skipper.

Now the bridge team waited. Meanwhile the weapons officer came on the bridge, then a couple more. Just to see what was up. But they didn't stay long. The captain thought the bridge should be quiet except for business. Left to their own devices, Sailors always were engaged in a good natured but derogatory banter with each other. The junior officers did it also – the exuberance of youth. But on the bridge there was little shooting the bull when the skipper was in his chair. Speak when duty called or the captain asked a question.

If it got a little noisy, the captain would often say, firmly,

"Business only on the bridge. You people keep it down. This is not a social club."

A little more than a half hour later,

"Bridge, combat, we have a new contact, designated skunk Charlie, bearing 084, range 17,500 yards."

Three minutes later, "Bridge, combat, skunk Charlie is on course 275, speed 11, range 14,200 yards (about 7 miles), bearing 079, recommend 080 to intercept."

"Very well," Dillan answered.

Dillan knew skunks were unidentified surface contacts, goblins unidentified submarine contacts, and bogies unidentified air contacts. Skunks were identified by letter starting at midnight each day with Alfa. Bogies and goblins were designated by number.

Dillan looked out on the bearing lifting the binoculars to his eyes. He could see a small contact, about a 30 degree port target angle, just visible through the perpetual haze.

"Come left steer 080." "Come left to 080, aye sir" "Steady 080 checking 083."

The captain said, "Come back to 078, we want to steam down his port side about 500 yards off, drop superheat, come around and tuck in on his port bow matching his speed, Mr. Dillan. Think you can do that?"

"Yes, sir."

Dillan thought, right now we have almost 38 knots of relative speed. The range closes 3800 yards every 3 minutes. We will be on top of him in 11 minutes. To keep from zooming by we better slow to 20, drop superheat, and keep to the right to allow room for our 180 degree port turn.

Dillan said, "Captain, I recommend we slow to 20, drop superheat, swing a bit more right and then swoop in for a port turn to station."

"Make it so, but let's go past him a bit before we make the station turn. And make our station about 45 degrees off his port bow at 500 yards. OOD set general quarters. Let's show off our gun mounts exercising to give him something to think about."

A bit of grandstanding, but he is the skipper, Dillan thought. And 500 yards was close, damn close.

"Bong bong bong bong… This is a drill; this is a drill, general quarters, general quarters. All hands man your battle stations."

The bongs were not so much like a bell being struck, more like a gong. They were electronically generated and distinctive on purpose. The sound sent out on the ship's general announcing system would penetrate everywhere. No one could say they didn't hear general quarters being sounded.[xxxi]

Dillan thought he was busier than a one arm paper hanger, checking the maneuvering board over the OOD's shoulder, on combat's case about continuous updates, and slowing and maneuvering the ship in small course change increments. The bosun's mate of the watch was breaking out battle gear: flack jackets, belt life vest pouches, helmets.

The captain said, "Secure battle dress on the bridge."

Since Dillan's GQ station was right where he was, he did not have to be relieved. The operations officer, good old LT Freddy Finistry the third, USN, relieved the OOD for GQ. Most of the other people on the bridge got relieved so those they relieved could make it to their stations.

"All stations manned and ready," from the bosun's mate of the watch. Six and a half minutes.

Skipper will not be pleased.

Four minutes was the norm, which did not include getting people relieved from one station and sent to another – just that each station was ready to do their job.

"A little slow to manned and ready, huh, Ops? Looks like an extra drill or two may be in order. All that plane guard and picket stuff must make the crew sleepy," from the captain.

"Yes, sir, a little slow, Captain," from Fred, binoculars to his eyes watching the AGI.

LARTER went by the AGI 650 yards to port, a bit closer than Dillan really wanted. Then a full rudder 180 degree turn to port, scuffing off more speed with a big heel, as the AGI swung across the bow left to right. And then a bit of a turn to starboard to approach station. A few moments later, LARTER was sitting 500 yards off the AGI's port bow, matching the AGI's course and speed.

After elevating and lowering the guns, training the mounts, and lighting up the AGI electronically with fire control radar, the captain said, "OOD, secure from general quarters."

"Aye, sir."

Over the 1 MC passed through out the ship, "Secure from general quarters, set the regular condition III watch."

The AGI looked tiny even this close. Painted a light but different grey, maybe with a slight blue cast, it looked like a medium sized fishing trawler. Mast painted white. She had some running rust down the sides at the scuppers, and lots of antennas, even a circular loop antenna above the bridge for radio direction finding.

No one visible on the main deck but through his binoculars Dillan could see a couple of figures through the AGI's bridge window, and one man, hatless, standing on the port bridge wing leaning on the rail smoking. At 12 knots her bow rose and fell to the slight swell and her mast swung back and forth with a moderate roll. Dillan figured it took real seamen to ride that thing.

It would probably rock in heavy dew.

Keeping station on the AGI was a lot of work. The AGI would make small course changes and speed changes just to make it difficult. And at 500 yards the ship was close. It was a chess game. The skipper loved it and with his years of experience could do maneuvering board in his head.

Fred was always critical. "You are drifting left of station Mr. Dillan. Better add a few turns, Mr. Dillan, he is creeping up."

It was done for the skipper's benefit. Not like Fred was trying to be helpful, just critical. Show the skipper that he expected perfection from his junior officers. Keep them on their toes. Make a good impression.

Is Fred ever just real?

Fred got relieved, but Dillan had this watch and so he stayed JOOD.

16

When 1545 arrived and Pete came up, Dillan was glad to see him. Feeling relieved figuratively and literally, he reported such to the OOD and went below; boredom to excitement. Right now he was tired and would take boredom. He went down to radio.

"Hey Mr. Dillan, heard the FT chief folded the game's tent," from Dillan's chief.

"Good. I like my poker right along with the next guy, Chief, but ashore only. Any of our troops get in over his head?"

"Not that I'm aware of, sir. I keep their little noses to the grindstone anyway – don't know when they'd find the time."

"Way to go, Chief, anything hot on the boards?"

"Your vacation starts tomorrow, sir – enjoy."

Dillan looked at the chief with a questionable face and the chief just smiled and handed him the message board.

There was a message on the board from the carrier. Helos to pick up and drop off junior officers for the 3 day cross deck training at 0900 tomorrow morning. Dillan went below and pulled out a small bag: clothing for 3 days, stationary, dopp kit, log book. The skipper would absolutely require that each officer sent keep a complete log of everything learned, in detail. And he would have LT Finistry check Dillan's. And check it he would.

Fred the checker would find fault. And make life difficult. Probably require Dillan to write a stupid report that no one but Fred would read. Fred and he were so different. Fred was always into his image and how the other department heads, XO and skipper perceived him.

Must have been a bitch growing up as the youngest in that family.

Dillan remembered another incident with Fred that occurred near the end of the shipyard overhaul.

Fred had called him in after quarters. Fred was in his desk chair, Dillan standing in Fred's stateroom doorway.

Fred said, looking up, in his disciplinary voice, "Mr. Dillan, I have been informed that you were seen in the enlisted club in civilian clothing with some of your ET's Saturday night?"

This was not illegal. On special occasions other officers had done the same, even some officers on LARTER that Dillan knew of, but not officers in the operations department. Fred took a very strict interpretation of the general prohibition against fraternizing. This prohibition existed to preclude friendships that might keep an officer from exercising discipline if necessary. You could not be someone's best friend and his boss at the same time.

And Dillan fully supported this – in fact, although not specifically defined in regulations, fraternization between widely different enlisted ranks, like a chief and a second class was also discouraged. At this club outing the chief and the first class and three second class, also in civilian clothing, were there even though the enlisted club was nominally for petty officers 3rd class and the non rated men below.

The chiefs had their own club, as did the 1st and 2nd class, the Acey Deucy Club. But this was a special event. It was a short department celebration for a job well done, and Dillan felt the troops deserved to be recognized.

Dillan answered, "Yes sir, these guys busted their humps 16 hours a day for the last two weeks straight. I bought them a beer and thanked them for all their hard work."

Loudly and with flaming eyes, "Mr. Dillan, you just don't get it. You have been fraternizing with enlisted men. Fraternizing. You are destroying the good discipline of this ship. Officers do not 'buy beer' for enlisted men. And you do not have to thank them for working. It is their job. I will not have my officers fraternizing. I will not have my officers fraternizing! Is that understood Mr. Dillan!"

A pregnant silence: *Oh shit. He is really serious.*

"Consider yourself in hack for the rest of the week. I'll clear it with the XO. By staying aboard maybe you can catch up on your paperwork which I am sure is behind. Maybe you ought to read Navy regulations about fraternizing also. Do you understand me Mr. Dillan? Do you understand me clearly?"

"Yes, sir"... *you miserable pompous bastard.*

Theoretically a department head could not restrict one of his officers from leaving the ship once the work day was done, critical work was up to date, and the officer did not have the duty. This was called being "put in hack", and only the XO or skipper could do it.

Practically, Dillan knew that Fred would come up with what ever story he needed to and the XO would go along since going along was always easier and the XO did not want to undermine a department head.

The Executive Officer, LCDR Chuck Peterson, USN was a nice guy from Minnesota. He was capable, competent, and had maybe a year to go before being in the zone for potential promotion to full Commander.

He had been on LARTER for almost 2 years and would be leaving soon. Tall, big, and very much a Nordic type, he had been on destroyers his entire career so far. He was married, one kid. Dillan respected him.

And Dillan could have pled his case to the XO. But this would only infuriate Fred more. Fred might even lose face with the XO. And a Fred who lost face was a terrible thing to behold. As it worked out, the XO, although not over ruling Fred's decision, might well have counseled Fred a bit in officer to officer and officer to enlisted relations.

Dillan did his time in hack, and Fred did not mention the incident again. But Fred rode Dillan hard.

In October 1967, just prior to Westpac departure, it was time for ENS fitness reports. Fitness reports were done annually, at the time of an officer's transfer, or the transfer of the reporting senior, nominally the Commanding Officer.

These reports were a big deal. Get poor ones and they would haunt an officer for a long time. Promotions to LTJG were essentially automatic after 18 months commissioned service as an Ensign. Promotions to LT and above were done by selection boards in Washington DC.

Although the boards looked at the most recent fitness Reports first, a bad one from years back could hurt promotability. Officers took fitness reports very seriously.

Reports were grouped. An officer was 'top 1%, top 5%, top 10%, top 30% etc. all the way down to bottom 30%'. As with all performance evaluation systems, there was reporting creep. Top 1% and top 5% officers always got promoted: top 10% mostly, all others no way.[xxxii]

Selections for promotion got more difficult the further up one went. For every CDR in the Navy there were 25 other officers below him. The pyramid got narrower as one moved up.

It was the captain's responsibility to write fitness reports on his officers, when due. From a practical viewpoint the captain had an officer's boss write a draft and the XO reviewed the draft prior to submitting it to the captain. So Fred was writing Dillan's fitness report although Dillan would not see it until the final formal sit down one on one with the captain where he got to see, discuss, and sign the official fitness report.

Dillan was dreading this. Fred had indicated that he was not very pleased with Dillan's growth as an officer. So when Dillan got called into the captain's big in port cabin for a sit down Dillan expected a 'top 10%'.

As a junior officer one knocked on the captain's door and waited.

"Enter." March in and stand at attention.

"At ease, Mr. Dillan, take a seat."

"Thank you, sir."

One sat at attention in the chair to the left of the captain's desk. The skipper's in-port cabin was enormous in Dillan's mind, lots of space, a desk, a brown leather sofa that opened into a bed. Dillan thought it must be 12 feet wide and 12 feet long. The forward bulkhead was angled on each side. It even had port lights, an attached head, even a brown rug on the deck. It smelled a little musty.

"You and Mr. Finistry have had some difficulties this year, Mr. Dillan. Mr. Finistry is a fine and dedicated officer. But he's young (only 1 plus years older than Dillan, or 26) and is 'a play strictly by the book officer.' He's still learning how to supervise other officers. It's in your best interest to work with Mr. Finistry and to remain respectful to him."

God, what had Fred told the skipper?

"All that said, you have done well as the EMO and so far are doing well as the communications officer. The new communications suite we got in the yards is a success in no small part due to your efforts. I personally want to thank you for that work. Many of my peer's new communications suites have not started up as well."

Dillan had heard absolute horror stories. One destroyer even had to be sent back to the yard for fixes, which got its schedule all screwed up and delayed its deployment. That was a very big deal since the scheduling officers at COMFIRSTFLT (Commander, First Fleet, the Eastern Pacific), and COMSEV-ENTHFLT (Commander, Seventh Fleet, the Western Pacific) did not like delays.

Delays were like dominos. Knock one over and a whole bunch of others followed. Other ships had technical representatives from equipment manufacturer's crawling all over them for weeks. LARTER had hit the ground running.

The captain went on, "You're quite capable in CIC watch standing and have a good grasp of tactics and CIC operations. The schools I sent you to prior to reporting have paid dividends. On the bridge, you have not progressed as rapidly. I'll sign you off as OOD for independent steaming by the first of the year, but you are not ready for the fleet steaming qualification."

Dillan knew that there were two types of underway OOD qualifications. One relatively easy one for standing OOD watches when the ship was out steaming along on it own in open waters. And one much more difficult one for steaming in company with other ships, which involved maintaining and changing station, assisting with underway replenishment, entering and leaving port, and, etc.

Since the OOD was essentially in charge of the ship as the captain's representative, and since maneuvering a destroyer at high speeds around other ships doing the same was dangerous, fleet steaming qualifications were a big deal. One had to be fleet OOD qualified to stand command duty officer watches in port.[xxxiii]

"I expect that I'll assign you to stand watches as JOOD more during our upcoming cruise, most of which will be steaming with a task group. It's in both of our best interests to insure that you complete your fleet OOD qualifications by the end of the cruise if not before."

"Remember, Mr. Dillan, that you're on the same career track as our academy graduates and will be leaving LARTER sometime next summer for another ship. I want to make sure that all the officers who leave LARTER are experienced and qualified to step aboard another ship and quickly take over as OODs, CDOs, and the other duties expected of a young career officer."

The skipper then handed Dillan his fitness report to read. Dillan was surprised, overall Top 5%. As he read the words and the detailed grades in specific categories, he saw that in professional knowledge he got a top 1%, most of the rest were top 1% or 5%.

Qualification progress got him a top 10, working relationships another 10. There were a few words about "accepting the inherent individual differences of people." It probably was an offhanded comment about his working relationship with Fred. But, overall, it was a very good fitness report and far better than he anticipated.

"Do you have any questions, Mr. Dillan?"

"No, sir."

"Then please sign at the bottom indicating that you have seen this report."

Dillan signed, and then stood up. "Will that be all, Captain?"

"Yes, and Dillan, try not to antagonize Mr. Finistry as much."

"Yes sir."

Dillan marched out of the captain's cabin and closed the door softly behind him. ENS Kirpatrick was standing outside waiting for his turn in the barrel.

"He in a good mood, Dillan?" he asked.

"A good mood, Jim? Yes, a very good mood."

Dillan went down to radio and into his crypto office. It took awhile to process this information. It seemed like Fred had downgraded Dillan but the XO and skipper had changed it. Dillan did not know if the XO or skipper had told Fred what the final version looked like. They were under no obligation to do so. It was his first real fitness report and a top 5. Even with the animosity between him and Fred.

Thank God for the XO, and skipper.

Dillan had received very good FitReps from his schools attended enroute to LARTER, but most report items were "Not Observed."

17

Back to the world of a destroyer shadowing an AGI: Dillan did a bit more work in radio, E-4 evaluations were due and he had to check over what the chief had written. The chief was objective and fair, but not very polished. So sometimes his marks were not totally supported by the wording.

Dillan was quite good at the verbiage and would spruce up the chief's words. Dillan knew from experience that enlisted quarterly marks (actually given semiannually in 1967) were as important to the crew as fitness reports were to officers. Without good ones, a man would have a difficult time making the next petty officer rank.

And Fred would review them carefully, ready to pounce on anything that did not support a good mark with some specific accomplishment. Dillan figured that Fred thought his job in life was to downgrade everyone else a peg, which would make him look like he was one peg up.

Then down to the wardroom, to sit and wait. There was a bit of banter and supposition about when LARTER would get back to Subic and the lack of mail the last few days. The captain and XO were probably still on the bridge.

Chris's comment: "So, someone upstream has decided that mail will be withheld until morale improves, again."

"Yeah, and the "chop" has doubled the salt peter ration to insure we all keep our thoughts pure," from Joe.

"Only in our food, never in his," from Eric.

"Not true you oversexed scum. I only add it to the coffee. Not my fault I don't drink the stuff," said Tony.

"We should put spanish fly in the chop's coke – then watch him beat himself to death," from Sam.

"Don't need self gratification, Greeny, but the girls in Subic better fasten their seat belts if you do it. Italian stallions are awesome when we get rolling," was Tony's retort.

One sure has to have his verbal saber sharpened to survive in this group. Good retort, Tony.

About 20 minutes late the captain walked in. "Attention on deck" "Carry on." The skipper and XO steamed in and took their seats.

After grace and while serving continued, the skipper told all that he had moved off to 2000 yards for the night, and that the AGI had settled down on a constant course and speed. He expected arrival near Yankee Station by 2000. After dinner, Dillan wrote his daily letter to Patty, and hit the rack. Sleep came easy.

At 2315 (11:15PM) he was awakened and stumbled off to the bridge again by way of the mess decks for a bowl of soup ('midrats' or midnight rations) and coffee. Since one had to make sure one's eyes were dark adapted, he had to wear the funny red lens goggles in the mess decks where the white lights were on.

Outside the mess decks or the engineering spaces, darken ship was in force and all passage way lights were red at night. Hatches to the weather decks all had light locks to keep any light from escaping. A white light at sea could be seen for miles. And submarines looked for it. A procedure left over from World War II.

Dillan went out on the bridge to relieve the watch. Pitch black. LARTER was steaming small figure eights at 5 knots. A steam turbine ship had to keep steam flowing to keep everything warm in case it needed to speed up. So dead in the water for a long period was not an option. The AGI was 2200 yards away and totally dead in the water, a black blob, only running lights visible swinging slightly to the swell. She was diesel driven and could light off quickly.

LARTER had her running lights on normal. The usual task group subdued setting was not for playing with an AGI. Normal brightness was required for international rules of the nautical road. It was a very dull watch.

And nothing changed. The clock slowly rotated to 0345 and there was Pete, ready to relieve. Relieved and back to the rack.

The next morning after breakfast and a stop in radio, Dillan was back aft. Helicopter transfers of personnel from or to a destroyer at sea were a real trip. LARTER's small DASH deck was not certified for manned helos. So the trick was to turn the ship into the wind to get a minimum of 10 knots over the bow.

A helo pilot would come in behind the ship and drop to a hover about 50 feet over the stern and move slowly forward against the wind. Then the helo would drop the transferee down, wearing a horse collar, by wire, as the helo hovered over the stern deck just behind gun mount 52 – the after mount. If there was no real true wind or seas this was even fun. With a strong true wind or seas, it was dangerous.

The helo came to a hover, and out of the side door came a guy in a khaki outfit, clutching a small bag, wearing a big orange kapok life vest, aviation type white helmet, and the orange horse collar, supported on a wire from a derrick above the helo's door. Down he went, and when close to the deck, he was grabbed by the flight quarters crew, the horse collar removed, helmet and life vest given up, and he was taken into the ship.

All this with the helo's down draft creating a hurricane. Wire back up, and out came another guy. Then it was LARTER's turn.

Billy went up first, then Dillan. Life vest, helmet and duffel in hand, ball cap in his bag, horse collar; clip on and up you went, quite fast. When you got to the top the helo crewman reached out, spun you around, grabbed you by your belt and dragged you backwards into the helo, butt scraping on the edge of the hatch and the floor.

Horse collar gone and you joined the 3 other similarly clad officers sitting on the deck, knees drawn up almost in a fetal position. The helo had a pilot and copilot up front, crewman in the open doorway wearing an olive green flight suit, boots, gloves, life jacket, and white decorated helmet, dark green visor down, with a trailing curled wire plugged into a jack on the bulkhead. This was a UH-1N, the Navy's version of the 'Huey.' A short range work horse aircraft that did everything from plane guard, anti-submarine warfare, search and rescue, to just being a taxi.

Even with his helmet on, Dillan couldn't hear anything but the roar of the engine and the whoop whoop whoop of the rotor. The helmet had a head set built in, but they were not plugged into the helo's internal intercom circuit.

Floor pitched nose down and to the right. The noise got louder. Up they went. Sea went by below, smooth but noisy ride. Then the sea changed to a dark gray solid surface and the helo landed with a jolt on the carrier's flight deck. They scrambled out and went across to the island hatch with heads down in a wind storm. They gave up their helmet and vest.

Well Dillan, your first helo ride and your first aircraft carrier. This thing is huge!

The LTJG who took the cross deck people below a thousand ladders and through 10,000 knee knockers, or at least it seemed that way, to their stateroom, said that there were 5,000 or so men aboard. It was a floating city. Once the gear was stowed, it was off on another trip through the maze to the junior officer's ward room.

The carrier had four wardrooms: senior officers, junior officers, warrant officers, and the flag mess. LTs ate in the JO's wardroom. Dillan figured Fred would not like that much.

The JO's wardroom was enormous. Lots of tables and a lounge with overstuffed chairs. Dillan went in and picked a seat with the 5 others – all destroyer types there for the cross deck. A LT came in and introduced himself.

He was the assistant first lieutenant, a title that harked back to the days of sail, but basically meant that he ran part of the crew that looked after the carrier's ground tackle (anchors and such), mooring equipment, and exterior safety equipment like life boats, liberty launches, etc. First lieutenant was an Ensign's job on LARTER: Joe Rederman's.

He dispensed with the housekeeping:

"Gentlemen, lunch is at 1230, dinner at 1745, all second seating. Breakfast is open seating and served from 0630 to 0745. Stay out of senior officer's or flag country. Lessons every morning and afternoon here 15 minutes after chow secures. Trainees to only stand day watches 16-20 as assigned, some in combat, some on the bridge, some in Prifly (where air launch and recovery operations were controlled) some in main control. Stay off the flight deck and hanger bay unless escorted. Questions?"

He passed out maps of the ship with names on them and staterooms and the JO's wardroom marked, along with a route to and from. Then he said, "Settle in and see you after lunch here, 1315. Dismissed."

They were on their own. Billy stayed for more coffee. On his way back down, Dillan heard "Flight quarters, flight quarters. All hands man your flight quarters stations, aircrews to the ready room."

The passageways were full of enlisted men wearing different colored flight deck jerseys, air crew in flight suits, and others scurrying along.

Passageways were narrow, so one had to paste one's self against the bulkhead often, to stay out of the way. Every 10 feet or so there was an oval opening about 5 feet high and two feet wide with a 3 inch steel lip around it. These were the passages through the frame bulkheads and were the infamous 'knee knockers.'

One had to be careful. The lip was low for the knees. But miscalculate, and your shin would show it for a week. Moving quickly through these passageways was like running the low hurdles. Only the hurdles did not fall down if you hit one.

Back in the stateroom with having only been lost 3 times, Dillan took a moment to write a letter. The stateroom was small, clean and a bit musty. There were bunk beds for four. Only two were made up. Unoccupied for awhile he thought. Light green walls, beige bunk covers, white overhead, dark gray furniture bolted to the walls, off white tile deck, green curtain door.

Two aluminum chairs with brown leatherette seats. Could be anywhere on any ship in the fleet. Maybe, just maybe, he thought, he could find the ship's post office, have them check for mail for him, and get his letter off.[xxxiv]

Before Dillan left San Diego, Patty and he agreed to try to write every day and number their letters sequentially, based on what they had heard from other Navy couples. Sometimes Dillan would get letter 8, 14, 16, and 3 all the same day, then a week of nothing.

It was very hard to communicate a thought from letter to letter. Dillan also had bought two small reel to reel tape recorders and once a month would make and send a tape. He had not received a tape yet from Patty. In past wars, outgoing letters were censored. Not in Vietnam, at least on ships.

After the letter writing, Dillan could hear a muffled whoosh and thump as aircraft went off the catapult. Otherwise quiet. He saw a small TV on the wall and turned it on. Channel 3 and a view of the flight deck from the island. The TV was black and white and had other channels with movies, even one with some petty officer reading the news.

Wow, their own TV station.

All one could get on the destroyer was Armed Forces Radio out of DaNang, or Hanoi Hanna, the North Vietnamese propaganda radio station. Hanoi Hanna was funny as she tried to disrupt American forces morale. The lies were so blatant that most Sailors or Marines were not impressed with her newscasts. She was good at welcoming new carriers and even some other ships and squadrons to the line – probably the AGI in action.

But Hanna did play some different and sometimes protest rock music. The troops liked it, but the skipper had forbidden Dillan from patching that radio signal to the ship's entertainment system – basically just a few speakers located in a few spaces, like berthing compartments and the mess decks. It was Armed Forces Radio only for LARTER. Hanna would be on a portable speaker in the ET shack, though.

Never underestimate the creativity of troops with access to communications patch panels.

Back to channel 3. F-4s moving into place, shoe engaged into the catapult, full flaps, engines turned up under the direction of a man in khaki wearing a hat like a barnstorming pilot with big bumps where the ears were, spinning his hand in the air. A big roar, a snappy salute, repeated by the pilot, a point down the deck, knee bent, with the 'yellow shirt's' hand, arm extended, and the F-4 went zipping down the deck and into the air. Then the shoe was pulled back into launch position again as the grove in the deck it ran on emitted wisps of spent steam. Repeat.

This was more than a CAP launch. The F-4's were carrying ground attack ordnance, since what were hanging from their wing hard spots looked like bombs, not air to air missiles. A strike Dillan guessed. He counted 8 outbound while he was watching.

The speaker emitted a Bosun's pipe attention chirp and, "Now secure from flight quarters. Life boat crew of the watch on deck to muster. Sweepers, sweepers, man your brooms. Give the ship a clean sweep down fore and aft," came over the 1MC.

Different.

On LARTER the skipper insisted on minimizing announcements. Normal daily evolutions were to happen on time without announcements.

OK. Time for lunch if I can find my way back. Otherwise I could wander the passage ways forever. Just like Charlie on the MTA. Ride forever 'neath the streets of Boston.

The US Navy had a system for identifying locations aboard ship. It was called compartment numbering.[xxxv] Using the map and compartment numbers on aluminum plates mounted over each doorway, Dillan worked his way back to the JO's wardroom. Many doors were painted with squadron insignias. Almost all had "Authorized Personnel Only" signs. Some with key pads like on the radio door on LARTER; sometimes a real office with a half door and men working at desks.

Every so often a fire main station, fat pipe riser painted red, big brass handled valve, rack of folded fire hose, brass nozzles and long low velocity fog applicators with a red pipe and a brass applicator nozzle like a small pineapple at the end, clamped to the bulkhead. There were big lockers for oxygen breathing apparatus (OBA), and stokes (wire basket) stretchers hanging alongside.

Passageways were not a straight line. They would zig 90 degrees left, run straight for awhile, then zig 90 degrees right as they dodged machinery spaces or stack chases. It was all pale green walls, off white overhead, and shiny beige floor tile. The handrails, so essential on a destroyer, were conspicuously missing on the carrier. A big ship which seldom experienced the movement destroyers did at sea.

Lunch was in the JO's wardroom: crowded and noisy. And all served buffet style. Grab your plate, take what you want, find a seat, eat, bus yourself, and leave. Just like a mess hall at OCS. Dillan figured that the carrier JO's, putting in 3 days on LARTER, were in for a lesson in table manners from the skipper.

Dillan and Billy met a couple of other Ensigns from ship's company and one from a squadron (embarked air group), and one LTJG, air intel, from an attack squadron now attached to the CarDiv commander's staff. There were even a couple of Marine officers. The ship's company guys all had jobs that on LARTER would be done by enlisted men.

18

At lunch there was a lot of talk about the Bob Hope Christmas Show that was on the carrier the day before. Dillan knew it had happened on the carrier but it sure didn't happen on the destroyers. Hope's crew had been ferried out from DaNang in big helos. The carrier's JOs were all talking about the women they had seen: Raquel Welch and others in tight tops and micro-mini skirts. They also mentioned how funny Hope was. But the women were the big hit.

Dillan thought, beautiful scantily clad round eyed women. Must be to remind the troops what they were fighting for. In case they had forgot.

Hell, I sure have not forgotten. The Brits used to say that the Americans were "over paid, over sexed, and over here." But I'm sure not over paid.

There was another intel guy who was a Security Group Officer, people the Navy called 'spooks.' These officers, designator 1610, were not line officers and could not assume command at sea. They, and their assigned communications technicians, did communications intelligence gathering and analysis: super hush hush.

"I can tell you what I do, but then I'd have to kill you," he said.

Funny, in a weird way. We all have to deal with classified material. But this spook stuff must be 'burn before reading.'

"So where do you guys normally go for duty, carriers?" Dillan asked.

"Naw, we don't spend a lot of time deployed to ships. Maybe every now and then a submarine or an assignment to fly on the EC121 shore based patrol aircraft. Then there are the AGER ships, like the Soviet AGIs. They're very small. I rode USS BANNER (AGER-1) for a month once. We have bases at different places around the world and do a lot of our work ashore."

"If this is TAD (temporary additional duty), where's home?" Billy asked.

"Kamiseya, in Japan; I've been there two years before getting assigned here for 6 months. Some SecGru officers work for the National Security Agency in Maryland. Hope to get a shot at that. I'm from the eastern shore."

"When I was in Bainbridge, heard that people from the eastern shore didn't think there was intelligent life west of the Chesapeake," Dillan said.

He laughed, "Yeah, my parents think that way. I found some people in the DC area that could walk and chew gum at the same time, but not many. Lots of women though, all those secretaries working in all those government offices, good ratio in DC."

"Visited DC a couple of times, the women all must live in the suburbs. After dark it's a dangerous place."

"Have to know where to go. Georgetown is good. Stay out of the east and south. SecGru is always looking for talent. You guys boat school types?"

When Dillan said that he was an electrical engineer, the spook indicated that Dillan could probably get a transfer to Security Group if he applied. There were lots of engineers and linguists in Security Group. And they needed more badly.

Something to think about.

Class time: break out the notebook. The first lesson was general and given by the ship's assistant operations officer, a LCDR. Obviously not pleased that he had been assigned to lecture a bunch of ENS and LTJG types. He gave a 45 minute monotone ship familiarization lecture with many slides and ship diagrams. Canned, but informative.

This was followed by a 45 minute overview from a LTJG from the embarked air wing staff. It was a lot more interesting. Carrier Air Wing 2, embarked on RANGER, had 7 squadrons, a few detachments, lots of air craft, and over a thousand men.

Dillan knew that all Navy fixed wing aircraft squadron's designations started with a "V" followed by one or more letters which identified their purpose, and their squadron number: "VF" for a fighter squadron, "VA" for attack, "VR" for recon. Helicopter squadrons started with an "H". That exhausted his knowledge.

But the lecture turned quickly to alphabet soup as "VAFs" and "RA5Cs" were mentioned. VAF was a combination attack/fighter squadron. The RA5C 'Vigilante' was a large photo recon jet. The primary fighter and attack aircraft was the F-4 Phantom, a twin engine, two person interceptor which could also do surface attack: the one with the slightly drooping black nose. There were multiple squadrons of these, a very versatile aircraft.

There were two squadrons of A-4 Skyhawks, a smaller but very effective attack aircraft, and a squadron of the new A7 Corsair II. The pilots called the A7 a SLUF (short little ugly f'er) since it was on a modified and shortened F-8 frame. There was a squadron of F-8 Crusaders. These were older and the precursors of the F-4 Phantoms. There was a squadron of A6 Intruders, a bubble nosed all weather attack aircraft with two aboard, pilot on the left, navigator/bombardier on the right, sitting roughly side by side. It was very effective as a night attack unit.

There were tankers for in-flight refueling, ASW patrol aircraft: the S2F or 'Stwof' twin propeller ones. There were air early warning (AEW) or 'Stwof with a roof' planes, and cargo aircraft, and a bunch of helos. The embarked squadrons also had all their own maintenance and administrative personnel aboard, their own workshops, and etc.

Then the air group and squadrons had their own air intelligence group, strike planning, bomb damage assessment, and administration. The ship's air department had all kinds of flight deck and hanger bay crews.[xxxvi]

Complicated and it would take awhile to learn. Aviation Sailors were called 'brown shoes,' for the brown suede chukka boots the flight deck crews wore. They were designed without nails so that there was no chance of a spark. The rest of the Navy was 'black shoes.'

Head spinning, Dillan was off for the combat information center for familiarization, and where he would stand his first watch. Billy was off to main control and damage control central for the same. Since there were 4 major watch stations and 3 days, no one got to see all four. Dillan was in operations department on the destroyer so the powers that be decided that combat, bridge, and prifly were to be his experience.

The CIC on a carrier was enormous. Used to a 20 foot by 25 foot CIC on LARTER, Dillan was surprised when shown into a very large dark space. Like a cave. Ceiling painted black like LARTER.

In CIC, white lights were minimized. They interfered with the ability to see the radar screens and the "bugs" on the horizontal surface plotting tables. On the carrier, there were bank after bank of green or grey radar screens, tons of side lit vertical plotting boards, radios every where, and lots of people in khaki and dungarees.

With a strike in progress, the plots were full of grease pencil marks, kept up to date by men standing behind the side lit Plexiglas boards, wearing sound powered headsets, updating aircraft positions given them by radar scope operators, and writing backwards on the glass. It took experience to write backwards so that the evaluators sitting in front of another bank of low 45 degree tilted scopes could see and read the plots.

One of the CIC watch officers took Dillan and another officer on cross deck through each area in CIC. There was flag plot, where the OTC's staff kept score, strike control, air plot, surface plot, electronic warfare, etc. CIC on the carrier kept track of every airplane for 250 miles around the ship. Behind the background of quacking radio speakers was a rumble of air conditioning units. The air had the normal CIC smell of cigarettes, after shave, burnt coffee, and hot electronics. And it was cold.

They keep this CIC about the temperature of a reefer! Could store meat in here.

After familiarization, Dillan, who was an air intercept controller (AIC),[xxxvii] although he had not done so for awhile, got assigned to work with an overweight 1st class radarman. He was controlling a flight of four A-4s returning to the ship after a bombing run over the South Vietnamese central highlands.

Dillan put on the extra radio headset and watched the radar screen in front of him. He observed as the aircraft were vectored back to the ship to a marshalling area by the controller. The very cryptic voice transmissions to and from the aircraft would be impossible for the uninitiated to understand. Navy standard radio telephone procedures sure did not apply here.

"Blackbear flight, Mango Station, port 060, take angels 10."

"Click swish, click swish." Many pilots acknowledged receipt of a transmission by just keying their mike once or twice, and not transmitting the official "roger, over." Dillan figured that flying a jet while trying to talk on a radio kept the pilots a bit busy. Blackbear was the flight commander's call sign. Mango Station the carrier's.

"Blackbear, Mango, bango button three."

"Blackbear, 3."

Changing the radio frequency from strike control to the vectoring working channel.

"Blackbear on 3, feet wet, angels 10, state 7."

"Mango," click.

Feet wet meant that he was over water. Angels 10 meant that he was at 10,000 feet. State was the amount of remaining fuel on board stated in hundreds of pounds: roughly 130 gallons. Not a full load but enough to get home.

The flight swung out over the coast, and was vectored to a holding station about 20 miles west of the carrier. A mid-air tanker was on site to refuel anyone who had taken a hit and lost some fuel, or was a bit low from high speed runs. Then the controller passed control over to another control station, and AIC and the aircraft were marshaled in for landing.

Dillan remembered his training. Observing was a good brush up.

Since Dillan was not a normal watch stander, he did not have to be relieved for chow. He had dinner, again buffet style in the JO's mess, then back to CIC for another couple of hours. Quieter this time, although a strike was landing. Only 2 CAP and an AEW aircraft were up.

Off watch and down to watch a movie on the TV, write another letter, and get some serious rack time. The last time Dillan, and for that matter Billy, had slept all through the night was in port Subic, almost a month ago.

When Billy came in Dillan was seated in a chair, leaning back on two chair legs, feet up on a fold down desk, eyes closed.

"Catchin a few zzz's?"

"Naw, just checking my eyelids for light leaks," from Dillan.

"Yeah, right, couldn't lean back like that on the can, would fall on your ass."

Tilting back down so all four chair legs were on the deck, "OK Rocky Top, skip the crap and tell Daddy about your watch."

"Main control was interesting. Eight boilers, 4 screws and this monster can do over 35 knots. Something the size of a skyscraper running along at over 40 miles an hour, I could water-ski behind her."

"Would require one hell of a long tow rope," from Dillan.

Billy was a 1967 Regular ROTC, political science, University of Tennessee graduate from Cleveland, Tennessee. Billy was a true southern boy or Tennessee Mountaineer, as he liked to say. One of 3 boys, all older, his family owned a small bar on the outskirts of town. The town itself was dry.

Billy had a girl, Belinda, finishing up her last year at UT in education, and he hoped to go see her when LARTER got back to the states. Billy was about 5 foot nine, average frame, and had red hair, a terminal case of freckles and a baby face. Billy was a bit of a red neck and could be loud when into too many beers. He looked down his nose a bit at Pete. Blacks were not supposed to be officers, he thought.

"Any idea when we'll get some mail there, Mr. D?" Billy said. "This dry spell sucks," as he tossed his hat onto the top bunk, ran his hand through his short hair and straddled the other chair backwards.

"I'm going to make a run at the carrier's PC (Postal Clerk)," Dillan responded.

"Belinda should know how her grades went for the fall semester. She's considering going on for her master's and a three five or better would get her a fellowship at UT."

"Good for her. You two getting hitched when you get back, Ridge Runner? You could use some full time supervision."

"Yeah, but not until I get out and she finishes school; and just what I need – full time supervision. She sure would keep my ass on the straight and narrow. She isn't into the Navy career stuff. I've got to go to June 71. God, that seems like a million years. But I needed the scholarship to get through school."

"This damn deployment seems like a million years already. Time goes fast when you're having fun."

"I'll take 15 days when we get stateside. Maybe I can talk her into coming to SD for the summer."

"Playing house for the summer; sounds like she has her hooks into you deep."

"Yeah, real deep. I called last time in Subic. Cost an f'n fortune but super. She indicated that a summer in SD may be fun."

"Good for you, nothing like a good woman to focus the mind. Patty sure focused mine."

Billy got a wistful look, "Tennessee seems so damn far away. Hell, San Diego was far away, my first real trip out west. Sure wish we'd get some mail. We get to play Navy and these bird farm pukes get to ogle Hope's girls and laugh it up."

"Easy boy, some one has to do the hard part. Besides, Belinda's probably better looking than those Hollywood starlets anyway."

"I sure think so, but then I'm just a mountain boy and only mountain girls count," Billy said as he leaned over, pulled his wallet out, fumbled for and withdrew a dog eared picture. He looked at it for a moment and handed it to Dillan.

Dillan took it and looked. "Wow. Never met a mountain girl but Belinda sure is a looker. You got lucky for a hillbilly. She'll keep you on your good behavior."

Big smile on Billy's face, "Thanks. She keeps me going," putting the photo away carefully. "Keeps me focused on the future."

Bet he looks at that 20 times a day, pretty girl, good for Billy.

Billy continued, "Belinda isn't like some of the other girls. One of my gunners mate's girl sent him a Dear John last week. Really tore the guy up. Sometimes I think the girls like that should just lie to the guys until they get back. Then dump'm when he isn't all they way over here. Paterson even talked about doing a swan dive off the fantail."

"Yeah, some guys really take it hard. Like their girl's their connection to the real world. When that goes belly up they flip. Heard that some guy off some ship last time we were in Subic took the quarterdeck watch's 45 and swallowed the barrel after a Dear John. Boom, and back of the head gone. Hope you or your chief got Paterson back to reality?"

"The chief spent some time talking to him, so did Chris. I think he's OK now, but bet he's headed for a serious drunk when we get back to Subic. Hope he doesn't get into trouble."

Damn, women, no girls – some not yet 18, sure can screw with a guy's mind if they just dump them in a letter. Some of the men are just kids and never really had to cope with much growing up. And their girl friends do not cope well with their boy friend being gone: messes with their social life just sitting around and waiting for a deployed serviceman to come home.

So they start to date again and soon, another boy friend. Then they write the break up letter. That thing that says 'distance makes the heart grow fonder' is crap. Yeah, fonder alright - fonder of someone else.

"Hope he doesn't. Interesting in DC central? This thing is big and I bet the damage control organization is huge."

"Yeah, their DC central's separate, not the log room like ours, and big; tons of diagrams. They have a lot more repair parties than we do, even some for the flight deck."

The LCDR DCA had taken Billy and one other officer. The Damage Control Assistant's job was to take care of the repair and maintenance of all ship systems that were not part of the main propulsion equipment. He had electrician's mates, machinery repairmen, damage controlmen, and etc. reporting to him. Any combatant warship had some very detailed procedures for controlling battle damage. And these ships also had redundant systems to insure that if one was out, the other could be used.[xxxviii]

Dillan had been through many Navy fire fighting schools when enlisted and one at OCS, where one had to actually enter a mock up of a couple of ship's compartments that were really on fire, usually an oil fire, and put it out with water or foam. The 1 ½ inch fire hoses used had to be snaked in through hatches and when charged were a handful.

On LARTER the DCA's job was filled by an Ensign, same year group as Dillan: ENS Sam Blongerinski. During general quarters, Sam was stationed in the log room (for all practical purposes the engineering department office, main deck amidships).

They called the station damage control central during GQ. LT Red Redmond, the chief engineer, was there also. Their job was to assess damage and minimize the effects of it using the two main repair parties stationed in the front and back of the ship for battle. There was a third repair party for the main engineering spaces.

In the log room were large plastic covered diagrams of the entire ship, with all plumbing, electrical, and interior communications systems marked on specific ones. Going to the log room and pouring over these diagrams was the best way to familiarize one's self about the ship, internally, and Dillan had spent many an evening doing so right after he reported aboard LARTER.

Although the engineering department was generally heard from but not seen, what Red and his officers and chiefs did kept LARTER afloat, under power, and in one piece. They were important jobs.

The next two days were a blur. Lessons on flight deck control, the ship's engineering plant, bridge procedures, even a 5 minute "hello" from the carrier's skipper. Dillan stood a watch on the bridge as assistant to the JOOD – not much different from LARTER only bigger - much bigger.

Since the carrier carried the OTC (CTF 77, now COM-CARDIV 3, a Rear Admiral), and therefore was the formation's guide, it did not have to keep station. It went where it wished and the destroyers kept station on it. It was an easy watch.

Prifly was interesting since it controlled the launching and recovery of aircraft with the air boss or one of his assistants running the flight deck. It had windows overlooking the flight deck. Like an airport control tower. Being assigned to the crew on an aircraft carrier's flight deck was one of the most dangerous jobs on earth. One mistake and get blown over the side, sucked into a jet intake, or cut in half with a broken wire.

They carried the pouch life vests, but one had to be awake to put it on and inflate it. There were steel mesh nets on the side of the flight deck and these caught some of the men, but not all.

It was like watching a ballet, aircraft moving around, placed into the catapults for launch and shot into space.

Meanwhile other men were rearming or refueling aircraft parked astern during launch. The deck was cleared and planes moved down the elevators into the hanger bay with wings folded prior to recovery. Dillan was told that recovery was the most difficult.

Aircraft came in as slow as they could and still fly, to pick up one of 4 wires crossing the deck and lifted slightly on springs, with their own spring mounted retractable tail hook. They used a mirror reflection of their landing lights to tell if they were on the correct glide path, instead of using the landing officer's paddles from World War II. They called it the "meat ball" or just "ball."

As the wheels touched, they hit full throttle so they could get airborne again if they missed a wire. They called this a "bolter." Catching a wire was a major stop, even if there were hydraulic shock absorbers on the wire systems. Well over one hundred to zero in 150 feet: major negative "g"s. Combat aircrews may be crazy bastards, as one could see at the Cubi Point Officer's Club when in Subic, but they were at major risk.

Dillan also got a tour of the hanger bay. Here most aircraft maintenance was done: aircraft with wings folded, jammed together, panels off, and men working on internals. The hanger bay had huge floor to ceiling sliding doors which could be slid shut to divide the hanger bay into a few separate areas. These were thick fire proof doors and would, when closed, limit a fire's spread to the enclosed area.

Dillan was told that it required hours of maintenance for each hour of actual flight time.

19

It was time to go back to LARTER, rested and glad to have 3 full nights in the rack. Dillan was also lucky enough to snag 6 letters for him from the very helpful postal clerk. He got 3 for Billy which made his week. He insured that all mail for LARTER would be on the helo taking him and Billy back to LARTER.

Wind and seas had picked up so the return helo flight was a bit rough. Dropping down to LARTER's deck which was pitching and rolling a little, he got bumped into a barrel on mount 52. *Ouch.* Billy had an uneventful drop. But back aboard, LARTER had been returned to picket duty as some other can shepherded the AGI.

Since it was 1400, Dillan had to go on watch and finish up his 12-16. After watch, Dillan went down to radio. Three days of messages to read.

My God, tomorrow is Christmas! Almost missed it, wonder if there will be a 'care package' from Patty?

Care packages sent from home were a special treat. But they had to be very well packed. A normal box of cookies would show up 2 months later as a box of crumbs, mostly infested crumbs. The best Dillan had seen was rum balls packed tightly in a sealed metal can, then wrapped in batting and double wrapped with brown paper. Even so the can was dented.

To have a care package by Christmas, Patty would have had to send it a couple weeks after LARTER departed. Dillan was sure there would be no care package this Christmas. Patty would have said something if she sent one.

Only one really interesting message: LARTER along with the rest of the RANGER task group was ordered to Subic in 20 days. They spent New Years at sea also. Christmas and New Years were just another day, but work was suspended (holiday routine) so one could sleep if one was not on watch or needed. Dillan slept a bit, wrote letters and caught up on the mountain of paper work that always was there, growing every day.

Someone told Dillan that when the USS NEW JERSEY (BB-62) was decommissioned, after the Korean War, they took 23 railroad cars of paperwork off that ship.

The US Navy thrived on reports and instructions that no one ever read. Every time someone made a mistake, the Navy generated an instruction with detailed procedures to keep that mistake from happening again. Usually requiring some monthly or quarterly report on how the instruction was being followed to the letter.

Over the years these things had grown to number in the thousands. Reporting only occurred if some senior command made a big deal about it. Most didn't. So the mistakes came back, generating a longer and more detailed instruction. It was an endless loop. But come an administrative inspection, the instructions all better be there, or the skipper, and therefore his officers, caught hell.

There was a story about this in World War II. A couple of junior officers, trapped at some backwater base on some rock in the Pacific, concocted a form and started sending reports showing the number of flies counted on flypaper in the base galley each day. After a couple of months of this, a message arrived from Washington giving all other bases hell for not making the fly paper report, and giving their base kudos for doing so. So a lot of the other bases contacted them requesting a copy of the nonexistent instruction and form.

The worst of this for real was the "3M" system: Maintenance and Material Management. Designed to make sure that all shipboard equipment was accounted for, repaired, maintained, and everything documented in quadruplicate, it pervaded everything associated with hardware. Special '3M' "chits" were required to draw a repair part. Repairs needed their own chit. And any work needed when the ship got back to Subic had to have work order chits. And one work order usually required lots of repair parts.

So the last few days prior to hitting port were a paper storm as Red, who was the chief work order worrier, had to get all the divisions to properly prepare all the work orders. Dillan and Pete, with their chiefs, dealt with communications, radar, and electronics stuff and normally had tons of work orders to get ready. Also, any equipment problem encountered at sea had to be reported, and then the reports sent off to multiple commands in the states: big shipment.

Fred caught Dillan waiting for the skipper for dinner in the wardroom lounge.

"Hey, Dillan," he said handing him an open envelope. "We got this last mail call. Looks like one of your troops can't pay his bills. Handle it please."

A quick glance: the letter was addressed to Commanding Officer, USS LARTER, FPO, 'Frisco. The return address was Guaranteed Collection Agency, San Diego, postmarked over a month ago. Dillan pulled the folded paper out of the envelope.

The letter was dated December 1, 1967. It alluded to the fact that one Signalman Seaman Groft had not paid his monthly payment to Jeffery Jewelers in downtown San Diego. It showed that he owed $368.65 past due, and that the collection agency was looking to the CO to force Groft to pay. Navy regulations were quite specific about Sailors who did not pay their bills. CO's were directed to insure that their crews were not deadbeats.

That is a hell of a lot of money for a Seaman.

After dinner, Dillan called the signal bridge, and asked the watch to track down Groft and send him to talk to Dillan in his stateroom – and bring any papers he had related to Jeffery Jewelers with him.

About 30 minutes later, there was a knock on the bulkhead.

"Excuse me, Mr. Dillan, you wanted to see me?"

Groft was about 19, tall, thin, short blond hair. He had been on LARTER for a year, a little less than Dillan. Should be up for 3rd next cycle. Groft was in dungarees, ball cap stuffed under his belt. Dillan pointed to the other empty chair and handed the letter to Groft.

Sitting down and reading the letter, "Damn. Sorry, Mr. Dillan. I've been making payments every month. Right after payday I get a money order from the PC and mail it. I never missed one!"

"OK, Groft, what did you buy and when?"

"I bought an engagement ring for my girl last summer. Gave it to her just before we started RefTra, and we're going to get married when we get back, sir."

"How big was it, and what did you pay?"

"It was a third of a caret, and I paid $499.00. I put $250.00 down and was to pay $30.00 a month for a year. I didn't think I owed this much," pointing to the letter.

Dillan did some arithmetic in his head. They were charging him about 30% interest. And $500 for an undoubtedly poor quality 1/3 caret diamond was robbery. Typical of the fly by night jewelry stores catering to young, love struck Sailors. The amount demanded was payment in full, plus interest, plus late fees, plus collection fees; a rip off.

"How many payments have you made?"

Groft took a look at his paperwork. He showed Dillan. It was a neatly annotated list of the date and amount of each payment starting in August, 1967, through January 1, 1968. And a small payment book with tabs torn off and their stubs marked. Sum on the original loan he owed was $170.00. The remaining $198.65 was fees and additional interest. A real rip off.

"I bet that as soon as they didn't see your payment right on the first of December, they turned the account over to the collection agency, Groft. Then the agency added late fees and big collection fees. And the same will happen for January. So the fees just keep adding up. Any way you can come up with $170 to pay this off?"

"Maybe, sir, I've been saving as much as I could for the wedding. I've got that much on the books, I think."

"OK. Here's what I want you to do. Get the DK to pay you the $170. I'll clear it with the supply officer. Then you get a money order payable to the jewelry store for $170 from the PC. I'll write a letter for you which will say this pays in full. We'll mail it as soon as we hit Subic."

"But how about all the other charges, sir?"

"Many of these collection agencies prey on young Sailors and try to use intimidation to collect big additional fees – especially on deployed Sailors. A letter to their CO scares hell out of them and they come up with the money, or take a big 'dead horse[xxxix]' to pay it. I think we can handle this so that they get off your case. When we get to Subic, I'll get on the WATTs line with NIS, you know, the Naval Investigative Service, in San Diego. I'm sure that a call from NIS will cause them to rethink picking on you."

"Thanks Mr. Dillan, thanks a bunch. I'll get you that money order."

"That's OK, Groft. But do me a favor. Don't buy any more jewelry from those people – go to the NEX. You can guarantee the quality, get a good price, and don't get dragged into an interest rate rip off. If you need to finance, NFCU (Navy Federal Credit Union) is better. You should know that I have to tell Mr. Finistry, the XO, and the skipper that you're paying the bill in full."

"OK, and thanks again, sir."

Dillan knew the assistant special agent in charge from San Diego, NIS. In the spring, 1967, there had been a theft of LAR-TER's test equipment from a warehouse when it was at the base electronics lab for calibration. He had to work with NIS then. They ultimately found the item and prosecuted a civilian tech rep who had a side business going in used test equipment.

Dillan had discussed the predatory nature of the down town jewelry trade over coffee with the agent. She said that they were starting to come down hard on those bottom feeders.

On January 10, 1968, after 42 days at sea, the task group left Yankee Station and headed east at speed, dodging around the 130 or so uninhabited rocks of the Paracel Islands.

Enroute message orders were received indicating that one LCDR Jim Henderson, USN, was to relieve LCDR Chuck Peterson, USN, as Executive Officer of USS LARTER. He was already enroute and Dillan didn't know, when questioned by the XO, why LARTER was getting the orders so late. Normally one got a 30 day heads up. But these were sent only yesterday.

Maybe someone in the funny farm in DC screwed up.

Not that Washington administrative screw ups were not normal. They were the rule, not the exception.

LARTER plowed along screening the carrier with two other destroyers.

20

Dillan overheard Red Redmond telling Chris Harcourt that he knew Henderson. They had served onboard USS BLACK (DD 666) in '56 for a few months together when Red was a boot. Henderson was a LTJG and the gunnery officer on BLACK back then.

"So what kind of an officer is Henderson?" Chris asked.

"Seemed like a good guy, academy 53, just like the XO, grew up on a farm in North Dakota," Red said.

"So, where's he been?"

"I'm not sure. Heard he went off to a department head's tour on some old DDR (destroyer - radar picket) out of Mayport, but haven't heard since."

"Sounds like he has a lot of destroyer experience which is nice, wouldn't want someone that spent their entire career in the gator (amphibious ships) Navy. I sure hope he's as good as Chuck is in keeping this outfit together."

Dillan hoped so also. And he felt the same way about the gator Navy. Amphibious ships moved the Marines and their gear around. It took a squadron (about 8) of them to move one fully supported Marine Amphibious Unit. The MAU could put a battalion of Marines, complete with artillery, amtracks, a few tanks, and all necessary logistics ashore across any accessible beach anywhere in the world: a powerful deterrent.[xl]

As the XO, Chuck was the 'voice of reason' on LARTER. Chuck walked that fine line between supporting the captain and the department heads, yet giving both suggestions that kept the captain from over traditionalizing everything, and people like Fred from running roughshod over JO's and enlisted alike.

As the one man in the middle, this was the traditional job of an XO, and Chuck did it well. It was a tricky path to follow, but Chuck had it down pat. Chuck would make a fine skipper for some ship after PG school, Dillan thought.

Dillan kind of expected a wetting down party might be in order when they got to Subic. Sam Blongerinski and Joe Reiderman had their 18 months in as of Jan. 1, and were sporting the silver bar of Lieutenants, junior grade. Traditionally, promoted officers had to foot the bill for a cocktail party.

These promotions elevated Dillan to "Bull" Ensign, and Sam gave him the bar, but Dillan didn't wear it and no one noticed. Dillan thought the big bar was ugly and the "Bull" tradition stupid for a destroyer with now only four Ensigns aboard.

About a day out of Subic, LARTER had a small fire. It was ten in the morning.

"Fire, fire, fire in compartment 3-57-2-S, supply storeroom. General quarters, general quarters, all hands man your battle stations. Bong. bong, bong, bong." Repeat.

At sea, US Navy ships set general quarters to fight a fire.

It turned out that it was a class Alfa fire (combustible material). Class Bravo was fuel, and class Charlie was electrical. Repair I went in and extinguished the fire quickly – in some paper goods - using only CO_2 extinguishers.

Red told the skipper that it was probably from careless smoking. There was lots of smoke but little other damage. Tony's storekeeps would be busy cleaning up the mess, painting out the compartment, and then ordering out replacement forms in Subic, Dillan thought. Not a lot of liberty.

"Tony, I want the damn smoking lamp out in the store rooms and enforced," from the skipper at lunch. "And you need to determine who was responsible for this fiasco and write'em up."

"Aye, aye, sir."

Dillan could anticipate a "dereliction of duty" charge and at least mast for the offender – maybe a summary.[xli]

A day later, LARTER tied up in Subic Bay.

Subic was jammed. Pier space was at a premium. Since LARTER was last there, a floating dry dock had been brought in. This would allow destroyers and smaller to be lifted out of the water for repairs without going all the way to Yokosuka. But it was huge and took up a lot of space.

LARTER was tied up outboard of the USNS HOPE, a naval hospital ship operated by the Military Sealift Command with mostly civilian ship's crew and lots of military doctors and nurses. Painted white, big red crosses on the sides and top, she towered over LARTER. To get to the pier one had to go through a side hatch on the HOPE, go forward along a wide passage, and cross to the other side's hatch.

As Dillan did this one morning early to get to the base communications center, he heard children's voices laughing. A quick look through the rubber bifold doors into another passage, and he just saw a small body duck into another compartment. More giggling.

So he went in, and there in a ward was a group of about 10 Vietnamese children age 5 to maybe 10, staring at him through sparkling big brown eyes. But there was something wrong, terribly wrong. All the children were missing a part: an arm, leg, foot, etc. Sometimes they were missing more than one part, and most were bandaged.

God, war is a bitch to do that to innocent children.

A moment later a US Navy nurse walked in. She was a Lieutenant Commander by the two full and one thin center stripes on her cap. She wore a starched white uniform, older but good looking, maybe pretty without the stern face, pulled back hair and skirt below her knees. She stood there for a moment, one hand on her hip, one holding a clipboard.

"May I help you Ensign," icily. "This is a restricted area."

"No, Maam, just crossing the ship," and Dillan split. The image of those children would haunt him for life.

He did make it to the phone center and after a long wait got through to Patty, at 1AM her time. Conversation was strained. She had had a lonely Christmas and New Year's.

"What'd you do for Christmas," she asked, a bit of antagonism in her voice.

"Just another day at sea, stood two 4 hour watches, wrote you a letter, caught up on some sleep," he answered. "We had a tiny tree in the wardroom and a big dinner for lunch but I was on the bridge so I ate in the mess decks prior to watch. How 'bout you?"

"Karen came over and we cooked a chicken after I got back from church. As I said, she wants to wait till February to move in when, her lease is up. What'd you do for New Years, go clubbing?"

Where the hell did that come from? She knows damn well that one couldn't go clubbing at sea.

"No, we were still at sea."

"Well, I was here all alone. Drank an entire bottle of wine and went to bed at 9. Alone, damn it. Didn't even stay up for midnight. Do you know we've never had a Christmas or New Years together? Never. I am lonely and I hate this. I want to quit my job, give up the apartment, and go home. I'll come back in April and get another place."

Oh shit! She is pissed. Quick, Dillan, think about how to answer this one diplomatically.

"What'll you do with our stuff? How about the car?" he asked.

"I'll put it all in storage. I hate being here alone! I hate it. I hate it. I hate it!" loudly and with a crack in her voice.

Time for some logic.

"When you get back, you probably will never be able to find an apartment even close to San Diego. We might end up living 2 hours away from the base. Remember what we were told happened to the Brookmans? His wife left during LARTER's last Westpac cruise, and when she came back ended up in a very dumpy apartment close to the border town with Mexico."

Silence, then a muffled, "Damn you."

"And we really can't afford storage costs, round trip air fare, and you with no job. Hell, Honey, I'll be home in a little over 4 months."

"Damn you," louder this time.

More silence.

"Don't the officers' wives get together? Why don't you call the CO's wife and find out?"

"I don't know. She called me a couple of weeks ago and there was some get together at the club in North Island. Since they live in Coronado it's close for her. But I was working and it's a long way over there on the ferry and all from work. And most of the wives have kids and are a lot older than me. I feel like a stupid little girl in that group," Patty said.

"How about Rita Donovan? We enjoyed getting together that time before the ship left."

"Rita went home for a month." *Oops!* "I am calling the storage company tomorrow to get prices."

"Patty, we have a lease. If you go we will still have to pay for the apartment until the end of May. That's a lot. Where will you stay back east?"

"I don't give a damn, and I'll stay with Mom. It won't cost anything."

Man, Patty must be desperate. It's almost 4 years since she lived at home. She and her mother fight.

She continued, "I'll just close up the apartment then, leave the car in the parking space and take a bus to the airport."

"I think you ought to stay in National City till I get back," Dillan said. Another silence, then 'click.' He stayed on the line dumbfounded. She had never hung up on him before.

"Sorry sir, your party has hung up."

Phone call cost $48 for 19 minutes.

Feel like a rat. Don't want Patty miserable, can't do a damn thing about it, trapped in the middle. The proverbial job - family trash compactor, this sucks.

He thought about calling her back – but not in her state of mind.

Dillan called NIS in San Diego on the WATTs line (at 10 AM San Diego time) and asked them to run interference on the Groft thing. The assistant special agent in charge told Dillan that this was not the first complaint against both the collection agency and the jewelry store. She promised to handle it.

Dillan wrote a letter to Jeffery Jewelers for Groft, as if Groft had written it. Then Dillan wrote one of his own to them, to go in the same envelope, on ship's letterhead, stating that he had turned the incident over to San Diego NIS and that the additional fees and interest on a deployed Sailor was extortion.

He questioned their business practices and inferred that it was their patriotic duty to treat young Sailors on deployment defending them with respect. He was not very diplomatic. He signed the letter but did not include his rank.

Dillan then wrote a note to the CO, via Fred and the XO, telling them that Groft had paid off his bill. Dillan did not mention his call to NIS or his nasty letter to the jeweler.

There was no further correspondence to Groft or the CO related to this incident.

21

LARTER had to get some badly needed maintenance done to her high frequency radio antennas. Caked with dirt, jet fuel and salt, they were starting to lose their effectiveness on transmit. Dillan had the ship's guard shifted ashore to the base communications center, and put his troops and the electronic technicians to work. He made an RPS run.

The new XO arrived. Turns out he had been flown to Subic by way of Travis Air Force base outside San Francisco, Guam, and into Cubi and had been there almost a week before LARTER arrived. At quarters[xlii], the first full day's morning in Subic, the old XO walked him around to each department's formation and introduced him. It was a very short introduction and done for the enlisted men more than for the officers. Then, after quarters, all officers were ordered to the wardroom for a meeting. Here the CO formally introduced the new XO to them.

"Gentlemen, this is your new Executive Officer, LCDR Jim Henderson, USN, a Naval Academy graduate class of 53. Jim has 6 years in destroyers, some on the east coast and the Med. He is a destroyer school graduate and most recently was the staff operations officer for DesRon 11 out of San Diego. He is the recipient of two Navy Commendation medals for his previous assignments. He and his wife, Sheila, and their 2 children, live in San Diego. Please join me in welcoming Jim to LARTER."

Then, "Department heads please introduce yourself and then your officers."

So, buy seniority, Red Redmond, then Chris Harcourt, and Fred Finistry introduced themselves and their division officers. Tony Carpiceso introduced himself.

Dillan responded with "Welcome aboard, sir," like all the others when his turn came and watched the new XO.

LCDR Jim Henderson was almost six feet, stocky and muscled. Growing up on a farm in the frozen north had undoubtedly hardened him at an early age. It was rumored, but unconfirmed, that he had played left defensive tackle for USNA for 2 years until his knee got messed up.

Dillan thought he looked the part, but maybe it was defensive linebacker. His neck was not thick enough for a tackle. Light brown short hair, firm but friendly face, light eyes. He looked Swedish or Norwegian. Not someone to run into in a dark alley.

Then the new XO said, "Over the next few days I'll be relieving LCDR Peterson, and will be meeting with you to understand the issues and challenges confronting each division. The captain has informed me of the excellent work you each have done on Yankee Station. I know Chuck'll be a tough act to follow. Thanks for making me feel welcome."

The skipper stood, indicating that the meeting was over.

"OK, men, our stay in Subic's short so get hopping."

Dillan did not get any face time with the new XO then. And he was a little apprehensive.

What will Fred tell the new XO about me? What will Chuck tell the new XO?

Three days later there was a short relieving ceremony after colors. When all officers, with the exception of the Commanding Officer, got relieved, it was usually a non event. Normally, even the XO's relieving would not involve a ceremony. But the captain insisted, even if it was very short.

When a ship was in port, watch stations and sections were different. The LTs stood command duty officer – essentially in charge of the ship in the skipper's absence. Other officers and some chiefs stood officer of the deck in port watches on the quarterdeck. The quarterdeck, another throwback to the days of sail, was basically where the brow was placed, usually amidships. This time in Subic it was where the brow connected to the side hatch on USNS HOPE.

When you had the duty you stood your watch on the quarterdeck attending the brow and checking the identification of everyone who came aboard. With nukes aboard, everyone had to be checked, and cross checked if unrecognized. It was usually just one watch a day. ENS Billy Hoffman was the officer of the deck for the 08-12 watch.

He had a 3rd class petty officer and a seaman with him as petty officer of the watch and messenger of the watch. The petty officer was armed with a 45 in a holster. After the suicide incident, the 45s did not have a clip installed, although one could be inserted quickly if needed. When anyone left the ship they would salute the officer of the deck, say they had permission to go ashore, step on the brow, face aft, and salute the ensign, and then leave. Coming aboard was the reverse.

Dillan needed to talk to Billy about another ammo recall message that had been received. Some lot of high explosive projectiles were all duds. Billy would have to check his records when he got off watch. If LARTER had some of that lot, a massive working party would be required to offload, and then replace the bad ones. So Dillan was on the quarterdeck talking to Billy.

The skipper had to make his formal courtesy call on the CarDiv Admiral on the carrier. One could wander around the base during the day in wash khakis but with the regular officer's hat (the one with the cover and bill). Ball caps were not appropriate for officers or chiefs ashore. On the Cubi point side, the officers and chiefs could wear the garrison cap (pisscutter) but not on the main base.

After 1600, one had to shift to a gabardine uniform, which, due to Subic's tropical location, was tropical khaki long. The skipper came down to the quarterdeck in tropical khaki long. As he left the ship, Billy had the petty officer of the watch ring: "Bong bong - bong bong" on the bell and pass, "LARTER departing," on the 1MC.

This was to alert all officers that the skipper was leaving. In most cases the skipper called down to the quarterdeck in advance so that anyone wanting to see him could as he was leaving. In this case the skipper had not called, he just showed up at the quarterdeck.

Dillan knew that the bongs came from some other old Navy tradition. A ringing of a bell on the quarterdeck passed over the ship's 1MC. Two raps, a space, and two more. Commanding officers always got bonged coming or going. Two bongs for LCDR and below, 4 for CDR and CAPT. There were six or even eight for Admirals and very senior Department of the Navy civilians.

The announcement was the officer's command, never a name. If one did not know who an officer was or what his command was, for officers of the same rank or above the ship's commanding officer's rank, the correct number of bongs and "Staff, gangway" was appropriate. In a nest, bongs were done for the commanding officers of outboard ships who were crossing, and were announced as crossing. In a nest an extra watch stander, usually a messenger, attended the brow connecting outboard ships.

As he left the ship the skipper said,

"Mr. Dillan, the CarDiv chief of staff called. He wants all task group communications officers to meet with the staff communications officer in the carrier's wardroom at 1000 tomorrow. I told LT Finestry. Go and see what's up."

"Aye, aye, sir," then the skipper was gone.

Later Dillan ran into Fred.

"The CarDiv CSO (chief staff officer) called a meeting for all TG comm officers for tomorrow morning," Fred said.

"I heard Fred; the skipper told me earlier, I'll head over tomorrow after quarters."

"So the skipper already told you did he Dillan? That must have been nice?" icily.

"Ran into him on the quarterdeck as he was leaving," Dillan said. Fred turned and just walked away.

God, I get a perverted pleasure from tweaking Fred's tail.

After quarters the next morning Dillan, in tropical khaki long, took the base bus around to Cubi Point. It wasn't much of a scenic tour since the ring road ran through storage yards and past warehouses. Once at Cubi, the bus ran down the pier towards RANGER. RANGER looked like a monster, dominating the pier area. There was another carrier space astern of her empty and desolate. And there was lots of activity with trucks delivering supplies and working parties, like a continuous string of ants, moving boxes up the forward brow. Dillan saw a sign which said "Quarterdeck" that directed one to the after brow.

To get up the brow one had to climb a bunch of steps like an open building staircase, then cross the bridge like brow to the carrier and ended up on an elevator. This was an aircraft elevator used for moving aircraft from the hanger bay to the flight deck, and located outboard – on most carriers there were four of them.

The aft elevator had been lowered as a 'quarterdeck.' Saluting the ensign and OOD, who was an ENS (being an ENS on a carrier had to be like being a fraternity pledge), he was aboard. Dillan had not met this one during his cross deck training. The Navy story was that there were Ensigns and there was whale shit.

Ensigns were junior. Dillan thought that really got rubbed in on a carrier.

The messenger of the watch took Dillan to the wardroom. This time it was the senior officer's wardroom, smaller, much more opulent, nicer chairs, paneled walls, ship's plaques everywhere. Looking over the plaques, maybe 100 of them, it was obvious that RANGER had seen a lot. She was older than some carriers. She was launched in 1956 and had been around a bit: mostly west coast out of Alameda.

Many of the plaques were from British navy ships. There was a little crown on the top. Probably from visits to Hong Kong, a British Royal Crown Colony, with its own small British fleet, Dillan thought.

Dillan was the first to arrive and got a coffee from a silver coffee service and took a seat. Soon another two single bar types came in, communications officers from the other cans now assigned. Dillan didn't know any of them, but after introductions all around, it was obvious that their radiomen and signalmen had been talking over the nets or semaphore.

The staff communications officer came in, a LCDR.

"Good morning."

"Good morning, sir."

"Gentlemen, I invited you here to discuss a problem. We've been missing numbers on our broadcasts every now and then, and I know you have been also. Since the carrier's antennas are higher, we haven't been missing numbers as often as you have. But we've missed some, also. And you have, as my watch chiefs tell me, been being a bit of a pain in the butt asking for sked scans and resends. I want to introduce someone to you."

Dillan had not seen the LT standing in the background.

"Gentlemen, this is Lieutenant Gregory. He is the propagation officer for NAVCOMSTAPHIL."

Dillan had been taught that there were Navy communications stations located around the world: small ones and large ones. They acted as transmission stations, on high frequency radio, for the Navy broadcasts. Many times the same broadcasts would be transmitted from the large powerful field antennas by two or more stations on many different frequencies. And these stations were connected by radio and even under the ocean cables. Naval

Communications Station Philippines was located on the west coast of Luzon, the closest NAVCOMSTA to Yankee Station.

Most broadcasts were multiplexed, where one radio signal could be broken down using special equipment into two or more individual broadcasts. A ship's radiomen had to insure that the station and frequencies they copied were reliable and usually had to shift stations or frequencies often. The naval message system was the communication lifeline for all ships and stations in the Navy.

"Lieutenant Gregory."

"Good morning. We collectively have a problem, a growing problem. Sun spot activity has been increasing since last June. It's getting worse. Almost all ships have been missing numbers. The number of requests we have gotten for sked scans and retransmittal has grown rapidly – now far exceeding our ability to keep up."

"We're a small base and handle all the traffic for 7th fleet in this area. We have to do something. Last week I talked to Pearl and we decided to institute a back up broadcast from NAVCOM-STAPHIL."

"Effective tomorrow morning, at midnight Zulu, NAVCOMSTAPHIL will mirror the normal 7th fleet broadcast 30 minutes later over the ASW broadcast. The ASW net gets very little use, as you know. You and the carriers copy ASW, and as soon as we can, other ships in the area will be provided with equipment, if necessary, and key cards to do the same. If we mirror the broadcast, you'll have two chances, offset 30 minutes, to get all the numbers. Does that seem like a good idea?"

"Yes, sir!" from all.

"Good, we thought you would like it. Is there anyone who can not copy ASW 24/7?"

One officer said, "Another broadcast to copy like that will eat up teletype paper at twice the normal rate."

"We anticipated that question, but thank you for asking. We have a limited supply that will be available in the Subic supply depot by the day after tomorrow. We also recommend that anyone who is using double carbon paper take it apart and use single sheet. Then you get 3 times as much."

Teletype paper, although a small item, was in very short supply in West Pac. Dillan had loaded out so much extra when LARTER headed for West Pac that boxes were stacked everywhere. Only using single thickness sheets was an invitation to losing something.

On LARTER, the last or bottom carbon was rolled up, and was their back up copy. Other copies and the top or original copy were torn off and routed on the message boards.

It was a good system. Dillan felt sorry for anyone who was so short that he had to go to single sheet. Unrolling and re-rolling 200 foot rolls would be a trip on a destroyer. And the logging of incoming numbers would stretch a small radio watch crew, especially with two broadcasts to log.

Following this there were a lot of discussions about propagation, its vaguerities, sun spots, and how they messed up high frequency radio reception, solar flares, which were bad news, and etc. Dillan took an active roll, since he had a lot of theoretical education in communications electronics.

The LT asked him where he had picked up so much information, and when Dillan told him he was an Ohio State NESEP, the LT said that the NESEP program was a great addition to the fleet. Although Dillan did not ask, he thought this LT must not be an academy type: they thought NESEPs were usurping the technical mystique of the Naval Academy.

Finally, the meeting was over. Dillan thanked the staff comm. officer and the LT from NAVCOMSTAPHIL, said good by, walked back to the quarterdeck and departed the carrier. They all took the bus back to 'fleet side,' the nickname for the side where the ships other than carriers tied up. There was lots of discussion on how to improve communications. Dillan thought it was a good meeting, and a backup broadcast would be a big plus.

22

Back on LARTER, Dillan told Fred what was up, and went to radio. Fred just made a face. Dillan called a radio meeting and passed the information on. When Dillan held radio meetings, the troops knew that they were two way. If they had a thought, they could express it once the presentation was done.

Dillan wanted his enlisted troops to feel that they could say their piece. There were some naysayers, as there are in any group, and lots of discussions on how best to set up for two broadcasts. After they came to consensus on the procedures, the chief stepped in and told everyone that radio would immediately set up to handle the double volume. Not that there was a choice. Dillan expected there would be something on the boards from COMSEVENTHFLT so directing by the end of the day.

He ran into LTJG Joe Rederman in the passageway.

"Hey, Mr. D, how they hanging?"

"Hey, Joe, low and slow; you and Sam going to do a wet down this time?"

"Naw, not this time, the skipper postponed it, too much going on with the XO getting relieved and all. You and Pete going to the XO's and Tony's Olongapo shindig tonight?"

"Well, we plan to go if Fred doesn't come up with some SLJO crap for me to do. Probably see you at the gate. Eighteen hundred, isn't it?"

"Yeah, see you there. It looks like the CO, new XO, and Fred are going to skip the bar scene."

"That's not a surprise. The CO won't go since his presence will put a damper on the fun. The new XO won't since it's the old XO's thing. Fred won't go since it wouldn't fit his self image to be involved in any wild time, especially with junior officers beneath his rank. So I guess Fred is standing by for Chris. And Eric and Ted have the duty anyway."

"Yea, figured Fred would beg off, see ya later, Gator," with a wave.

Subic Bay had a Philippine town just outside the base gate called Olongapo. One had to wear civilian clothing, go through the well guarded base gate, walk over a bridge above a cesspool river, and enter the most impoverished, dirty, smelly city Dillan had ever seen. The Olongapo side of the river was lined with shacks, some held up with sticks, some with flattened beer cans for roofs. The smell from the river was strong.

"Enough to gag a maggot," from Pete.

As they crossed the bridge, there were small boats floating with brown boys hunkered down on them yelling, "Hey 'ailor, toss quarter."

One of the guys in front of Dillan and Pete tossed a coin into the water and 3 boys dove for it. Dillan didn't have a clue how they could see in the murk, especially in the late afternoon sun. But one came up with it, holding it high to the cheers of his buddies.

Swimming in that water will make for a short life. But just living in Olongapo must make for a short life.

The city was mostly dirt streets crowded with carts, donkeys, a water buffalo or two, jeepneys (decorated jeeps covered in wild paint, tassels and religious medals), and people, lots of brown people. And there were lots of seedy bars catering to Americans. There was a rumor that a woman was running for mayor of Olongapo on a clean up platform. Dillan hoped she won.

The official language of the Philippines was English, but most spoke some dialect of Tagalog. And most spoke some combination thereof. There were tons of bars, and the bars were well populated with bar girls and whores. The joke on the ship was that if the world ever needed an enema, it would be administered through Olongapo.

The LARTER's officers, less the CO, the new XO and the duty section, took Tony Carpiceso over for a birthday party, and the departing XO over for his informal farewell party at a bar that Tony remembered. Lots of San Miguel beer, lots of strippers, and a floor show.

The Philippine government owned the San Miguel brewery, so it was the only beer in town, non-export. It had a different taste than the export stuff. There were lots of hanging on bar girls begging, "Big st'ong 'merican buy girl drink" Usually these 'drinks' were tea in a martini glass, and went for $5. The girl got $2 of that. Cost 2 cents to prepare.

The XO let his hair down a bit that night, doing the dirty boogie with a couple of strippers on stage. Tony really celebrated.

Two sometimes topless girls riding his legs, bouncing up and down singing "Ho'py Br'day" to him, one in each ear. Every now and then one would grab his head and bury it between her boobs. Then Mama San would yell and the boobs would be hidden again.

The guys got to singing "We all live in a yellow submarine," loud and mostly off key. Even the girls tried in their broken English.

Dillan had a few, then a few too many, then way too many. The phone call to Patty had set him up for a drunk, and he was going at it with a vengeance.

Beer was being augmented with a shot of rotgut whisky. Although beer was usually consumed directly from the bottle, the XO decided that 'depth charges' were in order. Fill a glass with beer, take a shot glass filled with whisky and drop it slowly into the beer glass, shot glass and all. Then as the beer glass was tilted to drink, the whisky slowly poured out of the shot glass to mix with the beer. It was a brutal way to get loaded.

Dillan had a girl in his lap for awhile. Sure felt different, and good. Nice stand up nipple when she discreetly popped one out of her dress. She would pull his head down and then rub one against his cheek. Felt real good. Then she started the "ets go upt'airs 'ailor me heally ike you" stuff whispering in his ear, nipple enticingly close to his mouth. His head was spinning.

He vaguely remembered being pulled up a rickety stair case and an awful smell in the scuffed wall hall way hidden only partially by cheap perfume. A tiny room with a rumpled bed and wall paper peeling off the wall, one small lamp emitting an orange glow from its tilted shade.

Then a brown girl stripping quickly and a warm body pressed against his. He slid his hand down the small of her back, then cupping a buttock like in a trance, his body responding automatically.

She pulled back, took his hands and cupped them around her breasts. She pulled his belt out of the loop and unbuckled it, pressing her hand against him, squeezing.

Oh shit. Here I am, upstairs with a nude girl rubbing against me and trying to get my pants off!

He pushed her away, and fumbled to refasten his belt.

"Mean 'ailor man not like Tinka? Tinka give good time."

Damn. She is maybe 18, long black hair, cute if she doesn't smile and show her rotting teeth, perky small breasts, creamy brown skin, soft and warm. Double damn. I sure could use some serious sexual gratification, maybe just this once. Stop that meathead. Think with your brain, not another part of your anatomy. You know damn well you will hate yourself. Get out of here!

"Sailor like Tinka, here take $20 dollars, Sailor go now," Dillan said, pulling a 20 from his wallet and handing it to her.

Tinka grabbed the 20, put on a big pout and wiggled her hips. She squeezed her breasts at him. She stepped forward, grabbed his right hand and rubbed it over a breast again, nipple hard against his palm, then down her belly into the fur. Warm. Maybe make more money.

He pulled his hand away and stepped back almost falling as the back of his legs hit the bed. She dropped to her knees and reached for his belt again. He side stepped her and held both hands in front of him, palms up and outward. She stared at him for a moment and sighed. Then she put the 20 in her teeth, bent over and picked up her dress and panties, stood and started getting dressed: other fish to fry. She said something to herself unintelligible.

Down the stairs and headed back to the ship went Dillan, holding on to the wall and dodging other girls pulling other Sailors up the staircase. When he got back to the first floor, he saw the LARTER table.

Mama San was sitting on Tony's lap. Mama Sans were the older women in charge of the girls. One per bar: usually ex bar girls themselves. They established prices, insured that the girls hustled the correct number of drinks, kept them from "giving" anything away that could be sold, and generally acted as den mother and hard nosed supervisor for the girls.

They took a cut. In the states they would have been called Madam, although they did a lot more than supervise whores. Every bar with bar girls had a Mama San. Sometimes Mama Sans stood at the door and hawked the bar's attributes.

"Wow, Dillan, you sure are a quickie," one of the guys yelled. Dillan just waived. Pete Donavan jumped up and said, "Wait, I'm coming with you."

They went out among the begging kids, advertising Mama Sans, and pimps; flagged down a jeepney, jumped in and Dillan said, "Main Gate, 5 dollar, no side trip, zoom, zoom." Many jeepney drivers had girls available and would make side trips to their homes if they thought they could augment their income.

Dillan had been briefed by Tony. Side trips could be dangerous. And away they went, dodging crowds of other jeepneys and ignoring stop signs: a quick trip. It was a long but peaceful walk across the bridge to the gate and then to the ship.

Pete asked, "What the hell happened up there. We thought for sure you were going to get laid."

"When I came to my senses, I wanted no part of it; I didn't want to do it to Patty or myself." It got quiet.

Then from Dillan, "I better watch my booze intake better."

They walked in silence for a moment, the fresh cooler air starting to make Dillan's mind at least a bit more functional. He took big deep breaths, still a lingering odor from the river.

"That was Joe that made the smart remark about you getting a quickie, he doesn't like me much."

"Hell Pete, he's still fighting the Civil War along with Billy."

"No, I understand that crap, lived with it a long time. It's deeper than that. Billy's just a kid born into it. With Jim it's worse."

"You think he doesn't just hate blacks?"

"I don't think very many college educated people just hate blacks. We make them nervous, we scare them. They pull their women closer if they see us on the street. No, I think he's nervous for some other reason. I make him nervous. He avoids me. Maybe some one in his family had an altercation with a black man sometime."

"Well, you make me nervous too Pete."

"Don't try to be funny or patronize me, Dillan. You are not prejudiced because you never grew up in an area that was. Hell, you never even saw us. Don't kid yourself. You are a good guy and I'm glad you're my friend. But you don't have a clue what it's like to be black."

Damn Pete, I think I do. "Course I do; I read that book in high school or maybe college. "Black Like Me" it was called. Don't remember who wrote it."

"Oh, God, you're such a stupid honkey."

"You don't have to be nasty."

"OK, only half a stupid honkey."

"I'd trade you one Fred for ten honkey hating black panthers."

"No you wouldn't. Fred's pretty much a flaming ass but he dislikes you more than me which is neat for me. I don't know if he's prejudiced against blacks or not. Probably is. But right now he's prejudiced against Dilláns. Besides the Black Panthers are real bad news for whites."

"What do you mean real bad news, just a bunch of punks."

"Damn dangerous punks Dillan, damn dangerous. They would slit a white man's throat just as soon as they could if they thought they could get away with it," making a slow throat slitting gesture.

"Why?"

"They think that because of slavery and discrimination, they have a right to turn the clocks back 100 plus years and fight back. Hell, it wasn't the whites that sold us into slavery; it was our own kind in Africa who did it for the money."

"But why do a lot of blacks hate whites?"

"They bought us. They treated us pretty much like the pigs they kept on their farm, probably treated the pigs better. They wouldn't allow us to learn to read. They raped our young women, and called their own children from such an encounter slaves. They worked us to death, sold us splitting our families, whipped us … . Damn you, I don't want to discuss this with a white man. Accept that you have no clue."

It was a quiet time.

Maybe I don't have a clue. Have to walk a mile in another's moccasins to understand for real. Sure haven't thought about what it's like to be black – or any other minority for that matter, beyond my experience base. Need to defuse this.

"Pete, were your ancestors slaves?"

"Yeah, they escaped to Canada from Virginia just prior to the Civil War. They were passengers on the Underground Railroad that went through Gettysburg. After the war they came back as far as Pittsburg, actually a small town on the Mongehela River called Turtle Creek. It's a rough place. Even as I grew up, the houses, streets, and even the trees were orange from the open hearth furnaces belching smoke. But as my dad said, when the stacks were belching there was food on the table."

"God, I'm sorry your ancestors were salves."

"You are drunk Dillan. I'm sorry your ancestors were Neanderthals. Just accept that we're friends. You and Patty come over and have soul food with us, and we'll come over and have Patty's Irish stuff with you. And I'll give you a rough time over Buckeye football and you can give me grief over Panther football. Accept that you'll never understand what it's like to be black. Don't try to turn a deep emotional experience into an intellectual exercise. Damn 'real' engineers, anyway."

I am drunk. Mind is sluggish. Real engineer huh – Pete is upset. In school we called Industrial Engineers 'imaginary engineers.' Never thought they had heard it. What do I know that will calm Pete down? He's a friend I don't want to lose.

"I read somewhere that if you took a white person and placed him in an area where it's hot like Africa, that 50,000 years later his prodigies' skin would be black just from normal adaptation. And it said the reverse is true also. So we all came from the same stand of trees, swinging along together making grunting sounds."

"Too bad so many people don't see it that way. Too bad whites don't listen to Dr. King's speeches like we do. Maybe they would understand. Maybe they would understand 'I have a dream,'" from Pete.

Pete's Doctor King is a rabble rouser, stirs up the blacks, although I never really listened to one of his speeches. Change the subject.

"So what does your dad do?" from Dillan.

"He works in the steel mill, the Edgar Townson works of United States Steel."

"A good job?"

"Yeah, now one of the few blacks in the union, started as a coke shoveler in the open hearth furnaces. A brutal 10 hour a day, 6 day a week job. Now he hopes to be an assistant foreman on the new basic oxygen furnace, maybe in 3 years. What's your dad do?"

"A rough carpenter, works building forms for road construction bridges – mostly only in the good weather. In the winter he's laid off. We used to go deer hunting to put meat on the table."

"Never hunted, never ate deer meat. Sounds like a tough upbringing. Good for you to get where you got. That where you got your 'Expert' ribbon?"

"Growing up with a rifle in your hand makes one a fairly good shot, made rifle 'Expert' in boot camp. Seemed a lot easier shooting at stationary targets than barking squirrels off tree limbs with a 22. But couldn't do better than Marksman with the 45 and haven't had the opportunity to requalify for that ribbon since."

"Couldn't hit the broad side of a barn with either, but I can throw a mean fastball. If I get in it, I'll just chuck grenades at the gooks."

They walked on, past the now closed Navy Exchange, windows dark and parking lot empty, and down toward the piers.

Dillan said, "Good for you to go to college, Pete. Get a scholarship?"

"No, Dad's very hard earned money. I screwed around a bit more than I should have in high school and didn't have the grades, too small for major sports like most of the other brothers. Came close to getting in big trouble a couple of times, tough neighborhood. And then I didn't sign up for ROTC, since I wasn't crazy about the military then. I lived at home and Mom watched kids during the day, also. He's a super guy. Someday I'd like you and Patty to meet him and Mom."

"I'd like that, and I am sure Patty would, also."

"What brought you to the Uncle Sam's Navy?"

"Choice, I wasn't married when I graduated from college and my lottery number had been called. Join up or get drafted and end up in an Army unit slogging through rice paddies with the rest of the blacks. That, and the fact that the recruiter was a black man, a big first class storekeeper, and talked me into it."

"When did you and Rita hook up serious like?"

"We dated a lot in college. Decided to get married while I was waiting for orders to LARTER. Figured I better marry her or she'd run off with some B-ball player. You know we're newlyweds like you and Patty."

"About a month or so less than us, I think. Why didn't you come right to LARTER out of OCS? Your DOR is early."

"Mid term graduation was in January; waited around till Feb for an OCS slot, got commissioned in May. Then they sent me off to Supply School in Athens. Right away I hated it and asked for a transfer to Unrestricted Line. It came through in early August. Meanwhile, they had me doing assistant admin officer crap."

"Yea, I remember. You went to EMO School enroute, arrived just in time for Reftra."

"My timing always sucks."

"Athens nice?"

"Deep south, lots of red necks. It's a college town. Although I didn't see any, heard that there had been a cross burning in town, still scuffling over integration of the schools. Thought Brown verses Board was a commie conspiracy. Thought Johnson was a carpetbagger. No place for a colored boy. Glad to get out of there."

Then, as they walked on, they talked about Olongapo and how thousands of Sailors with money far from home could corrupt a poor third world town and bring out the worst in its inhabitants.

"No wonder we're the ugly Americans," from Dillan.

Pete's comment, "The only difference is that they sell themselves, some one didn't capture them to sell them. But they are slaves anyway, slaves to the greenback."

Back to the pier and through HOPE to LARTER.

The Navy adage was that if you got laid, without protection, in Olongapo, go right to the corpsman – you have at least one type of social disease and most probably two. If you got laid with protection you still had a chance of contamination.

Another joke Dillan had heard, a Sailor was walking down the street with hands in both his pockets in Olongapo - and they were not his hands.

The hangover the next morning was one of the aspirin and rubber types. It was a major f'n headache. Dillan never went over again in Olongapo. Even the XO had that pained expression. For some reason Tony was immune to hang overs – unfair, Dillan thought.

23

Later he ran into Joe. "Hey there, Studly, either you have the quickest pecker in Westpac, or you couldn't get it up last night."

"Screw you, General," Dillan answered, "decided I could do without."

"Saint Patrick, huh? Trying to drive the snakes out of Olongapo? Depth charges screw with one's mind, Dillan, and with ones libido."

"Yea, still screwing with it, big head and small brain this morning."

"Better small brain than small tool. Going to the fare-well?"

"Duty calls, besides I could do with some time on the wagon."

"Don't tilt your head; your brain may fall out your ear. See ya later."

"Later."

Subic had a super officer's club with great Philippine food and lots of cold drinks. Dillan's favorite was lumpia: kind of a miniature egg roll. Sometimes one would see some round eyed women there with guys. Wives of men stationed at Subic, or nurses, Red Cross or DOD school teachers. Round eyed women were the exception rather than the rule since Hawaii, and not all that many there.

Dillan and Pete and a few of the other guys hit the club when they could. Chris Harcourt taught them to play 'liars dice' for drinks.[xliii] Thank God club prices were cheap. But the more you drank the tougher it was to figure the odds.

The last night before underway, there was a regular 'Hail and Farewell' dinner at the club for the new XO and the departing one. Dillan couldn't go, he had the duty. Ted said it was nice and the skipper gave a good speech.

All had pitched in and got the XO a nice salad bowl set, something Subic was known for, 8 small bowls, one big one, and wooden utensils. And a few not so nice gag gifts – like a simple monkey pod carving Tony bought in Olongapo of a nude girl and a guy with an enormous dick. Dillan figured that probably would not be on display in the XO's quarters back in the states.

Few officers really patronized Olongapo. But Tony loved it and went often. To Dillan's knowledge, he never slept with the girls or came down with anything; just played. Tony was from the South Bronx and had a bit of the goodfella in his genes. And he was big and a bit overweight. He seemed to handle himself well and was a favorite customer, so Mama San looked out for him, Dillan was told.

Dillan figured that he wouldn't want to be on Tony's bad side in New York.

Bet it would be a good way to get a set of cement over-shoes and a midnight swim in the East River.

Subic's weather was nice, even if a bit unpredictable. It would be sunny, then cloud up and rain like hell, mostly in the afternoon. Come down in absolute sheets. Then clear up and all the puddles would steam. Two hours later the puddles were gone and it was hot as hell again.

There also was a nice beach and club at Cubi Point. Swimming in the tropical waters was supposed to be wonderful and they even had a speed boat and would take you water skiing for $3, Dillan heard. There was also a small island where the guys could go to get free beer. Run by the Cubi EM club, boats would take and retrieve the Sailors from Cubi's pier. Carrier Sailors used it, but fleet side crews seldom if ever went. It was too far away.

The Cubi Point O-club's bar was another place however, populated with air crews. Like a wild fraternity party. They threw pitchers of beer into the fans, and held initiations for pilots that just made their 50th trap (landing on a carrier). The initiation required that the pilot get strapped into a castered desk chair, blindfolded, and then get pushed across the floor while every one else threw beer and popcorn at him.

Finally, he was stopped by a couple of guys with a rolled up table cloth stretched between them. It was all at maximum volume on the music speakers and maximum yelling. Lots of drunks passed out in the corner. A bit much, Dillan thought.

While in Subic, some new ships showed up. These were BRADLEY class destroyer escorts.[xliv] These ships, originally purchased in the early 1960's, were a poor example of democracy in action, Dillan thought. They only had one screw.

Dillan figured that BRADLEY class DEs would end up doing plane guard and picket duty and the older FRAM destroyers would get the more interesting assignments. That was a good thing. Plane guard and picket duty were boring.

USS RANGER, while tied up at Cubi Point, had a fire – in an aircraft tire locker – and it burned and smoldered for 3 days until it could be put out. Only a few injured, mostly from smoke inhalation. But no one put a ship on fire to sea. So the task group was 3 days late getting underway, and had a total of 9 days in port – unheard of in Westpac.

Dillan did get to make one more short phone call to Patty. Things were a bit better, but she was still lonely and mad at him.

"Why are you way over there instead of being right here in bed next to me where you belong, damn it?" There was at least a little tease in her voice.

"It won't last much longer, Honey, we're almost half way done. Soon I'll be on my way home."

"Come now. And why are you such an insensitive, bull headed, stupid man?"

"I don't know, just born that way I guess. You bring out my fine attributes. Besides, you are mostly not a pain in the ass. In fact, seldom a pain in the ass, my Honey."

"Oh, what a silver tongued bastard you are. Talk about an off handed complement: mostly not a pain in the ass, huh? Well you mostly are a pain in the ass," laughing.

"Part of my nature as a man, how is work going?"

"Fine, just being a teller is easy if you're careful and don't lose any money. And the head teller is OK. But I'm so lonely. I want to go home for awhile. Maybe I'll call my dad and borrow some money to fly home."

"You can do that if you wish."

She will not. She prided herself on never taking money from her parents.

"Yeah, right, Mister. You know damn well I'd eat dirt before I'd ask him for money."

"Hang in there, Baby, this cruise'll end and I'll be home."

"I'm hanging, Pat. I'm hanging, on the end of the rope. But I'm not happy doing it."

Dillan could say little but, "I'm sorry." And, "I love you."

He was feeling a little guilt over the Olongapo evolution. He vowed to get Patty a peace offering next time in Subic. Not that he would tell her he almost got laid, never. It would be a peace offering more to ease his own mind, maybe pearls. The NEX had some good deals on Japanese "Mikimoto" cultured pearls.

LARTER and the task group were underway again early on January 21st, headed back for Yankee Station. Speed of advance, 15 knots. It was a leisurely trip with a few exercises enroute. Intel summaries were indicating that the North Vietnam Army and Viet Cong were moving around more than usual. Chatter was up on their radio circuits.

24

At noon, on January 23, 1968, USS PUEBLO (AGER 2), a tiny US Navy research vessel a lot like the Soviet AGIs, was performing intelligence gathering operations in international waters off Wonsan, Peoples Republic of Korea (PRK), in the Sea of Japan. Some enterprising North Korean Colonel took a few PRK patrol boats out, surrounded the unarmed PUEBLO, opened fire, and boarded and captured the ship and crew. A messed up command structure, and contingency plan screw-ups, left no way to rescue her. She was sailed into Wonsan harbor and the crew interred.

LARTER heard about it in a fleet wide Secret message. The press went wild with the news when it leaked out, and even the 'filtered' daily news message the Navy sent out had a big spread. By late that evening, the RANGER task group had been turned around and sent, at best possible speed, to the Sea of Japan, collecting two DLGs and two BRADLEY class DEs scrambled out of Subic enroute.

Off they went, up through the Taiwan straits, and then through the Tushima straits into the Sea of Japan at 27 knots.

When LARTER left Subic, the captain shuffled the watch bill: spreading out the experience. Dillan was now standing the 04-08 and 16-20 in combat as CIC watch officer. This was a good watch and should allow for the most sleep. The chief engineer, LT Red Redmond, was the CIC evaluator with Dillan.

Another Ensign took Dillan's spot on the bridge as JOOD. Dillan still had to be on the bridge as JOOD for unrep and sea detail. His GQ station was now in CIC.

Red was a NROTC type from the University of Wisconsin. He was an industrial engineer, like Pete, so he had a good background. He spent 4 years active and then got out just prior to a divorce. He made LT in the reserves. Three years later, and after getting laid off, he went back on active duty and was augmented back to a USN commission.

He was a super guy, and Dillan thought that he would make LCDR in another 3 years. He gave Dillan a rough time about Ohio State football. The Wisconsin Badgers were big time rivals of Ohio State. Now he was remarried and lived in San Diego proper. He had been on LARTER's previous cruise and should leave the ship around summer, 1968.

Dillan wondered what triggered the end of his first marriage. Navy life would do that to some.

But not Patty and me. Not us.

Being in CIC was a lot more comfortable, and one was a lot more knowledgeable of the bigger picture. Watch standers could sit down. Now the data from the 200 mile air search radar was available. Surface contacts beyond visible range showed up on the surface search. Electronics countermeasures (ECM) data on incoming received radar and other signals was available.

The sonar stack was in the annex room next door. A Weapons plot readout was there. The Naval Tactical Data System readouts were available by teletype. Many more voice radio nets were monitored. The only other copy of the daily intel reports was kept there. One could understand and see most of what the carrier saw.

Dillan was primarily responsible for the surface plot, making recommendations to the bridge on station keeping and proceeding from one station to another. Watching other ships change station and keeping the bridge informed. LARTER's captain was a bridge man, having grown up in the Navy when it always happened on the bridge, although he would come into combat often.

The troops carried on a banter since Red did not enforce silence like the skipper did on the bridge. There was camaraderie in the CIC watch section – and even Dillan and Red got a good natured ribbing now and then.

"Hey there, Mr. Dillan, heard you almost sampled Olongapo's ichiban (Japanese for #1) attraction? Careful, careful – don't want an enduring reminder. Bad news as Morton here knows," from RD1 Roberts as he pointed his thumb at RDSN Morton.

God, this ship has a grape vine. Wonder who spilled the beans on my aborted adventure? Don't remember any other guys from LARTER in that dump. But I don't know everybody. And maybe someone overheard one of the officers talking about it.

"Not me Roberts. You got your wires crossed, must have been some Ensign off another can."

"Maybe, sir, but my source is reliable. Don't want anyone leading our Ensigns astray, bad for the ship's image. The chiefs tell me that Ensigns should be sweet little "wet behind the ears" types, never dipping their wick in foreign ports."

"I uphold the sweet tradition, but I've got more time in the chow line than most Ensigns have in the Navy, so wet behind the ears is not one of my traits," answered Dillan.

"Yeah, mustangs should know better. Save it for Hong Kong. There the girls are clean but pricy."

"Never been to Hong Kong, looking forward to it. You been?"

"Last cruise; best port in Westpac," from Roberts giving Morton an elbow in the ribs, "Classy young Chinese girls who really can send you on a round the world trip. Make ya speak Mandarin and glow in the dark. Save your pennies Morton, you'll need them if we ever get there. Need lots of 'm to get some in Wan Chai."

Red was sitting in front of the right air scope, reading through the order of battle about the Red Chinese fleet.

He looked up and said, "God, all you young punks think about is women, or rehashing old scuttlebutt. You should keep your minds pure like us old guys do. Save your energy for when you really need it."

He went on, "Remember the old joke. There was an old bull and a young bull standing on a hill top in a pasture. The young bull saw some heifers down in the meadow and said, let's run down and have one. The old bull said no, let's walk down and have them all."

"Yes, sir, Old Bull, point taken. Us older types should take our time and walk down," from Roberts with a smile.

"Alright, you perverts, get your minds out of the gutter and back to business. Back to the salt mines," from Dillan directed at the enlisted. "We have a course change coming up. Better be ready for a reorientation."

There were now 7 destroyers, two of them armed with surface to air missiles, steaming in company with the carrier at speed. Dillan considered this a bit risky, since at 27 knots, there was no way LARTER's sonar had a chance to spot a submarine at any appreciable range. He guessed that the task group commander thought that the speed would limit a conventional sub's approach from anything but ahead, so he had all the regular destroyers in bent line screen ahead, and the DLGs closer to him on the sides.

A part of the trip was within 50 miles of the Communist Chinese coastline, so things were tense. When the task group arrived in the Sea of Japan, it was not alone. Two other carriers were there with their complement of cruisers and destroyers.

Navy task groups traveled in formation. Defense in depth was the rule. In situations where threats could come from the air, surface, and submarines, one could think of a formation as a group of concentric circles with the main body, usually a carrier, in the center. Then there were anti air warfare ships, usually missile cruisers or large destroyers on the first ring, then destroyers looking for submarines on the second ring, and finally picket ships out on the third ring.

Coupled with airborne long range search aircraft to spot incoming enemy aircraft or surface ships, and if lucky, a US submarine looking for enemy submarines, the formation was effective. When transiting at high speeds, the destroyer circle was truncated to provide more destroyers in the direction of travel, since submarines would have to lie in wait ahead. They were not fast enough to come up behind.

This was a formidable force. And Dillan had no idea what was going to happen.

An air strike on Wonson, on Pyongyang? War with North Korea? What would the Soviets do if we attacked their crazy half assed ally? The Red Chinese?

So the task force steamed around as three relatively independent task groups, nervous as hell, and geared up. It was very cold, snow off and on, some icing conditions, and a bit rough.

The ship's air-conditioning system, so important in the South China Sea, had to be converted to heat, a slow process. And there was little else on earth as cold as a steel ship in a cold sea. Colder than a witch's tit in a brass brassiere, according to the RD chief.

Lots of foul weather gear had to be located in the store rooms and issued. If one went outside, one's face would freeze. And LARTER waited, and waited, and waited. Not bored with all the screen reorientations, imagined or real submarine contacts, which would require general quarters off and on all night, and the carrier launching and recovering lots of CAP 24/7. When they were not launching or recovering aircraft, the task group steamed at 12 knots.

The overall OTC insisted on lots of drills. And lots of maneuvering as courses were changed to accommodate air operations. Finally, things would settle down in the evening. Then the formation would just steam in a big racetrack loop north and south. A DLG was off to the north as a picket to watch for incoming air contacts.

This far north, the sun went down at 1630: a cold dark sea, a cold dark sky, and another cold dark night.

25

Another 16-20 watch in combat. It was about 1830. Dillan was preparing for the next destroyer screen reorientation due in about half an hour.

"Combat, bridge, sonar, I have a contact!"

Damn! This is not what one wants to hear when one is a screening destroyer for a carrier task group.

"Bearing and estimated range, Sonar!"

"Bearing 016, range 12,000 yards. Designate goblin one. Estimated depth 60 feet."

Periscope depth. Attack depth. Oh man, this could ruin my entire night.

"Bong bong bong bong, general quarters, general quarters, all hands man your battle stations."

GQ was manned and ready in under 4 minutes. The crew was very much on edge up here in the cold. If a ship got sunk from under them, they would last 20 minutes in the cold water, maybe less. One took a potential attack very serious.

"Combat, bridge, sonar, evaluate contact as possible PRK Whiskey class submarine."

Conventional, probably North Korean, old and noisy. But still not fun. We better get him before he gets us, if he's serious.

Chris was standing over the sonar stack operator's back.

"Go passive again; let's be sure it's not one of our own Sturgeon class boats. Intel says there are no JMSDF or ROK boats out here."

The task force was supposed to have two STURGEON (SSN 637) class, relatively new, fast attack submarines doing barrier patrol. These submarines were nuclear, quiet and deadly to enemy subs. But if this contact was not a Sturgeon class, then the only alternative was a Soviet, Chinese, or most probably a North Korean boat that had slipped by the Sturgeons.

The JMSDF (Japanese Maritime Self Defense Force) had some excellent new conventional subs – but they were pulled back to territorial waters right after Pueblo got gobbled up. Same for the few ROK (Republic of Korea) ex US Guppy class conventional boats.

The operator stopped pinging; now the sonar was just a large microphone. Lots of sea noise. All the US ships churning up the water didn't help. They watched the displays, a waterfall and the circular image. The ping image was gone. All they had was a faint prop signal, a spike, and a few sidebands on the screen.

Chris said, "I think it's a Whiskey for sure. Look at the prop side band; on battery. Slow, maybe 4 knots." Chris was good.

Chris Harcourt had been a LT for well over a year now and was another destroyer school graduate. He was married, one child, and short by Academy standards, but wirey. He had played short stop. Black hair, brown eyes, Dillan thought he had some Mediterranean or Hispanic blood in his ancestry. He had been ASW officer on an east coast can prior to DesTec and had lots of experience shadowing Soviet boats.

Intelligence had indicated that the Soviet Union had given at least 4 Whiskey class submarines to North Korea.[xlv]

Are we going to shoot? Not without authority. We're at DEFCON II. The skipper can't shoot without authority. Or can he?

The XO, after a discussion with the skipper, got on the ASW net.

"Beerbarrel, Beerbarrel, this is Quicksilver. Goblin, a hot contact, bearing 016 from Quicksilver, range 12,000 yards, at periscope depth, evaluate as PRK Whiskey, designate Goblin one, over."

"Beerbarrel, roger, out."

Back to active. Ping ..... ping ...... ping .... pong!

Sonar could send out a high powered acoustic wave from the big bow mounted transducer called a ping: a sound wave going out forward and to the sides like the ripples from throwing a rock into a pond. Power was adjustable. If the wave encountered a contact, the signal would reflect and be picked up by the transducer's waiting hydrophones. Like radar, but a whole lot slower and more susceptible to distortion. And no way did sonar have the range radar did.

"Got him again!" from sonar.

"Quicksilver, Beerbarrel, Hotcake 03 and Hotcake 04 enroute your location. Quicksilver designated on-scene commander. Rocketman to assist, break, Quicksilver, Rocketman, over."

The OTC wanted both ships to acknowledge, in alphabetical call sign order. LARTER was designated on-scene commander for ASW and USS BRONSTINE (DE 1037) was to assist. Normally, the on-scene commander was the ship with the first active contact, regardless of the seniority of the two ship's captains. Not that it mattered, LARTER was senior. The carrier had also sent two ASW equipped helicopters.

"Quicksilver, roger out."

"Rocketman, roger out."

From the PriTac speaker, "Streetgang, Streetgang, this is Beerbarrel, immediate execute, turn two zero zero, I say again, turn two zero zero, standby, execute, over."

The OTC had just turned the entire task group, less the prosecuting destroyers and helos, away from the submarine contact. If it was a conventional Whiskey class submarine, probably running on battery just below the surface, it would be slow and would never catch the task group. Normally, a task group turn was far more complicated, and the destroyer screens were first reorientated to the new course, and then the main body executed the turn.

That was a quick fix to a close conventional submarine threat. The boss man takes it seriously.

The helos were invaluable. Able to use dipping passive sonar, really glorified waterproof microphones on retractable cables, they could be positioned such that their bearing data, coupled with LARTER's and BRONSTINE's active and passive sonar, would pretty much pinpoint the submarine's position, unless he could go deep and hide under a thermocline.

Combat was in full ASW mode. The sonar data was fed to the NC-2 plotter table. It was a frosted glass horizontal screen with a tracing paper on top. It was big: 3 feet by 5 feet. This was a geographical plot, not a relative one, and the ship's course and speed were input into the central bug.

Another bug (red) showed the approximate submarine position based on sonar's input. The position of BRONSTINE was plotted along with the helos. The XO had a reasonable picture to evaluate, including a history of who was where and when. A little inaccurate since most data was generated from inaccurate sensors, but close enough. The skipper came into combat.

"Captain's in combat" was announced. He took a long hard look at the plot.

"If we lose him we're going to have to go to a sector search or spiral search. I'll get the OOD to look up the signals. Hell, we may even do the old Acorn and Oaktree; old tactics but effective against conventional boats."

Then, "Since he is 10,000 yards away, this would make a perfect ASROC shot, Weaps. Let's make sure we're ready to drop a 44 on his head."

"Yes, sir. ASROC is ready. Cell 3 has a new 46 and is ready to go, Captain," Chris said. "We have a good solution and the launcher in ready. All we need is weapons free, and I'll turn the key and snap the switch.[xlvi]"

OK, here we go, getting ready for a shot.

After a pause, the captain answered, "I don't know if the OTC will want to risk weapons in the water unless the sub shoots first. Although we think it's a PRK Whiskey, it could be Soviet. Keep the OTC informed and ask for weapons free. We'll see."

The XO took the encrypted voice handset, transmitted LARTER's evaluation again, and indicated ASROC selected. He requested weapons free.

"BRONSTINE, LARTER, this is Oscar Tango Charlie, weapons tight unless fired on, repeat weapons tight, acknowledge, break BRONSTINE, LARTER, over."

"BRONSTINE, acknowledge weapons tight, out."

"LARTER, acknowledge weapons tight, out"

"Damn! We had him!" the skipper said. "But let's not start another war. We have enough to deal with now. Sure would have liked to feed him a 46 though. So now we play hold down."

Then, "I'll be on the bridge, XO. Keep his head down. Sonar, keep on your toes. He might try a snap shot. Maintain an ASROC solution. If you hear a torpedo from his bearing, shoot – got that XO?"

"Yes, sir. If he tries a snap shot, it will be his death warrant."

"And Chris, better get a DASH ready with a couple of 44 war shots."

"Yes, sir, but I'd like to keep it in the hanger until we know we're going to launch. It's cold out there and it might not start even with the electrical cable."

"Roger that. We'll use ASROC or the tubes as primary," from the skipper as he left combat for the bridge.

The OTC had just precluded LARTER and BRONSTINE from putting weapons in the water unless shot at first, a 'rules of engagement' thing. Actually, the entire task group was steaming under Defcon II (Defense Condition Two, War Expected), weapons tight. The radio message from the OTC was just a reminder: Let's not start something unless actually attacked. But at Defcon II, units were permitted to return fire if shot at.

There was always the remote possibility that a trapped submarine would try a snap torpedo shot at one of the destroyers. A destroyer was a small target, and difficult to hit, but it was a distinct possibility. And the longer the sub commander was trapped, the more likely it was that he would try a shot. It was very definitely a war of nerves.

Torpedo sounds were very different than a slow moving sub's sounds. Like an alarm bell for the sonar operator. Listening for a torpedo's high speed prop scream along with the normal pinging and passive listening was important. And if a sonar operator was listening passive, he could hear the thump and whoosh of a sub opening its outer doors, flooding his torpedo tubes, or expelling the torpedo with compressed air. The North Korean Whiskeys used older 'dumb' torpedoes. Dillan had heard that the Soviet Whiskeys used wire guided torpedoes. Wire guided were bad news since they could be "flown" into a target. Dumb torps just ran in a straight line.

No MK 46 homing torpedoes were launched. LARTER and BRONSTINE were ordered to do a hold down evolution. They were to maintain contact with the sub and not let it get far enough away to surface or pop up its snorkel. This was going to be a long term exercise, lasting hours, while the sub tried to sneak away and LARTER, BRONSTINE, and the helos tried to keep that from happening.

26

Ted managed the plot with help from Dillan. Dillan's main job was to use the surface search radar to control the helos as the XO and Chris directed. Move to this range and bearing from LARTER. Stop and dip sonar, listen, and report. Pull up dipping sonar, move to another location, dip, listen, etc. Helos were relieved on station with further and further to go to, and from the carrier.

But as the range to the task group proper increased, Dillan finally had to stop using helos. They were using up on station time with the longer and longer runs back and forth to the carrier. And LARTER's helo refueling rig had not been deployed. It got in the way of the after ship refueling station and cluttered up the DASH deck. After two hours, no helos.

The task group steamed off to the south. LARTER and BRONSTINE chased the submarine. And the sub faded in and out. Sometimes they had a good contact by one of the destroyers, often a faint contact. And sometimes it was gone all together. The sub was maneuvering and changing depth. First go one way, then another, but trying to work his way back north.

"Combat, bridge, sonar, lost contact, lost contact. Last bearing 341 range 3,300 yards."

The XO said, "Damn" and grabbed the ASW net handset, "Rocketman, lost contact," looking over the plot, "datum bearing 341, range 3,300, over."

The bridge had a speaker on ASW so they could hear also. Rocketman rogered.

"Go passive sonar. Bridge, recommend come left to 350, and slow to 3 knots."

XO wants to minimize our sound.

"Combat, bridge, sonar, no passive contact, just background."

"He has pulled something, XO," from Ted.

Dillan had marked datum, and used a compass to swing a 400, 800, 1200, and 1600 yard circle around datum – the distance the sub would go at 4 knots, his last speed, in 3,6,9, and 12 minutes. Assuming he was trying to work north and west, LARTER would move that way slower than he was going. And if the sub presented her stern to LARTER, passive sonar should pick up prop sounds easier.

BRONSTINE had swung around and was working her way west, again slowly but at 6 knots to make a barrier. Neither ship had contact.

Slowly LARTER approached datum, on course to pass it to the right.

Ted said, "I'll bet he stopped and hopes we go by."

"If he stopped, he'll be almost behind us and to the left," Dillan said.

The XO took a long look at the plot. As he did the messenger announced, "Captain's in combat."

Then there were six faces illuminated from the plotter, and the small spotlight above, staring down at the trace. Two enlisted, wearing sound powered phone headsets, were leaning on the plotter, receiving information and plotting. So were Ted and Dillan. The skipper and XO were on opposite sides. Plotting took training and the tracing paper was on rolls, advanced when it ran off the chart and restarted. Each plot was annotated and saved. Then the action could be recreated for training or investigation. Sonar was also tape recording any sounds received from the Whiskey.

The skipper said, "Think he stopped XO, just lying DIW (dead in the water – just drifting) and hoping we go by?"

"That's our theory skipper. Figure he went bow on to BRONSTINE who was pinging active and then stopped. BRONSTINE lost him and we went active and then lost him. And passive just shows background. Lots of junk, the Sea of Japan is a noisy place. He must be just sitting there silent. Maybe below a thermocline we can't see."

The skipper pushed the 21 MC button, "Bridge, come left to 270 and go to all stop as soon as we get around," he said.

Slowly the compass repeater over the plot table swung left. Then the knot meter started dropping numbers.

"Chris, we have stopped. Make that passive sonar do tricks," from the CO.

Dillan checked the stop watch. *If he had not stopped he would be out to the 1600 yard ring in another 30 seconds.*

"Could be at the 1600 ring soon, XO," he said.

Datum was bearing 263 at 1,400 yards. Close. Not quite a mile. Dillan drew some more circles at 2000, etc.

The skipper picked up the encrypted voice handset.

"BRONSTINE this is LARTER Charlie Oscar (CO=Commanding Officer), over."

A short wait and, "BRONSTINE, Charlie Oscar, over."

"We think he went DIW and went down."

"You may be right, want us to haul out to the Northwest and set up a barrier?"

"Roger that. Passive. We're going to sit right here. I think we're almost on top of him. There may be a thermocline between us and him and we'll do a BT drop. If he hears us go DIW maybe he'll move," the skipper said while waving his hand at the XO.

"BRONSTINE, roger, out."

The XO turned to Chris. "Get a BT drop to 300 feet quickly."

"Aye, sir." Chris went into sonar and had the phone talker notify the BT team.

Dillan knew that the bathythermograph (BT) was a cylinder on a wire, swung out on a small davit. It was weighted and would record the sea temperature at different depths and graph it on a chart. It would take about 15 minutes if they did it quickly, from whichever BT station, port or starboard, the weapons group was using. Then a messenger would run the chart up to combat. It would be done so quickly the data would not be great but would show a thermal inversion, if one was there.

And they waited. Dillan helped plot BRONSTINE as she slowly opened her range to 5,000 yards to the Northwest.

Chris came out of sonar, "We have lots of residual noise from the task group to the south, and even a whale off somewhere northeast. Otherwise just plankton. It's like he just vanished, which we know isn't true."

And they waited some more.

A messenger came barging into combat in a foul weather jacket, out of breath, with a metal canister in his hand. Chris took it and quickly pulled the top off and removed a strip of paper. He stretched it out on the plotter, just a ragged line on wax graph paper, with one small kink in the line.

As Chris pointed to the kink, "Small thermocline at 120 feet. He has to be hiding under it. But it doesn't look like enough to stop active. I think we ought to give him a good dose of active, XO."

"What do you think, Captain?"

"You may be right, Chris. And if he is only 1400 yards away, a full power ping is going to rattle him."

As Chris turned for sonar, "Hold off till I tell BRON-STINE."

The skipper got on the encrypted voice and filled BRON-STINE in on the plan. BRONSTINE would remain passive and hope to pick up LARTER's refracted ping off the sub, or hear the sub start to move again.

"OK, Chris, full power and ping for about 5. If you don't see him active, go passive."

"Yes, sir," and Chris went behind the curtain.

Ping... ... ping... ... pooong! Not a crisp echo, but there.

"Got him! Combat, bridge, sonar, Goblin 1, bearing 285, 1600 yards."

"Chris, stay active and rattle his cage good," from the skipper. Ted plotted the contact, very close to where they expected him to be.

The XO got on the radio and told BRONSTINE.

"Combat, bridge, sonar. Goblin 1 is on the move. Estimated course, 288, speed 5."

The skipper said, "Combat aye," then on the 21 MC, "Bridge, come to 290, speed 4 knots."

"We will sit on his tail, XO. I'll bet that first high power ping made that boat ring like a bell."

"Yes, sir, Captain."

"Good job, men," the skipper said, waving his hand around. "Good job."

Then, "Chris, you can back off on the power a little, no need to scramble all the eggs in his galley."

And on it went. When contact was lost again, the last ship with contact set up a datum, and the two ships started specific search patterns. The destroyers would go round and round, one pinging, both listening. And sooner or later, one would pick up the submarine again, and then both would alternately ping, bracketing the sub between them.

The XO said, "Well, that proves it. This has to be conventional. A nuke would have just gone deep and run off and left us here. And by now the sub skipper knows that we're not going to feed him one. We've given up multiple opportunities for a shot (either from ASROC, or the tubes: torpedo tubes mounted three in a pack, port and starboard on LARTER), so he can just continue to play with us."

Essentially they had the submarine trapped.

It was a deadly game that would only end if the OTC pulled the destroyers off, or the sub surfaced to be photographed – a major coup counted for the USA. The other option, of course, was for the submarine commander to somehow trick the destroyers into losing contact again and then sneak away.

Dillan was sure he was still trying, but without the enthusiasm of before. And the longer the game went on, the lower the submarine's battery would be and the slower he would have to go. And he would not try DIW again. The high power ping right on top wasn't something a sub wanted again.

This is still intense. And tiring. Some one once said that ASW stands for "Awfully Slow Warfare", and I believe it.

Chris said, "Sooner or later, he will have to pop a snorkel.[xlvii] If he is within 15,000 yards, it might show up on radar. Besides, a snorkeling submarine running its diesels is very noisy, and passive sonar will key on it in an instant. And water conditions are great. As long as we keep him inside 10,000 yards he won't get away. He doesn't want to go real deep to lose us, and probably couldn't anyway. And he knows damn well that we'll fire if he tries a snap shot."

Ted's comment, "I think we took the fight out of him. He just wants out and to surface and get some fresh air in his boat."

Five hours and well into the mid watch, and the game continued. Everyone was getting a bit punchy. The sonar operators had to be changed often to keep their ears sensitive. Plotters were rotated.

I'm getting punchy right along with the rest of the guys. More coffee, just what I need is more of that potent CIC coffee. I'll be flying around combat like a just released balloon. But the body longs for the sugar. Wish I had a Snickers.

147

On the bridge, they also remained very busy circling slowly with the other ship in the dark, or doing submarine search patterns. The skipper would stay on the bridge as long as they had an active contact, and come into combat to discuss strategy with BRONSTINE's CO if contact was lost.

Slow speed was essential to keep from making so much noise that it hurt the sonar operator's ability to pick out the contact. When the sub got behind or on the quarters of the ships, the ship's own propeller noise blanked out the sub's contact. It was called "getting the contact into the baffles".

One never wanted to do that, because it was a good way to lose the sub again. Anti submarine warfare in 1968 was not easy, even playing hold down with a conventional submarine.

By 0300, the task group was over 100 miles away. Well out of UHF radio range. Over the 7th fleet long range HF net, "Quicksilver, Rocketman, Beerbarrel, break off, I repeat break off, return to station, over."

"Rocketman, roger out." It took a moment for the XO to find the appropriate handset. Then, "Quicksilver, roger out."

Now LARTER had to take a guess as to where the main body was and head that way in offset column, double normal spacing, LARTER as guide, back at speed. The bridge handled the signals on PriTac. But after 9 or more hours of trying to slip away and running fast sometimes, the sub's batteries were very low and the sub's skipper had to sneak off, surface or pop a snorkel and recharge batteries. And with all the aircraft that were definitely going to be looking for him at sun up, he did not have long to do it and get back under the waves before first light. With the sea state, a snorkel was not very practical. So he was going to have to show himself.

Once he had finished some charging, he would dive again. The S2 ASW aircraft from the carrier would be making runs on him with their magnetic airborne detection gear and sonobuoys. So he would have to go deep and hope to slip away. And if he collected a Sturgeon class shadow, he would have to get well out of its operating area prior to trying anything else.

Essentially, he had tried to penetrate the task group's destroyer screen and had failed. Now he was in for relentless persecution.

Big whoop, but one point for the USA!

27

On LARTER everyone was relieved to be secured from general quarters. The men in the gun mounts and repair parties had long since started naps. Sailors who were not required to be alert could go to sleep anywhere and in any position, even standing up. Some even with their eyes open.

Sitting on the deck, quietly at their station during an evolution when nothing was happening, almost guaranteed a nap for all but the phone talker and group leader. But the bridge, CIC and sonar people had been at it full court press and they were exhausted.

The captain came into combat from the bridge,

"Gentlemen, good job. I am going to establish holiday routine tomorrow – or, that is, today so people can get some sleep. This turkey may try another penetration tomorrow night. We need to be ready. Good job again, men."

"Hey, XO, we almost had one of the little bastards huh? It either took balls or stupidity for a Whiskey to think he could sneak by. And it was good to have the team get some real contact time. Not much of that over here chasing carriers."

"Yes, sir, Captain, a good drill. Sure would have liked to have sent him a present. I'm going to put off field day for tomorrow also, shift it to Saturday."

Then the skipper went into sonar and said good job to the sonar operator who found the initial contact. Dillan could hear him giving Chris a kudo also through the curtain. Chris sure is good at ASW, Dillan thought.

Dillan had been in combat since 1600 the preceding day, with 25 minutes out for supper, and now it was 0300. Eleven hours. He had to back at 0345.

This will be a zero sleep night.

The Navy did issue strong stimulant pills to the officers for themselves and their men in cases of severe exhaustion concurrent with extreme risk: "Bennies," or legal speed.

Maybe I should, but after the high came a downer like one never wanted to experience. No, a trip to the mess decks for a cup of thick soup and just lots of coffee so that I will be jumpy, but awake.

He had a quiet 04-08 as LARTER and BRONSTINE ran at 25 knots back towards the task group, rendezvousing about 5AM, and then taking bent line screen stations again. Keeping awake was a bitch, lots of coffee and cigarettes.

At first light, the carrier launched S2's and Dillan could tell from the air scope and the radios that they scoured the sea for the PRK sub. By 0700, the sub had surfaced and was headed Northwest on diesel. Multiple photos of the black shape moving out at 17 knots, no hull numbers or other distinguishing marks visible were reported.

Dillan figured that the OTC would try to keep an S2 with the sub as long as he could. Always better to know where they were. But as soon as the PRK sub's batteries were fully charged, he would go deep again and try to slip away. And probably be successful.

Dillan also figured that there was no way of being 100% sure it was PRK and not Soviet. The sub sure wasn't advertising. It was just a black Whiskey like the other 250 in the world. Dillan assumed the OTC would contact the Sturgeon subs.[xlviii]

Dillan got relieved at 0730. Then he hit the rack. Slept like a log until 1400. He went back to the mess decks for more soup. He was living on it, that and crackers and of course copious quantities of coffee and cigarettes.

Other cans had sonar contacts and prosecuted them on an average of every other night. The PRK subs were definitely persistent. LARTER got lucky and did not get involved, playing screening destroyer instead. The Secret intel summaries were calling the subs PRK Whiskeys. So there must have been additional source data. But still the destroyers were precluded from attacking them.

This is being micromanaged in Washington again. Sinking a PRK sub would be a good retribution for PUEBLO and the PRK won't even know – just a sub that fails to return messages or return to port. It would be a hell of a morale boost. But someone in DC will run off at the mouth to the press, and then the PUEBLO crew in captivity will have to pay. Get the crap beat out of them if lucky. Get dead if not. Maybe better just doing hold down. Damn.

Naturally, all this running around the ocean chasing subs and launching aircraft burned fuel like crazy, and even the carrier had to come alongside oilers to take on fuel and JP5. Usually the carrier would be on one side, and a destroyer on the other, steaming along at 12 knots, parallel courses, less than 200 feet apart in less than a perfect sea state. An unrep in those cold conditions was brutal on the deck hands that had to haul the heavy hoses over on the wires which were passed between the ships and connected them.

Steering during unrep was difficult. Helm orders were measured in half degrees and the most experienced helmsman aboard had the watch. Speed control was essential. Too far ahead and the oiler's bow wave tended to push the destroyer's bow away. Too far back and the oiler's prop suction tended to pull the destroyer's stern in.

All the while they were connected by two tight thick wires with fat black hoses hanging from them on saddles pumping fuel like mad. FRAM destroyers had two stations, one forward, just behind the bridge on the main deck, and one aft by the DASH deck.

FRAM I destroyers carried 204,000 gallons of fuel oil – basically a poor kerosene, officially called Navy Distillate. The old Navy standard, or bunker "C" fuel oil, previously used by the US Navy, had changed for a more refined fuel to eliminate black smoke and improve boiler maintenance. Restricted by regulation to dropping to no less than 60% reserve meant refueling for destroyers every 3 to 4 days.

For this reason, normal task group steaming speeds were 12 to 15 knots, increased to whatever was required for flight operations. The 60% reserve requirement was left over from World War II. A few cans had run dry during a big Pacific storm. Then, just drifting, they had ended up taking the seas on the beam, and had been capsized and sunk. Over 700 men were lost. So the strategy was to keep all with at least 5 days standard fuel reserve.

The unrep OOD and sometimes the JOOD had to be on the unprotected cold bridge wing closest to the oiler, watching the distance line. A small marked line from ship to ship that at least gave the conning officer some indication of position.

The US Navy was one of few navies in the world to do underway replenishment. Even the Soviets did it by stopping and floating a hose over on a barrel. But it was effective, fast, and really added to the capability of sustained operations at sea.

Dillan thought his ears were going to freeze the first time. After that he carried a black enlisted watch cap he borrowed from a signalman that he could pull down over them in his foul weather jacket pocket. That, and some warm rough wool lined leather gloves. Then, only his feet and face froze.

Another thing happened. An ALNAV (All Navy) message was received indicating that the time in grade requirements for advancement from Ensign to Lieutenant Junior Grade were reduced from 18 months to 12 months. Dillan had just over 15 months in as Ensign.

Super! Now 1 and ½ stripes, and change the little gold bar for a little silver one. More in the paycheck. There is going to be one hell of a wetting down party when and if LARTER gets into port again.

Dillan and his radiomen put in a lot of hours dealing with the changes required by the PUEBLO capture. For them it was a class five pain in the ass, squared. Lots of off line encrypted messages. Dillan, Tony and the chief spent hours in crypto breaking messages.[xlix]

After about a week in the Sea of Japan, LARTER was notified that she was now part of Operation Formation Star. There were 34 US ships. And it got a lot more interesting.

There was a Soviet task group steaming around over the horizon to the north, a standoff. Dillan had picked up from the intel summaries that shortly after PUEBLO had been captured, the USS YORKTOWN, the first US carrier on scene, had played tag with a Soviet Kashin class can and had a few Soviet over flights.[l]

If it comes to fist-a-cuffs it will not be pretty for either side. And if the crappy weather does not allow us to launch big air strikes, or keep tons of CAP aloft, we might not do so well. The only saving grace is the 2 Sturgeon class submarines somewhere out there between the task force and the Soviets. Still scary, enough information to worry the admirals, let alone a lowly boot JG. Good training for Pete's electronic warfare troops though: lots of Soviet emissions to identify and take bearings on.

Around the task groups went, churning up the cold water. CTF 71 (the TF commander) got ordered to disengage, move south towards Japan, and put some water between him and the

Soviet task group. This was probably to keep some testosterone poisoned individual from starting World War III.

The news said that the UN negotiators had met with the PRK at the Panmunjom table. The PRK indicated that they would only let the crew of PUEBLO go if the US admitted violating their territorial waters and apologize. And the PUEBLO itself would not be returned until later. When the US refused, the PRK negotiators walked out.

At dinner, the skipper, usually not a political person, went into one of his rare lectures,

"Those crazy PRK bastards have captured a US Navy ship. The last time that happened was the Civil War. And all we do is talk and steam around in circles. Those McNamara idiot kids just wring their hands and strut around like peacocks. They have no sense of history or honor. No wonder the Red Chinese call us paper tigers."

Dillan knew that most officers on LARTER thought the whole thing was a travesty. He sure did. On February 7, LARTER was detached from the RANGER task group and assigned to the ENTERPRISE task group, which was then ordered south, again at best speed, leaving RANGER and YORKTOWN in the Sea of Japan. Dillan figured that there would be no attack on North Korea.

Off LARTER went, screening another carrier at speed. LARTER was detached and ordered to steam independently at best speed to take up gunfire support duties off the I Corps region of South Vietnam. One other FRAM destroyer was headed to the Vietnam coast also, to join the four already in place.

Although there were indications in the message traffic, Dillan had not paid a lot of attention to what was being called the Tet Offensive, which started with major coordinated attacks by North Vietnamese Army (NVA) regulars and the Viet Cong (VC) the last two days of January 1968. It turned out to be a big deal, and the NVA had overrun lots of places. LARTER was headed to help the Marines and ARVN (Army of the Republic of Vietnam). Tet was a traditional Vietnamese New Year's holiday, this year officially 1/31/1968, and historically the NVA and VC had done a stand down during it, but not this time.

28

Finding an oiler a bit south of Yankee Station, LARTER, now below 60%, topped off and headed for the assigned station point. She hadn't done any Naval Gunfire Support (NGFS) since the short Reftra certification at San Clemente Island, in August 67. So Red and Dillan put their CIC watch through drills to sharpen up.

The weapons department scrambled to make sure both guns in both mounts were ready. Spotting was to be done by incountry Naval Gunfire Liaison Officers (NGLO) embedded with the Marines and small aircraft. LARTER's 5 inch guns could shoot at targets up to 18,900 yards from the ship, just under 10 nautical miles. So if LARTER got in close to shore, a fairly large portion of the coast could be targeted.

Meanwhile, USS KITTY HAWK (CVA 63), and now USS TICONDEROGA (CV 14), having just arrived on Yankee Station, were doing major flight operations. ENTERPRISE would be back by mid February: quite an armada there also. The NGFS area was identified, and air strikes were restricted to areas inland of the NGFS area.

There was a standard section on NGFS in the COMSEV-ENTHFLT operations order. The captain and appropriate other officers, including bridge and CIC watch officers, each had to review it and initial the cover sheet.

Arriving off the South Vietnam shore early on February 10th, LARTER reported to First Marine Division in DaNang by radio. An hour later, she was ordered 30 miles south, and after a mad 25 knot dash, reported on station where she dropped super-heat and cruised parallel to the coast 3,000 yards off in 60 feet of water at 5 knots.

This was close and from the bridge one could see trees and vehicles. They could even see human faces quite clearly with the binoculars.

Things were quiet until about 1000 when the NGFS radio net speaker in combat came on.

"Quicksilver, this is Blackbeard, report when ready for a mission, over"

Blackbeard was one of the NGLO people. The Evaluator grabbed the handset and answered,

"Blackbeard, Quicksilver, wilco, out"

The evaluator made a quick call to the captain on the bridge and soon, "Bong bong bong … general quarters, general quarters. All hands man your battle stations."

Dillan scrambled from radio to combat. Fred departed for the bridge, and the XO and weapons officer came into combat. Chris was there primarily to manage the weapons control equipment and actually fire the guns from a remote hand held trigger at the end of a thick coiled wire.

When manned and ready, the captain told combat to advise Blackbeard that they were ready to answer all missions. The Confidential Vietnamese topographical map, with sector grid lines, was on the dead reckoning tracer plot table. The map was lighted from below.

Here, just like for ASW on the NC-2 plotter, a brighter under lighted "bug" would show the ship's position as it moved. Properly set up and calibrated one could see the ship move on the water portion of the map in real time.

Sectors were 10 kilometer square chunks of Vietnam and the surrounding sea out 20 kilometers. Red was north from the southwest sector corner, green east. One would establish a gun target line (bearing from the ship to the target) and it was cross checked and loaded into the gunfire control computer – a large older 1950's vintage mechanical computer which worked quite well.

It was an amazing device with whirring motors, disks, shafts, and micro switches. Windage from the bridge wind indicator, and the target's elevation taken from the topographical map were preset by the weapons plot group.

The weapons officer would also convert meters to yards when necessary, since the computer only thought in yards. Ten kilometers was only 9,144 yards, so this conversion, from tables, was essential. The area of probable shell impact was roughly an ellipse, centered on the gun target line long ways and on the spot crossways.

"Quicksilver, Blackbeard, mike posit sector Yankee Delta Five Four, Red 1 point 3 break Green 0 point 2 over."

The spotter's position was acknowledged and quickly plotted on the map. Dillan handled the radio.

"Quicksilver, Blackbeard, target 01 suspected NVA trucks, sector Yankee Delta Five Four, Red 7 point 3, break, Green 3 point 2, break, one round, HE fuse quick (High Explosive, fuse set to go off on impact), nearest friendlys mike posit, over."

"Quicksilver, target 01, possible trucks, Yankee Delta Five Four, Red 7 point 3, break, Green 3 point 2, break, one round HE fuse quick, nearest friendlys Blackbeard, out," Dillan sent.

Transmissions were repeated to insure accuracy. After the initial call up, one only identified themselves at the start of a transmission. With possible friendlys in the area, and the spotter and his Marine guards, this check helped prevent blue on blue incidents. Ted plotted the target location.

The spotter was roughly 7 klicks (kilometers) away from the target – about 5 miles southwest. Moderately close. This area had been badly over run by NVA.

The XO requested "guns free" from the captain on the bridge and got it.

When set, and after a couple minutes of updates to insure the computer was tracking, the XO felt comfortable and nodded to Dillan.

Dillan transmitted, "Quicksilver gun target line 242, one round HE fuse quick, out."

Meanwhile mount 51 was ordered to load one round. The computer trained the mount and set the gun elevation. When advised that the gun was ready, and after checking the feedback on the mount bearing and elevation (no need to screw up and drop a round on the spotter), Chris pulled the hand held trigger.

Boom. Out a round went from gun number 1, mount 51. The boom was muffled and low frequency in combat – almost more of a vibration than a sound, but distinctive.

Dillan transmitted, "Quicksilver, shot ... out." The ... was a delay to allow the round to cover the trajectory to the target so that the spotter could stay hidden and then pop up just prior to impact to see the results. At 15,000 yards this was 43 seconds. Dillan used a stop watch to time the flight based on what the computer indicated, and transmitted the "out" 5 seconds prior to expected impact.

Mount 51 reported one round expended, bore clear, no causalities.

"Blackbeard, left 200, drop 300, one round HE fuse quick, over."

"Quicksilver left 200, drop 300, one round HE fuse quick, out."

This was the spotter, adjusting the fall of shot but from his position. Ted used the 'Comanche Board,' a plastic plot ring with two sets of grid overlay rings on it, one transparent and moveable, to convert to range and bearing from the ship. This was loaded into the computer. Mt 51 loaded and Chris shot another round.

"Quicksilver, gun target line 245, break, (boom) shot ..., out."

"Blackbeard right 100, drop 50, fire for effect, 20 rounds HE fuse quick, over."

"Quicksilver, right 100, drop 50, fire for effect, 20 rounds HE fuse quick, out."

The final corrections made, both mounts were ordered to load and fire twenty rounds, ten each. The computer took into account the relative position of the mounts. This was rapid continuous fire, and the guns went bang as soon as the breech slammed shut.

Boom, boom, ... "Quicksilver, gun target line 249, shot ..., out," Dillan sent for the first round.

By the time he had finished, there were a lot of booms. Twenty rounds went out in rapid succession, 4 almost immediately, and the rest as reloads occurred, all 20 out in less than 30 seconds. The last round fired before the first arrived on target, and before Dillan sent the delayed, "out."

Having seen mount 51 fire from the bridge a few times during Reftra, Dillan knew the guns were belching a torch of orange fire and a puff of gray smoke each time. Out there the sound was like a shot gun going off close. It was a deeper boom than a rifle's crack. LARTER shook at each shot. Even in combat one could feel it. Some dust drifted down from the overhead.

These were essentially beam shots, at almost a 45 degree elevation. So LARTER was pushed slightly sideways and rolled a little, but too little to really notice. The ventilation system picked up some of the cordite smell and the normal odor of combat was altered by the smell of burnt powder. Mount 51 reported 10 rounds expended, bores clear, no causalities. Ditto for 52.

"Quicksilver, 20 rounds expended, bores clear, out."

"Blackbeard, 19 rounds on target, one dud, one vehicle destroyed, one damaged, no secondary, standby for target 02, over."

"Quicksilver, standing by, out."

A dud, damn.

Chris remarked that, "Many of the lots of projectiles we received at load out at Seal Beach were quite old, some World War II vintage."

So a dud is not unanticipated. According to the spotter, we have just destroyed an NVA truck and damaged another. No secondary explosions: odd for gasoline powered trucks, possibly with ammunition in them. There are probably NVA causalities, but that damage assessment would have to wait for some ground or air recon. My first ever shots fired in anger!

Quiet for awhile. LARTER made a slow turn to seaward and then resumed cruising off the coast. The captain came into combat and was announced.

"Good shooting boys, our first opportunity to shoot at the enemy. I bet we're kept busy. The Marines have been up to their asses in NVA and VC the last ten days. Too bad we were up north. We might have made a difference earlier. Keep the crew on their toes, XO."

"Yes, sir, Captain, on their toes."

Yes, sir, right on our toes. I sure would like to have been in a helo watching our rounds hit. NGFS is a lot like shooting at a target in a shooting gallery while wearing a blindfold.

After the skipper left, Chris added, "If the NVA and VC are strong enough to launch coordinated attacks, they are a lot stronger than we have been led to believe with the intel summaries. Hell, I thought we were winning this stupid war. Sure doesn't look like it from here."

From the XO, "Sure doesn't, always the way though. Never enough troops or fire power to really win, only enough to be a token. We got whipped real good at the start of the Korean War when the Chicoms came over the border for the same reason. Pushed our butts back to Pusan."

"Then it took years to fight it back to a stalemate. We never seem to have the balls to go for the knock out punch like we did in the big war. Now I bet there is another troop build up, but not enough to win. Politicians should just decide the goals and let the military decide on the winning strategy like we did against the Japs. Those dips want to have both guns and butter to get re-elected."

Ted's comment, "We should either win this thing, or leave the damn rice paddies to the gooks. All those US body bags have to count for something."

Dillan knew morale was suffering over the entire ship. First the Formation Star fiasco, now coordinated attacks in Vietnam. And all the time the news and letters from home were talking about more and more war protesting back in the real world.

Does anyone back there really want to win? If they don't want to win, then what the hell are we doing over here?

No more calls from Blackbeard. LARTER steamed slowly in her assigned area.

29

LARTER had gotten lucky on her first mission. Firing 20 rounds, even in 30 seconds, and having them land on target was a miracle. The spotter was being generous. Maybe the flying debris took out the truck. Although LARTER was quite accurate against surface targets or air targets using the fire control radar on the director, NGFS was firing at a spot on a map from a moving platform. Not so accurate.

Even with a good set up and excellent ammunition, twenty rounds shot 15,000 yards would spread out over an area bigger than a football field.

Then it started again. This went on for 5 more hours, sometimes taking spots from Blackbeard, sometimes from War Eagle about 10 miles up the coast. LARTER would crank up to push all there was without super heat, and then slow and start the next evolution.

By then it was almost dark. The crew had been at general quarters since 1000 and only box lunch sandwiches had been distributed to stations during one repositioning run.

LARTER had expended 41 rounds of HE and 54 rounds of VT frag. VT frag was an anti aircraft round with a small internal radar transmitter in its nose, developed during World War II. It would detonate a fragmentation shell upon sensing the proximity to an aircraft – basically smart flack.

However, shot at land, it would detonate 15 to 20 feet above ground and shower a fairly large area below it with hot shrapnel. It was great as an anti-personnel round and sometimes called the 'weed cutter.'

Ninety five rounds total. Not a lot. In fact very little as NGFS evolutions went. It was important to insure, once firing was completed, that the bores were clear. LARTER got lucky and all rounds fired that day. When the gun barrels were hot there was always a chance of a misfire. A projectile trapped in a hot barrel would cook off. Not good. So a misfire was a big deal and the primer could be a total dud or just a hang fire, where it would take a few seconds to ignite the powder. So one waited with held breath.

After 30 seconds, a water hose would be stuck in the business end of the barrel while the gun crew tried to retract the powder / primer casing, pitch it over the side, load a 'short charge', depress the gun, and then pop the projectile over the side a few hundred yards.

A hot projectile, especially VT frag, had a tendency to detonate a little way clear of the barrel which could spray the ship with shrapnel. Naval gunfire was not for the uninitiated.

"Now secure from general quarters, set the regular condition III watch", came over the 1MC.

Now almost 1800 and Dillan had the 16-20 CIC watch officer watch. As the joke said, turn your hat around and relieve yourself. A few minutes later the captain came into combat and discussed the days shooting with the XO, weapons officer, and Dillan. He seemed pleased.

"Good shooting again, boys. Ops will be drafting a message report, give him your input, Weaps," and he was gone.

Fred came into combat and talked to Chris. Then to Dillan,

"Well, Mr. Dillan, hope you have been pitching in and helping in here. Have to get you back out on the bridge again soon to get your qualifications completed. Don't want you to fall too far behind."

Chris said, "Dillan has been doing well in here, Fred. He handled some of the NGFS plot thing and did all the net stuff. XO is pleased."

"Good." Then Fred was gone.

Always on my case, always. Wonder what I have to do to get an "ataboy" from him. Probably walk on water and then turn it into wine. Leap tall buildings in a single bound. Dip shit.

About 20 minutes later the NGFS net squawked.

"Quicksilver, War Eagle, can you do H&I (Harassing and Interdiction fire), over."

Dillan answered, "Quicksilver, H&I, roger, over."

"War Eagle, H&I sector Alpha Whiskey Red 3 to Red 4, Green 3 to Green 4, flood 20 rounds VT frag, friendlys 10 klicks west, to sunrise, over."

Dillan answered, "Quicksilver H&I sector Alpha Whisky Red 3 to Red 4, Green 3 to Green 4, flood 20 rounds VT frag, to sunrise, friendlys 10 klicks west, out." *Damn, screwed up the sequence.*

Harassing and interdiction fire was to essentially deny the enemy the use of a piece of ground, this time overnight. A random round of VT frag was quite effective at doing this. And a stupid enemy may well be at the wrong place at the wrong time. The NVA and VC were not stupid. And they understood H&I. A round or two and they vacated. They didn't go in much for testing their luck. Beat feet now and live to fight another day.

Red called the captain in the wardroom.

The captain said, "OK, I'm sending Weaps up."

Chris came back into combat to insure the watch set up the plot location; gun target lines, and etc. correctly.

Then handing the trigger to Dillan he said, "OK, Dillan, put a round of VT into the 4 square kilometer area roughly each 40 minutes on a random basis. Plot your placement to cover the square at random locations over the next 10 or so hours. Give Mount 51 a few moments notice, then order a load. Spread the wear between barrels. Call me if you have problems or questions. Pass these gun orders on to the remainder of the watches. I'll go talk to the OOD, so he knows what we're doing. Red, the skipper wants to steam up and down the coast here about 3 miles out at 5 knots all night."

"Understood, sir", Dillan said.

The weapons officer would be in CIC as evaluator for the 00-04 anyway. But the 20-24 needed to be brought up to speed.

Red and Dillan and the enlisted watch standers in CIC got hopping on placing a piece of tracing paper over the map, laying out the square (2x2 kilometers) to be targeted, and plotted 20 points within the square to cover it all but to remain 200 yards inside. One did not want a shot to wander too far out of the square.

Once everything was set, and cross checked, Dillan and Red grabbed extra old box lunches and ate stale sandwiches for dinner. They could be relieved for dinner if they wanted, but it wouldn't come till late anyway. And since no cooking went on during GQ, it might well be after 2000 before the crew's mess secured, and they could grab a bite if needed down there.

As he chomped away on an almost stale white bread, ham and cheese, Dillan said, "Wonderful cuisine Red, my compliments to the chef. But where's the wine?"

"The Navy lost their liquor license in 1862. And even before that it was just grog, not wine, maybe Port for the officers, awful stuff. And the chef isn't up to 5 star standards either. But it's a hell of a lot better than starving."

"I guess you're right. Everything is relative. We could be plopped in a rice paddy, mud up to our necks, eating C-rats. Go Navy. It's not just a job, it's an adventure. Anyway, this is going to be interesting doing the H&I drill ourselves."

At 1906, Dillan put his first round on target. Thirty five minutes later, boom again. At 1945, his relief arrived, and it took almost a half hour to fill him in and get relieved. Go over everything twice. At 2013 Dillan left CIC and headed for radio, tired, but he still had to meet with the chief and check the boards before he could think about the rack.

And he might not get to stay in the rack his allotted time. Some cans had taken some inaccurate NVA mortar fire this close to the coast. Dillan figured that the skipper would set GQ if there was any incoming to deal with.

No letter tonight. Sorry Patty. My ass is dragging.

The after action message from DaNang about the days NGFS spotted targets was on the boards. LARTER was credited with 2 trucks, a BTR 152, and 13 NVA KIA (Killed in Action). Some of the other destroyers on the gun line had had a better day. One even got a big secondary explosion when an ammo dump went up. Most had more KIA.

KIA numbers were a bit on the exaggerated side to say the least. But the top brass loved big enemy KIA numbers, and one gave them what they wanted – even if inflated.[li]

When this war is over, someone at the funny farm will add up all the enemy KIA reports and find out that the entire population of Southeast Asia was KIA three times.

While in radio, Thomas, 2nd class electronics technician (communications), or ET(C)2, and his striker (non rated helper), were replacing a couple of UHF radios. Dillan knew Thomas well from his days as the EMO in early 67. LARTER usually copied or had a listening watch on 8 to 10 UHF (ultra high frequency – short range line of sight) voice circuits at any one time, and these "new" modularized non crystal units, installed during the recent shipyard overhaul, were always drifting off frequency.

The heat in radio didn't help much. They were manufactured by Collins Radio, and Dillan was sure they worked great in an airconditioned rack ashore. But here they were always drifting. Dillan and Pete Donavan had picked up an additional half dozen spares when first in Subic. Seventh fleet kept a supply that were exchanged between ships going home and new ones coming into the area.

And the ET gang worked 3 shifts 24/7 in their shop retuning them to keep 10 up and running out of the 20 total on hand. LARTER also had picked up a couple of Marine VHF (Very High Frequency – also short range) pack radios for talking to spotters. "Prick tens" they were called, short for AN/PRC-10. Most NGLO officers used these, but some aircraft used UHF. On LARTER, a long whip antenna was temporarily mounted outside of combat on the signal bridge rail, and battery packs were kept charged for the prick ten.

"Hi, Mr. Dillan. How is it going up there on the bridge? Congrats on making JG," waving his hand in a half salute.

Waving back, "Hey, Thomas, thanks, I'm in combat now, but things are fine. You guys keeping busy?"

"Sure are. These friggen 9s (AN/URC-9 the UHF transceivers) are still giving us fits. Wallace here," referring to the striker, "is coming along good though, maybe make 3rd next cycle."

"Good for you, Wallace, go get it. You can if you study," Dillan said.

The kid beamed. Seldom was he even addressed by an officer, especially one on one. A little encouragement went a long way.

This kid will do it. Thomas is a super people developer.

The tests for advancement were quite difficult, and men had to study. They not only concentrated on equipment aboard one's own ship, but all non airborne communications equipment the Navy had. So hitting the books was essential.

Dillan picked up a message board and started flipping sheets. He was looking for info on lots of HE ammo recalled. If he found any he would give them to Chris Harcourt and Billy Hoffman. Not his job but he didn't want any more duds.

Thomas was talking to the 2nd class radioman. "That gunfire today did a number on ET berthing. Two light fixtures fell and one whole stack of racks broke off the overhead and ended up on deck, dirt from the overhead all over everything. What a mess. The DCs are trying to weld them all back now."

She is an old girl. Vibration damage is SOP for the first sustained firing. Welds fatigued, and the shock caused a lot of minor damage. ET berthing is just aft of mount 51 on the main deck. They got it good there.

Closing the aluminum flip up message board, Dillan said, "I bet the ET compartment isn't the only one where welding will be going on tonight. After crew's berthing, just aft and below mount 52, is known for shock damage when 52 fires."

"You're right, sir. Some light fixtures fell, and a water line to the aft head cracked, heard it was a big mess back there, also."

30

All night long there was a bang every now and then, all from mount 51. Not loud in after officer's country but the ET's must have had a noisy night. Otherwise, it was a quiet night – no incoming. Dillan was back in CIC at 0345 the next morning and got to finish out the last 3 H&I rounds.

By 0730, LARTER was off to the races again. About 20 miles south, got a spotter call, this time from a small single engine prop aircraft, essentially a one person Marine Piper Cub, aluminum tube and fabric.

Now those are some brave Marines. Fly a tiny paper airplane over enemy positions slow and low to spot. Those people take a lot of ground fire. They have some armored plate installed inside on the floor, but it's still very dangerous. Most come back with lots of holes in the wings and fuselage, if they come back. I sure wouldn't want to do it. I don't have a death wish.

Overnight, some NVA, maybe a company, had tried to surround a Marine platoon and had mauled them a bit with mortars. Enter LARTER. Lots of rounds on spotted targets; and then establish a 200 meter wide line of fire, and then march it in a requested direction, like a ladder, 100 meters each time, for quite a time period.

Over 200 rounds just at that target and all VT frag. Essentially, the spotter was getting LARTER to plaster a NVA group as it tried to move. There wouldn't be much standing over 2 feet tall along that ranging ladder's swath.

Later, there was more ground spotter action, and a request to shoot up a fishing village that, reportedly, the NVA were using to smuggle supplies in right at the coast. Dillan sure couldn't see it from combat. But the bridge had visuals.

The captain elected to do direct fire from the gun director. The gun director was a box on the 03 level that could be trained like a gun mount. It had the fire control radar dish on the front plus a fat tube sticking out of each side that was the optical sight. The director watch officer sat on a metal "tractor' seat inside, looking through the optical range finder sight, and could send signals to the gunfire control computer or monitor the radar as it did so.

LTJG Len Ottaway was in the director for GQ and used the optical sight. The plan was to use HE to tear up the huts and switch to VT frag, if there were any troop movements. LARTER was 6,000 yards off shore, so it was almost point blank range. Boom, boom, boom and it went on for 30 rounds HE.

Later, LTJG Joe Reiderman, who was the GQ JOOD now, told Dillan that he could see the detonations, that there was lots of black smoke, and shredded "hooch" parts flying all over. Joe had watched the fall of shot from the bridge wing with binoculars, along with the CO, XO, and Fred. Some one thought they saw movement, so the captain had Len work the village over with 10 rounds of VT frag also.

"Did you see any enemy? Dillan asked while talking with Joe.

"I think the village was abandoned, I sure didn't see anything like a human. Saw a stray dog though – wonder how he managed to stay out of the pot?"

"Did a number on the village, huh?"

"Totally obliterated the village, nothing left but sticks, straw and craters in the sand, trashed the place good. Thought the skipper might use some willy peter (white phosphorous) to start some fires, but I guess he thought the VT was enough."

Maybe a little overkill - poor dog.

Secured from General quarters at 1720: a big day, 464 rounds expended, almost all VT frag.

Relieve myself again. God my butt's dragging. Sure could use a decent night in the rack, and a chance to write a letter. Patty must be wondering where we are since my last letter was just after the Formation Star stuff. The papers will be carrying all the Tet shit, though. Bet she figures we're involved somehow. When do we get to dock this can? Seems like we have been underway forever, should change the name LARTER to Flying Dutchman.

The entire crew was bone tired. But LARTER had a problem. Over the past two days, 669 rounds had been expended, again mostly VT frag. Although not out of ammo, another 300+ round day would start scraping the bottom of the magazine's VT frag supply soon.

LARTER carried some 1600 rounds, but that was divided up into special rounds (star shells, white phosphorous, etc.), VT frag, HE, AA Common (old anti-aircraft stuff but usable for troop concentrations if the VT was gone) and some light armor piercing. Rearming was indicated. Knowing this, the Navy had an AE (ammunition ship) steaming up and down the coast about 30 miles out.

So off LARTER went at 20 knots towards its last reported position. This was euphemistically called an 'unrep of opportunity', and LARTER would do a lot of them, for ammo, fuel, and even, occasionally, for stores. When near to reported position, CIC started looking for surface contacts that "squawked" the USS MAUNA LOA (AE-8)'s Identification Friend or Foe (IFF) code.

This IFF signal would show up on a radar scope as a few arches or lines of dots and dashes at the unit's location, a separate dot-dash code for each unit, when the scope was set to read IFF. In actual practice, the dots and dashes on the radar screen were very hard to read and one better have a well tuned radar repeater, and a real good idea of the approximate location, especially in a target rich environment, to pick out who you were looking for.

All ships and aircraft in the North Atlantic Treaty Organization (NATO) had IFF transponders and, when queried by the proper interrogation signal, would automatically respond with the unit's 3 digit code if the transponder was turned on.

Tonight there were a bunch of IFF returns all in the expected area. Individual ones were unreadable. The scope looked like someone had sprinkled salt on it there. Dillan assumed MAUNA LOA was a busy ship tonight. Range 17 miles, bearing 056. This was the far far edge of the radar's range. When Fred came into combat, he asked Dillan where MAUNA LOA was, and Dillan told him.

"I'm not totally sure, but we have a bunch of faint IFF contacts about 060. They all merge into a cluster of confetti so I can't be sure. But that's roughly where she is supposed to be, and there will probably be other cans there loading up now." Dillan said.

"Yeah, that's probably her," Fred said looking over the scope operator's shoulder at the screen. "That's the area she said she would be in." He waited for a couple more sweeps, nodded, and went into air plot.

No derogatory comments for Dillan?

Fred then looked up MAUNA LOA's call sign on the status board, checked the board for the UHF voice radio unrep net channel number, and dialed the channel button using the 'telephone' dialer that would change a radio's frequency.

When the remote's number clicked to the dialed channel, he transmitted, "Firebox, Firebox this is Quicksilver, Quicksilver, over."

Shortly, "Quicksilver this is Firebox, over", came out of the speaker.

"Firebox this is Quicksilver, request rearm 500 each 5 inch 38 VT frag, 150 each 5 inch 38 HE, full rounds, over."

A short delay then, "Quicksilver, Firebox, can do, you are third in line, unrep corpen 200 speed 12, take starboard waiting station and advise. Send confirming request circuit 27, over."

"Quicksilver, roger, out."

"Dillan, get radio to send a teletype supply requisition on 27. I think that is unrep TTY (teletype). Get Tony to give you a rec (requisition) number."

"Yeah, that's the UHF unrep TT net, and I'll send it right away. Wouldn't want to try for any freebees." Then Dillan called Tony, then radio.

Each ship was 'charged' for supplies. And a requisition was required to keep track. Later the ship's 'Optar' or operating target budget, would be adjusted, based on operational assignments. Even the US Navy, in a war, had thousands of accountants counting beans. Tony was the banker and bean counter for LARTER.

Fred went out to the bridge, undoubtedly to talk to the skipper. A few moments later, Fred came up on the 21MC intercom and said,

"Combat, bridge, we're coming to 060, give us a solution for waiting station 3 at 20."

"Combat, aye," Dillan replied.

Dillan did the maneuvering board solution for intercept 1500 yards astern and about 200 yards to the right of MAUNA LOA, and advised the bridge. Dillan calculated about 50 minutes to station allowing for time to slow to 12 knots. A bit later he recommended slowing to 15kts to the bridge. They ignored him.

Everything LARTER did was the go like hell then slow down to keep from overshooting station method. MAUNA LOA was headed almost right at LARTER at 12 knots. LARTER was going 20 almost right at her. That meant 32 knots of relative speed or closing 3200 yards every three minutes. Slowing to 15 would cost 5 minutes. And they had station 3 wired anyway. But full court press was the 'destroyer' way.

Hurry up and wait. The Navy's real motto.

One had to plan for the distance the ship went when speed changes were ordered – speed changes were not instantaneous and large turns tended to slough off speed. Then there was the ship's advance and transfer: the distance it took to make a turn into station, i.e. forward and sideways travel until one was steady on the new course, like a turning radius that was different for each speed and rudder angle.

This would be a 180 degree starboard turn into station. And LARTER had to keep clear since she would be crossing in front of MAUNA LOA, a ship "engaged in a mission that precluded her from maneuvering" according to the rules of the road.

I sure don't want to come close. The AE's skipper will get bent if we even make him think we're close. And he is probably a 4 striper. Careful, careful.

Dillan started to work on a 2000 yard clearance in front, then a slow turn to pass 1000 yards down the starboard side of the can replenishing, then a swing into waiting station. These factors were not easy to predict accurately and took experience and 'Kentucky windage', sometimes called intuition, sometimes luck.

Once he had a solution, he called the bridge and recommended slowing. They ignored him again.

These people may have lost the picture since they ignored my recommendation to slow down twice.

He asked Red if he could go out on the bridge and discuss it with the OOD. Red said OK.

Combat was always, day and night, kept dark. But they did use some low white lights over the work table, and the plotters generated an upward white light. Knowing he would be blind since, it was dark on the bridge, Dillan grabbed a red lens flashlight, his maneuvering board page, and left combat.

On LARTER it was only about 12 feet combat door to bridge hatch. When he got there, there was still a tiny little after sunset light. There was a glow on the western horizon. But pitch black in front of the bridge windows with the exception of the AE, which was a bright white spot – lit up like a Christmas tree.

Walking up to the OOD, Dillan said, "Excuse me, sir, but combat worked out a solution, to pass 2000 yards in front of the replenishment group, pass 1000 yards down their starboard side, and then swing into station 3. Combat recommends we slow to 15 and drop superheat at this time. Recommend coming left to 030."

From the captain's chair came,

"Let me see that. It's you, Dillan isn't it?"

"Yes, sir," handing the sheet to the captain.

The skipper pulled out his red lens flash light, took a quick look, and said, "OOD slow to 15."

Then, "Super heat hasn't been up all day, Mr. Dillan. Refine this. I want to go 2500 yards in front and stay 1500 yards away. No need to show off for the other cans and get MAUNA LOA nervous, right? OOD, you do a solution also, so we can cross check. No need to make a mistake that makes us look foolish."

As Dillan scurried back to combat to redo the solution in what now had to be record time, he heard the JOOD say,

"All ahead standard, indicate turns for 15 knots."

Well that was stupid. Of course superheat wasn't up. We can't steam around at 3 to 5 knots banging away with it up. Looked like a dip in front of the old man – again. Stop shooting yourself in the foot, Dillan.

When Dillan got back to combat, LARTER was now close enough that the radar had sorted out MAUNA LOA from the tin cans in waiting station one and two, but the can alongside just blended into MAUNA LOA's return. They were now 15,000 yards away and Dillan recommended coming left to 025 to make it obvious to MAUNA LOA that they were not going to try a close bow crossing. At this rate they would be at the 2500 yard point in less than 25 minutes. Then he started the maneuvering board drill again.

The bridge came to 030. The skipper was coaching and doing maneuvering board in his head again. Although Dillan kept up his work, he pretty much knew that the skipper would eye ball this one in with small course and then speed changes to do what he wished and to give the OOD and JOOD a lesson in ship handling. He wouldn't actually take the conn. Just make suggestions to the conning officer.

Dillan had never heard of the skipper actually taking the conn himself with the exception of making an approach to a nest of other moored cans in difficult wind and current conditions.

The bridge made some course corrections. Sure enough, LARTER passed 2500 yards in front at about 16 knots; made a sweeping right loop turn, passed the unrep ships off their starboard side 1500 yards, and swept towards waiting station three on the money.

The skipper is quite the ship handler.

At the same time, just as Dillan was about to get relieved by the on coming 20-24 watch, a bosun's pipe attention chirp and,

"Now station the underway replenishment detail for re-arming, now station the underway replenishment detail for rearming."

Oh goody, I've been up since 0330, and now probably a 3 hour unrep. Lucky if I get 4 hours sleep tonight.

Dillan's unrep station was still as JOOD on the bridge, with his boss, LT Finistry, as the OOD. There was a massive shuffling of people on the bridge and in CIC. Not all ship's company had unrep stations. But a lot did, especially for rearming.

172

31

When relieved in combat, Dillan went on the bridge. Now a glow from ahead through the windows lit it up a bit. At first he still couldn't see shit. Slowly he felt his way around the chart table with its red light, and using his red light flashlight walked up to the OOD standing next to the captain in his chair.

Out front the AE was lit up. That was the glow seeping through the bridge windows. Fred was there also. And slowly his eyes adjusted. The previous OOD now had the conn and was making the final careful approach to waiting station three. Relieving during a complicated evolution was not permitted, so Dillan and Fred waited till LARTER had snuggled into station.

Shortly there after, a destroyer pulled away, and everyone moved up. An hour and a half later LARTER was in station 1 watching the previous ship start to pull away.

The captain said, "Mr. Dillan, do you want to make the approach?"

Now this is a fix. I've never made an unrep approach, let alone at night.

"Thank you for asking Captain, but I would rather my first try be during daylight."

This is a bit of a cop out since the AE is lit up like a night football game.

An odd silence…

"OK, Mr. Dillan, if you do not feel confident. XO take us up. Dillan can supervise the helm and lee helm."

Underway replenishment was such a tricky maneuver that a qualified JOOD or OOD had to stand behind the helmsman and lee helmsman, listening to the commands of the conning officer and insuring that no one made a mistake.

While a ship was alongside, a 3 degree rudder error would mean an almost instant crunch. One had to stay 150 to 200 feet from the providing ship. Much closer and the vortex of water rushing through the gap between ships would cause a suction that could bring the ships together. The conning officer was on the port bridge wing, so he used the voice tube for commands. This allowed the helm and the lee helm to hear commands a lot better than yelling from the bridge wing over the wind noise.

In addition, the conning officer usually gave commands alongside like "come right to 201 and one half or add one turn" which were not normal helm or lee helm commands. Getting it wrong would, at the best, strain the rig or dip an ammo pallet into the drink.

At the worst, if a rig broke, men on deck could be hit or swept over the side in an instant. Finally, there was always the chance of playing bumper pool with the providing ship. Skippers had been relieved for sideswiping the unrep providing vessel. So an extra insurance policy was necessary.

I will get hell from Fred, when out of the captain's ear shot, for not taking the opportunity. And he will say that he would have been right next to me on the bridge wing guiding me on the approach and station keeping. Having had Fred 'help' me with an approach to a wide open pier in Pearl Harbor, I'll get shouting in my ear 'help.'

The shouting makes me nervous and even more uptight than I already am; makes it hard to think straight. I did get LARTER along side the pier, kind of sloppy like, and got a frown from the skipper. But it was a bitch. No thanks. If I was being chased through the woods by a bear, Fred, I would rather you helped the bear.

So the new XO, an accomplished seaman himself, brought LARTER alongside perfectly. A wire was passed, pallets of projectiles were transferred, and when on deck, broken down, and projectiles carried one at a time per man. Then they were passed, fire brigade fashion, man to man, down the ladders and into the forward and aft magazines.

Heavy work since each projectile weighed 54 pounds, over 17 tons of ammo. And even though the fuses were set to safe, and had protective caps, dropping one would make a big dent, injure some one or at least make a few men's heart stop for awhile. One did not want to have fingers under a dropped projectile, either.

Dropped projectiles tended to be squirrelly, usually due to internal fuse damage. So a dropped projectile would have to be tossed over the side once clear of the AE and the other ships in waiting stations behind. Dropping one on its fuse could cause a detonation, so they were always carried fuse up and cradled in the arms like a fat baby. Two hand pass to two hand accept, man to man.

Then came the propellant and primer cartridges in their aluminum tube cases, a bit less weight, about 28 pounds each. Finally, all was stowed and reported secure. It had taken hours.

The captain said, "Good job, XO. Ops take the conn and let's pull away smartly."

A destroyer tradition was to do every maneuver with timeliness and precision. Zip into station and match ordered speed hitting station right on in range and bearing. Maintain station plus or minus 100 yards and 2 degrees. Change station with the minimum number of safe legs, crisp turns, and at ordered stationing speed. The "Navy way" or "like a real destroyer" the captain called it. There was a right way, a wrong way, and the Navy way.

So once all the wires and lines were clear, LARTER went right about 3 degrees and increased speed. The skipper saluted the AE's skipper bridge wing to bridge wing. A short blast was sounded on the ship's whistle, and there was one puff of black smoke from the stacks. Break the 'house' flag. For LARTER, this was the California state flag, again, a tradition. Once past the AE's bow wave with the stern, goose it, crisp takeoff for station.

It was 0150. "Secure the underway replenishment detail set the regular condition III watch."

When Dillan was relieved, he stumbled down to his rack for an hour's sleep. At 0330, back into combat. At 0730, when relieved in combat, he almost fell down the ladders to his rack and climbed in clothing and all, kicking his shoes off as he went. No stop in radio; no breakfast.

If they really want me they know where to find me. Don't know if the skipper set holiday routine, and don't give a damn.

But at 0900, off went the bong bong bong of general quarters again. Dillan stumbled back to combat looking like an old rag doll.

The next days were an exhausted blur. NGFS all day and some H&I at night, unrep to rearm every 3rd or 4th night depending on the number and type of rounds expended. They did an unrep for fuel once, again at night. There were lots of hours at general quarters. The only people getting any sleep were the 08-12 / 20-24 watch. They could get at least 4 hours. Everyone else was living on 2 or 3 hours in 24. People started to make stupid little mistakes.

In CIC for GQ, the XO, Ted, and Dillan had to start cross checking each other's calculations and plots, and then get Chris to agree. Nerves were frayed.

From the XO, "Dillan, that gun target line does not sound right."

"Yes, sir, I'll check it again," leaning over the plot table.

Using the parallel arm protractor, moving bug center to the requested target point,

"I get 274 degrees at 15,200 yards, XO."

"The 274 seems a bit off, check this, Ted."

Ted checked. "I get 283 degrees, XO."

"Damn, it's different every time," from the XO.

Dillan watched. *The bearing ring was moving!* He re-zeroed it. Then he had to get a screwdriver and tighten the locking mechanism. It did not tighten enough. *Damn thing is not holding.* Finally he took another bearing holding his thumb on the ring to keep it from moving.

"Now 268, XO, the bearing ring came loose."

"Much better. We better overhaul that protractor or get another one up here. We're all getting punchy. And if our gun target lines are not right, we will be shooting somewhere else, not on target. Ted, call supply, let's get a new one installed ASAP."

"Yes, sir."

Ted sent one of the RD men to supply. Then he called Tony on the growler. With a heads up to the supply officer, the SKs would be motivated to find the part in a hurry.

Putting a round out with a wrong gun target line is dangerous for the spotter. Such a little thing as a loose bearing ring and our exhausted and overtired crew could cause a major incident. Blue on blue. Every now and then it happens even with all the cross checks. But seldom admitted, or if admitted, seldom publicized. Friendly fire incidents get lots of unneeded press.

Once, by missing the round count, mount 52 loaded a round into a hot barrel after a fire mission had expended all the rounds asked for. Now there was a projectile in a hot barrel and no where to shoot it. A few tense moments while the powder casing was removed, and a short charge rammed home. They depressed the gun all the way and shot the short charge.

Joe told Dillan that the projectile went out and skipped when it hit the water 500 yards from the ship but did not explode. Then back up in the air tumbling, skipped once more and hit the beach, big bang. There were some fishermen down the beach a ways and it scared hell out of them. They jumped in their boat and paddled like mad. Last seen headed south.

Once, a powder casing split when fired and got stuck in a hot chamber. Took hours to get it out, because as the unusable gun barrel cooled, and with it the chamber, the chamber contracted and made the jamb even worse. The breech block was dinged up and the gun logged "down" except for emergencies. LARTER was down to 75% gunfire capability.

Finally, the captain saw the light. He requested and received permission for a 24 hour stand down, promising to get back to 100% over the interim. LARTER went off shore 10 miles and steamed back and forth at 5 knots, everyone but the watch and some gunner's mates and machinery repair men on holiday routine and in their racks.

By now it was February 20th and LARTER had been underway just short of a month and on heavy NGFS for days. Dillan slept like a dead man. But the young recuperate quickly, and the morning of the 21st, LARTER was back on station and busy again. Slowly but surely, the number of fire missions fell off. The NVA had been driven inland, and by what the message traffic said, most of their captured cities, towns and villages in I Corps recaptured.

The Marines were having a rough time recapturing the provincial capital at Hue, Dillan read. Although not specifically noted, one could read between the lines in the situation reports: heavy causalities. The Marines fought for Hue until the end of February.

But for LARTER, life got easier. Only 1 or 2 fire missions each day. More transit time between spotters, less rounds expended. Even less H&I at night. They got one job "escorting" a truck convoy up the coast. LARTER remained on the gun line for almost 3 more weeks, finally being ordered to Subic. When she arrived in Subic, she had been at sea continuously for 54 days. March 16, 1968.

During the relatively uneventful last week on the gun line, Fred called Dillan in for a 'talk.'

"Pat, (Fred almost never called him by his first name) the CO is not happy with your progress towards becoming an officer of the deck for fleet steaming. You are OK in combat, and we need you there, but as soon as he gets a chance, he wants you moved back to JOOD on the bridge. And when you are on the bridge for unrep, neither of us or the XO thinks you show enough initiative."

"You have, on two occasions, (*2?*) turned the skipper down on an opportunity to make an approach. To be recommended for destroyer school in a couple of years, you must get your fleet OOD quals completed. Your division is functioning well, but your professional qualification progress is slipping."

"One Annapolis JG, just 6 months your senior, is already qualified. You have to get off your butt and get on with it. You can't sit in combat all the time and ever become a capable career officer. I know that in the enlisted ranks, qualification is not as big of a deal, but as an officer, you have to play by our rules."

Oh great. I have been busting my butt but that must not be enough. And the enlisted comment was a cheap shot. Qualifications for enlisted, although different, are just as important as they are for officers. Maybe I should tell Fred that all the yelling in my ear makes me nervous. But I know Fred well enough that all that will do is alienate him further. Will think I am shifting blame.

Fred is a master of ducking shit when it hits the fan. No way will he accept that. And the Annapolis comment is another hit below the belt. But I can't fight this shit. I'll just make it worse.

All Dillan could say is,

"Yes, sir, I understand, I'll try to show more initiative."

Fred said, "Good, any questions?"

"No, sir."

"OK then, dismissed."

Bastard.

Dillan went up to radio, locked himself in crypto and wrote a long letter to Patty, a lot of which was about what a flaming asshole Fred the III was.

Good thing letters are not censored.

32

Arrival at Subic was uneventful. The XO made the approach to the nest and did it perfectly, again, quite a seaman.

Even better than the skipper at pier approaches, but no one would dare utter such blasphemy.

There was major work to get done. LT Chris Harcourt had gotten the captain to request two new barrels for mount 51 and have a tender look-see at the repaired chamber. A barrel was supposed to be good for about 4000 rounds and these only had about 2,000 on them, but he wanted to be sure. The 5 inch 38 was technically not a 'rifle' because it did not have a lot of rifling (groves) inside the barrel, and was not long enough.

The 38's were about 16 feet long. Billy Hoffman told Dillan that there was some noticeable evidence of wear. These barrels were maybe half through their useful life since LARTER had not done any NGFS on her last cruise. The ones on 52 were also dated from the FRAM conversion. Original barrel fabrication was probably World War II.

The barrels weighed about 3,000 pounds each, so replacing them was a major evolution. LARTER was moved pierside for that so the crane could help. While alongside the pier, the weapons department did a hush hush transfer of two ASROCs out of the launcher, and some other canisters. Then two new ASROCs were reloaded. Must have been nukes they pulled, Dillan surmised, with all the armed guards on the pier. Seventh fleet must be stockpiling some, he thought.

But in any nest of destroyers in Subic, daily shuffling of ships, usually in the early morning, was common as some departed. By the afternoon others arrived.

Red Redmond was busy as hell getting the #2 evaporator fixed. LARTER had been on water rations for the past three weeks, since it went belly up. Feed water for the boilers had priority. Fresh water to showers was secured most days. Since salt water was used for flushing, it didn't take any. But fresh was required for cooking and even the final rinse in dish washing and the ship's laundry. Not a lot was left for crew showers.

And salt water showers, even with the special soap, left a sticky irritating coating on the skin. Most started fresh water wipe downs after salt water showers, using water from the scuttlebutts (water fountains). Now in Subic, they took on fresh water from the pier, and the crew could enjoy a real clean up.

Most Navy enlisted were very clean, showering and shaving every day. If a man started to emit body odor, the crew would make it obvious that they did not approve. In extreme cases the offender was treated to a forced shower with scrub brushes and Fels-Naptha soap. It usually took only one of these to convince anyone that a shower a day was appropriate.

Typical for a stop in Subic: major working parties trundling boxes of food aboard on their shoulders from trucks on the pier. Most food and supplies arrived by this route. Tony would pre order by message, so trucks could be staged when LARTER arrived. Some fresh veggies but the meat was all frozen and boxed and mostly from Australia.

The skipper, XO and Fred were off to meetings with the admiral (CTF 77) on board USS TICONDEROGA (CV-14), who was tied up at Cubi. TICONDEROGA was an old lady. She had seen service in World War II and Korea, had been deactivated, and then re-commissioned.

Dillan was buried in RPS stuff and got Pete Donavan to help him. So much had to be offloaded and destroyed (burned) and destruction witnessed. So much new stuff had to be checked out, page checked, and loaded. New crib circuit boards had to be installed in the broadcast equipment. This would make the main broadcast secure again.

Dillan sent a message acknowledging the change. When all Westpac ships had executed this change, the main broadcast would be good for Secret again. LARTER was one of the last to do the change. Busy busy.

But the crew's moral was high again. Any day now LARTER would be released, team up with a carrier headed home, and start the long slog across the Pacific headed east. By schedule, they were due to be back in San Diego April 30th. And at best it was a 20 day trip from Subic. LARTER had to head home in 21 days to make it.

Maybe that is what the CO, XO and OPS are discussing with the CarDiv admiral? A week or two on Yankee Station chasing a carrier and homeward bound. The April 30th date is not set in concrete, but soon thereafter. Please?

Dillan did get to the phone exchange. Patty was in better sprits. It was mid March and she knew LARTER should be coming home in a few weeks. The nightmare was about over. Dillan teased her,

"The second thing I'm going to do when I get home is to set down my suitcase."

She laughed. "Sure it'll not get in the way?" she said.

He had always found intimacy to be wonderful. Dillan longed for it. He thought about it often.

Cuddle and make love, then cuddle some more. Stop that thought process idiot. You are horny enough, already!

"Looks like Hong Kong is out," she said.

When LARTER left San Diego, it was expected that she would make a port call in Hong Kong. Hong Kong was known for all the neat stuff to buy. They had made a list together. But it looked like Hong Kong was out – not enough time left.

"Yeah, the PUEBLO thing probably squelched that. But I would rather come home."

"Me too. Come home right now! Is there anything worth getting in Subic?"

"They do have some monkey pod carvings and some rattan ware."

"What's monkey pod?"

"Like teak only softer. They have carvings of a man bending over all the way with his head up his butt. Maybe I ought to get one for Fred. It looks just like him."

"Ha, maybe not, he would put you in hack and you would never get off that damn ship. Get some rattan place mats, maybe 6. And save the rest for vacation. Want to go to San Francisco?"

So they planned a super vacation for the honeymoon they had never had. Dillan thought maybe Frisco would be too expensive, so they settled on Lake Tahoe for a week. They had some good deals at Tahoe, since they figured people would make up for any freebees by gambling. Dillan and Patty were not much in the way of gamblers. Their budget couldn't afford it.

"Remember", she said, "Let's each save our pennies so we can have a super vacation. I'll start looking for hotels. There are always ads in the paper."

"Combat pay and making JG makes us not quite so tight with our budget. We can have a super delayed honeymoon. Sleep all morning and play all night. I'm going to make love to you so much you'll walk funny."

"Promises, promises, promises," was her retort.

When in the war zone, all hands got a bit extra each month for combat pay. The trick was to have at least one day out of a month in the zone, so even the Formation Star thing allowed for combat pay those partial months. Dillan had received combat pay since November 1967.

Dillan had always sent Patty an 'allotment' from his check each month. Allotments were deducted automatically and sent the first of each month to the spouse at home. Although Patty was working, she had to pay rent, utilities, a car payment, gas, insurance, etc.

Patty said her brother had stopped in. Her brother had enlisted in the Air Force and had been stationed in Thailand. She said he didn't look good and was getting a medical discharge. Said it was some bug he picked up over there, probably malaria. Dillan knew that malaria was an occupational hazard incountry and very difficult to cure.

She said Dillan's dad had called and asked when Dillan would be home, and wanted to know if they were coming for a visit. Dillan had not seen his dad since the wedding, but that was not quite a year ago.

She said, "I didn't know what to say to him, so I told him you would get back to him. Then he said he never gets letters from you." It sounded like a strained conversation to Dillan, but Patty knew that his relationship with his father sucked, to say the least.

"I'll write him a short letter and say that we can't come until we get orders."

"Good, orders. A stop in Ohio followed by a short one in Middletown, enroute to wherever. Any ideas yet?"

"No, filled out my dream sheet and asked for Mayport, or Key West."[lii]

"What are the chances?"

"Needs of the service, you know. With our luck it'll be another can in SD."

"As long as it's not headed west right away. I wouldn't mind staying here if you're home."

"Me too. Soon, Baby, soon."

Dillan and Patty ended with the normal, "I love you and miss you," things and it was over. Lasted 46 minutes, cost $75. Price was coming down.

God, I miss her. This Navy career stuff may not be all it's cracked up to be.

When the CO, XO, and OPS came back from the carrier, no one said anything. Dillan at least expected Fred to have a department meeting and tell Dillan, Ted, and Pete what was up. Dillan worried but was very busy.

On the exterior, LARTER looked like a rust bucket: lots of running rust stains on the sides, main deck, etc. Right around the mounts the deck non skid was scratched up pretty good from shell casings. As soon as they were ejected from the gun after firing, the hot case man pitched them out.[liii]

LARTER's superstructure had a lot of aluminum so rust didn't show up there, just white fuzz where it got scratched. And there were a lot of fuel oil stains around the unrep receiving stations. All the time at sea took a toll. Joe Reiderman's deck hands were busy scraping and putting red lead primer and then deck gray paint over the deck scratches, and cleaning and touching up where the oil spills were. Yellow zinc chromate was put on the aluminum as a primer. They even went over the sides in boson's chairs and rolled paint right over the running rust, so much for proper preparation.

Dillan, Pete, and a couple of other guys went to the club for drinks one night. And then there was the wetting down party. Dillan, Sam Blongerinski, Jim Kirpatrick, and Joe Rederman had all made LTJG. Their dates of rank were not the same however. Dillan's and Jim's were November 1, 1967, backdated to the 1 year commissioned service point.

Sam's and Joe's were back dated to July 1, 1967: Naval Academy types. They had effectively been promoted in January 1968 anyway, and before the reduction in time in grade. But LARTER was at sea, and their wetting down party was overshadowed by the new XO's arrival and workload during the stop in Subic, before the Formation Star trip.

The wetting down party was fun. And with 4 officers sharing the cost, it was a lot cheaper than it could have been. Even Fred came since Chris had the duty.

"Well, Dillan, your first promotion as an officer. You new guys got lucky. I was an Ensign for 18 months. But I did make Lieutenant in 4 years instead of 5. So keep out of trouble, watch your self regarding looking out for the enlisted, get fleet OOD qualified and bust your buns and maybe by the end of 1970, you can be a Lieutenant."

"Maybe I'll get a spot and be a Lieutenant sooner," Dillan said, taking a pull on his Scotch and water.

Spot promotions were for officers serving in a billet in the war zone, one grade down – like a LTJG serving in a LT billet. In that case, the Commanding Officer could request a spot promotion for an officer, and, if approved, the officer would be promoted to the billet rank.

But spots did not shorten the time to the next following rank – they only allowed for stripes and pay early for the billet rank. If one got transferred after a spot, the spot stuck. No return to previous rank like occurred in the Army.

Fred shrugged, "There are not many spots available, maybe incountry. You want a tour incountry?"

"No way, but there are spots on ships or staffs to be had."

"Few, damn few. Plan on a full 4 years commissioned service. That is, if you don't screw up, and only if you don't screw up."

"I have no intention of screwing up. And I intend to continue being an advocate for the enlisted, if I think they're getting screwed over."

"Unfortunate, Dillan. We all look out for the enlisted – just because you were one does not give you license to coddle them. Be careful. That's not the way to higher rank."

He tipped his glass and polished off the liquid. "I need a refill, especially if it's free," shaking the ice in his glass. Then he turned, and walked towards the bar.

Discussion over. God, Fred is so myopic. Maybe the Navy will cut the time in grade to Lieutenant like they did for JG?

By then it was time to get underway again. Total time in port was 5 days. Gun barrels replaced and full ammo load out. The crew was getting jumpy. And so was Dillan

The plan for the cruise home should have been at least leaked, if not announced by now, instead: total silence. We're like mushrooms. Kept in the dark and fed bullshit.

It was now March 21st. "Now station the special sea and anchor detail," over the 1MC; usually, the cans went out first, then the carrier.

Line handlers were on deck, and a piloting team was set in combat and on the bridge to navigate out of the channels. An anchor was readied for letting go in case of a problem. Dillan's station was JOOD like unrep. OOD was Fred, also like unrep. The ship was manned and ready, and main control was told to stand by to answer all bells. Once everything was set the skipper said,

"OK, XO you got us in here, get us out."

33

This was going to be a bit tricky. LARTER was now the second closest to the pier in a nest of four. The two outboard cans were pulled away from LARTER by pusher boats. Pusher boats in Subic were small landing craft, probably with bigger engines, and black rubber bumpers over their bow ramps.

They were tied bow on to the front and stern of the two outboard destroyers and then pulled in reverse to pull them clear of LARTER while the two ships were still tied together. Meanwhile, Fred ordered the brow taken in and all lines singled up. The inboard ship had rigged a couple of big fenders along side and ¼ back from her bow.

The XO took in all but the forward line, held the starboard aft facing forward spring line, and went ahead for a moment on the port engine with the rudders right full. The stern swung out and the bow turned in. Then take in all lines and, "Underway, shift colors" was passed on the 1MC. Then rudder amidships, and all back 1/3 was ordered. Three short blasts on the ship's whistle and LARTER backed into the fairway. The XO never touched a fender.

LARTER went down the channel at 10 knots, and increased to 15 when clear of the point to starboard. Soon she was up to 20 and "Secure the special sea and anchor detail, set the regular condition III watch," was passed. Back at sea again, headed 270, due west for Yankee Station. It was 0820. Dillan figured that they would steam out about 12 miles to 'Point X-ray' and then slow and wait for the other cans and Tyco.

The XO had done a nice job. Ship handling in tight places with all the fleet watching was tough. Even a little screw up lost large amounts of face for the captain, even if he wasn't driving. A captain was responsible for everything his ship did, every message it sent, and every thing its crew did. If the lowest seaman from a ship got picked up by shore patrol for being drunk and disorderly, the captain could expect one of his peers who heard about it to mention it – normally when there were even more peers around. All those Commanders were competing for a smaller number of full Captain promotions.

Seamanship, that's a real sailor's game. So the XO did the skipper proud.

As soon as LARTER had cleared what the skipper thought was audible sound range of shore, he got out of his chair and walked over to the 1MC microphone station. He pulled out a folded sheet of paper, and asked the bosun's mate of the watch to sound attention on the bosun's pipe. Then he took the mike, and put it to his lips.

"All hands, this is the captain speaking. I know all of you are looking forward to getting back to your loved ones at home. I am also. But the tempo of air strikes against North Vietnam has increased and we have been ordered to be the shot gun destroyer for a cruiser on northern search and rescue station. This is an important job saving our pilots and air crew that have to come down in the Tonkin Gulf. We all need to be on our toes up there because there have been attempted PT boat attacks in the past."

"I have asked the staff of Destroyer Squadron Fifteen in San Diego, to contact your loved ones using the telephone numbers you turned in prior to our departure, and to tell them that LARTER is performing an important mission and will be a few weeks late. I am confident that each of you will put your disappointment behind you and will do your jobs to the best of your ability. Once our job on north SAR (search and rescue) is successfully completed, we should be headed east. That is all."

It got real quiet on the bridge as each man tried to grasp what the captain had just said. First, there was no way LARTER would be in San Diego by the 30th of April. Maybe the 15th of May? Their loved ones were expecting them in April. Where was LARTER going? Northern Gulf of Tonkin was up between North Vietnam and Communist China.

Great f'ing place!

Minds wandered. Not having been relieved yet, Dillan, although seething inside, had to say,

"Helmsman, mind your helm," when the ship's course started to drift.

"Sorry, sir."

"Very well, try keeping your mind on what you're doing, Kaplin, OK?" from Dillan.

"Yes, sir."

The captain gave Dillan a look for that one. "Mind your helm" was the correct procedure. The rest was fluff.

I'm due for a thumping, Dillan thought. So what? Kaplin is human and probably has a young wife waiting. Show some compassion for the guy.

LARTER set the regular underway Condition III watch. Dillan was relieved and went below for the 3 hours until he had to be back in combat. He really expected that the skipper would send him back to the bridge watch bill after this in port period. And was wondering why he had not. Now it was a bit clearer.

Northern SAR was all about the air picture and the long range surface picture. And Dillan was 1 of 4 qualified air intercept controllers on LARTER. He needed him in combat.

Dillan went down the ladder to radio, dejected.

God, is Patty going to be pissed! And she will quiz the caller, who can not answer questions on an unsecured land line. And then she will be more pissed. If I write a letter tonight, God only knows when she will get it – a month? Longer? Damn, damn, double damn.

He walked into radio and as he did, Fred was right behind him.

"Keep the fluff out of your helm orders, Dillan. And make damn sure you don't screw up in combat. This is a serious assignment."

Could have expected it. Fred, with no female attachments is more interested in staying where the action is anyway. Maybe get a medal?

Dillan remembered what Fred had put him through after he had gotten married. It was mid summer 1967.

An officer was obliged to request "permission to leave the ship" from his boss on days when he did not have the duty and the work day was done, officially 1600. Dillan was desperate to leave the ship on the few occasions when he did not have the duty and the ship was in port. Fred continued to find something else for Dillan to do.

"Mr. Dillan you may go running home to your wife after I have the E-5 evaluation drafts in my hand. They are due next week, you know, and I have to have time to insure that you and your chief are grading the men objectively and not padding their evaluations."

Dillan couldn't fight this crap, although it made him furious inside. Fighting it only got another job heaped on top of the one he just was assigned. Dillan knew that his time with Patty was very limited prior to departing on the 6 month Westpac cruise. And Fred, on purpose, restricting this time even further, was inflicting cruel and unusual punishment; his way of 'whipping Dillan into shape' without having to go to the XO.

Dillan took to finding Fred at 1500 to ask if there were any last moment things that Fred wanted done today. This worked for a couple of days but soon Fred would only say,

"You know what needs done, Mr. Dillan. I can't be supervising you all the time."

OK, try another tactic. Dillan knew that Fred wouldn't be sharp with him if there were others, especially other department heads in ear shot. Fred might not look professional. Fred might lose face. So Dillan would wait until Fred was having a discussion with another, and then do the "everything is done and I'm going ashore boss" bit with a wave. Usually Fred would frown but almost never say anything.

Then Fred would give him a lecture the next day,

"Mr. Dillan, did they not teach you manners at OCS? You do not interrupt a senior when he is having a conversation with another officer. You should wait until he has concluded his business."

"If I waited, I could be standing around for an hour or more. And you're a busy man. Maybe if you are busy after 1600 and my work is done, I should just ask the XO and tell him you are tied up."

And Fred knew the XO would be leaving the ship as close to 1600 as he could. By tradition, he had to wait for the captain to go ashore. But the skipper was also married, and left promptly at 1600 unless there was a major problem.

Checkmate.

34

Now, after the "fluff" comment, Fred blew past Dillan into radio looking for the Moverep board.

All ships in the fleet, everywhere, had to file movement reports or 'Movereps.' These were specially formatted short Confidential messages that told the Navy where they were and where they were going. Not that a ship could just go wandering off somewhere. There was an advance quarterly schedule, subject to revision and sometimes after the fact, like was currently occurring for LARTER, which pretty much dictated a ship's schedule. So Movereps were mostly a day to day confirmation.

When a ship joined a task organization, it sent a report "chopping" to the task org's OTC. As long as a ship was assigned to a task organization the task organization commander was responsible for the Movereps for the task organization. Get sent off independent, chop back to yourself, and submit Movereps again. One could also "modlock," which was to say I will be in a XX nautical mile area of such and such latitude and longitude.

Fred was looking for a modlock Moverep from an oiler, so LARTER could top off as close to Northern SAR as possible. But oilers did not go up there, so the unrep would be slightly northwest of Yankee Station at the best.

It was obvious the guys in radio were not as surprised as Dillan was at the captain's speech. Not happy, but not as surprised. Dillan could tell because they went about their business with out as much solemnity as he would have expected. They must have gotten a head's up.

Dillan walked up to the chief with a questioning look on his face. The chief said nothing, just handed Dillan the outgoing message board. There on top was a Moverep undoubtedly drafted by Fred and released by the captain. Very cryptic but translated it said: Underway XX time, go west, then north, rendezvous TU 77.4.3 at location XX. Chop to CTU 77.4.3.

The date time group sent indicated that it went out just as the special and sea and anchor detail was set. Date time groups (DTG) were a number like "202104Z MAR 68." It was the date and time the message was transmitted and was assigned by the radio watch just as it was transmitted. The date was first and the time was in "Zulu" time or Greenwich Mean Time. The sending unit's name and date time group were used to reference messages.

So that is how radio knew. The chief has been around long enough that he can read a Moverep as good as any operations officer in the fleet. And task units are listed in the 7th fleet opor-der.

Fred, muttering to himself, made some pencil notes of oiler Moverep locations, and left for combat to do some plotting.

Dillan pulled the intel board, a rack with lots of message tear offs. By reading through the mountain of intel summaries and then, on another board, the mountain of sitreps, he could glean a lot. Better bone up on what was going on in the air war. Soon he would be in it up to his eye brows.[liv]

The North Vietnamese had been playing at the Paris peace talks for a long time. Arguing over what shape table to use, arguing over who sat where. There were endless protocol discussions and seldom any real progress. And if there was progress, the North would set everything back to zero just for the sheer audacity of it. Find an excuse and walk out of the talks.[lv]

LARTER is at the end of the yo-yo string again. A jerk from Washington and off we go, up and down.

Now there were three carriers on Yankee Station, and significant Air Force fighter/bombers stationed in Thailand. Lots of ordnance delivery options.

The B52's from Guam, or even further away, were always another option. But the Soviet provided surface to air missiles (SAM) the North possessed, probably with Russian or Chinese crews or at least advisors, were a significant threat to them at normal bombing altitudes. Just what the SAMs had been developed to shoot down.

The air campaign against the North had to rely on smaller, low flying, maneuverable, fighter bombers. Use the 52's for carpet bombing the VC and NVA in the south and for rearranging the Ho Chi Minh trail – not really a road, actually hundreds of dirt roads all intertwined. Slip the 52's into the north if conditions dictated. They could carry a significant amount of ordnance. But a downed 52 in the north would be a very bad news day.

Washington was upset. Now all bets were off. National Command Authority was mad as hell and was not going to take it any more. When you screw with the bull, ultimately you are going to get the horn.

Bomb the crap out of them, kill them all and let God sort it out. Well, probably not that drastic, but a major bombing effort anyway.

To Dillan and the other officers on LARTER, the general reaction was 'about time.' They thought that the USA had <u>not</u> been successful in the World War II by asking the Japanese permission to attack islands or to fire bomb Tokyo. Most thought that the war was being fought with one hand tied behind their backs.

Anyway, President Johnson and his administration, especially McNamara, were serious now. So the US military was obliged to kick butt and take names.^{lvi}

After blowing almost all his work time reading intel and sit reps, Dillan finally understood. North SAR was going to be for keeps. One super thing was that up there the rules of engagement were relaxed. Assume all surface contacts unless otherwise identified were hostile, weapons free. That might just save their butts for a trip home.

He went down to the wardroom for lunch.

At about 10 minutes to 12, as the stewards were just serving the main course, the messenger of the watch knocked on the wardroom door and entered. Obviously very nervous, twisting his ball cap in one hand, a small pack of papers in the other. He came in and stood at attention looking at the captain. All officers gave him their attention.

"Good morning, Captain. The officer of the deck sends his respects and reports the approaching hour of twelve. All chronometers have been wound and compared. Request permission to strike eight bells on time, sir," he said. He then handed the captain the papers.

The captain said, "Very well, permission granted, and you did that well."^{lvii}

"Thank you, sir." The kid beamed, and he turned and left the wardroom.

A messenger had to do this report every noon, finding the captain if he was aboard and the command duty officer if he was not. The papers given to the captain were the noon position, fuel state, fresh water and feed water levels, magazine temperatures, and any others that the captain had asked for.

It was tough on the young messengers, usually junior seamen only 18, since they had to memorize the words, were seldom allowed in the wardroom, and had little interaction with the captain.

Lunch was interesting. The captain was obviously pumped about the up coming operation. Not much small talk.

Did he volunteer LARTER? A good showing on North SAR would look nice on a CDR's fitrep.

35

Right after lunch there was an "all officers meeting," something that happened seldom. The skipper even pulled the evaluator out of combat and the director officer down. Even all engineering department was there. The only ones missing were the OOD, JOOD and CIC watch officer, two guys from weapons and Pete from operations.

Fred came in with a flip chart on which a topographic map of the northern gulf was posted. Right in the middle of the west side of the northern gulf was a star, with a ring around it which came awfully close to the North Vietnamese coast – like 12 miles.

The captain stood and said, "We have been assigned an important role. Over the next few minutes the XO and Fred will take you through what we expect. COMSEVENTHFLT and CTF 77 are placing a lot of trust in LARTER to do this job and to do it well. Pay attention. XO." Then he took a chair in front.

LCDR Jim Henderson took the floor, "Thanks Captain. We do have a major assignment. North SAR is a two ship operation. LARTER will be riding shotgun for USS MENAUL (DLG 25)."

Dillan knew that MENAUL was a 'double ended' DLG (destroyer leader guided missile) and a large ship, over 500 feet long. In WW II she would have been classified as a cruiser. The double end related to her twin rail Terrier surface to air missile launchers, one forward and one aft. Although she carried ASROC, sonar, and some ASW gear, she was an anti-air warfare ship primarily.

No guns. But the key attribute was that she had the Naval Tactical Data System, a computer system that could track lots of contacts, and she had a ton of radars, including height finder radar.

The XO continued, "MENAUL will track all strikes going in and coming out. We want to insure that we don't get more out than in." There was a muffled laugh.

A couple of the NVA air corps MiGs tried to tag along on a returning strike a time or two before. Probably the ones with Soviet pilots 'on loan' although not advertised. But these adventurous pilots didn't make it. Some F-4 Phantom jockeys got their first kills. It taught them a lesson.

"Then there's search and rescue. Our pilots, and the Air Force pilots out of Thailand, know that if they're hit and they can get out over the sea prior to punching out, we will be there to pick them up. Not so much with the ships themselves but with helicopters vectored in from the carriers or DaNang."

"MENAUL and LARTER will be doing in flight refueling for these helicopters while they hover over the flight deck, or stern in the case of MENAUL," the XO went on. "Mr. Harcourt assures me that we have all we need to set up for that and tomorrow will get the refueling system rigged and ready to go."

LARTER had special tanks of JP-5 just for this. Same fuel DASH used. The in-flight refueling rig was a small portable tower mounted in the center of the DASH deck that had a flexible hose connection on top. Helos could hover over the tower and the hose could be extended and coupled to their belly mounted refuel connection.

"MENAUL may have to refuel the larger helos like a SH-3, which will go in low over the land to pluck an air crew right from under the NVA's nose if the opportunity presents itself. We can do the UH-1s, new UH-2s and SH-3s in a pinch. MENAUL will do the HH-3 Jolly Green Giants out of DaNang. And the admiral has insured us that SAR CAP (special CAP who would shoot up the area big time to keep the NVA's heads down) will be available."

"Remember, the North Vietnamese navy takes a dim view of downed pilots, who they consider to be their property, being plucked out from under their noses by the ships or helos just off their coast. In many cases, it'll be a race to see who gets to the air crews, in their little orange life rafts, first. And punching out is rough on the air crews. Generally beats them up a bit, so they're in no condition to fight back. Also, the NVN will spray a lot of machine gun fire around. If they can't get the crews then no one should."

"Our rules of engagement in this case are 'no rules.' Any surface craft near or going towards the pilots or us is a target."

There was a round of applause.

Right on.

"And at night we can and should expect a visit from PT boats determined to disrupt our tranquility. We're going to have to keep on our toes."

"LARTER's job is to ride shot gun for MENAUL, go get a downed air crew if necessary, and keep the PT boats away. But that's not all. Mr. Finistry'll fill you in on the other jobs and discuss order of battle. Please save your questions for after his presentation," Then looking at Fred, "Ops."

Fred got up and started, "Thanks XO," a nod, "Captain."

"Gentlemen, in a major SAR situation, LARTER can also expect to be controlling aircraft as a back up or addition to MENAUL. When this happens, Mr. Brunshall, Chief Goldman (the radarman chief), and RD1 Foster, will be in the controller's chair. Mr. Dillan, you are the back up controller. Bone up on procedures before we get to station. Think you can do that?"

He looked at Dillan, and Dillan nodded.

What an ass, the "think you can do that" crap was a dig. Of course I can.

He went on, "As the only two US Navy units up there, we're always an inviting target, by air or surface. Intel indicates that the north does not have any subs, thank goodness."

"However, a MiG attack is a remote possibility. To counter this we have to rely on MENAUL's missiles which can reach out and swat a MiG from over 20 miles away. And there will usually be some CAP around to ruin the enemy's attempt."

Air attacks on North SAR ships are scarce. It's the night PT boat stuff that's a concern.

Fred continued, "Although not advertised, North Vietnam does have a few ex Soviet Komar class small missile boats. These carry two of the SS-N-2 Styx cruise missiles and have a 25 mile range although reality is probably closer to 13 miles. These boats have to have a good radar return and course and speed solution to launch. Then the bird flies on auto pilot. They have terminal radar homing. To date, these have not sortied, which makes us think they have Soviet crews, or at least Soviet advisors aboard."

"The Styx can sink a destroyer, so air recon keeps really good track of their where abouts. Remember, just over a year ago, an Egyptian Komar sank the Israeli destroyer ELIAT. If the Komars come out, the recommended tactic is to run right at'm full bore using the FC radar and as much VT frag as we can put in front of them, then make a 90 degree course change if they launch. Unless of course we have CAP available and close."

"Then there are P-6 patrol craft with torpedoes and 25mm guns. P-6's are small and fast, although they have to be on a steady course awhile to get a solution to launch one of their two side mounted torpedoes. These are dumb torpedoes. Any surface contact that comes fast or right at us will immediately be taken under fire."

The P-6 was a class developed in the 1940's and parceled out to all their friends by the Soviet Union. The ones in North Vietnam had probably been built in China. These were the ones, and some smaller P-4s, that had attacked USS MADDOX (DD 731) and later her and USS TURNER JOY (DD 951) in 1964. This was the infamous 'Tonkin Gulf Incident' that triggered the first air strikes on North Vietnam.

"Finally there are a bunch of small, wooden 'fast' junks. Take a small junk, add a big engine, install a couple of 7.62 RPK light machine guns, a 12.7 machine gun, or even a 25mm open gun, and have an instant patrol craft. These carry RPGs (rocket propelled grenades) also, so our helo pilots have to watch for them. These junks are usually used to snag downed air crews. These are especially nasty since their low wooden hulls will not paint on our surface search radar until they get real close. Sharp eyes on the radar, gentlemen, and we'll be doubling the visual lookouts and send two to the signal bridge at night."

Not that the machine guns could do a lot of damage. But with LARTER's thin superstructure and hull plating, they could punch a bunch of holes and hurt some people, maybe damage some equipment. The 25mm shells were explosive so they could do some significant damage.

"LARTER is in for an interesting assignment, and we'll be relieving USS JOESPH KINKAID (DD 769), our sister ship out of Pearl. The MENAUL is already on station."

The captain stood up, "OK men, any questions?"

"Captain, will we be going to general quarters at night or staying at Condition III?" from Billy Hoffman.

Not a great question. It would depend on the situation.

"Mr. Hoffman, we'll go to GQ if conditions warrant. Since it takes time to station GQ - lately maybe too much time" –

pause for effect – "I expect the evaluator to commence fire immediately if we have a potentially dangerous surface contact."

Wow, shoot first and ask questions afterwards.

"Captain", Eric Ebersole asked, "Has the KINKAID seen any action?"

"Good question, yes, KINKAID and MENAUL have experienced either actual or feint night surface attacks on 3 occasions over the past two weeks. These they easily repelled with gunfire. They also have been involved in 6 SAR situations recovering 4 pilots and air crew."

He went on, "Sadly, two pilots didn't get out to sea far enough and were picked up by the enemy. We also lost a helo and 3 men attempting an inland pickup south of Haiphong."

The questions went on a little longer. Then the captain adjourned the meeting. As everyone was leaving Fred said,

"Mr. Dillan, the comm. officer for the staff told me that many ships had experienced broadcast interruptions while at North SAR, even with the mirrored one. Insure that doesn't happen to us."

Dillan didn't answer, just looked at Fred. Fred turned, and was gone.

What could one say to this? What kind of interruptions? What caused them, etc.? But Fred sure didn't understand the technical side of radio wave propagation. Asking him detailed questions about this is like asking a golf pro to explain an Apollo capsule. Not that Fred isn't smart, he is very smart and a competent operations officer, damn him. But most complex communications technology exceeds his knowledge base. Besides, he really doesn't want to know, he just wants me to fix it.

36

Dillan had about 45 minutes to check with radio prior to assuming the 16-20 watch in combat. He wanted to give the chief a heads up on Fred's comment.

Maybe write a letter after watch. That'll be a tough letter to write. I can't tell Patty about where we're going exactly, only that it's another operation. I'll mention search and rescue, since it will at least seem like a humanitarian thing to her. By the time she gets the letter, maybe weeks from now, she'll have already gotten the telephone call from DESRON 15, anyway.

Dillan went down to his stateroom to get his notes on air control out of his small desk safe.

Might as well bone up on what'll be a dull watch in combat.

He poked his head into Tony's stateroom.

"Hey, Pork Chop, any hot skinny?"

Tony looked up from his paperback, "There was a fist fight on the mess decks last night: RD3 Fister and MMFN Fredrick. Troops are getting squirrelly since we're extended."

"I heard it mentioned when I was in combat. Fister was locked up in the brig and didn't stand his watches," Dillan said. "What was it over?"

"Not sure, one of my SKs told the chief that he thought Fister was hitting on Fredrick."

"Wow, if that's true, that would be our first major queer incident this deployment."

"Yeah, there were a couple of other independent rumors but the men handled it themselves. This one got a master at arms attention after a full scale fight erupted. Headed for mast I think," making a hanging gesture.

"Isn't mast required since pre-trial restraint is involved? Maybe even a summary? Just what we need out here headed for SAR."

"The log says "locked up in protective custody" so it isn't really pretrial restraint. Anyway, the XO called me and told me to do an investigation. I'll get started after chow."

"Good luck," with a wave, and Dillan headed for combat.

Damn. A potential homosexual dust up, just what we need. And RD3 Fister, he looked a little effeminate, but I wouldn't have guessed that he would hit on another man. Can't picture Fredrick.

Every so often there was some yelling or, at worst case, a wrestling match or a few punches thrown between enlisted men. Being trapped in close quarters for extended periods exacerbated personality differences. And the sleep deprivation didn't help much either. Fighting was dealt with harshly and the master at arms force and senior enlisted kept the lid screwed down as tight as possible. Even some young officers would have their verbal disagreements. But usually these were quickly stifled. Officers were supposed to be gentlemen and even the slightest squabble was immediately stomped on by department heads and the XO.

Steaming independently, the watch was quiet. The RD enlisted kept the surface plot up to date. Only a few contacts in what was an American ocean. The air picture showed a lot of contacts as the carriers on Yankee Station were doing major ops. The air search radar could reach out to 200 miles so some long range, high altitude contacts would show up when LARTER got to 180 miles of Yankee Station.

FRAM destroyers had no height finder radar. So an air contact's altitude had to be guessed from the radar's lobe pattern chart. An aircraft would fade as it moved from one vertical lobe to another. This was very inaccurate. And the air search (AN/SPS-29C) put out lobes that normally did not follow the earth's curvature, so low distant contacts were invisible.

Dillan took the opportunity to explain his underway replenishment approach to Red.

Talking to your boss' peer about your boss is maybe a little unethical. Approach carefully.

"Red, I'm sure you have heard that I'm in the doghouse with the old man for not being aggressive enough at my fleet OOD qualifications?" Dillan asked. LARTER was a small ship, and besides, Red was the senior watch officer, the one who made up the officer's watch assignments with the skipper's agreement.

"I've heard a little. The skipper wants you to get some more JOOD time. He told me so, was not happy when you turned down an approach. But with our North SAR assignment he needs you here. I agreed with that. You're good here in combat, and did well last trip out during the 'Star' fun and to NGFS," Red said.

OK. Now I get to stick my neck out.

"With all due respect to Fred, the guy drives me crazy standing at my back and yelling in my ear as I try to conn the ship in tight situations. When he does that, my confidence shrinks and I make stupid little mistakes. You might have heard about my sloppy run at the pier in Pearl?"

"Well, I can't get in the middle between you and your boss."

"I understand that, sir, but I've thought about this since we got back to Subic and I have an idea that might help."

Silence.

"I've really been impressed at the new XO's ship handling. He's so smooth and seems to be at ease making approaches for unrep or to a nest," Dillan added.

"Oh, he's good alright, I've heard. Even the skipper has lots of confidence in him."

"Maybe I can get the XO to be my coach on an approach." Dillan said.

"Coaching the JOOD is Fred's, the OOD's job, hard to dodge that one."

"I thought that maybe a word from you as senior watch officer to the XO might help?" Dillan had dropped the bomb.

"Let me think on that awhile."

Oh shit. We will be alongside an oiler tomorrow. I hope it doesn't take too long to think. Anyway, that conversation is over now.

"Thank you, sir," and Dillan went back to watching the surface radar repeater.

Then, about 10 minutes prior to the reliefs showing up, Red waved Dillan over, pointed to a seat and said,

"OK, I'll put a bug in the XO's ear. If he's willing to do it, then he can ask the skipper. Fred will not be pleased, but it can be sold as the XO learning more about the capabilities of his officers. But if you get asked to make an approach, even if you're not sure it'll be the XO coaching, you better do it."

"Yes, sir. And thank you, sir," from Dillan as he got up. Red smiled.

OK. You may be getting your chance. Or you may be getting your chance to screw up royally.

The 04-08 watch in the morning was uneventful. Fred came in just prior to 0730 to tell Red that he was setting up an unrep for noon that day with USS MONONGAHELA (AO-42). As he left combat, Red gave Dillan a wink. *OK, here we go.*

When Dillan got to radio, sure enough, there was a message on the boards to MONONGAHELA requesting a rendezvous and fuel. Dillan worked in radio, distributing the next day's key cards and codes since they changed at 0000 Zulu time, or 0800 local. He did this every day. And he worried.

If this works out that I get the XO to coach, then I have to do it well. And if Fred is there yelling in my ear, I still have to do it well. Got yourself between a rock and a hard place again. Bloody brilliant. But you really don't have a lot of options. Dig deep boy. Yes, you can. Stop being a whimp.

Lunch in the wardroom was at 1115, a half hour early and was rushed a bit.

At 1200, "Now station the underway replenishment detail, now station the underway replenishment detail for refueling."

Dillan went to the bridge. The AO was visible and LARTER was headed for waiting station. There were no other ships unreping. It was a relatively nice day, just a little sea running from the Northeast. As Dillan relieved the JOOD, who had the conn, he learned that the signaled unrep course was 030, speed 10.

Slow also. I can do this he thought – hopefully with out Fred!

Completing the formality of changing of the guard, Dillan had the conn and slowed to 10 knots, swinging into waiting station 500 yards back and a bit right of the oiler on the same course.

From the captain's chair, "Well, Mr. Dillan, now it's daylight, ready to make an approach?"

"Yes sir," Dillan said. Fred looked surprised.

"XO, you be the coach. Time you learned some more about the abilities of our JO's."

Jack pot.

"Ops, you watch the helm."

Dillan and the XO went out on to the port bridge wing, Dillan trying not to look at Fred. Dillan stepped up onto the single step platform next to the wing pelorus, opened the voice tube and put the funnel on it. He took in a big breath of the salt air. Humid, but it was clean and clear. The Romeo (R) flag was at the dip on the AO's starboard yardarm flag halyard; this meant preparing to do underway replenishment.

Then he leaned over to put his mouth near the tube and said, "Helm, voice tube check."

The helmsman said, "Loud and clear, Mr. Dillan."

The XO leaned over to Dillan and said quietly, "OK Dillan, tell me your plan."

Dillan stepped down and said, "Once the AO two blocks[lviii] Romeo, I'll increase speed to 13 knots and start forward, watching for the AO's stern prop bubble, so it doesn't pull us in. I may have to come right a degree, then back to base course when her stern is about amidships. I'll then slow enough to insure that I don't go by, probably dropping to 11 knots. As we get alongside, I'll drop to 10 and try to be 200 feet away, adding or dropping turns, and coming left or right a half degree or so, to end up with our bow just behind the AO's bow wave. By then the distance line should be in hand, and I'll keep station right there."

"Very good. But we want to be 150 feet away. Sea conditions are very good and it makes handling those hoses a lot easier for the crew."

"Yes, sir." The Romeo flag went all the way up on the AO. Romeo closed up meant replenishment operations were in progress.

"OK, Mr. Dillan, make it so," the XO said. The skipper was standing on the wing also, arms folded on top of the wind brake, looking at the AO. It was bright, but no real sun, the Tonkin Gulf haze.

Now's the time.

He stepped up, "All ahead standard, indicate turns for 13 knots," he said into the voice tube. "Come left steer 027."

LARTER started forward. Dillan felt the AO's props pull the bow a little. The Romeo flag was all the way up on LARTER also.

"Come right steer 030, all ahead two thirds, turns for 11 knots."

Slowly LARTER crept forward.

"Indicate turns for 10 knots, come right steer 031."

Dillan thought he was a little close. The XO said, "I would stay at 029. You need to move in a little."

"Come left, steer 029 and a half, add two turns." LARTER was drifting back a little. "Come right, steer 030."

The distance line was over. It showed 160 feet.

Not bad. Seems a lot closer.

LARTER was on station.

"Good, Mr. Dillan, now that wasn't all that hard was it?" the skipper remarked. "Now keep us here."

"Yes, sir," from Dillan, eyes swinging from the distance line to the surging water between the ships. Other lines were fired using line handling guns from LARTER to the AO, then messenger lines followed by the heavy wires were pulled back to LARTER.

"Now the smoking lamp is out throughout the ship while taking on fuel," was passed. The signal bridge ran up the Bravo flag, indicating fuel or ammo transfer in progress.

The "smoking lamp" was another old Navy tradition. In the days of sail, a smoking lamp was used to light the crew's pipes. If it was out, no smoking was allowed. In 1968, most of the officers and crew smoked, usually cigarettes. Cigarettes were cheap, a carton for $1 when purchased at the ship's store at sea. And smoking tended to help keep one awake.

Navy fuel oil, officially Navy Distillate, the more refined fuel used in 1968, was not all that volatile. At room temperature one could probably drop a lit cigarette into it and the cigarette would just go out. But prudence dictated caution. JP5 was a bit more volatile, but LARTER didn't need any this time.

Smoking was authorized in all but a few spaces. Precluded in berthing areas after taps, and in ammunition areas or when transferring fuel. Most spaces, including the bridge and combat, had round metal 'butt kits' that served as ash trays.

The ship was well ventilated, but combat would get smoky sometimes, especially when a butt kit caught fire and filled the space with a stench. Someone would poor a half a cup of coffee into the small hole in the butt kit's lid to put the fire out. It made a mess to clean up later. Smoking was precluded during general quarters, during meals in the wardroom, and at other times.

The skipper and Fred did not smoke. All the other officers did to some extent. Dillan was a pack a day man, usually Salem, if he couldn't get Newport Menthol filters like his wife smoked. The menthol helped with the chronic sore throat he got if he smoked regular filters. Many of the enlisted smoked unfiltered Camels or Pall Mall. They were too strong for Dillan.

Once the wires were in hand and connected, the black hoses were slid over to LARTER, draped on saddles riding the wire. For the next hour Dillan kept station on the oiler, XO beside him. A tiny screw up when the wires and hoses were across could ruin your entire day. A ship couldn't just sit there. It took effort to stay. The AO would wander a bit. A larger than normal wave, hitting both ships bow on would slow LARTER more than it would the heavier oiler, so one had to be tweaking all the time.

"OK," the XO said, "How are you going to get us out of here, Dillan?"

"Once all the wires and lines are clear, I'll come right 2 degrees and increase speed to 15 knots. It'll take a while for the speed to build. The oiler's bow wave will push our bow out another degree or more. I'll have to watch to insure our stern doesn't come close to the AO's bow. Once our stern is past her bow, I'll increase to 20, and we'll go out about 1500 yards before we come left to get back on track for North SAR."

"Very good, the lines are all clear, there goes the distance line, get us out of here."

"All engines ahead standard, indicate turns for 15 knots." Dillan waited a few seconds until he could see LARTER moving forward.

"Come right steer 032. One short blast on the ship's whistle."

He could hear the house flag flutter above him from the signal bridge; a puff of black smoke from the #1 funnel; a short blast.

The skipper stood at attention and gave a snappy salute to the AO's skipper on the AO's starboard bridge wing. AO's were considered deep draft vessels and had 1st or 2nd year full Navy Captains for skippers. The AO's skipper returned the salute.

Once clear of the AO's bow, "Right 5 degrees rudder, come right, steer 040."

From the helmsman, "My rudder is right 5 degrees, coming to 040, sir."

"All ahead full, indicate turns for 20 knots."

"All engines ahead full, indicate turns for 20 knots, sir."

"Engine room answers all ahead full, turns for 20 knots, sir."

"Steady 040, checking 043."

"Very well."

"OK Mr. Dillan, you did well," from the skipper as he walked back into the bridge. "A little tentative in the approach and the break away, but well; doing it with a little more destroyer flare will come with experience, huh XO?"

"A little tentative, careful. I like my JOs careful, Captain. Then experience will allow more zip," from the XO.

"Secure the underway replenishment detail, set the regular Condition III watch."

As they left the bridge, Fred said, "About time Dillan. Thought I was going to be admiral before you got up enough nerve to make an approach. But that was an easy one, ought to try one down wind at night."

Screw you very much, sir

Verbally, "Yes, sir."

Hope you get a personality transplant prior to making admiral. That would be a major operation, maybe have to replace your entire head. Maybe I should take up a collection. Bet most of the men on this ship will contribute.

After he was relieved, Dillan walked out the back of the 02 deck, leaned against the rail and looked aft: pale grey haze coming out of the stacks, and some FTs with a panel open working on the ASROC launcher. The AO was disappearing astern, LARTER's white wake converging in the distance and more sun than normal. A warm wind; he took off his ball cap. The breeze felt good ruffling his short hair, a few deep breaths of the salt air.

Did well, thank God that first one is behind me. It wasn't as bad as I thought it was going to be and, without the yelling, I felt a lot more confident. The XO made me feel confident.

One of the ship's IC strikers came up the ladder, carrying a black multimeter, and a tool belt hanging from his hip. Dillan looked at his name stenciled on his shirt.

Dillan said, "Hey, Moraski, chasing grounds on the sound powered circuits, again?"

"Yes, sir, Mr. Dillan. Seems like a never ending battle."

"Understood. Back when I was an EM striker, a million years ago, my 3rd used to make me do it. Not one of my favorite jobs."

"Yeah, I'd rather PMS[lix] the internal circuits. Salt air raises hell with the top side ones."

"Make third, and someone else will get the opportunity," as he replaced his hat and turned around.

"Yes, sir, maybe in the fall."

Dillan turned and walked back to the 02 hatch. The man went up to the signal bridge to continue his work.

37

Back to radio, Dillan had an hour or so before he had to be back in combat. He intended to thank Red then.

The next 20 hours were without incident. There was a meeting in combat for evaluators and CIC watch officers held by Fred. The CO and XO were there also even if they did not actually present. Going over the CTF 77 Operations Order related to North SAR again.

Dillan talked to Tony, "How goes the investigation?"

"Looks like Fister's in deep shit. Over the past two weeks Fredrick has been hit on a lot, and Fister even was waiting by Fredrick's rack after the 20-24, night before last. MM2 Bond warned Fister and roughed him up a little – but he kept it up. The CO is going to set up a summary and Chris will have to do it."

"Fister still in the brig?"

"Yeah, still protective custody. XO thinks if we let him out he's headed for an accident."

"How's Fister coping locked up?'

"He knows he'll get his clock cleaned if he's out and about. So he just reads and sleeps. Wouldn't admit anything to me, just said he really liked Fredrick, and was trying to be friendly."

"Yea, waiting by his rack - real friendly - the pervert. Good to keep him on ice. Someone may just schedule an unauthorized swim call. When's the summary?"

"Sometime tomorrow. Meanwhile he stays in the cooler."

Dillan spent time in radio and even a couple of hours in the ET shack with Pete and his ETs and the chief ET, getting the radios ready and aligned for SAR. LARTER would be copying 12 UHF voice circuits, and so all the radios had to be working well. The ET's were going to 6 on and 6 off watches in the shack to keep after them 24/7 with enough staff each shift to add 30% to their maintenance workforce. Not a lot of sleep but what was required. The ET berthing area would be designated a day sleeper area.

Then Dillan spent some time on the signal bridge. The signalmen reported to him, but they had a super first class that ran the show up there. Dillan let him mostly run the place, a good group.

Signalmen took care of all the non radio communications outside the ship. They looked after the search lights with shutters for sending Morse code by flashing light, and the 'flag bags,' large lockers, port and starboard, where the letter and number signal flags were kept. In the days before radio, signal flags were the primary means of communication and there was a signal book that showed all kinds of signals made up of two or more signal flags. This book was even used on the PriTac radio circuit: Allied Tactical Publication II.

When LARTER was in company with a task group, transiting like to Formation Star, signals from this book were what were used to station screening destroyers and cruisers. There were also tons of administrative signals. These were used seldom, if ever. The task group UHF teletype net was encrypted and was used for most administration.[lx]

There were only 7 signalmen aboard, including the 1st class. Although LARTER rated a chief, Dillan was sure the 1st class would make chief soon.

Then there would be a chief's initiation as the other chief's aboard put the new, or boot chief, through hell for a few hours at the chief's club. Dillan had been dragged into one of these initiations as 'Defense Counsel' for one of the guys from the ET gang who had made chief the previous summer.

Damn expensive since the 'judge,' the senior chief aboard, a gnarly old Master Chief Machinist Mate, had fined the hell out of Dillan every time he opened his mouth in the boot chief's defense. It was traditional and expensive for the boot chief's division officer to be defense counsel. The fines paid the bar bill. Other officers, like Fred and the XO were invited.

Fred thought it was an "archaic tribal rite" and hated attending, but the XO insisted. He got fined a bit also, although it sure didn't hurt his net worth. Even the XO got fined. But Dillan took most of the crap from the judge. Dillan even got fined for being dumb enough to give up a perfectly good enlisted career to become a lowly Ensign – something all attending got a big kick out of. When the next chief's list was promulgated, Dillan was sure his 1st class signalman would be on it.

Better save up.

Around noon the next day, March 24, 1968, LARTER arrived at North SAR. There was a strike headed in but no SAR situation was expected for a couple of hours since the strike had just left Yankee Station, and the morning strike was marshalling for recovery.

With weather conditions good, LARTER lowered her motor whale boat and Fred and the XO went over to MENAUL. They were gone just over an hour and then back. KINKAID had also sent a boat. It was as close to a relieving ceremony as there was to be. By Dillan's 16-20 CIC watch, LARTER was it and KINKAID was headed south.

When Dillan assumed the watch, there was a SAR situation being coordinated by MENAUL. He had been briefed that an A-4 Skyhawk was shot up and had gotten out over the water after a strike on a bridge in the North Vietnamese pan handle. He was being picked up by the helo out of DaNang. No trouble from any North Vietnamese boats.

Once it got dark, CIC was quiet and all professional. Extra lookouts were on the signal bridge wearing sound powered phones and scanning the sea with binoculars. Everyone was a bit jumpy.

This is what we trained for. I doubt that there is fear in the troops. Hell, we know we're good at what we do. Besides, bad things happen to others, never to us. Rationalizing, Dillan, but necessary mental hygiene.

Chris came into combat to check the intel skeds. When quietly questioned by Dillan, Chris would say nothing about Fister's summary.

"Can't comment until the skipper approves the verdict," was his answer.

Red and Dillan talked their watch people through how to tell the difference between a surface contact and a friendly helicopter. Friendly helo pilots took a real dim view of being mistaken for a PT boat and getting shot at. And on a surface radar scope, a low flying helo and a PT boat at speed looked a lot alike.

But the helos went faster and knew that they needed to go faster, especially at night. So the key was to get a course and speed on a contact quickly. If it was going slower than 30 knots, expect it to be unfriendly. Faster than 50 knots and it was most probably a friendly helo.

The helos at night also tried to keep in radio contact and to identify themselves and their positions on a regular basis. Not that there were a lot of helos running around after dark. Almost never. Strikes normally went in at dawn or mid afternoon. Hard to see targets well enough in the dark. They were watched on the air search radar.

The MENAUL had a 'Tacan.' A Tacan was like civil aviation's Omnirange system. It sent out a VHF radio signal that could be received by US aircraft. The receiving instrument on the air craft would convert this signal to a bearing from the transmitter. There was also an enhancement to this signal that the civilian world called DME, or distance measuring equipment.

This would give the air craft's pilot a range to the transmitter. This was very handy. An aircraft could come up on the radio and say, "on your 230 radial at 12" which translated meant that the aircraft was bearing 230, range 12 miles from the Tacan transmitting ship.

It sure made it easier to sort one particular aircraft from all the other ones seen on the air search scope, and the helos would use it to vector themselves to North SAR for refueling and for keeping the ships aware of their location at night.

An air search scope did not present targets as blips. They were more like bananas, or little arches, fatter in the middle and hooked down a bit at the small end, like little quarter moons with the inside of the curve facing the center of the scope. The further away, the larger and fainter the banana.

The actual aircraft being painted was at the center of the inside edge of the arch. This was because long range air search radar ran at relatively low frequencies for radar, pumped out a lot of power, and had a slower sweep or antenna rotation rate and wider lobe patterns in the signal.

There was a story that if one was standing in front of an air search radar antenna when it was radiating, that they would become sterile.

Yea, right, first get blind, then dead, then sterile.

A lot of microwave power.

Since LARTER could be a minimum of 12 miles off North Vietnam, and since North Vietnam was quite mountainess, especially the northern portion, an air search radar would paint mountains as airplanes, and anything over land would be lost in the massive clutter. But with the 'moving target indicator' on, only targets that actually moved would paint. Dillan could sit at an air scope and watch strikes going in.

It was a jumpy watch but no real excitement. Dillan went down to radio, wrote a letter, mostly "I love you and miss you stuff", and hit the rack.

God, I miss her. Get this SAR thing completed, then home-ward bound. Home! Yes.

No excitement or gun fire overnight. When Dillan relieved for the 04-08 watch, he was told that the 20-24 had a few tense moments when a slow speed contact showed up about 20,000 yards (10 miles) out at 346 and faded in and out and wandered around a bit out there. The evaluator, Chris Harcourt, had thought about opening up on it if it had gotten into 18,000 yards, but that didn't happen.

Fred was the off-going evaluator from the mid watch and said all had been quiet on his watch. No verbal shots at Dillan.

Maybe he is too tired?

38

By 0600 the strikes were on again. Lots of aircraft headed inbound to rearrange Hanoi: real estate redevelopment by explosives. LARTER was ordered to move 20 miles west to a position about 15 miles off shore. By the time Dillan was relieved, he could see the mountains on the coast north of Haiphong on the surface search radar screen, if he cranked the range out.

There were some small targets fading in and out just about 6 miles from shore, and CIC watched these very carefully. Probably just fishing boats, but the bad guys had been known to hide among the fishing fleet. The radar was very well tuned to paint these small targets at extreme range.

Dillan went down to the wardroom, got a cup of coffee, and then back up to radio. While in the wardroom the XO was there, getting coffee, also.

"Any excitement up top?" he asked as he poured a cup from the side handled pitcher. Dillan told him that he could see the mountains on the scope. "Never seen it," the XO said. "I guess I'll look in on combat and see what's up."

The XO is a nice guy. LARTER had gotten lucky. Two good XO's in a row.

When Dillan got to radio, the chief was there and the chief ET also.

"Mr. Dillan, we lost the main broadcast at sunrise, and then the secondary went down for a bit. We got'm back but missed 8 numbers that we just couldn't get from the backup. MENAUL lost both for even longer and we're checking the numbers we have to help them. We're going to have to send a message to PHIL to check the missing ones. MENAUL'll transmit it for us."

"Thanks, Chief, why is Chief Summer here?" Dillan asked.

"I asked him to come up. We're going to try and look at the spectrum for better frequencies. When the sun comes up, propagation gets messed up real bad, but maybe we can find something that'll hold the signal."

The ET chief must be very good tuning broadcast receivers, and that is respected by the radio chief. When the skipper, or

Fred, finds out about MENAUL's message to NAVCOMSTAPHIL, I can expect a question. MENAUL will send it 'radio to radio.' Even so, I better give them a head's up. The poor propagation conditions reported previously are rearing their ugly head again.

Fred will make a fuss, but he will be really bent if he finds out from someone other than me. And some of the radiomen might spill the beans just to get on Fred's good side. Fred is a bit of a pain in the butt about recommending people for advancement, so some think a little brownnosing might pay off. Not that it ever had.

Dillan went to find Fred. He was in his stateroom/office. Once Dillan told him, Fred bristled.

"I thought I told you to keep that from happening?"

Yea, right, I am supposed to do something like keep the sun from coming up.

"We're doing out best, but we do not have control over the ionosphere," Dillan said.

"Don't get smart with me. Your job is to keep this ship in communications. You better do it. Now get back up there and insure that they are doing everything possible, Mr. Dillan."

God, Fred never changes.

"Yes, sir," and back to radio.

At least one broadcast stayed up long enough to keep from missing numbers for the rest of that day. Dicey, a time or two, and thank God for the back up broadcast. And for the chiefs, who chased frequencies most of the day and into the night. Once the sun went down, things stabilized.

When Dillan went back up for the 16-20, strikes were over, no SAR action, and LARTER was back steaming around at 5 knots about 2500 yards from MENAUL. It was a quiet watch and no sneaky little surface contacts.

After watch, Dillan ran into Tony. "Fister was found guilty of conduct unbecoming and will be helo transferred tomorrow to a carrier and then a COD to Subic. Headed for a general discharge. Skipper approved."

Good. Get him off the ship quick like before this thing turns ugly. If the troops get him alone, bad things might happen.

"Thanks, Tony."

"My den mother's job."

It was 2130, and Dillan just in his rack for almost 6 hours sleep.

"Bong bong bong bong ... General quarters, general quarters, all hands man your battle stations." *Oh shit!*

When Dillan got to combat, the XO was there and the CO. All staring at the surface scope. Dillan could see a grease pencil plot on the scope face showing a relatively slow moving contact closing slightly at 18,000 yards, bearing 275.

The electronic warfare (EW) technicians had reported a possible "Pot Drum" radar on roughly the same bearing. But it came and went. The older Pot Drums were enemy patrol craft surface search radars, named for the round dome that covered the antenna. The newer version, called 'Skin Head', was on the Komar and Osa class missile boats: bad news. According to Pete, this one drifted around in frequency and was probably an older and not very well maintained one. Asked how sure he was that it was a Pot Drum, Pete said 60% confidence factor, not very sure.

Since they had been on North SAR, they had picked up some weak surface search and air search land based radars. Pete's GQ station was in the electronic warfare (EW) shack, which was manned by men who were specially trained and could use their equipment to receive and analyze incoming radar signals.

Most radar had a specific frequency range and pulse repetition rate. So a type could be identified. The EW equipment would also give a bearing to the transmitter. Not real accurate, and of course, since it was passive, there was no range information available. One made a guess based on signal strength.

The skipper looked at the surface scope for awhile and then said,

"That's a P-6 testing the water XO. Let's go get the little bastard!"

How did the skipper know for sure it was a P-6 patrol craft? Yes, it had to be bigger than a junk and made of metal to give a small clean blob on the radar return. And what would a fishing boat be doing all the way out here alone, with maybe a Soviet Pot Drum radar?

There was zero intel on any freighter inbound for Haiphong. And a freighter would be a lot larger blob and be using another larger radar for surface search. Process of elimination? Experience?

The XO went to the encrypted voice handset, "MENAUL, LARTER, prosecuting a surface contact at 275, range 18,000 yards, over."

"MENAUL, roger, out."

"I'm going on the bridge; you may commence fire when we get to 16,000 yards, XO. I'll go at him slow, say 15 knots, do not want to spook him if he sees us coming full bore. Feed him VT frag, Chris, and I'll go around to his north so we can unmask both mounts and see any buddies he has. If he turns towards us or MENAUL, or increases speed, give it to him."

Then turning to Dillan, "Keep a sharp eye out for company. Most of these people don't try this alone, got that Dillan?"

"Yes, sir."

The skipper left. "Captain left combat," from the messenger.

"Combat, bridge, coming to new course 285, speed 15."

Dillan could feel the heel and the slight speed vibration increase.

Four minutes to firing range. This really is shoot first and ask questions afterwards!

As Dillan watched, the little blob on the screen started to drift left of track.

"Bridge combat, skunk November is in a port turn, looks like the same speed. He may be turning towards the MENAUL," Dillan said into the 21MC. Using the maneuvering board to refine the new course and speed, Dillan was a bit surprised when,

"Gun director has locked on," Chris said.

The FTs have been keeping it in excellent tune. Good for them, nothing like being in a real combat environment to focus the mind.

"Let'm have it," said the XO. Not quite to the 16,000 yard mark, maybe closer to 16,900.

"Mount 51, rapid and continuous fire, VT frag, commence fire."

A moment, then, bang bang bang...the ship shook.

From the bridge, "Coming to 300."

Trying to unmask mount 52? That'll take awhile. The contact's off the port bow now. LARTER is on a course that ultimately will allow both mounts to fire, but not for a long time.

This went on for another couple of minutes. Range now 13,800 yards. Bang, bang, bang. Slight smell of cordite in the air-conditioned atmosphere now. Dillan could feel the vibrations in the deck through his shoes. *We're really giving it to that P-6.*

"Mr. Dillan, the contact has changed course to starboard, and his speed is increasing. Looks like he's bugging out," the scope operator said.

Dillan watched as the grease pencil dots placed on the scope's plastic face by the operator showed a hook to the contact's right.

"Combat, bridge, the lookout reports an explosion off the port bow and an orange glow on the horizon."

"We hit him, XO," from Chris.

"Don't just concentrate on November", Dillan said to the scope operator, "keep a sharp eye out for his friends."

Not quite a minute later, "Director has lost lock on".

Chris said, "Cease fire. Cease fire." Mount 52 never got a shot off.

"Combat, bridge, the orange glow has faded."

"Mount 51 reports 148 rounds expended, bores clear, no causalities."

Being on the receiving end of all that hot shrapnel, almost 8,000 pounds shredding your boat, would not be fun. Turn the ocean into froth like a blender set on frappe. And at 13,000 yards, LARTER was quite close. Just over 6 miles away. Shots, with a director lock on a target, would be close to right on top.

Dillan had seen 20 rounds chop up a towed sled target at 10,000 yards when the required offset had not been dialed in during REFTRA. One was not supposed to blow up the target sled. One was to dial in an offset in the computer, so shots went behind the sled. Skipper had to apologize to the tug and was not amused.

From the scope operator, "Skunk November faded." Dillan leaned way over to confirm. When the sweep went by, there was nothing on the scope where November had been. The XO leaned over also. They carefully watched two more sweeps.

The XO got on the 21 MC. "Bridge, combat, we've lost lock on and the contact seems to have disappeared from the radar scope."

"Bridge, roger that. We were watching the orange glow. When it faded, we figured that he went down," from Fred.

Mount 51 reported a foul bore. Chris said, "Bridge, combat, we have a projectile in 51 port. We intend to use a short charge to expel."

Mount 51 had loaded one gun just prior to ceasefire. It was a hot gun, and once the projectile lands started to engage the rifling, there was no extracting it. *Why had they reported bores clear?*

"Bridge aye, skip the short charge; train 045 relative, max elevation and fire."

"Weapons, aye."

The projectile was expelled, this time it went out without a close aboard detonation.

"Combat, bridge, coming to 120, speed 10."

LARTER headed back to station, but slowly in case another P-6 showed up. Radar operator intent over his scope with the RD1 standing over his right shoulder.

Good. We don't want to feel so smug over sinking the first one that another gets to sneak up close.

"Captain's in combat," the watch messenger announced.

"Anything else out there we can shoot up tonight, XO?"

"Not that we can see, Captain."

"Good shooting, Weaps, and the rest of you," waving his arm. "I think we must've set off one of his torpedoes. The orange glow was probably the end of him."

Then to the XO, "XO, it looked like a P-6 huh, what do you think?"

"Probably Captain, about the right size return, with the Pot Drum it was a give away. And that turn towards us was a give away. When he decided to get the hell out of Dodge, he kicked it up to over 20 knots just prior to going sinker, and when we got a secondary, another indication. Yeah, probably a P-6 out to make a name for himself."

The captain said, "He gets a name alright, on a temple wall some where. Sure would like to go over there and do a search light drill for debris. You got a position plot on the datum, didn't you, Dillan?"

Although datum was an anti-submarine warfare term, here the skipper meant where the contact was when it disappeared from the scope so that the location could be found. Since the ship had been firing and running at the contact on a relative basis, geographical data was not used.

But to find the location again, geographical data would be important. All Dillan could do is to take some guesses based on LARTER's assumed geographical position when the fun started, her courses and speeds since then, and the range and bearing from LARTER when the contact faded. The resultant position was 'datum.'

"Yes, sir, at least a good approximation," Dillan said.

"Good. We'll put it in the after action report. Ops will be in once we get GQ secured. XO, we will be going back to station on MENAUL. She is probably getting nervous without her hired gun by her side. Then maybe in the morning we can get a helo over for a look see. What do you think, XO? Maybe we should change our call sign to 'Paladin', you know – have gun, will travel." Reference to a 1950's TV western.

I enjoyed that show. All black outfit. 'A knight without armor in a savage land.' Richard Boone.

The skipper was bubbling over. The first encounter at sea and a probable kill. A kill that did not get an opportunity to get close enough to shoot back. Dillan was surprised that the P-6 was alone. Usually it was a matched pair, from the intel reports.

A few minutes later GQ was secured. Dillan had to wait for Fred to give him the plot data. Chris had this watch anyway so he let Dillan go first.

Fred said, "Well, Mr. Dillan, think you know where the P-6 was when he went down?"

"I have made an approximation from our DR track," Dillan said.

"Approximations are fine for enlisted men, Mr. Dillan. But professional officers have to be far more accurate than that. Show me what you have done."

So Dillan went over it with Fred, seething inside.

Fred accepted it with a frown.

"I guess we'll just have to run with what you've got, could have been a lot more accurate."

Then Dillan went below for some rack time. This was going to be another 3 and one half hour night. But Fred had the mid. He would get no sleep till 0400, and then only 3 hours.

Dillan ran into Eric in the stateroom. Eric looked like he had taken a shower with his uniform on. Smelled like a wet dog.

"Took your sweet time chasing that P-6 off," he said, pealing his shirt off.

"We sank his ass. Stuck in main control for the duration, huh? Thought you had AC in the hole?"

"Yea, when the damn thing works. Broke again, hot and crowded. To think people actually pay to sit in a sauna. What took so damn long?"

"Wasn't long, just seemed like it. Initially he wouldn't fess up and wanted to play hide and seek. Sorry. My butt's dragging. Need some serious rack time. I've got to be back up there for the 4 to 8."

"OK, OK, but next time sink the bastard quicker so I can get out of the hole more. Really feel like a gopher."

The engineers had to go down a scuttle into the engineering spaces and called it the gopher hole.

"At least you're a short gopher and being in the hole, you get more damn sleep than I do."

"Not short enough, and being a sewer rat (another name for the engineers) is getting old," climbing up into his top rack.

Dillan was asleep before Eric turned his bunk light out. Slept like a brick.

39

Dillan's 04 – 08 watch was uneventful. He really had to hit the coffee to keep awake. At 1000 the next morning, MENAUL had a helo from the carrier take a look. It took the helo a bit of a search to finally find the remains. Yes, it was a P-6, or at least the bits floating on the surface looked like they came from a P-6.

Must have been shredded like cabbage for cole slaw.

Heavy bits like hulls, engines, guns, etc. sank. Usually not much left on the surface. But the helo found some of the NVA block cork life vests, one occupied by a deceased individual face down wearing the odd khaki/blue/grey of the NVA naval branch, papers, an oil slick, and some other unidentified flotsam.

Not being float equipped, the helo could only look, photograph, but not recover. And when it got close, the rotor wash blew stuff around a bit. MENAUL sent out an after action report to CTF 77 calling it a confirmed sinking of a North Vietnamese P-6 patrol boat that was closing on North SAR.

Feather in cap for the skipper.

The helo refueled from LARTER and took Fister onboard.

At lunch the skipper said, "OK, Weaps, get your gunners mates to paint a P-6 silhouette on the director."

There are a couple of those around on other destroyers, but not many. Will be a nice topic of conversation when the skipper is having a drink with his peers in Subic.

A couple of uneventful days, with the exception of the sunrise broadcast unreliability. Another 15 missed one morning. MENAUL missed 12. MENAUL did the radio to radio thing to NAVCOMSTAPHIL. Dillan told Fred and got a scowl but no ass chewing this time. The skipper was less generous.

"Damn it, isn't there anything you can do to stop this crap?"

"We're doing all we can think of and then some, Captain."

"Better be," was the retort.

He had been in such a good mood after the P-6 incident. Now a bit grumpier than normal. Wonder what's bugging him?

It was 1100, day three after the P-6 incident. LARTER had just refueled a helo. Dillan was in combat making sure the code books were turned to the correct page. Not that it was his job, but he liked to check now and then. It saved time if a location code, or authentication, needed broken in a hurry. And the code book page changed every day. He would put the black metal clip over the current time.

There was a small strike underway over the outskirts of Haiphong, and LARTER was 10 miles west of MENAUL. Chris Harcourt and Ted Brunshall had the watch.

From over the "Guard" radio speaker came:

"Mayday, mayday, mayday. This is Redrobin six. I'm hit; I'm hit, losing altitude. Don't know if I can make it to the coast."

Guard was 243 MHz, the military air distress frequency. There was also a VHF distress – International Air Distress, 121.5 MHz.

"Redrobin six, Kingfisher on guard, state position, and fuel state, over."

Kingfisher was the assigned search and rescue CAP. Up for each strike, SAR CAP orbited just off shore and were there to help pilots with a problem. They were usually F-4 Phantoms, but sometimes, the older F-8U Crusader. The Crusader was the preferred air craft for this mission, since it was smaller and more maneuverable than the F-4. Typically armed with Zuni rocket pods and lots of 20mm cannon ammo. It was also there to deter enemy patrol craft or fast junks trying to scoop up air crew who managed to punch out over water. The F-8s, like the F-4s, could be refueled in flight.

"Kingfisher, Redrobin leader, six is 10 miles from the coast heading 110 about 20 klicks south of harbor entrance, over."

Chris had grabbed the call sign book.

"Redrobin is an A-4 flight off the TICONDEROGA," he said.

"Kingfisher, roger, six say state, over."

"Six, loosing altitude fast."

"Six, leader, have to leave you with SAR CAP. No juice. Hang in there Longhorn, you will make it."

"Roger, leader, keep your fingers crossed. Lots of vibration."

"Kingfisher, Redrobin leader, am breaking off; take care of Longhorn, over.

"Roger that leader, Redrobin six, say state, over."

"Six, this bitch doesn't want to fly anymore, help meeee!"

The hit the Skyhawk had taken was probably ground fire and not a missile. If it had been a SAM, an instant punch out was typical, if the pilot survived the missile hit. So his aircraft was still flyable – at least somewhat. His engine might have ingested some metal and was not delivering the thrust required to keep flying fast enough to maintain altitude. Panic in his voice.

Just like it would be in mine, if I was in his fix.

"This is Kingfisher; we'll get you a ride. Hang on and get your feet wet, say state, over."

From the encrypted voice circuit, "LARTER this is MENUAL. We have a SAR situation. Move towards a position 15 miles off the coast bearing 295, range 15 miles from your current position, best speed, contact Kingfisher on guard, over."

Chris answered, and then passed the information to the bridge on the 21 MC. He then called Kingfisher on guard and told him LARTER was enroute.

The bridge came to 295 at 25 knots. Reality was that without superheat, maybe 20, assuming a quick light off, the last of the run towards station would be faster. LARTER was roughly 45 minutes from station.

There was some more chatter on guard, Kingfisher trying to keep Redrobin's hopes up. There was still no answer on state. Redrobin indicated that he was whole – was not wounded. Voice was calmer.

Finally, "Redrobin six, feet wet about 3 miles out, down to angels 2, bitch is vibrating apart. I'm out of here. Somebody please come get me!"

"This is Kingfisher; roger, can you give me a position over." No answer. Redrobin had punched out at 2000 feet, roughly 3 miles from the coast. SAR CAP was going to have to find him. It would not be hard once his chute opened. The A-4 did a nose down right roll and impacted the sea surface. Sank like a brick.

Dillan looked up. The captain and the XO were standing there. Dillan had not heard the obligatory "Captain's in combat."

The skipper must have stifled the messenger. Dillan stood in a corner.

This is not my watch and I do not want to be in the way.

From the encrypted voice, "LARTER this is MENAUL. We have a pilot in the drink. CAP confirms a good chute. Position 3.6 miles off the coast, bearing 279, range twenty point four miles from your position. I am vectoring Ploughman 3 to that location. Continue at best speed to take up station 12 miles off coast, over."

Chris answered again. LARTER was headed for a spot 3 miles closer.

Dillan figured Ploughman 3 was a helo configured for SAR from Yankee Station. It was normal for one or more to be sent up as a strike went in, to be controlled by MENAUL. MENAUL and LARTER could also refuel them and did a lot. They only had a 170 mile range and burned 70 of that up enroute from the carrier. So they refueled upon arrival.

The skipper said, "This is the area where the little yellow bastards hide the fast junks in among the fishing ones. We need to be prepared to put down some covering fire."

Then he walked over to the 21 MC and said, "Bridge, this is the captain, set general quarters. Come to 279 and get main control to give you all they can. Take her up to 27 knots, more when you can on all 4. Push her, but don't break anything."

Main control is going to light off the other 2 boilers and push superheat. They have a chart on just how much fuel they can burn without pushing cold boiler tubes so fast they blow or come loose from the drums. Careful, careful!

Bong, bong, bong ... *Here we go again. At least I'm already here.*

In fact, as far as the officers were concerned, combat was almost manned already. Chris, Ted who looked after the air picture at GQ, Dillan who looked after the surface picture, and the XO as evaluator. Pete was not there yet.

LARTER was still over 20 minutes away from the new station when the encrypted radio came up again, "LARTER, MENAUL. Ploughman 3 has the pilot in sight but has taken fire from one of the fishing boats 3 miles north."

That boat may have a 12.7mm AA gun, good for maybe 1500 yards max so he sure is not going to hit the helo unless he gets closer; maybe just an intimidation trick. Spray a few tracers around and keep the helo away.

"LARTER, MENAUL, I am vectoring SAR CAP to make some low passes and see if they can sort out the bad ones. I have pulled Ploughman back. Be prepared to provide covering fire on arrival, over."

The XO acknowledged.

We will be shooting right over the pilot. Station will be 16,800 yards from him. Max range is 18,900 on a good day. He will sure hear the detonations.

"XO, lets go north 5 degrees to close the range to the junks. I don't want to shoot over the pilot any more than I have to," said the skipper. The XO called the bridge and made it so. Dillan checked the knot meter; they were up to 25 knots.

Less than 8 miles to station. Less than 20 minutes.

"LARTER, MENAUL. SAR CAP spotted two suspected fast junks, still among the fishing fleet but moving south. Took one under cannon fire and he returned fire. When on station, LARTER to place barrage, Ploughman will act as spotter. SAR CAP has less than 10 minutes of station time and will keep their heads down, over."

The XO answered, "Roger, out."

This was going to get touchy. The SAR CAP was low on fuel and would have to go high and find a tanker. They would orbit the pilot and make runs on the fast junks to keep them at bay. But in less than 10 minutes, they would have to go. Even with a quick refuel turn around, taking turns, the pilot was going to be vulnerable for awhile. LARTER was going to have to open fire soon.

"Weaps, set Mount 51 at elevation for max range," the skipper said. Then to Ted, "You got Ploughman on the scope, Mr. Brunshall?"

"No sir, he must be low, negative IFF."

"How about you, Dillan?"

"No sir, he's probably 15 miles away and small, no squawk."

"Damn." He grabbed the encrypted handset, "MENAUL, LARTER give me a position on Plowshare please, over."

A moment later, "Ploughman is on my 275 radial, 31 miles, you may take control when you hold him, over." The skipper had screwed up the call sign but MENAUL knew who he was talking about.

"Got that, Dillan, XO? Find him on the surface scope. Ted, any SAR CAP around that we might hit if we open up with the guns?"

"Yes, sir," from Dillan.

"No sir, they are well south now," from Ted.

Dillan did a quick plot from MENAUL, then converted it to range and bearing from LARTER. If multiple staring eyeballs straining could get the helo to show up, it would. Dillan drew a grease pencil circle on the scope face.

"If he is there he is inside that circle," Dillan said.

"LARTER, MENAUL, SAR CAP has cleared. Put down covering fire. Go get him, over." XO answered, "Roger, out."

A minute went by, seemed like an hour.

There he is!

"New contact bearing 273, range 14,300 yards, designate skunk Golf," the scope operator announced.

"Got him XO, but he fades in and out," from Dillan. "Not a skunk, I think he is a friendly, our helo," to the scope operator.

Ted transmitted, "Plowman 03, Quicksilver, check your parrot over."

"03, parrot up, sorry, over."

Dillan used the surface scope IFF. "That's him. Bearing 272, range 13,800," he said.

"Call him, Mr. Brunshall, get a range and bearing to the pilot and the fast junks."

"Yes, sir."

Ted came up on the helo air control frequency again and asked for data. The pilot was 4000 yards at 010 from Ploughman and the fast junks were 8000 yards at 020. Dillan quickly plotted this on the maneuvering board, only 4,000 yards apart.

If the junks want him they can probably go get'm. They are just over 7 minutes away if they crank it up.

The skipper took a look. "Combat, bridge, come to 310."

"Bridge Aye." They were 3000 yards from the 12 mile limit and going like hell.

The skipper is going to go in closer to the coast and keep the pilot off LARTER's port bow, running right at the junks.

"Range to the fast junks, Mr. Dillan."

"We do not hold them on radar, Captain. Estimated range 13,500 yards, bearing 302."

"Brunshall, tell the helo we're going to lay down a barrage, stay south of the pilot." When Ploughman rogered that, Ted did a thumbs up. The skipper turned to Chris,

"Weaps, commence fire, 20 rounds VT frag, at 12,000 yards and on 305." *We're firing blind.* It took a moment for Chris to set the computer, tell the mount, and then bang, bang, bang.

The skipper was watching the sweep second hand on the combat clock.

"Mount 51 reports 20 rounds expended, bores clear, no causalities."

"Weapons, 10,000 yards bearing 300 and again 20 rounds VT frag, fire when ready." A moment to set the new bearing and range and bang, bang, bang ... again. LARTER was 10 miles off shore and closing at 28 knots.

In 20 minutes we will be a landing craft on a hostile shore. Sooner if there is shoal water.

"Brunshall, have that helo go get that pilot." Then to the XO, "let's slow to 17". The XO did the 21 MC thing to the bridge. Speed started to bleed off. Dillan had been maintaining the plot as best he could.

Keep track of the pilot's assumed location, the helo, and the fast junks assumed location. Do it right, Dillan. Do it right.

"Mr. Dillan, another range and bearing to the fast junks."

"301 at 7,800, Captain. We have some small contacts on the surface scope there."

"Bridge should have visuals. Weapons 301, 7,300 yards 10 rounds VT frag, fire when ready."

"Yes, sir." Bang, bang, bang ..... It was almost point blank range.

"Combat, bridge we have a visual on the helo and some small contacts off to the right. We can see our shots detonate near them."

Silence in combat. The second hand on the clock seemed to move, oh, so slowly.

"Plowman has a swimmer in the water and is hooking up the pilot," Ted said.

"Combat, bridge, the helo dropped a swimmer."

"Mount 51 reports 10 rounds expended, bores clear, no causalities."

"Bridge, slow to 15," the skipper said into the 21MC.

"Mr. Dillan, what are those small contacts doing?"

"Nothing sir, most are just sitting there DIW. It looks like some are moving northwest now. Doesn't seem to be as many."

"Looks like our intimidation trick worked."

"They got him!" from Ted. "Bringing him into the helo now. Ploughman is bugging out to the south," Ted added. A cheer in combat.

We did it! It feels great, like winning a big game. Elation.

"Great, vector Ploughman back to MENAUL."

"XO, lets come around and head back to station, slowly." "Weaps, to mount 51, good shooting. To mount 52 sorry boys you didn't get in on this one, maybe next time. Stay ready. We may get to shoot on our way back, and you are the mount to do it."

The skipper went over and picked up the encrypted handset and called MENAUL. He filled the MENAUL's captain (and CTU 77.4.3, one and the same) in on the action. MENAUL planned to refuel the helo and vector it back to TICONDEROGA. The pilot was fine, wet, and cold, had been worried about sharks as he bobbed there in his life preserver, and had "enjoyed the fireworks."

The pilot probably never knew, unless he deduced it from the SAR CAP runs and all the VT frag a couple of miles away from him, that he came real close to having a very bad day.

Then a few minutes later, Dillan watched the helo head southeast for MENAUL on the surface scope.

LARTER had expended 50 rounds, built a wall of hot shrapnel between the fast junks and the pilot, and convinced them that they didn't want to try a pick up. Reality was that with the timing, a lot of the VT frag was quite close to the junks. And bursts were about 30 yards apart. There had been major shrapnel flying around. LARTER had saved a pilot from capture and a long stay in the Hanoi Hilton, maybe death.

A good day. We may well have ruined some North Viet-namese fisherman's day however. If one was under a burst, bye bye. That's what we're here for. Saving our pilots.

The Skipper turned as he was leaving combat, "XO, The after action report will have to say that LARTER may have violated the claimed territorial waters of North Vietnam, the 12 mile limit. At the turn we were probably less than 6 miles out in thin water. The coast was sure clear on the scope, probably a good visual from the bridge."

He continued, "Not that we give a damn, but Washington might have to answer questions when the North Vietnamese do a press release claiming that the 'American pirates violated their waters and shot up their innocent fishing boats just fishing to feed their poor families.' Ops'll be in soon to draft the report. Help him with it."

Then he was gone. "Aye, sir," from the XO to his depart-ing back.

There is always press, always a leak somewhere. This damn war is being fought in the press as much as it is here. But the reporters back home sure are not getting shot at, just reporting every action like paperback writers. Patty is seeing and reading their stuff – knowing her, probably glued to the news. Hope she remembers me telling her to believe only half the crap they put out. But which half?

Shortly thereafter, GQ was secured and Dillan had time for a quick trip to the mess decks for a cup of soup from the always available steam kettle. He didn't want to try a very late lunch in the wardroom. Then back to radio. The skipper came up on the 1MC and told the crew about the action. Cheers and lots of happy faces.

So far, LARTER had not been in a situation where she was not the 500 pound gorilla. The joke was that if you asked a 500 pound gorilla to dance, she got to lead. LARTER had been leading a lot. She had shot up a lot of countryside on NGFS and now a P-6 and some fast junks, and had never taken return fire.

When Dillan went up for the 16-20, nothing was happen-ing.

40

There was almost a week of relative quiet. LARTER had been on North SAR 18 days. Seemed like forever. One night LARTER and MENAUL took off and ran south to pick up an unrep. The AO had pushed a bit north to reduce the trip. LARTER was close to 40% then due to all the charging around. They had to send a message so noting. It was a midnight effort. It took awhile since they also had to take on JP-5 for the helos.

Dillan made his first night approach with the XO coaching without incident. Then he passed the conn to Sam who the skipper let do station keeping and the pull away, again with the XO coaching. The skipper allowed for holiday routine the next day, since so many in the crew got 3 hours of sleep or less. Dillan slept like a rock after his 04-08, slept till almost noon.

Strikes still went in but were limited to one or two a day and mostly small ones. There was an A6 strike on Hanoi one night, but no SAR situations. Every sunrise the broadcast went down, and there was a mad scramble to retrieve numbers. Many times it was noon before it settled down. Dillan kept Fred and the CO informed.

By now Fred just scowled and the CO said, "Again, Mr. Dillan?"

Dillan was coming out of the ET shack after another re-view on the URC-9 retuning – the never ending battle.

"Mr. Dillan, please report to combat." Seldom if ever did anyone use the 1MC to page anyone. It was strictly verboten by the skipper. Enlisted, if ever paged, were obliged to "lay to combat." Officers were "please report."

This must be a major awh shit.

Scramble up the two ladders, two steps at a time, a man backing out of the way, "Sorry, Mr. Dillan."

Wonder if I'm in it? Now what did I do wrong?

When he walked in, there was a SAR situation underway.

Fred was there. So were the skipper and XO. Dillan re-ported to Fred.

"Hope your air control skills are sharp," said Fred. "We have an Air Force F100 pilot down in the mountains north of

230

Haiphong, and with the weather over the mountains, this looks like a long term thing. We've decided to put you, Ted, Chief Goldman, and RD1 Foster on port and starboard, two of you per watch. Get the bubble and then get some rest, you and the chief need to be back in here in 3 hours."

"Yes, sir." *WOW! Watches 4 on and 4 off air control, must be a bunch of aircraft involved in this one for us to be using 2 controllers and probably 4 at a time on MENAUL.*

Just then on VHF air distress, "Hellfire 4, Hellfire 4, come up beeper."

Hellfire 4 was the Air Force pilot's call sign. Beeper was slang for the 121.5 MHz hand held emergency radio pilots carried in their ditch kits. A little bigger than a paperback with a pull out whip antenna and a battery. It sent out a beeping signal but could also allow for voice transmissions.

The beeper allowed SAR CAP to triangulate his position. But he was on the ground in enemy territory and he did not dare to use beeper much. It was not like the NVA didn't know about beeper and have their own ability to triangulate. So the rule for a down pilot was do a bit of beeper and then move.

Hellfire 4 was down in some rough country. He had been down about an hour. On the topographical map there were lots of mountains and valleys: some 3000 to over 4700 meters. Like 15,000 feet. It was very rough country. Like the middle of the Rocky Mountains.

And Dillan learned that there was an overcast which went part way down the mountain sides.

Getting a helo in there for a pick up is going to be hairy.

The air scope had lots of contacts. The two controllers on duty, Ted and RD1 Foster, were controlling using the radar display, and switching to IFF often. There were contacts coming and going everywhere.

Once Dillan had the bubble he went down to radio.

When he came back up for the 16-20 (at least his first 4 on 4 off was his normal watch) Dillan sat in RD1 Foster's seat. It was still warm. He had a 45 degree angle air scope, with IFF in front of him, and a radio headphone. The job was to get tankers from the carrier to refueling stations, and get tankers back to the carrier when empty.

However, with all the SAR CAP up, tankers were busy from arrival to departure at refueling station. And it took time to get tankers back and forth to the carriers. Dillan had one tanker coming, one on station refueling, and one on the way back all the time.

Grabbing the authentication code book and sliding the clip window to the current Zulu date and time, Dillan transmitted, "Whitehall 06 this is Quicksilver, new controller, I authenticate Foxtrot November as Golf Tango, over."

One used authentication, a coded letter substitution, to insure that the pilot knew that the new voice in his headset was really a bonifide controller, not some NVA English speaking turkey trying to vector an aircraft to the wrong place – like into a SAM envelope. It had happened before.

The code changed every 5 minutes, so once an enemy heard a code, he really couldn't use it to make him sound official for long. Besides, there were 5 two letter groups for each time, so it could be cross checked. And one never requested an authentication using a specific alphanumeric, since a blind request like this was never answered. Never let the enemy get you to give up good code. If one needed another station to authenticate, they just asked for authentication, and the authenticating station had to pick the alphanumeric and its correct code.

"Whitehall 06 roger." Tanker pilots, usually flying the KA-3 tankers, tended to be a bit better using radio telephone procedures than the cryptic fighter jocks.

"Whitehall 06, Quicksilver, squawk flash, over."

This was asking the pilot to turn his IFF to flash – an emergency signal that put out 5 clumps of IFF. It was great for quickly identifying which one of the multiple contacts on the screen was really him. But one only did it for a few seconds because it cluttered up everyone's screen.

"Whitehall 06, flash." *Got him.*

Dillan put the offset cursor origin on the IFF signal and then switched to normal air scope. There was Whitehall's banana paint on the air scope.

One couldn't direct aircraft very well at all using just IFF. The air search view was much more accurate showing the actual radar paint of the aircraft. And the tankers were big. Dillan was vectoring the tanker to the rendezvous spot for in flight refueling.

Once he got it there a controller on MENAUL would pick him up on another frequency and keep him on station while bringing in SAR CAP to refuel. When the tanker was getting dry he would be returned to Dillan to vector home to the Yankee Station marshalling area.

"Whitehall, Quicksilver, port 003 to station. Take angles 20."

"06," click, schuss.

OK, so much for radio telephone procedure.

Dillan had told him to turn left to course 003 (magnetic) and insure he was at 20,000 feet.

"Whitehall 06, Quicksilver, station 003 at 30, over." Bearing and range to his station.

"Whitehall 06," click.

And so it went, all watch, tankers back and forth. And in the background always,

"Hellfire 4, Hellfire 4, come up beeper."

"Hellfire 4, Hellfire 4, come up beeper."

The SAR CAP did get some responses. Then they had to ask questions by voice radio. Questions like "What is your biggest problem?" (my mortgage), or "mother's maiden name?" (Williams). This was done to insure that it really was Hellfire 4, and that he had not been captured, or killed, and some NVA guy was using his or another captured beeper to get a helo into his gun sights.

All pilots prior to take off filled out a sheet with this info on it and by a couple hours into a SAR situation, the SAR CAP had it. LARTER could not hear Hellfire 4, only the SAR CAP, so it was like listening to one side of a telephone conversation. But SAR CAP would retransmit the gist of his contact with Hellfire 4 on his controller's frequency, being careful not to say location or other information. The NVA listened to guard and as many other frequencies as they could. Air control frequencies were changed often.

Once, Hellfire 4 had indicated bad guys to his south, and SAR CAP had tried to make a run on them. But with the awful weather conditions, all they could do is drop some napalm as close to Hellfire 4's position as they dared from altitude. SAR CAP could not go flying down the valleys under the overcast. Air navigation was not good enough to drop through the overcast and end up in a valley, instead of smack into a mountaintop hidden in the clouds.

Hellfire 4 was moving around a lot to keep the NVA from finding him. And he didn't dare use the beeper much.

As night started to fall, Hellfire 4 must have just wiggled his way into cover, and did not respond. Dillan figured it was probably cold and wet there anyway.

But CTG 77.7 kept 4 SAR CAP on station, along with the required tankers.

At 1945, Ted and the RD1 were back and Dillan relinquished his seat.

Stiff, have to pee like a judge, and emotionally shot.

Dillan stumbled down to his rack and collapsed. No dinner.

Will have to get midrats. Must keep blood sugar levels up to maintain the old brain functioning well.

"Hellfire 4, Hellfire 4, come up beeper" running through his head like a broken record.

At 1130 he was awakened, and was back in the saddle for another 4 hours of the same, with a cup of thick bean soup at hand.

The aircraft call signs changed, frequencies changed, and one had to keep up with each aircraft's state, along with any remaining pay load. Controllers kept a note pad to do this. They also had the aircraft ride the cursor.

The air search repeater scope had an off set cursor. One could put the origin on the aircraft's blip, and then use the cursor to point in a direction one wanted and told the aircraft to go. As the aircraft tracked to station, his blip would ride the cursor. Every minute or so, Dillan moved the origin back on the aircraft. Using the range bug on the cursor, one could determine not only direction but range from the aircraft to station. Station was a geographic position. With LARTER moving slowly, the air scope was essentially a geographic plot at distance.

Off at 0345, back at 0745. Time just went on. Dillan had no understanding of day or night. Day was when the passageway walk to combat was white light, night when it was red light. Not that he could just hit the rack between watches. One had to eat to keep energy up, and every now and then a stop in radio: conditions normal – sunrise propagation grief.

The CO, XO, Fred and other officers stopped in or had the watch every now and then. Dillan didn't hear much. With the headset on, and his mind at 20,000 feet 30 miles away, he was not really of this earth.

Amazing how one can have an out of body experience like this. I feel like I'm actually floating along above the aircraft I'm controlling, can picture it in my mind; can picture the top of the pilot's helmet. My body wants to lean into a turn.

Talking with the other AICs, Dillan learned that they all felt that way after awhile in the hot seat. Once on his way down after a watch, he ran into Red.

"How's it going up top?" Red asked.

"Lions 27, Christians 3, mid 3rd quarter," Dillan answered.

"That bad huh?"

"The crummy weather in the mountains is screwing us big time," Dillan said.

"Keep the faith, you may get him out yet."

"Right on, Red, keeping the faith. Later, I need some zzzs."

"Later."

On Dillan's watch, the RD chief, two seats but one scope to Dillan's left, was busy with helos. There was always one SAR helo on station making figure 8's in the sky about 30 miles off shore. These had to be vectored back to MENAUL or LARTER for refueling, and then back and forth to the carriers for relief every few hours. Normally he was dealing with 3.

MENAUL was controlling the SAR CAP, and usually had 3 flights of 4 in some position or heading home or coming out. SAR CAP also had responsibility for making sure the helos had some air cover. The NVA air arm didn't try to tangle with US aircraft often – very bad for their health. But one might try a low level run at an orbiting helo.

Not that this was only 3 things to control. On top of a down pilot, a SAR CAP group would be split up to do low level cloud top search, beeper triangulation, and even a suppression run, if they could find a hole. Then there was always a malfunction or two requiring one to break off and go home.

To keep a minimum of 3 on top, there was a lot of shuffling back and forth to mid air refuel. An F-8's combat radius was only about 600 miles, an F-4s, 760 miles. So some of the SAR CAP were F-4s.

With Dillan and Ted essentially off the normal watch bill, Red had shuffled things a bit. The CO did not want to give up the director officers since North SAR was still subject to night incursions. He did allow for daylight pulling of them down to relieve the JOOD sometimes. So the XO took a shift as evaluator, and Red went on the bridge, it screwed up every normal watch.

About midway through Dillan's 08-12 watch, CTU 77.4.3 decided to attempt a pick up. Hellfire 4 had come up on beeper and felt he was away from the bad guys and the overcast was breaking a little. SAR CAP got a fix and one helo was vectored in by SAR CAP and dropped slowly through the clouds into a wide spot in a valley. They ran right into NVA ground fire and got shot up quite a bit. They pulled up, and made it out to 8 miles over the sea and had to ditch. Now they had two SAR situations going at once.

SAR CAP got a fix on the down helo and MENAUL vectored another for a pick up. There were a few tense moments. The pick up helo was then vectored to MENAUL and ended up lowering one badly wounded crew man to MENAUL prior to refueling and heading back to the carrier with the other 2 men. The wounded man needed stabilized prior to an hour helo ride south. North SAR was short on helos until more arrived.

Dillan just shuttled tankers. On his 16-20, CTF 77 cut SAR CAP back to two. They had not heard anything from Hellfire 4 since the aborted helo try. Things got a lot easier with only 2 aircraft orbiting. The "Hellfire 4, Hellfire 4, come up beeper" still continued.

Dillan's mid was the same. The next morning on the 08-12 CTF 77 pulled the plug. No one had heard from Hellfire 4 in 20 some hours.

All that and we lost him. Captured, or dead. Poor bastard.

Dillan knew that the pilot had about a 50/50 chance of survival even if captured. The NVA would take him in. But the irregulars, the NV National Guard, were poorly trained, had been taught that Americans ate babies for breakfast, and they got trigger happy. Pilots were told that if confronted by anyone armed, a very un-antagonistic posture was essential. They were to curl up in the fetal position. Then they did not look frightening and maybe would not get sprayed with AK-47 rounds.

Combat was silent. SAR CAP and the tankers were vectored back to the carriers. MENAUL took over the helo control, and the SAR effort for Hellfire 4 ended in what was essentially a defeat.

The old Condition III watches were re-established. Back to normal. At lunch, the captain told everyone who had participated "good job," but the wardroom was less than animated. It was as if LARTER had lost a shipmate.

The Lions had won. Ate the Christian. Defeated.

Dillan wrote a long letter to Patty trying to get his feelings out.

Probably not fair to Patty, who will not understand all my exhausted ramblings. She knows that I'm sensitive – even if I hide it well. She won't understand the details, but she will understand how I feel frustration, sorrow and compassion for the pilot. Sorry Patty, have to do this to retain sanity.

Although there were still some strikes going in, and had been going in all the time during the SAR situation, the well defended targets were ignored. Dillan felt that targeting was trying not to risk another SAR situation on top of the Hellfire 4 incident. Once Hellfire 4 was over, strikes built again, but still only one a day.

Conditions returned to normal. LARTER would set flight quarters about every 3 hours or so to refuel a helo from the pole mounted in the center of the DASH deck. Turn into the wind, bring the helo into hover and slowly descend until the articulated probe could be inserted, and lock into the port on the underside of the helo.

The probe was attached to a hose for flexibility once connected. Then the helo could move around at least a little. Pump JP-5 like mad. Take back suction. Release the probe and off the helo would go for a while longer. JP-5 spills on deck to be treated with the ever present kitty litter. Then they were vacuumed up so the litter would not become a dust storm for the next helo.

At night, refueling was a bit hairy and the DASH deck was lit up with down lights and colored lights on the ECM shack just forward and higher, so the helo pilot had a reference. It took some real skill for a helo pilot to do an unrep from a moving destroyer.

The Navy news message summary had a big article about the murder of Dr. Martin Luther King Junior on April 4. Pete took it hard.

"Bastard red necks, I was afraid this was going to happen, some Klan thing. Every time a black man asks to share the American dream, someone wants to kill him. Maybe the damn panthers are right," from Pete to Dillan.

"So sorry, Pete, I know you really respected him."

Panthers? Wow Pete. You are upset. What the hell is wrong with America, our President and now a preacher getting gunned down on our streets?

"I did. We all, or at least most, hoped that he would get the yoke off our necks without resorting to violence. Now I don't know what'll happen."

"Think the Black Panthers will strike back?"

"Don't know – maybe - hope not. If they do, it's war on the streets of the ghettos. And war there just hurts the innocent black poor caught up in the violence. The Watts thing in 65 killed over 30 and trashed almost 600 buildings."

"Think there'll be riots?"

"Yeah, but no idea where. But there will be some, frustration and anger boiling over. Ignorant bastards."

41

Two days later, as Dillan came off the 16-20 and stopped in radio, the chief handed him a message from NAVCOMSTAPHIL. There was a solar flare.

This will disrupt communications big time.

Dillan took it first to Fred who was in his state-room/office.

"What does this mean, Mr. Dillan?"

"Solar flares put out a lot of energy and strongly affect the ionosphere. It could significantly disrupt all high frequency communication world wide. The worst time will be just prior to sunrise as the ionosphere starts to lower in the atmosphere."

"Again, what does this mean Mr. Dillan?"

"We will probably lose the broadcast and be unable to get NAVCOMSTAPHIL on HF to ask for retransmit."

"We better not lose the broadcast. The skipper is waiting for an important message from CTF 77. Our orders, Mr. Dillan, and the orders for our relief destroyer. You better not lose the broadcast."

Silence.

Right, I can control this. Bull shit.

"Take this to the skipper."

"Yes, sir"

Dillan went out on the bridge. Pitch black again. It took quite awhile before Dillan, even with the red flashlight, could see the dark shadow in the skipper's chair that was him. No one, ever, but the skipper sat in that chair. And the empty one on the other side of the bridge was for a squadron, or destroyer division commander or such. Essentially, covered with a tan canvas cover and never used.

The skipper lived in his chair, sometimes sleeping in it at night. But mostly always there, maybe reading messages, maybe reading a paperback. The skipper loved pulp westerns and would always have one tucked behind his binocular rack.

Handing the message to the skipper, "Captain, we're going to have communications problems," Dillan said.

"OK, Mr. Dillan, explain it to me without all your engineering words."

So Dillan tried.

"OK, you better get down to radio to insure that we do not, repeat do not, have communications problems."

Oh goody – now I have to stop solar flares.

"Yes, sir," and Dillan left. He went to radio and he and the chief did some brainstorming. They got Chief Summers up. They did a 'radio to radio' with MENAUL. Consensus opinion was that they were in very deep shit. Dillan finally hit the rack at 0045.

Dillan was up at 0330 for watch in combat, a quiet watch, and lots of coffee.

At 0610, the 21MC went off, "Combat, radio, Mr. Dillan up there?"

"Dillan here."

"Mr. Dillan, we lost both broadcasts 20 minutes ago and can't get them back even trying frequencies for every COMSTA in the Pacific. MENAUL is down also. We're missing numbers big time," the chief said.

"Thanks Chief, I'll be down at 0730 when I get relieved. Start going through all the frequencies again and even try some Frisco ones." Maybe long range would work, Dillan wished.

Oh shit. Telling Fred and the skipper is going to be fun.

He picked up the sound powered hand set, turned the 'growler' to the station for "OPS OFFICER" and gave it a good crank. This would cause a 'growl' to come out of the unit in Fred's stateroom over his desk. Fred had the mid and had been in the rack for maybe an hour and 10 minutes. Dillan had to crank three times until he got another growl on the phone, "Mr. Finistry, sir."

Dillan told him the wonderful news. Fred flipped.

Not one to swear but, "God damn it, Dillan, you have really screwed the pooch this time. Get off the line; I have to wake the captain."

About 5 minutes later over the 21MC, "Combat, bridge the captain wants to see Mr. Dillan right now on the bridge."

Skipper must be sleeping in his chair again.

Although only 12 feet, it was a long walk to the bridge, red flashlight in hand, dawn creating a line of light at the horizon to the east.

"You wanted to see me, Captain."

"Mr. Dillan, missing numbers is not acceptable. You are to abandon your watch and get to radio. You are to stay there until you stop missing numbers. You may only leave to use the 01 level head. Otherwise you better be in radio fixing this problem. Do you understand me, Mr. Dillan?"

What was one to say to this total nonsense?

"Yes, sir."

"Well? Get out of here!"

Dillan walked off the bridge, stuck his head in combat and told Red what had just happened, and went down the ladder to radio.

As he walked in the chief said, "Mr. Dillan, how did you get off watch?" Dillan took him aside and told him. The chief was awestruck.

If all problems look like a nail, the only management tool one needs is a hammer. And if that doesn't work, get a bigger hammer. Fred was that way. But the captain was not normally that way. Had Fred been filling him full of crap that I could fix it if only I applied myself? Probably. Anyway, here you are, Dillan, playing nail head. OK, you're in it now. Let's see how, in detail, the two chiefs have been attacking the problem. Maybe we can get lucky.

"Chiefs, take me through everything you've done to get the broadcasts back."

This took awhile. They had done a lot. First they had tried every frequency, and there were quite a few, that NAVCOM-STAPHIL transmitted both broadcasts on, white noise, basically nonsense static.

They tried the same for NAVCOMSTAPEARL, where the really big transmitters were, then the smaller ones in Guam and Japan, then San Francisco, another big one. They even tried some Atlantic Fleet ones, nothing but white noise.

They coordinated with MENAUL, searching frequencies for that tell tale high speed rattle that was the audio signature of an encrypted teletype signal. White noise with a few pops interspersed, the radio signature of a solar flare.

The radioman chief had his watch sections continue to look at, over and over, all frequencies. MENAUL was doing the same. The flare was even making the short range UHF teletype circuit between LARTER and MENAUL go screwy. The teletype would for no reason shift to upper case so a message would look like: COMMUN&*7^%4#. Radio had a crib sheet for the upper case shift but it took awhile to decipher a badly garbled message.

And time went by. The mess deck sent a breakfast tray with hot coffee. By lunch, another. By dinner, a third.

By 1800, the entire crew had heard that Mr. Dillan had been locked up in radio by the CO. The knowledgeable crew told the unknowledgeable. The radiomen off watch and the ETs were a major source of information to the rest of the crew.

When someone came to the radio door window to drop off messages they said, "Tell Mr. Dillan the SKs are sorry for him."

This really surprised Dillan. Most of these people he had not dealt directly with over the past year plus.

Fred came in every now and then. The conversation was usually short.

"Got the broadcast back yet?"

"No, sir"

The chief changed the push button combination of the radio door. Now anyone who wanted in had to knock. This really pissed Fred off and he accused Dillan and the chief of deliberately doing it.

But the chief told him, "No, sir, Mr. Finistry, no sir. The damn thing has been giving us trouble for awhile and just decided to stop working. I've asked the SKs to dig out the spare, but they're having trouble finding it."

Never, ever, underestimate the creativity of the enlisted men. Hell, on some ships, maybe even this one, they have poker games and even stills in compartments the officers don't even know exist. Maybe the DCA or chief engineer know the compartments are there but never go there, down two normally closed scuttles into a void.

Dillan remembered that on VULCAN there was a still run by the boiler tenders in a void only reachable through a 30 foot scuttle and three locked hatches. The hatches looked locked but the locks had been cut in a way no one would notice. One little jerk and open. The product of that still would take one's breath away. Ferment some soaked corn and fruit, then distil same: white lightening.

Fred was visibly angry. He had a very dark look on his face when he walked out of radio. Being had infuriated Fred.

The XO came in twice. "I'm sorry this is happening to you, Mr. Dillan but the captain wants that broadcast back up very badly. How's it going?"

"Sorry, XO, but all we get is white noise on all frequencies. We've even tried LANTFLT frequencies."

"Well, keep at it. Get your troops to get you a mattress and some blankets. You'll probably be sleeping here tonight."

"Yes, sir, XO," Dillan said.

The chief ET said, "We have a spare rack in the ET compartment, I'll be back."

"Thanks Chief, and let me bum a pack of smokes, I'm almost out."

"Sure, back in a bit."

Ten minutes later one of the ET strikers showed up at the radio door with a thin foam rubber mattress, complete with cover (enlisted called the covers 'fart sacks'), pillow with cover, and two of the Navy's dark grey wool blankets. The enlisted slept without top sheets.

The chief came back with a pack of Winston, shoved burn bags around, found a spot 6 feet long by 2 feet wide on the deck up against a bulkhead and made Dillan a place to sleep. It would be in the light, behind a short wall of bags, and it would be noisy, but at least it was a place to lie down. By midnight, Dillan was propped up on one elbow and fast asleep.

Dillan got about 5 hours of fitful sleep. By 0600 he was awake with an aching right arm. Coffee and breakfast from the mess decks again. His last shower was 36 hours ago, lots of stubble for a beard. Uniform looked like one big dirty wrinkle. He sent a radioman down to his stateroom for a clean one.

"Chief, first thing this morning either replace or fix that damn door lock. Mr. Finistry'll be watching and will expect it to be fixed by then. He has the mids so he shouldn't be here until 0715 or so."

"OK, Mr. Dillan."

"And Chief, thanks for all your support, but I don't want to see you in trouble with Finistry. He makes a very bad enemy and has a mean streak."

"Oh, I know that Mr. Dillan – the entire crew knows that."

Oh good, a mutiny. Not in my division.

Fred was back at 0720, right on time. The door lock worked. Dillan looked at least presentable and the breakfast tray had disappeared. But Fred said nothing. One could tell instantly if the broadcast was still down. When it was up the teletype racket was always there, after the mirror broadcast two teletype rackets. Now radio was eerily quiet. Not perfectly quiet but the background racket was missing. Fred just scowled and left.

And the radiomen slaved over the receivers both in radio and in the secondary radio space across the passageway from radio central, sitting on the deck, headphones on, slowly twirling dials and listening.

At 1000 a miracle happened. RM3 Eberly got a high speed rattle out of his headphones on an odd NAVCOMSTAPEARL frequency. Patched it through the multiplexer and crypto gear and a teletype started chattering. All upper case and with blanks every now and then but the main broadcast was back.

RM2 Stephy, the watch section leader, immediately wanted to call the bridge on the 21MC.

Dillan said, "No Stephy. Let's make sure it stays up. Send a radio to radio to MENAUL and let'm know."

It won't stay up. Bet it won't stay up. Don't jump the gun and tell the skipper just to have it go belly up again.

It didn't stay up for more than 10 minutes and was badly garbled. For the next couple of hours they kept trying. By 1200 the signal from NAVCOMSTAPHIL was back, and reasonably solid. The broadcast was back on line. They had missed well over 1500 numbers. MENAUL got a high frequency point to point link, again 'radio to radio,' up with PHIL. PHIL was buried. Every ship in the fleet had been out for awhile. North SAR was the longest outage.

The PHIL radiomen were standing 12 and 12 and going through the skeds. They had missed numbers themselves, even with their huge field antennas, and were going back to Washington and Pearl for numbers. The undersea cable was very busy. It might be days until it got sorted.

Fred was on watch in combat. Dillan called him on the 21MC.

"Thank you Mr. Dillan. About time you got your act together. How long until we get all the missed numbers?"

Dillan told him the NAVCOMSTAPHIL story.

"We must get them as fast as possible. Can you assure me that you are doing everything you can to do this Mr. Dillan? Everything?"

"Yes, sir."

"I will inform the captain."

Five minutes later, the growler went off in radio. Seldom did anyone use the growler. Stephy took the handset out of its rack.

"Radio central, RM2 Stephy speaking, sir."

Stephy got an odd look on his face. "It's for you Mr. Dillan, it's the captain," passing the hand set over.

"Dillan speaking, sir."

"About time, Dillan. You can get out of your cage now. Go get a shower and then come talk to me on the bridge."

"Yes, sir."

42

Dillan left radio for the first time, less head calls, in almost 30 hours. Down to after officer's country. Tony was in his stateroom doing paperwork and playing music.

"Hey Mr. D, got out of your brig I see. This a full pardon or a work release?"

"Don't know, Chop, but I'm out for now, probably on probation."

Dillan took a hotel shower. Normally Navy showers were restricted to wetting one's self, turning off the water, soaping down and turning the water back on to rinse. It saved a lot of scarce fresh water. A 'hotel shower' was letting it run.

Screw it – this makes up for two days.

He turned it on as hot as he could stand and let it work some of the aches and pains out.

Showered, shaved, another clean uniform. As he walked back towards the bridge, almost every enlisted man he passed would do, "Hello, Mr. Dillan." And smile. He was surprised at the support he felt from the crew.

But I shouldn't be. The crew has a special bond they feel with 'mustang' officers. Not that I'm anything special. Hell, I screw up with the best of them. But to the crew they feel it's important for an officer to really understand what it's like to be enlisted by having lived it in a past life.

Not all mustang officers were good ones. Some got a big head and used their knowledge of the enlisted ranks to come down on people. Crews developed a special dislike for them. And if a crew really disliked an officer, they could make his life unhappy in so many subtle ways. His paperwork would get misplaced. His uniforms would come back from the laundry with stains or holes.

His mail would get lost. A care package for him would find its way over the side. His pay record would get fouled up, or his coffee cup, especially if he had one with his name on it, would go for an unexplained swim. While he was in the shower the hot water would get secured at a remote valve.

In extreme cases, his fitness report would get changed or never get mailed to Washington, his leave record would get double charged, or even his shoes would disappear over the side while he slept.

Fred had been through a little of this until Dillan told his chief to put a stop to it.

The chief denied having any knowledge but Dillan had just said, "You chiefs run this ship – and you can stop this crap, I know you can. It's a form of mutiny and you don't have to do that. Never fear, a bad officer always gets what's coming to him in the end. This subtle stuff is unethical." Fred never knew but some of his frustrations went away.

The enlisted men usually gave officers the benefit of the doubt until proven otherwise. There was a grapevine on a ship as good as, or better, than any informal communication system in existence.

I guess that I have a good reputation with the troops – generally passed on word of mouth from the ETs, RMs or SMs I bet. Probably the CIC and bridge people also. It isn't brain surgery. Treat the men with respect. Lots are under 20; some are not much over 17. Understand that they bust their buns just like officers do.

Support the hard workers. Kick the slackers in the butt. Tell the troops not only what to do but why. Trust their judgment. Look out for your troops. Keep the system from screwing them over when you could. Be firm but fair. Treat'm like you would want to be treated.

When Dillan got to the bridge, the skipper was into a western. One did not interrupt the skipper when he was reading unless it was a major item. Dillan waved to the OOD and JOOD, and stood by the skipper's chair.

"Oh, there you are Mr. Dillan, clean shave and all. Got a little ripe in radio, huh?"

Then, "OK, tell me how we got the broadcast back and if we're OK for awhile? Did it take magic? You got a voodoo doll? It sure took long enough. Ops told me that we lost 1500 numbers. That's a bunch. I'm looking for a message that'll get us out of here."

"I'm sorry, Captain, but the solar flare essentially wiped out high frequency communications over most of the world. MENAUL and LARTER got it the worst in our area according to PHIL. PHIL's backed up big time, lost numbers themselves and are getting Pearl and Washington to resend. We have a firm signal now, but we can't guarantee that we won't take a hit as the sun goes down or tomorrow morning just before sun rise."

"And why is that, Mr. Dillan?"

"The ionosphere, where HF signals are reflected back to earth, moves outward during the night and then contracts during the day. Long range HF must bounce off the ionosphere. This is not a mirror but a layer. And the cosmic rays from the flare screw up the layer a bunch. And when it shifts, it gets worse."

"I'm sure it all makes sense to you, Mr. Dillan, but it far exceeds my communications course at PCO[lxi] almost 2 years ago."

"Sorry, sir."

"Don't be sorry, Mr. Dillan. And glad to have you back from radio. I'm very interested in any message from CTF 77 to the TU, so alert your troops to route it to me ASAP."

"Yes, sir, they have already been so advised."

The captain opened the paperback that was sitting upside down on his lap and looked down at it.

Guess this discussion is over. Better get back to radio.

The 16-20 in Combat was dull. For some reason there were no air strikes on North Vietnam. Dead quiet. North SAR did not even have a helo. MENAUL and LARTER steamed around at 5 knots 3 to 4 thousand yards apart and contemplated their navels.

Red and Dillan BS'ed a bit. Red wanted the low down on why the broadcast went down. Dillan was not a hot shot on propagation, but knew enough to be dangerous. They talked for quite awhile.

After watch, Dillan went by radio. Broadcast still up.

"We almost lost it when the sun went down, had to change frequencies twice, been running two freqs and 4 teletypes. Using paper like there is no tomorrow. One would drop, then the other. Thank God for the 30 minute delay on ASW," the chief said.

"Great job, guys, keep it up," as he looked around at all the tired faces. "You don't want me cluttering up your deck again. And thanks Chief, and thank Chief Summers for me. I'll be in crypto for a bit."

Although dead tired, Dillan wrote a letter.

Almost out of here Patty, headed home soon. Love you and miss you.

Reasonable night in the rack, 2100 to 0330, six and a half hours. Like a vacation. The 04-08 in the morning was an instant replay. Dull. Dillan was hungry and went to the mess decks for bean soup – for breakfast, ran into RM2 Stephy.

"Broadcast still up, Mr. Dillan, and we got that message the CO was concerned about, being routed to him now. We're going to Hong Kong!"

Shit. Dillan was up to radio in a flash. As he walked in the door, the chief immediately handed him the message tear off.

Am I that predictable?

Skipping all the US Navy message header stuff, it was from CTF 77 to CTU 77.4.3, copy TU 77.4.3, and others.

CONFIDENTIAL //3000//

SUBJ SEVENTHFLT SKEDCHG (U)

1.(C)NCA PRECLUDES AIR OPS NVN UFN. ABANDON NSAR 1200 LOCAL.

2.(U) DISESTAB TU SEVEN SEVEN PT FOUR PT THREE. ESTAB TU SEVEN ZERO PT FIVE PT TWO. MENAUL CTU. ASSIGN USS MENAUL, USS LARTER.

3.(C) PCD AND RPT SOPA BCC HONG KONG FOR SEVEN (7) DAYS R&R. PORT CLEARANCE CERTIFIED.

4.(U) BZ. RADM MAHONEY SENDS.

It was a schedule change. Translated this meant that National Command Authority (the President or someone on his senior staff) had halted all air strikes to the north until further notice. North SAR was to be abandoned at noon, and the North SAR Task Unit was to fold its tent. Another task unit was formed with MENAUL still as the Task Unit Commander.

The TU was to proceed to the British Crown Colony of Hong Kong, report to the Senior Officer Present Afloat, and commence 7 days of Rest and Relaxation. Bravo Zulu was Navy lingo for good job. Rear Admiral (upper half) Mahoney was CTF 77.[lxii]

By 1000, the skipper got on the 1MC and shared the news with the crew, including the admiral's comment. The skipper added a "well done" from him. Most of the ship was pumped.

At noon, with LARTER 1000 yards behind MENAUL, North SAR was abandoned. As the crow flies, Hong Kong was close. But the Red Chinese would not like two US Navy destroyers transiting their territorial waters between the mainland and

Hainan Island. If there was deep enough water to even fit. So the TU had to take the long way around. They needed an unrep for fuel anyway. No AE, so no ammo available even though LARTER was some rounds down.

Dillan ran into Pete in the wardroom,

"Haven't seen any news of unrest in the streets Pete, and I saw they got King's killer. With the broadcast back, we get news again."

"Hope he gets a real trial and not some southern white-wash."

"Should, with all the media attention, they can't pull a fast one. Besides, the justice department'll be all over the prosecutor. But better keep him locked up. Remember Oswald."

"Yea, some black man may try to even the score. Maybe they can find out who's behind the hit, the bastards."

"Maybe."

Then the skipper came in and it was time for lunch.

43

Late the following day, just as Dillan came down from CIC to radio, the petty officer of the watch handed Dillan a message.

It was from CTF 70 (CTF 77 and CTF 70 were one and the same, the admiral wore a 'double hat', 70 being a general purpose organization) to LARTER "eyes only". This message was off line encrypted and for the captain only. Dillan had to go to the bridge, tell the captain and the captain followed Dillan back to radio.

Dillan took the skipper to the tiny crypto room, set up the off line equipment with the day's preset, and showed him how to set the rotors from the key code, with the door open. Only one person could fit at a time. He told the skipper to type the 5 letter code groups into the machine slowly. Then Dillan was obliged to leave the captain in the room behind a locked door alone.

Dillan could hear the slow kachung kachung of the machine as the skipper typed one finger at a time. Twenty minutes later, the captain came out with folded papers in his hand.

"Thank you, Dillan," and he left radio. The machine's rotors had been reset to zero, and Dillan disassembled it and put it away.

Now just what is that about? Our orders back to the states? Why "eyes only"? Of course it could be something about Fister or another administrative matter that the admiral determined that only the skipper should see. But it was the first "eyes only" that I have heard about since I've been comm officer. Intriguing.

Hong Kong was a British crown colony on the south east coast of China. The British extracted a 99 year lease which would not run out for over 30 years. A big, over crowded metropolis, it was a business and financial outlet for Red China and a free port. No duties.

Hong Kong had a British governor, and a squadron of the British Far East Fleet. Commodore Hong Kong was the senior British officer with a huge white home up on the hill over looking the harbor on Victoria Island. There was also a large area of peninsula called the 'New Territories' with the city of Kowloon across the harbor from Victoria Island.

The approach to Hong Kong harbor was narrow and had some current. MENAUL and LARTER went in carefully. All hands were in service dress blue and the troops were at quarters, a formal port visit. Since the British were still wearing blues, even though it was warm, the US Navy was obliged to do the same. The first time the troops had been in Service Dress Blue since leaving Yokosuka.

LARTER dropped anchor at her designated anchorage at 1100, on April 20, 1968. The senior US officer present afloat (SOPA) was COMINEFLOT ONE (Commander, Mine Flotilla 1, a very senior four striper) embarked on USS CATSKILL (MCS-1), a mine sweeping command ship out of Sasebo, Japan. CATS-KILL was SOPA Admin and did all the work. Dillan had heard the station ships did this for 6 weeks.

Six weeks of station ship in Hong Kong. So that's how the other half lived?

Once they anchored there was the obligatory motor whale boat, the Captain's Gig, trip to CATSKILL. The CO and XO went. Standing on the 03 level, Dillan could see that their Gig was enroute from MENAUL also.

Hong Kong harbor is amazing. Enormous freighters anchored or coming and going. Hundreds of lighters serving the anchored freighters, junks every where. Neat green hull white top ferries running back and forth between Victoria and Kowloon side.

And Victoria was mountainous and there were tons of high rises, and smaller buildings perched on the hill sides. Dillan saw a tram going up one of the hills. The city stretched as far as he could see to the left and the right, only the buildings got lower to the left and right.

The radarman chief standing next to him remarked, "That low area over there is Wan Chai, the bar capital of Hong Kong. And Mr. Dillan, you should check out the China Fleet Club. It's a British navy club up on the hill over there and drinks are really cheap! And they have a lot of good shopping there, also."

An hour later, LARTER's Gig was headed back. There was an all officers meeting in the ward room.

"Gentlemen," the captain began, "Hong Kong is every Sailor's dream. There is everything here. The best shopping west of the International Date Line. Great restaurants – let me recommend Jimmy's Kitchen on Kowloon side. Menu is like a telephone book and the oysters are superb. There are lots of bars, thousands of good looking bar girls, big trouble, and expensive. Ten times the price of Olongapo, at least. Remember men, thousands of GI's from Nam come here for R&R with 6 months pay in their pocket. Two weeks later they go back to Nam broke."

"Fleecing Americans is the colony's number one sport, more important than cricket. If your troops are going to get into trouble, this is the easiest place. Getting drunk and busting up bars is not allowed. I ask each of you to meet with your divisions prior to liberty call."

"There are drugs available that we have not even heard of. Prostitution is legal but very strictly controlled. The VD rate's high and most types are unknown to modern medicine. Tell your men that condoms are essential if they choose to partake. The corpsman has free samples to pass out. Tell them that we will prosecute anyone who becomes incapacitated from VD for destroying government property."

A laugh.

Always the same threat going into a foreign port, not that anyone I knew about ever was.

"OK. Try to discourage conjugal visits with prostitutes. There is enough excitement here to keep your troops busy without getting ripped off, or collecting some social disease."

"The Hong Kong police are all Chinese, and have a very low tolerance for drunk and disorderly. This place has more people than a large city stuffed into one third the area. The New Territories, outside down town Kowloon are strictly off limits. So is Macau. Out there Americans disappear, probably behind the bamboo curtain, never to be heard from again. This place can be fun, and the crew deserves it. But your troops have to be careful, XO."

"Thank you Captain. We'll be on holiday routine throughout the visit, modifiable by department heads to meet the needs of the ship. Three section duty just like in Subic. Only the duty section will be required to work. No one, I repeat no one, will restrict any one to the ship during their liberty time with out my consent."

"Liberty call each day at noon expiring on board at midnight for all enlisted less chiefs. Officer's and chief's liberty will expire on board 0730 the following morning. I will entertain requests from officers and chiefs, using the buddy system, to spend the night ashore in one of the major hotels down town. The Hilton and Mandarin are good but pricy. If I agree, the subject officers or chiefs who don't have the duty may forgo the 0730-1200 period on the ship the next day providing they return on time for their duty day. The uniform for all hands on liberty is appropriate civilian attire."

"We must provide one officer and 4 petty officers to shore patrol each day noon to midnight. Mr. Redmond will assign officers and enlisted to shore patrol from the duty sections. Shore patrol will muster at the regional police station downtown at 1230, each afternoon. This assignment will last until midnight. Some may be assigned to patrol Kowloon side."

"We will not run ship's boats. We only have the gig, and CATSKILL's boats will not be used. There are numerous ferries called water taxis, which make a living servicing visiting ships. They go from the main boat landing to the ships and back essentially continuously. Fare is two Hong Kong dollars, about a quarter. The last boat is just prior to midnight so make sure your troops don't miss it. They'll be counted as AWOL, since the first boats do not run much prior to 0700."

"The Commodore Hong Kong holds a weekly cocktail and dinner party at the China Fleet Club for all officers of visiting ships. It's Tuesday night. Uniform is service dress blue. It's possible that a royal navy boat, but maybe just water taxis, will take those attending to the British fleet landing, and buses will take us to the club."

"The captain, department heads, and I'll be attending. Other officers are welcome, if they do not have the duty. Len will be CDO for Tuesday evening so all the department heads can attend."

Dillan did some forward thinking.

Shit, I have the duty. Would be nice to see how the Brits entertain, heard it's quite the splash.

"For those interested in calling home, there's a telephone exchange at the China Fleet Club. Rates are more than Subic, about like Yoko was. I don't have to remind you, but you must remind your troops that our past operations and naval operations in general are confidential and must not be discussed on unsecure telephones."

"Your troops will ask when we are going home to tell their loved ones. We don't know. I would expect shortly. LARTER got this trip to Hong Kong for doing a super job, with MENAUL, on North SAR. Never fear, COMSEVENTHFLT knows that he has to send us back to Eastpac. His lease is up."

Laughter.

"OK, go meet with your troops. Liberty call at noon. Any questions see me later."

Dillan's head was spinning.

What will I say to Patty? Will we get sent from here back to Subic and pick up a carrier for the transit home? Should I ask Pete about a night in a hotel ashore? God, I would sure like to get off this damn ship for 24 hours. What was it that Patty wanted me to buy here, linens maybe?

Today was Saturday. Dillan had the duty.

OK, go ashore and call Patty on Sunday – actually Saturday night her time.

44

Dillan went down to radio and had the chief get everyone together including the signal bridge. He then gave them the same speech, with exceptions, that the skipper and XO gave. He left out the part about prosecuting.

"Any questions?"

"Will you be signing stand by chits, Mr. Dillan?"

When enlisted wanted liberty, and someone else of equivalent qualifications was willing to swap duty with them, it required a stand by 'chit' signed by the chief and division officer.

"Yes, I'll sign stand by chits – but if I hear of someone selling a swap, both the seller and the buyer will get restricted to the ship for the rest of our time here. A trip to Hong Kong is not an opportunity to make money. It's an opportunity to get a little R&R. If you wish to stay aboard that's up to you. But no selling."

This is hard to prove. But some men would stand-by for others as often as they could and charge them for it. The going rate was $10 but here in Hong Kong, that will probably triple. I want all my men to have some time ashore to decompress. Selling a swap is not teamwork.

Dillan said, "There are a lot more things to do in Hong Kong besides getting loaded and getting ripped off by bar girls. The shopping is super. There are good places to eat, and lots of sights to see. The chief engineer has a bunch of brochures in the log room, grab one and try to see a little besides the inside of a girly bar. If you want to drink and eat cheap, go to the China Fleet Club."

"Can we spend dollars here?"

"No, exchange your money with the DK (Disbursing Clerk) prior to going ashore. The XO brought a lot back from CATSKILL. The Hong Kong dollar's the official currency, about 8 HK$ to 1 US$. If you need more to make purchases, exchange money at the China Fleet Club or a bank. Don't exchange money on the street. Most is counterfeit and you'll get ripped off. They even split the money so it looks like real but it only has one side. Purchases at the China Fleet Club can be made in dollars."

Thanks to the RD chief for giving me a heads up on that one. Red China is accumulating US dollars. That's why the US Military in Japan and Korea use Military Payment Certificates not dollars. Then, every so often, the series is changed and only ID card holders can convert to the new series. The superseded series is worthless. Keeps the locals honest. Wonder why MPC isn't used here? Probably too much of a pain in the ass to administer.

"And make damn certain you use protection if you get laid here. The corpsman has rubbers for the taking. There are strains of VD here that have no cure. Better if you only look but don't touch."

Some of the unattached men would partake, Dillan knew. And some of the older men would think it was their duty to insure that the younger ones did, even jump for the girl if need be. Like an initiation ceremony.

There were a few more questions, then they dismissed. Dillan went down to the wardroom for lunch, and then to his stateroom to see if he could find Patty's shopping list for Hong Kong. He ran into Red.

"Dillan, I want you to be the shore patrol officer for your section today."

"OK. Service dress blue?"

"Yes, and the boat leaves at 1300, think you can make it?" Dillan looked at his watch. 1240. "I'll give it a try, how about the petty officers?"

"Hope they can make it, also. Here's the list. Department heads are passing the word. I'll hold off having the OD flag a water taxi until you all are on the quarterdeck. Stop by the log room and pick up enough arm bands for 5, and some billys."

Shore patrol wore white arm bands with a black 'SP' on it. Petty officers were issued a 2 foot long black wooden billy club on a leather thong, carried in a white web belt loop.

"Yes, sir."

Ashore in Hong Kong and I'm going to be a cop! Great. Good thing I had had my uniform re-striped with the JG stripes in Subic.

This would not be Dillan's first go round as shore patrol. He had pulled it a couple of times in Norfolk, when on VULCAN. But as a 3rd class he was very junior and did what the 1st class or

2nd class told him. Granby Street was not a great place. Once in a close brush with a hurricane when the fleet had not sortied, the city of Norfolk was shut down.

Not the bars on Granby. Water a foot deep and they were still open. There were bars, whore houses, combinations, bar fights, drunks who couldn't walk, etc. Shore patrol duty didn't seem all that exciting to Dillan. But at least in Norfolk then, Sailors from visiting ships had to wear uniforms ashore.

How the hell was he to tell Sailors from civilians here?

He didn't know at the time, but an American Sailor in civilian clothing stood out like a sore thumb. Close military hair cut, usually plain toed black military shoes, and usually a cheap shirt and cheap plain trousers, mostly crumpled or with fold creases. They looked out of place in their clothing.

Dillan had to go by the DK's office to get some HK$. He had head of line privileges.

The water taxi left at 1320. Dillan had to pay the fare and would get reimbursed. The water taxi driver didn't understand or wouldn't understand anything. They went to the main pier instead of the police boat pier and they had to walk to the main Wan Chai police station ten blocks away. They got some funny looks from the locals. This was going to be almost a 10 hour shift.

He was met by a Chinese police officer who spoke fairly good British English and had a couple silver stripes and a crown on his soft shoulder boards. Light blue uniform with jacket, badge. Blue officers hat with a red band. A silver crown emblem and a silver chin strap.

A Lieutenant?

Dillan would ride with him, the watch officer, in a small square white Toyota van with a gum ball machine on top. Dillan's other shore patrol petty officers were parceled out one to one with Hong Kong police patrol officers. They did 12 hour shifts also. The pairs would walk beats in Wan Chai.

And off the patrols went. Dillan sat in the office for awhile. Finally, after getting the beat cops off and running, the Chinese watch officer came back.

"Welcome Hong Kong, Lieutenant Junior Grade Dillan."

"We're going to be together for awhile, how 'bout just Dillan?"

"You American so informal. But as wish, Dillan. Hong Kong glad have US Navy here. As our allies, is our duty insure your crew has good time. But there many temptation Hong Kong and trouble happen every night. We will be, how you say, 'paddy wagon' Wan Chai tonight. Hopefully we have quiet night."

"My officer all have radio and if trouble happen, we get call. We drive around Wan Chai, but traffic very bad. We use siren and I drive. If there is problem, I handle Chinese people. Do not touch them. Not acceptable their culture. I handle Chinese. You handle American. I help you if I must, but do not wish do."

"I not arrest American Sailor, you arrest. We transport back fleet landing, and police boat escort American back ship. One American petty officer, first class I believe, big first class, assigned ride police boat. Sometime American drunk to remember ship. If so, he spend night detention cell here. Once American back aboard ship, American deal with them they see."

"Recommend your representative when man brought aboard, he not come ashore few day. In case injury requiring hospital, we transport and American treated. We try be fair and understand that young American at sea long time and want have fun. Fun acceptable. Destruction personal property or fighting, not."

Dillan said, "When will my shore patrol for LARTER return here?"

"All patrol collected mid night. Visiting ship not allowed enlisted crew ashore beyond midnight. You meet police landing and police boat return you ship."

"Who covers Kowloon side?"

"Another officer and petty officer already detached Kowloon side. From CATSKILL I believe? And MENAUL shore patrol Aberdeen till 8 and then help us Wan Chai."

"OK, I understand. You'll fill me in if I need other information as we go along?"

"Yes, Lieutenant junior grade Dillan, I fill in."

Firearms are probably illegal in Hong Kong. The Chinese carry a very short stick in a leather case. Probably some judo thing. And a portable radio with a hand set in a purse like satchel. This is going to be an experience.

The Chinese officer's name was something something Chan. They talked as they rode around – well maybe the right word is sat - in massive traffic jams on streets with 6 story apartments with balconies covered in laundry, and past road side carts cooking stuff Dillan did not recognize and probably did not want to, or parked. People everywhere, weaving in and out of traffic and 8 deep on sidewalks built for 3.

The smells are unrecognizable – some mixture of cooking meat and vegetables, noodles, sweat, truck exhaust, and God knows what else. And noise – always the noise, like a bee hive. But an oriental bee hive – with the sing song mutter of Chinese in the background.

Chan was a Hong Kong native. His dad was a tailor. Short commercial for tailor-made suits. He had 2 brothers and a sister. One brother was in England. Chan was married, no kids.

He said that with sadness. Must want a family, but in this ant hill? I might not be in a hurry to have kids.

Chan said he went to the police academy and worked his way up to Captain and had been on the force 12 years. He sure looked younger than that when Dillan did the math in his head. He had been on the shore patrol liaison detail for 6 months. It was a good step and he had an opportunity to meet and talk with Americans. Help him perfect his English.

This assignment would help him make Major. When a carrier came in, Hong Kong was flooded with Sailors and it was a long week. Sometimes an Australian ship would come in. Chan said the Aussies took their reputation as hard drinkers seriously.

The radio chattered in Chinese every now and then, but Chan ignored it. Dinner was picked up from a small storefront restaurant and was a paper box with some bean curd noodles, and pork with vegetables. Or at least Dillan thought it was pork. It could have been anything. Chan did not ask Dillan what he wanted. He just handed it to Dillan and said, "Here, eat." Chan brought Dillan a plastic fork but Dillan chose chop sticks – a skill he learned at Ohio State years ago. There was a challenge to pick up one uncooked rice grain or chug.

The food was hot and good, strong tea in a paper cup, and no dessert.

"You do well chop stick, better many occidental," from Chan.

"A skill acquired in college to keep from always having to drain the glass, Captain Chan. I enjoy eating with chop sticks and do it whenever I have the opportunity," Dillan answered.

"Parent insisted I learn fork when child. But still feel natural with chop stick," spinning a pair in his hand, "more sanitary. Never eat with ivory chop stick like they sell junk shop. Ivory chop stick for funeral – picking bones of dead. Wood chop stick for eating, big one for cooking. Most use cheap wood chop stick eat only once, then throw away, very sanitary."

"Thanks for the heads up," from Dillan.

The sights and sounds were interesting. Neon everywhere and people everywhere. At 1800 they were called to a bar: an altercation between some Sailor and a mama san. The Sailor wanted the girl but did not want to "buy her out" of the bar. Things got loud. Mama san called the police. The patrol couldn't handle the Sailor because he got belligerent.

Dillan walked up to him while Chan was talking to his patrol and mama san was screeching in the background. There was a big crowd.

Dillan said, "OK, Sailor, what ship are you off of and what's the problem?"

"USS MENAUL, sir. The girl agreed to go with me but that old bitch over there said I had to pay 200 Hong Kong to buy her out of the bar. That's slavery. I don't want to buy the girl, only have some fun. I'll pay the girl the 300 she wants and I'll have to jump for the place. I don't have another 200, sir."

"What's your name and rate Sailor?"

"QM3 Richards sir, from the MENAUL, N Division." A 3rd class Quartermaster from the navigation division.

"Well, Richards, I'm from the LARTER and both of our crews deserve a good time. But the system here is to buy the girls out of the bar where they work, then make your own deal with them for anything else you want. Not playing by the rules gets you in trouble with the local cops. And you don't want that do you Petty Officer Richards?"

"But damn it sir, buying someone isn't right."

"Think of it this way, Richards, when you take the girl out of the bar, the bar loses all the money she would make hustling drinks for the rest of the night. So you aren't really purchasing her, just renting her. Now if you wanted to wait till 2200, it might be a lot cheaper."

"Oh shit, pardon me, sir, but I'll be way too drunk by 2200."

"Well, Richards, you sure can't have her now without ponying up the 200."

"To hell with this sir, I don't want her that bad. I'll just go down the street. Is that OK sir? I'm not under arrest or anything am I?"

"No Richards, you are not under arrest, but it's obvious you've had a few. Take a break and eat some dinner. Things will look better afterwards. I know you were cautioned to go ashore with a buddy and to stick together. I recommend you find your buddy or another MENAUL group to pal around with. And I'm the shore patrol officer all night here. If I get another call on you, then you are headed back to MENAUL with a report chit for disobeying a direct order – understand?"

"Yes, sir, and thank you, sir." Richards walked away. Dillan heard some Chinese girl yell, "ailor, come back, me love you." But he kept on going, pushing his way through the onlookers and gone.

Dillan went over to Chan and the patrol. He filled Chan in. Chan said mama san was not happy and wanted the Sailor arrested, but that he finally had to tell her "no." No harm done. Dillan thanked Chan for previously telling him how the bar scene worked in Wan Chai. End of event and back in the van.

"You handled well, Lieutenant Dillan," Chan said.

"Thanks." *Was I just promoted?*

Over the next few hours Chan told Dillan about the Hong Kong experience for the GI's who came for R&R.

He said, "Your soldier flown charter commercial from South Viet Nam to Kai Tak airport. There many government and private group who want give them grand tour, take them dinner and so. But sadly, are also 'agent'; I think in America you call them "pimp." Agent pick up soldier when arrive and take hotel in Kowloon. There soldier can pick Chinese girl for week or longer."

"Girl get maybe $600 US for week. Agent get $200 US so soldier pay $800 US. Best looking girl cost more. We hear one

American officer pay $1200 US per week for two week for very beautiful girl."

Wow, well over 3 months pay for an Ensign.

"Soldier also pay hotel room, food, drink, entertainment. Usually here Wan Chai. Cheaper and safer than Kowloon side. Girl sleep with soldier all week. Give grand tour Hong Kong. Agent compete and soldier tell other soldier."

"Agent make lot money and ride big car with driver. Girl make lot money. Average Chinese Hong Kong not make $50 US in month. Many girl college girl and can make enough two month, go college all year."

"Good Hong Kong family never want daughter be prostitute. But some family, especially poor one, pretend not happen. Some family sell girl to agent. Good looking girl can make enough support big family. Agent girl make lot more than bar girl or street girl. Agent buy fancy dress for girl. Send hair dresser."

"Agent teach girl English. Agent have girl under doctor care and give pill. But never drug. Not allowed. Girl must have head OK for work. Girl work 3 week out of 4. Girl want fancy agent and, as you say, 'high roller' client."

"We know this happen. But not get called. And we not stop. Prostitution not illegal Hong Kong long as girl not on street or caught working bar fancy hotel down town. But that rule not enforced for high class girl. Big shot like high class girl hotel bar. Prostitute must register police and have monthly examination."

"We have problem with social disease Hong Kong and try keep under control. We think many new strain brought here by GI from Vietnam, but government not wish make wave. And bar Wan Chai not allowed have whore house. Bar girl take client poor hotel. Many poor hotel rent room by hour."

He continued, "If soldier beat up girl, agent take her away and we never know. Last month we think soldier kill girl. But no body and no evidence. We think agent give girl family $5,000 Hong Kong. No one talk us."

"Americans come Hong Kong and think is "World of Susie Wong". Movie about Hong Kong 10 year ago. Not today. Lieutenant, you see rickshaw?"

That's right. I never saw a rickshaw. "No."

"Rickshaw very restricted Hong Kong. Few license given out and only tourist trade down town. No license Wan Chai."

"How about business men? Seems like there are lots of Japanese company neon signs," Dillan said.

"Japanese big problem down town, I work down town area before. Think they have right any girl and throw lot money around. Japan lost war but now buying Hong Kong. Get very drunk. Total separate system from soldier or Sailor. Mostly older call girl working down town hotel. Girl move up and agent still handle."

"I haven't seen any strip clubs."

"None here Wan Chai. Japanese come looking for strip show. None here bar. Not allowed. Counter culture. Only agent have what they call "private party." Charge Japanese attend. Most stripper Filipino or even Australian. I hear also some German and American. Japanese want occidental and pay big."

"Customer get watch strip show, then get girl big money. Most your soldier and Sailor can not afford. Some strip club Kowloon side. Dangerous. Big one Macau where lot drug are. Macau not part Hong Kong. Portuguese colony. Lot communist influence. Even gambling there. Very dangerous."

"It seems so crowded, so many people."

"We have major over crowding problem Hong Kong. These apartment," indicating the overhanging steel balconies above them, "have whole family one room. Some people live poor wood house hill side. When rain monsoon, house slide down. Sometime many die. Government knock down. Poor build back faster than can make down. Many poor people Hong Kong."

Must be tough being a cop here. Must be tough living in all this over crowding. Chan probably lives in a tiny apartment.

Then Chan got quiet for awhile. And he lightened up.

"Other side mountain, Aberdeen. Many people live junk and sampan there. Some say these people live entire life never walk land. There big floating restaurant. Food very good, very expensive."

"We also have Tiger Balm Garden. Take tram up hill. Garden built many year ago play park for rich Chinese man grand children. Now public park. Rich man sell herb medicine for body ache. Company still sell. I use."

"I think I have heard about Tiger Balm even in the states, never used it though," Dillan said.

Then Dillan asked about shopping for things like linens. Chan told him there were much better bargains on linen on the Kowloon side but only in daylight. Another commercial for tailor made sport coats, suits, shirts and even shoes.

Once I can get some liberty I'll go to Kowloon side and try to get some linens. And yes, a tailor made sport coat from Chan's. But no shoes. Got enough already. What else? Sure need some peace offerings for Patty.

Chan has a great vocabulary, but could use a course in colloquial English; maybe a course in prepositions and plurals also. Not that I am any hot shot in English. Grammar and spelling were always my worst subjects. Learning another language must be tough.

45

Around 2000 they got another call. The streets of Wan Chai were jammed. It took 15 minutes to go the 5 blocks, with the up down warbling siren wailing its insistent call. It was a seaman off LARTER. In the bar there was lots of yelling in Chinese. The LARTER's 3rd class shore patrol told Dillan that the man's wallet had been stolen and that he had no money to pay his bar bill. And it was an $80 US bar bill: almost half a month's pay for a seaman.

Wow, must have been a lot of tea drinks in a martini glass to run it up like that.

The bar owner had run out and pulled the patrol into the bar. A big Chinese guy was standing in the door and would not let the seaman go. Chan talked to the Chinese. Dillan went over to the ashen faced seaman. Dillan didn't know him but he was told the man was Seaman Gates from LARTER, first (deck) division. He was one of Joe Rederman's men.

When Dillan walked up to him he said, "Sorry Mr. Dillan, but they stole my wallet. I have no money to pay. What'm I going to do, Mr. Dillan? Me and Mike here," indicating another Sailor, probably a seaman also, Dillan at least remembered his face. He had been a lookout in Dillan's bridge watch section for awhile. "We were just having fun with a few girls. Mike just has enough to pay his bill."

"OK, Gates, you sure ran up a big bill. Think they saw you coming? How long you been here? When did you notice your wallet was missing?"

"We been here since about 1400. When we went to leave and had to pay up, sir"

"You been sitting with the girls?"

"Yes, sir, one on my lap and one rubbing my back. They seemed like nice girls, sir."

Right, nice girls, they liquor him up and then keep him busy loving him up and allowing for some exploration while a hand slips into his pocket. And the wallet is long gone. We will never be able to prove a thing.

"You didn't get your ID card stolen did you?"

Gates reached into the watch pocket of his pants and pulled out an ID Card. "No sir, here it is."

"Good, losing an ID card can get you in a lot of trouble."

Losing an ID card was a major screw up. As far back as Dillan could remember it was drilled into enlisted men to keep their ID card in a safe place and *not* in their wallet when ashore. ID cards were worth a bunch on the black market and suitably doctored could give someone access to US military installations.

Dillan indicated the other Sailor. After asking his name, he asked him questions. The story was the same, although the other Sailor was obviously not quite as loaded as Gates.

"Wait here," Dillan said and walked over to Chan and told him the story. Chan said that there were a lot of pick pockets working the Americans in Wan Chai. It didn't happen in bars very often.

"I take care this, Lieutenant," Chan said and walked over to the bar owner. Soon the girls were all lined up in front of Chan. All in tight sprayed on high collar dresses with micro mini skirts. So much for the Susie Wong slits. Dillan understood not a word. But the girls got a firm lecture from Chan. They stood there with heads down. Then Chan had a sharp conversation with the bar owner.

"OK, Lieutenant, no one admit seeing wallet, let take your men police boat. Just ride home. Not want them come back here tonight. Something bad happen."

Dillan told the men, "OK, boys your liberty for tonight is over. If you come over again never go near this bar. That big Chinese bouncer could put a hurt'n on you big time, understand."

"Yes, sir," together.

"What about my wallet, Mr. Dillan? Can you get it back for me?"

"Not a chance, Gates. It's probably out of the bar and empty by now. Nothing super important in it was there?"

"Just about $130. Oh, and some snap shots and my Colorado driver's license."

"Well the $130 is gone, along with the pictures and the driver's license. You can apply for a duplicate license when you get back stateside. I hope you were smart enough not to bring all the money you had this first night?"

"No, sir. I have a little more money back on the ship."

"Good. OK, let's get in the wagon, and we'll run you back to the police boat landing."

"We don't get put on report do we?"

"No, your punishment for forgetting yourself and getting your wallet stolen is a $130 fine. Chalk it up to being naive and thinking that those girls really enjoyed your hand sliding up their inner thigh. Next time put your wallet in your front pants pocket. It's a lot harder to get out without you noticing."

Why do all young men have to climb fool's hill for themselves? Why can't they take any telling from their seniors? I found out about the front pants pocket when I was 18. Not by screwing up but from my 3rd class. The bars on Granby Street were notorious for picking Sailor's pockets, but I had a heads up. Of course if one was in uniform, the old 13 button pants pocket was so tight and small the Sailor himself had a very difficult time extracting anything from it. The guys who just hung a fat wallet from the uniform waist band lost it quickly.

After the men had been dropped off to be taken back to LARTER by the police boat, Dillan asked Chan what he had said to the girls and the bar owner.

"I ask if anyone would give me stolen wallet. I say I not press charges someone just throw on floor. No one do. I tell them bar closed for rest night. My patrol check insure door locked fifteen minute. And my patrol make close watch bar rest week. Any infraction, bar closed for two week."

"I told them if American wallet stolen again this bar I take all girl jail until someone admit stealing. And I have bar shut down and lock for ever. Shutting bar hurt them. Girl who work bar that get shut down by us, have very difficult time getting job another bar."

"But I not sure American lost wallet this bar. Could be pickpocket on street. So I talk tough, but bar owner understand that some threat "bluff" as you American say."

So far, shore patrol is interesting but not challenging.

That was about to change.

At 2130, they got a call. It was a fight in another bar. Backup needed. Chan made a few radio calls. There was a big crowd in the street outside the bar and it took Chan, running the up and down wailing siren with the flashing blue lights, and yelling out the window, to squeeze the van through. An additional police patrol van was there already. Two Chinese police officers were trying, somewhat unsuccessfully, to push the crowd back. Dillan heard more sirens. More help on the way?

When he and Chan walked into the bar, there were tables turned over, chairs broken, and two groups of Sailors separated by the patrol team glaring at each other. Glass and liquid on the floor. Bar girls and a couple of Chinese men in the background. And there was a big overweight middle aged mama san with her hands on her hips, letting out a torrent of unintelligible sounds. At least to Dillan they were unintelligible.

The lights were on bright, probably done by the bar owner or mama san to stop the fight. Usually bars were dimly lit so the bar girls could work the guys in relative privacy.

There were 4 Sailors on one side and 3 on the other. Dillan looked them over.

Damn, the group of three are LARTER Sailors. And one of them is RMSN Kilmer. One of my own division's men. With a nice bruise on his left cheek.

When the LARTER men saw Dillan they looked at the floor.

Oh boy, there will some captain's masts for this one.

Chan said, "You deal with American." He obviously was not happy.

Dillan went over to the group of 4. "OK, guys, what ship are you off of?"

Quiet. Then an older looking one said, "CATSKILL."

Dillan looked him right in the eye. "CATSKILL what Sailor?"

"USS CATSKILL, sir!"

Better. One needs to establish authority quickly. The men were probably well lubricated, and a scuffle could break out again in an instant. The patrol had done an excellent job getting them separated. SK2 Wilson, the LARTER shore patrol guy, did well. And his Chinese counterpart must have been pretty good also.

Dillan knew that the shrill whistle the Chinese carried tended to stop everyone in their tracks. And Wilson was slowly slapping the palm of his hand with his night stick. And he was a big man. That may have put a damper on the fight also. Dillan didn't see any bleeding heads but wouldn't be surprised if there were a few bumps on the noggin or sore stomachs here and there that he couldn't see.

A skilled shore patrol man could swing a billy club on its leather thong and deliver quite a blow with the end of it to the solar plexus: took the fight right out of most drunks.

"OK, all of you, break out your ID Cards. Wilson, take'm and write down all names, rates, and service numbers."

The men started fumbling for their cards.

"Now," turning to the CATSKILL group, "you start. Tell me what caused Sailors from the same US Navy to fight with each other."

The older one said, "When we came in here at 9 o'clock they was sitting with our girls. When we tried to get'm back the fat one," pointing to a 3rd class FTG Dillan knew, "got pushy."

"Yea", said another CATSKILL Sailor, "they was with our girls and wouldn't give'm up."

Dillan stared at him. "Sir," he added.

This CATSKILL group is surly lot.

Dillan turned to the FTG from LARTER.

"Is that how it went down, Sailor?"

"No, sir, the three of us were having a quiet drink and talking with these here girls," waving at the group of mini skirted Chinese girls. "Then these guys came in and told us we were messing with their girls. We didn't see any signs around the girl's necks saying they belonged to anyone." There was a snicker from RMSN Kilmer.

Turning, "Listen Kilmer, this is not funny. Read me loud and clear?"

"Yes, sir," sheepishly.

"OK, go on."

"Well, then the fat old one over there", indicating the older CATSKILL man (and a nice retort to being called fat before), "started pushing Kilmer around and tried to drag the girl on Kilmer's lap off. Kilmer got up and pushed back. Then one of the other guys kicked me and told me that we should get out of their bar."

"Who threw the first punch?"

"The fat old guy," said Kilmer, "Sir."

"Did not!"

Dillan spun around. "Listen Mister, keep your mouth shut unless I ask you to talk, got that?" "Got that?"

"Yes, sir."

"Anything else, Kilmer?"

"Yes, sir, then they jumped us and the fight started. We were outnumbered, Mr. Dillan, and they threw a chair at Levet," indicating the FTG. "Then one of'm took a swing at Morton," indicating SN Morton from 1st Division.

God, like kids fighting in a sand box. But have to give each side their say.

"OK, CATSKILL, who do you think started it?"

"They did, sir, the one you called Kilmer kicked me when I tried to get my girl off his lap. Yeah, and then they pushed me over a table and broke the chair."

Dillan thought for a moment. *OK. There is no way I'm ever going to know the whole truth. Let's finish this thing and get both groups back to their ship.*

"Listen up, all of you. Fighting is unacceptable. And you all know that and were briefed by your superiors. It makes the US Navy look bad and you have damaged private property in a foreign country nice enough to allow us to visit them. Each of you will be charged with violating the UCMJ, that is for disobeying an order, and damaging personal property."

"You'll be taken to police headquarters, and I'll write up the charges personally. Then you'll be escorted back to your ships and the report documents will be given to your officer of the deck. Your liberty, for tonight at least, is over."

He continued, "Give me or the police any trouble and I'll have you clapped in the Royal navy's brig, instantly."

Then a long stare at each.

"One more thing, CATSKILL. I know you are station ship and have been here awhile. But to my knowledge, these girls do not belong to anyone. They're just trying to make a buck. Better remember that. The next shore patrol officer may decide to just lock you up and throw away the key."

"And you guys from LARTER, you've just added significantly to my personal workload. That does not make me happy."

He walked over to Chan. Chan was of the opinion that a night in the tank might be good for all of them. Dillan talked him out of it.

"With the reports signed by an officer, all these guys are going to captain's mast, and probably lose a stripe, get fined, and get restricted to the ship, at the least. If we lock'm up they'll have all that and being absent with out leave on top of it," Dillan said.

"OK Lieutenant," and then something in Chinese to his men, now numbering 5. Each of the fighters was taken out and placed into Chan's van (the CATSKILL group) and another van, in thumb cuffs.

Chan was talking to the bar owner. Then he came over to Dillan. "Bar owner intend submit claim damage American Embassy," he said.

Great, all this and an international incident too. The skipper and the XO are going to be pissed. The punishments to be metered out at captain's mast just went up. Oh, well, they had been warned multiple times about fighting and busting up bars. They all know better. And so the long swift arm of military justice will rap them aside the head. Maybe they'll learn something.

Chan and Dillan went back to headquarters. After unloading their charges, the other van headed out. All the men were locked into a big holding cell, still wearing the thumb cuffs. These cuffs were small but very effective. The thumbs of each hand were inserted with arms behind. And then they were latched. Don't fiddle with them and they did not hurt. Try to get them off and they hurt like hell.

SK2 Wilson helped and Dillan uncuffed and interviewed each man and had him sign his charge sheet. They had sobered up a bit by then and were docile. Then Chan took each group separately to the police boat.

By 0020 it was over. The rest of the LARTER shore patrol was standing by. Dillan thanked Chan and got another commercial for suits. Chan asked if he would be back another day as shore patrol officer again. Dillan said he didn't know. Dillan stumbled into his rack at 0130.

46

The next day, after giving the XO and appropriate division officers a heads up, and filling his chief and Fred in, Dillan and Pete caught the 1230 water taxi for fleet landing. From there they took a cab to the China Fleet Club. Fred just scowled and didn't comment when Dillan told him about Kilmer. The Radioman chief was bent and Kilmer was in for a tough work day.

Dillan and Pete went into the telephone exchange. The wait was short. It was 10 PM in San Diego, the previous night. One could not make calls one's self. It was like the Philippines, give the number to the attendant and go sit on a bench until called and given a booth number.

"Hello, Patty?

"Where the hell are you? Where have you been, for God sakes?" *A bit hostile?*

"I'm in Hong Kong. Sorry about the time, but I just got off the ship and came over to the British place to call you."

"What the hell are you doing in Hong Kong, when you're supposed to be here or almost here?"

"Didn't the Squadron Staff call you? We got extended."

"Oh, they called alright, some JG. He said you were on some fancy national security mission. When I asked him what mission and when you would be home, all he would say is, an important mission and he didn't know when you would be back. I yelled at him good. Served him right. Damn Navy screwing up my life again. Damn Navy. I didn't know when you were coming or when, or even if, I would hear from you again. I was worried sick."

"Did you get any of my letters lately?"

"A couple, maybe 4, some old ones, only one since you went on search and rescue.

That was a quick turn around. Maybe 3 weeks was very fast for a letter, especially from North SAR.

But Dillan knew the helo air crews were real good at taking a mail bag back to a carrier after refueling and seeing that it got on the next COD flight to Cubi.

"When are you coming home, damn it?"

"Honey, I don't know for sure. They sent us here for a week's R&R because they thought we did a good job. I expect they'll send us to Subic to pick up a carrier for the transit back to the states."

She was being, oh, so tough and antagonistic. Words came out of her that he had never heard from her. But that was not Patty, not at all. It was just the frustration coming out.

But if I am a bit patronizing, she will flip. I taught myself to not show emotion. A shitty childhood taught me that showing emotion was a weakness that others could exploit. Patty had not been down that rough path. Her emotions are a lot closer to the surface.

The telephone was quiet for awhile.

"I, I … can't take it much longer Pat. I love you so much. But it hurts so much. I've been married for a year and you have been here five months, and most of that gone. Our first anniversary and I spent it alone, alone damn it. I'm lonely, I miss … miss you so much"

Her voice was broken; she was trying to suppress a cry. *God, I feel like a bastard.*

She continued, "Pat, I want to be a good wife. I went into this with my eyes open. Lots of my friends had naval officers for fathers. But this unknown stuff is so … so difficult. I never know if you are dead or not. Sometimes I think you'll reach out to me if you are in trouble. Then I'll know. Other Navy wives go through the awful experience of having two guys in uniform show up at their front door."

It got quiet for a moment. Then in a cracked voice she said, "Pat, Frank Norstrand, you remember … his wife Tammy called me the other day. He was on an incountry tour, remember? She said he was killed in a firefight in the Delta. God, I can't cope. I feel so sorry for Tammy."

Oh God, Frank was the communications officer before me. I relieved him. We were friends!

She went on, "Tell me you'll be home soon. Tell me we'll be the 'two Pats' again soon. Tell me you're OK and love me. I need that so much."

"My sweet Patty, God I love you. This'll end soon I think. Soon all of this shit will be a forgotten bad dream. I'm coming home, Honey. I'm coming home."

That eased things a bit. Frank getting killed had really done a number on Patty. They talked a bit about how he would buy the things on the list since he was in Hong Kong. It ended with the usual love and miss ending and she was gone.

I have not had enough of her voice. Maybe I should call her back? She won't be asleep. When she gets upset she can't go back to sleep. But I want her to get some rest. It's Saturday night there, and she usually goes to church at 9 Sunday. Maybe she will fix herself a glass of wine.

His core ached – like having a heart attack. He sat in the phone booth alone for awhile, just staring at the graffiti on the wall. Like so many others before him.

I miss Patty so much. Frank gone. Damn Gooks. Damn war. Poor Tammy. Patty will feel Tammy's hurt almost like it's her own.

When he came out, Pete was there. He looked melancholy also. A phone call home would do that. So close but so far. But Pete didn't know Frank. Pete arrived after Frank left. Dillan told him because Pete had at least heard about Frank.

Pete said, "Poor guy. I need a drink, a big one, a double."

This was going to be a tough day. It was only 4:30 PM and Dillan wanted a big drink at least as bad as Pete did. They went into the China Fleet Club bar. The bar was dim, lots of paneling. Lots of draft beer taps that Dillan didn't recognize, only a few guys at the bar. They grabbed a table.

Walls were covered in ship's plaques. More than Dillan had ever seen. More than even the carrier had, popular place for lots of navies. No service, so they moved to the bar. Pete ordered a Guinness and a Bushmills, very Irish. Pete sure was not a paddy. And Dillan didn't even know black men drank Guinness. Dillan ordered a Johnny Walker Black up and a Bass Ale.

Wow. Serious boilermakers. That's a way to get it on! OK, so much for shopping.

They talked a bit. Pete's wife had been upset also, he said. The DESRON staff had not handled the telephone calls with much diplomacy. Then they played a couple of games of snooker, an odd pool game on a table the size of the carrier's flight deck.

Little balls and one had to get a red one in prior to going for a colored ball. Dillan had never played before, but Pete had. It was a lot more difficult than playing 9 ball for quarters. And the pockets were so small! It took hours.

Dillan had a major buzz. They had dinner at the club: some overcooked beef, potato, no salad. By 2030, they were headed back. Dillan saw double – maybe triple. Up the gangway and finally back aboard at 2130.

Rack. Oh God, where is my rack? Stumble through the hatch. Down the passageway weaving. Into stateroom. Drop clothing on the deck. Crawl into rack. Pass out.

"Now reveille, reveille. All hands heave out and trice up."

About 30 seconds after Dillan went to sleep. Or at least it seemed like it.

Out of the rack 0600, oh goodie, I got almost 9 hours and still feel like shit.

He took a quick shower and fresh wash khakis, then went up to the wardroom for a coffee before quarters. Dillan couldn't look food in the eye with out a major eruption. He probably should have closed his eyes before he bled to death.

"Good morning Mr. Dillan!" *Damn the skipper is still at the table.*

"Looking a little rough around the edges this morning, are we?" *God, I hate the un-hungover.*

"Yes, sir, please no loud noises. My tongue is asleep and my teeth itch." It was a saying from an old comedy routine.

"Sit here," indicating the empty chair to his right. "Once you can tell up from down, Mr. Dillan, the XO wants to see you about RMSN Kilmer. Our troops got in deep shit night before last. We have to deal with it now, you know."

Great. Let's crucify him. Why are you so apparently happy, Skipper, when one of your crew is in deep shit? Has Fred been blowing sweet nothings in your ear again? Have to keep the enlisted crud in line? Not fair. The skipper was not at all that way and even Fred wasn't a total ass, only half of one. Give him a big nail and a hammer and he would pass it to someone else. He would not want to participate in a crucifixion. Just watch. Shut your mind Dillan. In your state something might leak out of your mouth!

"Yes, sir. We'll see at what I assume will be a mast?"

"You bet ya, Dillan. People like that we have to deal with firmly. Make an example that'll keep the rest of the crew on the straight and narrow. Your radioman and the other two have caused problems for a lot of people. We got notification from the embassy that a claim has been filed."

Goody. That was quick. Kilmer's ass is grass, and the skipper is going to be the lawn mower.

"When are you going to schedule mast, Captain?"

"Tomorrow morning. We can't let these things fester, don't you agree?"

"Absolutely, Captain, never let things fester."

Then, quietly, leaning over to the skipper, "Captain, I talked to Patty yesterday. Tammy called her and told her Frank Norstrand was killed in Vietnam."

The skipper just looked at Dillan, like he wanted the words to go away.

"Shit. God damnit – sorry, thank you Dillan. Frank was a good man. How?"

"Some dust up in the Delta. I think he was assigned to a PBR. Heard they're in it a lot."

"Yes, they are. Fine young officer. It's not fair. Hope his wife is OK?"

"Don't know, hard to be OK when something like that happens. They were only married about 3 years. Patty's going to see her. Tammy's packing up and going back home. Frank'll be buried there."

"I'll ask my wife to see her also, get her to call Patty. Maybe they can go together."

"Yes, sir."

Patty will not want to see Tammy with the CO's wife; too much Navy and not enough compassion.

Dillan excused himself and went looking for Fred.

"Fred, my wife told me yesterday that Frank Norstrum was killed in Vietnam."

Fred just looked at Dillan with a weird expression and said, "Thanks for telling me. You didn't have to."

"I told the skipper at breakfast. Figure he will tell the others."

"I'll tell Ted and Pete."

"Don't need to tell Pete, he was with me when I found out."

"OK," and he just stood there for a moment. Then he turned and started back down the passage way.

Dillan just watched him, then turned and walked towards radio.

Human emotions Fred? You never cease to amaze me.

Dillan told the chief about what he knew about Frank Norstrand. The radiomen that had been aboard last cruise would all know him and would be sad to hear how he was killed. The chief would tell the rest of the men who had known Frank.

"Damn, Mr. Dillan, damn. Poor bastard."

Death is not a big deal until it hits home. There are lots of causalities in Vietnam, so I'm a bit jaded. But when it is someone I know it bothers me. Gives me the willys, makes me think about my own vulnerability. Don't think about it.

Then, "OK, Chief, we got work to do. Get Kilmer in here right now. We need to brief him," Dillan said.

When Kilmer arrived, complete with a nice mouse around his eye, Dillan and the chief took him through what to expect at mast.[lxiii]

Dillan and the chief's primary efforts were to get Kilmer to act totally contrite and ask for forgiveness. The hard nosed skipper had a soft heart, and Kilmer needed to appeal to it. Then the chief and Dillan went over what they would say about RMSN Kilmer's performance of duty to date. A good man that had performed his duties well and had only this time transgressed, usually made out a little better. Kilmer was such a man.

Someone who was a repeat offender might even get a Summary Court Martial. If a man was found guilty in a Summary Court Martial, punishments could be harsher.

For major screw ups there was Special Court Martial made up of a panel of officers and, effectively, a real trial. Finally there was General Court Martial for things like murder, rape, etc.

There was some good news this morning, however. A message sked change on the board from CTF 70 indicating TU 70.5.3 was ordered to Subic at the completion of the 7 days R&R.

Right on. Team up with a carrier and head home. I'm more than ready.

Pete and Dillan didn't go ashore. They worked a bit, and ate in the wardroom. Only Chris Harcourt, sitting at the head of the table, and maybe 6 other officers were aboard. Dillan was still so hung over he could hear the sound of one hand clapping. Pete was better off, but hurting none the less. They tried watching the officer's movie in the wardroom at 2000. But by 2015, Dillan was out of there and headed for the rack. He had seen "Blue Hawaii" a hundred times before anyway.[lxiv]

Movies were shown by one of the duty electrician mates or interior communications electricians. If Dillan was going to watch a movie, he would normally let the duty man off, and show it himself. He had been qualified as a motion picture operator as an enlisted man. But tonight, he let the duty man show the officer's movie.

Tuesday morning. Dillan and Pete had the duty with Red Redmond. At quarters, the skipper asked each division to hold a moment of silence just prior to colors, for Frank -- a former shipmate lost in combat.

Dillan noted that the disagreement between the skipper and "Mary Sue's Side Painters" had been resolved and her crew was busy painting the ship. She had also been permitted to set up a place to sell Cokes on the fan tail (extreme back of the ship).

Mary Sue was a fixture in Hong Kong. For an old heavy 3 inch diameter nylon mooring line, a couple of brass fire nozzles, and permission to sell cokes on the stern, she would have her crew in sampans give the ship's sides and guard rails a wash coat of haze grey paint provided by the ship. All ships allowed this. After months at sea, ships needed painting. The paint job would not last very long. But it did spruce up the ship.

The Chinese coolly crew that worked for Mary Sue spoke no English and worked sun up to sun down from their little sampans, with long poles and paint rollers. Some would come aboard and paint the guard rails with their bare hands dipped in the lead based paint. An awful job and they probably got $3 a day.

In the case of LARTER, the skipper did not want the two or three Chinese camping out on the stern 24/7. Mary Sue insisted. A short middle aged Chinese woman decked out like an empress and ferried to the ship in a small but beautiful wooden sampan. It was a standoff.

Water taxis started to skip LARTER on pick up runs, troops ready to go on liberty lined up on the quarterdeck. Mary Sue had some clout.

Finally the skipper had her aboard again, to the ward room for tea, and agreed, although he did rope off the area and post an armed guard at mount 52. So the painting and coke selling started. And the coolies selling cokes always had an ad or two for bars in Wan Chai, or even special 'parties' to pass out to the crew with their cokes.

47

Now it was 0900. "Now lay before the mast all malingerers and charged men," went the 1MC: captain's mast.

Men lined up outside the captain's in-port cabin, master at arms making sure that the men looked good and that their division officers and chiefs were present. This was one of the very few occasions where men wore their hats inside. Even so, in the US Navy, no one ever saluted inside, and never without a hat, although the bridge was traditionally considered outside even though enclosed.

When the case was called, the man's division officer and chief formed up in ranks, to the captain's right. The captain, with his officer's cap on, scrambled eggs (gold braid) on the bill, standing behind a podium. Yeoman (essentially a secretary) standing by to record notes. XO at attention on the captain's left. The accused was marched in by the master at arms and stood at attention in front of the captain. When ordered, he uncovered (took his hat off).

"Radioman Seaman Kilmer reporting as ordered, sir."

"Seaman, you have the right to challenge this Article 15 UCMJ proceedings and you may, if you wish, request that charges be submitted to Court Martial. Do you wish to proceed with Non Judicial punishment?"

"Yes, sir."

I have never, ever heard of a man ask for a court martial.

Under the UCMJ Article 15, Non Judicial Punishment could be refused, but punishment was limited by the UCMJ and according to the rank of the captain. Far more serious punishments could be metered out by Court Martial. No one ever really considered skipping mast.

"Seaman Kilmer, you are charged with violating the Uniform Code of Military Justice Articles 92, failing to obey a lawful order, and 109 destruction of property. Along with the rest of the crew, you have previously been specifically cautioned about fighting. You were involved in a fight involving property damage in a liquor establishment in the Wan Chai district of Hong Kong on the night of 20 April, 1968."

"You were taken into custody by the shore patrol and returned to the ship. Shore patrol issued an infraction report. The establishment owner has filed a claim for damages against the United States Government. The charges against you were signed by one LTJG Patrick Dillan, USN, and an official shore patrol officer at the time of the incident. Do you, Seaman Kilmer, understand the charges brought against you?"

"Yes, sir, and sorry I embarrassed the ship, sir."

"Excellent, Seaman Kilmer, do you have anything to say on your own behalf?"

"Only that I really fouled up, Captain, and I know it was wrong to get in a fight. I'm sorry, Captain."

"Mr. Dillan." Dillan front and center to stand next to the man.

"Mr. Dillan, as this man's division officer, tell me what kind of a Sailor he is."

"Captain, Seaman Kilmer is an excellent Sailor. He hasn't been in trouble since he came aboard. He's always on time for his watches and evolutions, works hard, and did well when he was assigned to mess cooking. He's a good man, sir, who fouled up this one time."

"Thank you, Mr. Dillan. Chief." Front and center alongside Dillan.

"Tell me, Chief, what kind of Sailor Kilmer is."

"Captain, Seaman Kilmer is a good Sailor, sir. He never gives his petty officers any grief, always looks ship-shape, and works hard. We were going to recommend him for 3rd, maybe next cycle."

"Very well. Seaman Kilmer, you should consider yourself lucky that your division officer and chief think so highly of you. You are going to have to wait a while longer for a chance at petty officer. You must understand that the charges brought before me are serious. Fighting and causing property damage in a foreign port brings discredit on the US Navy and the United States of America."

The CO leaned over and scribbled on a paper on the podium in front of him. Then he looked up.

"You are found guilty of the charges brought against you. You are sentenced to a reduction in rate to Seaman Apprentice and forfeiture of one half of one month's pay. I will suspend the pay forfeiture. Consider yourself lucky. I usually deal more harshly with Sailors that embarrass this ship."

Silence for awhile, probably to allow it to sink in a little.

"Seaman Apprentice Kilmer, you are dismissed."

From the master at arms, "Seaman Apprentice Kilmer, cover, to, (put your hat on), left face, forward march."

Dillan and the chief marched out behind Kilmer. It was over. As they left, he saw Billy Hoffman and Len Ottaway waiting in the passageway with their 2 offenders.

As the door shut, Billy whispered, "Dillan, how did it go?"

"Better than expected," Dillan whispered.

After they went down to the main deck, Dillan turned to Kilmer, "Kilmer, you got off easy. I was sure that you were going to get restricted to the ship, also. Maybe busted to Seaman Recruit. So you may go ashore again while we're here, if you don't have the duty. But if you get into trouble ashore again, expect a much harsher sentence. Understood?"

"Yes, sir, and thank you and the chief for standing up for me. Do I lose half my pay?"

"You're welcome, Kilmer, and no, that portion of the sentence was suspended, which means it'll not be enforced unless you get caught screwing up even a little. Three months from now, if you keep your nose clean, that part of the sentence'll go away. And 3 months from now you can take the test for Seaman again. If you pass the Seaman test and continue to walk the straight and narrow, maybe you'll get a shot at 3rd next year. Now get up to radio and get to work."

"Yes, sir." As he walked away the chief said, "The skipper was quite lenient, I think. Figured he would be hard on him. 'Penetration, however slight' you know. How 'bout you, Mr. Dillan?"

"Yeah, it could've been much worse. We can thank whatever lucky stars look down on poor dumb young Sailors. It's obvious that the captain understands that it's been a long cruise, with few opportunities for liberty. He gave him a break. And Chief, I know we have to cough up another mess cook soon. Put that new signalman striker on next and let Kilmer have a by for 3 months."

The chief looked at Dillan with a question in his eyes. But said nothing.

"I know you think Kilmer really messed up, but I was there. He got dragged into a situation. He didn't start it. You can send him mess cooking next go round."

"Yes, sir, Mr. Dillan, OK."

Dillan heard that Billy's man got busted also. Len's got busted and restricted to the ship. He had been to mast a year ago for dereliction of duty so the skipper was harder on him. The rest of the day was uneventful. Pete got assigned as shore patrol officer.

At least Red was spreading the fun around. Dillan told Pete about his experiences again. They had discussed it in detail at the club but both were too loaded to remember it well. Dillan told Pete to say hello to Chan, and find out how quickly a sport coat could be made.

At 1700, the captain and other officers attending, in service dress blue, were picked up by a 40 foot utility boat flying the Royal Crown Colony pennant forward and the white and red Royal navy ensign on the stern. Off for the Commodore Hong Kong's shindig.

"Bong bong – bong bong, LARTER departing."

Dillan had the 20-24 on the quarterdeck as officer of the deck. In a port like this, with liberty expiring at midnight ("Cinderella liberty," the crew called it); most of the action would be on that watch. Sure enough, by 2130 the water taxies started depositing well lubricated Sailors on the small platform at the bottom of the gangway.

Getting in or out of a water taxi required some coordination. All the boats running around Hong Kong harbor generated lots of wakes and water taxies bounced around. Some wakes even sloshed over the ship's lower gangway platform. Dillan was amazed how the men got out, up the gangway stairs, stood at attention on the top platform with ID Card in hand, and requested permission to come aboard without falling into the harbor or down the stairs.

Dillan looked the men over quite well and looked into any parcels they had. Bringing booze aboard was a "no no". And Hong Kong did have drugs available: some marijuana but also some serious stuff like opium. Getting caught trying to get booze or drugs aboard was a captain's mast offense in small quantities and a Court Martial offense in larger quantities.

Marijuana use was rampant incountry, and to a much lesser extent, on ships. Picked up in Olongapo, every now and then it showed up aboard. Usually spotted by someone due to the distinctive smell it left when it was smoked. LARTER had only one small quantity incident prior to Formation Star, and the offender was treated to mast, extra duty, loss of a stripe and restriction.

At 2300, Dillan caught sight of the police boat, blue light flashing, headed his way. Sure enough, it came along side, and a big 2nd class sonarman that Dillan did not know walked a stumbling Sailor up the gangway.

A salute from the 2nd class, "Permission to come aboard, sir?"

"Granted."

"Sir, this man was stumbling around and creating a disturbance."

"OK, Sailor, let's see your ID Card." It took a long time while the man fumbled for it and then handed it over."

BMSN Miriam, one of Joe Rederman's boson mate strikers, quite drunk.

Dillan asked, "Any report chit on this man, petty officer?"

"No, sir, Captain Chan and the Ensign just had us pick him up and transport'm before he got into trouble or robbed."

"My compliments to Captain Chan, tell him LTJG Dillan sends, and thanks."

"Yes, sir," and a snappy salute, "Permission to leave the ship, sir?"

"Granted," Dillan said as he returned the salute. And the SP was gone down the gangway to the police boat.

"You got off lucky, Miriam. Messenger of the Watch, please escort Miriam to his rack. He probably can't make it on his own."

"Yes, sir." And off they went, the watch trying to propel a stumbling drunk in the correct direction.

"Should I log this sir?" from the Petty Officer of the Watch.

"Log the time and that a police boat delivered a crew-member to the ship. No charges, and leave Miriam's name out of the log."

"Yes, sir.

At 2330, the 40 foot utility boat came back with the CO and others. They must have had a good time. After taps, there were no bongs.

"Quiet watch, Mr. Dillan?"

"Yes, sir, Captain, a quiet watch."

"Good."

Then Fred came over. "You have been writing up men who came back drunk, haven't you?"

"Yes, sir, but we haven't had any tonight."

"Really, Mr. Dillan?" with a questioning look.

Hell, Fred, you have at least your main sails up and drawing. Maybe I should write you up.

"Really, sir."

That was the only other incident. Dillan was relieved by Chief Michael, the EM chief at 2345.

The next morning, Pete said he had had a relatively uneventful shore patrol. No real fights. Lots of drunks transported. Pete said one was a black Sailor off CATSKILL.

"He was ready to tear the bouncer in one bar a new asshole, Pat. We got there just in time."

"Did you write him up? And why was he ready to take on a big bouncer?"

"Don't know for sure, something about a girl getting uptight over him not buying her a drink. I think she ordered it on her own, and he wasn't about to pay. Bouncer told him to pay or else, grabbed his collar. The man got away. Owner went out and grabbed a patrol off the street. When we got there he was in one corner with a beer bottle, ready to defend himself, wouldn't listen to the patrol."

"You didn't write him up for fighting?"

"There was no fight. Blacks, liquored up, can be a handful. Some of the seething inside tends to spill out under the influence. But a black officer can say the right words to bring them back to reality that a white officer can't."

"So what are the magic words?"

"Appeal to his sense of family pride, tell him that he is making all his black compatriots look bad. But don't try it yourself – you don't have the complexion for it."

Chan had advised Pete that a sport coat took about 24 hours to make. Dillan would have expected a few days and since LARTER was to depart on Saturday, and this was Wednesday, he didn't have many days.

48

Pete and Dillan went ashore at 1300. First they went to Chan's recommended father tailor for a fitting for Dillan for a blue blazer. Pete ordered a light brown one. Then they took the Star ferry to Kowloon side. Big oval shaped ferry with mostly open decks covered with a metal roof.

The ferry ride took about a half hour, went fairly close to LARTER, now about two thirds painted, sampans and painters busy. MENAUL was anchored to the right and had just about been painted, more sampans. Dillan saw some power junks flying the red with a big and four small gold stars in the corner flag of The Peoples Republic of China.

Hong Kong was a great outlet for the Red Chinese. A lot of their exports were shipped through Hong Kong and a lot of their money flowed through the banks in Hong Kong. If Hong Kong had not existed, the Reds would have had to invent it.

There was a Portuguese colony up the river a bit called Macau. A high speed ferry made the run. Gambling there and lots of opium and prostitution, but it was strictly off limits to US military personnel. Few, if any, ship board people risked it.

On Kowloon side, Dillan and Pete stopped for a drink at the Princess Hotel. Most expensive drink they ever had in a stuffy Victorian bar. It even had overstuffed sofas. Then they went shopping for linen. There were a lot of shops. Most linen probably made in Red China.

US military personnel purchasing things in Hong Kong were obliged to get a "Certificate of Origin" from the vendor to insure that articles had not originated in Red China. These would be required for the US Custom's officials when LARTER got back to the states.

It was a known fact that one could get a certificate of origin that said anything one wanted it to say. A piece of paper with some Chinese characters, an official looking stamp and lines filled in by hand in English noting what the article was and that the country of origin was the British Crown Colony of Hong Kong. Some stores would even give a purchaser a bunch of forms for an extra few $HK.

Hong Kong had lots of factories making clothing and cheap toys. But most of the stuff, especially linens, listing Hong Kong as the origin country, came over the border from Red China and then were creatively converted with a label or certificate into acceptable items. The prohibition on Red Chinese merchandise was just another unenforceable rule.

By 1700, and after obtaining embroidered table cloths, embroidered napkins, some lace, and even some embroidered pillow cases, Pete and Dillan were tired and their feet hurt. They went to Jimmy's Kitchen for dinner.

The menu must have been 50 pages in a bound book, too many choices. They settled on Kobe beef steaks. Kobe beef was a Japanese thing, but it really meant very finely marbled melt in your mouth steak, probably from Red Chinese cows. Smelled wonderful and tasted like ambrosia. They ended with a caramel cream tort-like dessert and a brandy to go with a cigar. It was even a real Cuban Montecristo cigar. Another prohibited item in the USA, but the brits liked them. And so did Dillan.

They talked college football for awhile. Then they discussed their plans for leave once the ship got back stateside. Pete and Rita were flying back east to see family.

Back to the Star ferry, across to Victoria, and then back to the ship on a water taxi.

The following day was Fred's CDO duty day. He and Red had spent the previous night ashore. After quarters he was in a very good mood. He was telling Dillan, Ted, and Pete about what a great hotel the Mandarin was, and what great food their restaurant had. Getting away from the pressure had been good for Fred.

Did he get laid? He sure could have used it. I could probably take up a collection and make enough to pay for a girl for Fred, anything to make Fred more human.

Thursday was the last day ashore for Pete and Dillan. A quick telephone call home to tell Patty about what he had bought and that they had orders to Subic. It was 11 PM Wednesday night in San Diego. The call went well.

But Patty said, "I'll believe it when you're here, not before. As long as you're over there anything can happen."

"Well, it'll be soon now, Patty. XO says our lease is up and 7th fleet has to let us go."

"Not soon enough. The CO's wife called and asked me to go with her to Tammy's. I begged off due to work. Then after work I went alone. Tammy's taking it hard. Her mother was there. She flew out to help Tammy ship things. Tammy's life is over, at least for awhile. I don't know if she will ever get over Frank. Good thing they didn't have kids."

"Don't think anyone who has a spouse die like that ever gets over it."

"Well, her mother seemed nice. She leaves early next week. I probably won't see her again. Frigging war. I saw Rita day before yesterday. She's back."

"Yeah, Pete told me. You all set to take some time off?'

"I told my boss that I need a week. Haven't been there long enough for vacation so it will be a freebee, but she'll let me off."

"You can make reservations for Tahoe as soon as we have a date. I'll call you as soon as I know anything."

"Good, call me, I've got some ads I clipped out of the paper."

"OK, love you, bye."

"Love you, bye."

A few drinks at the China Fleet Club, a little shopping. Dillan picked up his sport coat – fit like a glove, $40. Pete got his. Dillan bought a big green painting of a junk for $40 after haggling the street vendor down from $60 (480 $HK). It was going to be hard to stow when he got it back to the ship. He dropped it by Chan's office but Chan was not there. Sam had the SP duty with him and they were probably out and about in the van.

Then Dillan and Pete took a little ferry around the island to Aberdeen and had dinner in a floating restaurant. The harbor was amazing with literally thousands of junks jammed together in a big mass: the floating city. There were little sampans running around every where. Some with little open motors, shaft sticking out the back into the water. Putt putt putt. Poor man's outboard. Many with just a single sweep oar, driver standing up and moving the oar back and forth like she was born doing it.

The food was Chinese and was good but expensive. A crispy skin duck, pork, noodles, vegetable medley of many things Dillan had never seen. Not like a Chinese restaurant in the USA.

Dillan showed off his chopstick routine for Pete. A few Johnny Walkers for Dillan and Jack Daniels for Pete. Then they took the ferry back to the municipal landing, and walked to police headquarters to pick up Dillan's picture.

Chan was in his office and the detention tank was about 1/3 full. Sam was not there.

"Good evening Lieutenant Dillan, Ensign Donavan, heard you availed self father tailor shop?"

"Sure did, Captain Chan, sure did. Nice material and tailoring and a good price done quickly."

"We try please customers. Happy customers tell shipmate. I see you purchased painting. Since wrapped, local artist?"

"Young, I believe," Dillan said.

"Ah yes, S.T. Young, quite famous paintings of junk Hong Kong harbor and Aberdeen."

"An easy night?" from Pete.

"Wish quieter. Was fight in bar. One Sailor off CATSKILL had go hospital. Your Ensign at hospital with him."

"No one off LARTER involved I hope?"

"No, only CATSKILL. Station ship here too long I fear. After month or so Sailor always more trouble. CATSKILL has another week, then Royal Australian navy cruiser take over for three week."

"Well, Chan, this was the last day for Pete and me, we have the duty tomorrow. But we'll not be back for shore patrol. Our senior watch officer is spreading the fun around so you can expect Ensign Bill Hoffman tomorrow night."

"Last night sometime very busy; hope Ensign Hoffman ready?"

"He should be, we both briefed him."

"Good, as Queen's navy say, fair wind and following sea to you both. Maybe sometime I see you again when return Hong Kong."

"Thanks, Captain Chan, but for us we hope it'll be a long time before we have to come back to the Far East on a ship. Hope you are a General by then."

"Understand, stay home with family. If you wait I get General – very long wait, maybe Major," with a smile. "Good-bye."

Then they took a water taxi, back aboard 2145, their last outing in Hong Kong.

Friday was a duty day. It rained off and on all day. Dillan had the 12-16 on the quarterdeck, black raincoat, getting the few going ashore off in water taxies. Most of the officers, including the CO and XO, went over. It was the last day in Hong Kong. Dillan wrote a letter, found a place in secondary radio to stow his painting, and watched the movie with Red. Pete had the 20-24 quarterdeck watch. Dillan was in the rack early.

At breakfast Dillan asked Billy if there was a lot of action on shore patrol. Not much, he said. LARTER and MENAUL crew's wallets had been bled dry. So they mostly stayed on board or returned to their ships early. A couple of drunks transported back to CATSKILL, but from the China Fleet Club. CATSKILL's funds had been depleted, also.

Wan Chai will have to wait for financial reinforcements.

Billy said Chan was taking the weekend off, his first days off in 3 weeks.

49

Saturday morning right after quarters, held in service dress blue, "Now station the special sea and anchor detail."

Bring up the gangway and, "The officer of the deck is shifting his watch from the quarterdeck to the bridge." It took awhile to pull up the hook to short stay. And the deck crew had to wash the chain down with a fire hose: black muck. Dillan was back on the bridge as JOOD. The skipper had decided that Red was to have Dillan on the bridge for watches, sea detail, GQ, and unrep. Goodbye combat.

Finally from the 1JV sound powered telephone talker, "Anchor's aweigh."

"Underway, shift colors. All hands to quarters for leaving port."

Anchor aweigh meant nothing more than it was no longer attached to the bottom. They sat there for awhile as the anchor was brought up the rest of the way and stowed in its hawse pipe. The bow crew had to use a fire hose to wash the muck off it, also.

Then Dillan conned the ship slowly out of the harbor, while the foredeck crew passed the stoppers. The two cliffs at the east entrance looked awfully close. Would not want to meet a big freighter coming in at the same time we were going out, Dillan thought.

Out into the fairway, Red China to port. "Secure from quarters." Once 12 miles out, LARTER slowed and waited for MENAUL. Senior ship came in first, left last.

"Secure the special sea and anchor detail, set the regular condition III watch."

Dillan got to turn his hat around and relieve himself. He had the 08-12. Len Ottaway came up in wash khaki and relieved Fred as OOD. Dillan would be stuck in blues until he got relieved.

When MENAUL was about a mile away, the 21MC squawked,

"Bridge, combat, signal bridge: Signal in the air at the dip from the OTC. Charlie November 3, tack, corpen 165, speed 15."

The MENAUL was using flag hoist. Len checked the signal book.

He said, "Form a column at 1000 yards spacing on the guide. Course 165, speed 15 knots. Not a bad formation but why so slow?"

From the skipper, "OK, make it so when executed, smartly now."

"Yes, sir."

Flag hoist signals were placed at the dip or not all the way up to mean that it was an execute to follow signal. Then it would be closed up. When it was hauled down that was the signal to execute it.

Dillan did the maneuvering board. Combat did also. When executed they needed to turn left, increase speed to 20, make a circle, and pull in behind MENAUL. It would only take about 10 minutes to get on station. MENAUL was already headed 165.

"Bridge, combat, signal bridge, signal closed up."

Dillan walked out to the port wing. He could see the flags on MENAUL come down smartly.

"Bridge, combat, signal bridge, execute."

Dillan ordered, "Left standard rudder, come to new course 090, all ahead standard, indicate turns for 20 knots," as he reentered the bridge proper. And it was repeated. LARTER heeled to port and off they went to station.

Otherwise, it was a boring watch keeping station behind MENAUL. Lunch and Dillan ate in the mess decks. Most officers hated doing this. Dillan didn't mind and took Ted Brunshall's sampling for him today. The food was quite good: chicken and mashed potatoes, salad. Lunch and dinner were both full scale meals. There even was some chicken noodle soup. The fried chicken was greasy and Dillan noted this.

By tradition, the on-coming officer of the deck was to sample the crew's mess. This was supposed to be done for every meal. The officer sampling then had to write comments in a log book about the preparation, appearance, and palatability of the meal.

A couple of times in the past Dillan had not been pleased. Most notes in the log said things like "Fine meal." And an officers initials followed by LTJG, USNR or such. Dillan knew that many just looked at the food, signed the log, and went to the wardroom to eat.

But Dillan took the job seriously, having been eating in the crew's mess full time in another life. At sea, meals, and maybe the crew's movie, were the social and enjoyment event of the day.

Navy crews were supposed to be fed well. It was one of the things that allowed the Navy to exist almost totally as a volunteer force while the US Army was drafting like crazy.

So Dillan had gotten on the chief mess serviceman's case over his use of grease, especially on hamburger and meatloaf, and for mashed potatoes the consistency of library paste. Tony had even talked to Dillan for being hard on his cooks. But Dillan persisted, and things got better.

Dillan was in radio, actually crypto, going through some more of his Registered Publications Custodian stuff when there was a knock on the door. It was the chief.

"This message just came in, Mr. Dillan, from the MENAUL. We're routing it to the captain right now."

Dillan took the copy from the chief, and started reading.

270146Z APR 68
PRIORITY
FM   CTU SEVEN ZERO PT FIVE PT TWO
TO   USS LARTER
CC   CTG SEVEN ZERO PT FIVE
       CTF SEVEN ZERO/CTF SEVEN SEVEN
       COMSEVENTHFLT
       CTE SEVEN SEVEN PT SIX PT TWO PT ONE
CONFIDENTIAL //3000//
SUBJ ORDERS (U)
A. CTF SEVEN ZERO 180606Z APR 68.
1.(C) USS LARTER DETACHED. PCD IND AND RPT IAW REF A. GOOD HUNTING.

And that was all. What did that mean? So we're detached. What was the good hunting comment?

"What do you make of this, Mr. Dillan?" the chief asked

"Well, obviously, we have been directed to do something else. I have not seen any other orders. What is that date time group referred to?"

"Don't know, sir. The DTG is better than a week back. We're checking our log."

"OK, Chief, let me know when you find it."

What the hell was going on? Are they being sent to rendezvous with a carrier and not even stop in Subic? That would be great. But they have a lot of Westpac gear to off load. No, it isn't that. What then?

A couple of minutes later the chief came back. "Mr. Dillan, we found it, it's that off line encrypted "eyes only" that came in before we got to Hong Kong."

Shit. Shit, damn, piss. The skipper got secret orders and knew about them but told no one all the time we were in Hong Kong. Secret orders are not for sending ships home. This is really going to suck. He was probably precluded from telling us because he knew we would call and tell our wives that we were getting extended again. It's April, 27, and we're still screwing around on the wrong side of the pond.

"Thanks, Chief. I get the feeling we'll find out what's up soon. And we may not like it."

At 1100, the skipper came on the 1MC.

"This is the captain speaking. I know all of you are looking forward to heading home. I know all of you expected that we were going to Subic and then head east with a carrier. And that will happen. But not right away. We have been asked by COMSEVENTHFLT to take on a Sea Dragon assignment prior to being released. Once we complete this assignment we will go to Subic and then team up with ENTERPRISE or another carrier for the transit home."

"This new assignment is complex and may be dangerous. For those of you who do not know, Sea Dragon is an operation using destroyers to shell the North Vietnamese coast. We will be working in tandem with USS JEFFERY C. GLOVER (DD-791) our sister ship who is enroute from Subic now. We will be doing an unrep for fuel and another to top off on ammo. Expect to be on station day after tomorrow."

"As we did in the past, COMDESRON 15 will be telephoning your loved ones again with the news. I'm sorry that we have been extended again, but I'm sure each of you will do your duty. Over the next few days enroute we will be holding GQ drills and briefings to make sure everyone is ready for this challenging assignment. That is all."

There it is. Another damn extension and a bad one. Sea Dragon is not activated very often. And when it is, ships take a hit sometimes. When one bangs away at the North Vietnamese coast, the bastards shoot back. And at night there are always patrol craft or the damn fast junks to be concerned with. Not as bad as North SAR since Sea Dragon concentrates in the pan handle away from the major ports. But fast junks can operate out of a bath tub. Patty is going to be talking in tongues again. When in hell are we going home?

Fred came into radio with a quickly drafted Moverep outgoing: proceeding to central gulf of Tonkin, chop to CTE 77.6.2.1, the Sea Dragon task element.

They rendezvoused with USS SACREMENTO (AOE-1) just north of Yankee station. The new AOEs were big, almost as long as a carrier. They could refuel from both sides and transfer ammunition using CH-46 Sea Knight twin rotor helicopters at the same time. Pallets were slung under the big helos and set down on the DASH deck. Then they were broken down and the ammo was man handled below.

This should go quickly and without incident. It's a lot safer than high lining ammo pallets over.

Dillan made the approach. It was like making an approach to a carrier. SACRAMENTO was big. They even had a small band playing while LARTER was along side.

She sure has some bow wave. Since she is so long, I don't have to get close to it, thank goodness.

When using helos for vertical replenishment concurrently, one had to go up wind, regardless of the sea direction to insure the helos had favorable wind for their close quarters maneuvering with pallets dangling under them. In most cases, seas were generally coming from the direction of the wind source, but not always. On this day, they were 30 degrees to the right, which made it a bit more interesting. The receiving ship tended to wallow more in the swells, especially as they reflected off of the SACREMENTO.

LARTER was only using the forward fuel station, or station 2. Station 4 was not being used because of the helos.

Dillan was on his toes keeping station. The helo ammo transfer was over quickly.

Then Mr. Murphy struck. The SACRAMENTO had rams that automatically kept the primary wire, the one that the shoes rode on that slung the hose, at the right tension. Tight enough to keep the hoses out of the water, loose enough to keep from pulling the destroyer into her. This was a new innovation.

And it started pulling, hard!

Dillan noticed it, since he was always checking the distance line and looking at the river of water flowing between the SACREMENTO and LARTER. And Fred and the CO noticed it also.

"We seem to be getting closer, Mr. Dillan." Fred said.

"We are, come right a half," from the captain.

Looking at the messenger standing by the bridge hatch and his grease pencil board to refresh his memory on what the last ordered course was, Dillan said into the voice tube,

"Come right, steer 214 and a half."

"Come right, steer 214 and a half, sir. And immediately, "Steering 214 and a half, checking 216, sir" from the helm.

They were swinging more than usual for this sea state, and wallowing. Then the XO noticed a little list to port.

"That damn wire is too tight. Look, it's creating a port list."

Dillan looked. *Sure enough, there is a little port list and the wire is like a bow string. If it breaks, men are in trouble down on deck on both ships. And each time LARTER wallows it gets tighter. We have to get out of here!*

"Captain, that wire …." The XO looked at the captain for a moment.

"Damn, execute emergency break away!" from the captain. This was an emergency exit. During unrep, either ship could call it. The receiving ship had to disconnect the hose, trip the wire, and get out of there.

They had practiced this during refresher training, but this was the first one for real. And Dillan had just watched, then. Now he had to do it.

"Sound five short blasts," Dillan yelled. "Emergency break away, emergency break away," was passed over the 1MC. It was also passed over the sound powered telephone line strung from ship to ship with the distance line.

Dillan could not just pull away. SACREMENTO had to relieve all tension on the wire, or when its pelican hook attached to LARTER was tripped, it would go flying back at SACREMENTO like a rocket, with 200 feet of flailing wire and hose with it. Men would die or be swept into the sea and equipment damaged.

At the whistle signal, SACREMENTO hit the tension release while LARTER shut the fuel valve and tripped the probe connector. Connectors were mushroom shaped probes with automatic shut off valves. During unrep, the probe was inserted into a connector on the receiving ship which opened the valve. But they all leaked. In a normal breakaway, the delivering ship took back suction on the hose prior to trip.

A moment later, a Bosun's mate hit the pelican hook trip with a hammer, and LARTER was free. SACREMENTO scrambled to recover hose and wire, oil slick on the water. The distance line was let go.

"Come right, steer 216," Dillan yelled. "All ahead standard, indicate turns for 15 knots." And LARTER started pulling away.

"Bridge, unrep station 2, we have an oil spill." The captain leaned over the rail on the wing, and said,

"We sure do, I'll bet there's 50 gallons of fuel oil on the deck or running down the side, maybe more. There goes our Mary Sue paint job."

"Station 2, bridge, let's get it cleaned up. Good job getting us away, Mr. Dillan."

"Thank you, sir." Even the XO gave Dillan a smile. Fred just frowned.

Then, the skipper walked into the bridge and said into the 21MC, "Main control, bridge, we need a fuel state. We had to break away."

"Main control, aye, we have to wait until the tanks have settled. We're transferring fuel aft, estimate 93%." Later it would be determined that it was closer to 89%.

"Damn, but I'm not going around again," from the captain. "OK, Mr. Dillan, lets get out of here. Back to base course."

"Aye, sir. All ahead full, indicate turns for 20 knots. Come right steer 220." Helm and lee helm answered up. LARTER moved out and away from the AE.

"Quartermaster of the watch, course to station please?"

"Recommend 320, Mr. Dillan."

"Very well," and Dillan looked back to port to insure he was well out in front of the AOE's bow,

"So be it, Helm, right standard rudder, come right to 320."

"Helm Aye, right standard rudder, come right to 320."

"My rudder is right standard, coming to new course 320, sir."

Later, "Steady 320 checking 326, sir."

"Very well."

From the captain, "Mr. Finistry, I'm going into combat to talk with the SACREMENTO skipper."

"Yes, sir."

"Captain left the bridge," from the messenger.

"Mr. Dillan, lets head a bit more north to pick up GLOVER," from Fred. "Try 330. And crank it up to 25, we will do it the destroyer way."

"Yes, sir," And Dillan made it so.

"Now, secure the underway replenishment detail with the exception of station two, set the regular condition III watch."

Underway replenishment is dangerous, even in good sea conditions. Glad to get out of that one with out someone getting injured, or something damaged on either or both ships. SACREMENTO is going to have to figure out what is wrong with the automatic tension control on that ram.

LARTER's station two team, under the direction of Joe Rederman, had to use a fire hose to wash down the deck and as much of the port side as they could reach. Then kitty litter to try to soak up the remaining slick on deck. Finally another go round with the fire hose. The darker grey stain would be there until LARTER could repaint.

After he got relieved and as he was leaving the bridge, "Good emergency break away, Dillan," from Fred.

"Thanks."

Did his experience in Hong Kong make a human out of Fred? I sure was apprehensive when we were alongside and that wire was pulling. But no one took the conn away from me. Theoretically, Fred, the XO, and the CO could have. So I guess they have some confidence in me, confidence that I don't have, yet.

Dillan went to radio for a few hours of pouring over the intel skeds again, coupled with a brush up on the COMSEVENTH Fleet Operation Order, Sea Dragon Annex.

The radiomen were apprehensive.

RMSA Kilmer said, "Mr. Dillan, I hear that Sea Dragon is dangerous?"

"Not any worse than SAR, I think. Anywhere up in the gulf has its exciting moments. Look at it this way. We get this done, and then we finally get to go home. Taking some leave when we get stateside?"

"Yes, sir, home to Tulsa to visit my folks. I get out in November 69, so I need to start lining up a job."

"A year and a half to go; a little early for a job search, isn't it?"

"Yeah, maybe. But my uncle has a landscaping business and I want to be sure."

Kilmer is already thinking of getting out. Nothing like a small run in with the system to pour cold water on any thought of a Navy career.

50

They rendezvoused with GLOVER and commenced Sea Dragon operations, awaiting a targeting message. Since GLOVER's skipper was senior, GLOVER was the OTC.

Just south of Thanh Hoa, at a small point called Nho Quan was a cove with a beach. Air recon had determined that some of the fast junks would operate out of this cove, sitting on the sand at low tide or anchored. And an opportunity to catch them there and shred them good was important to preventing them from going after shot down pilots. LARTER and GLOVER were given this target as a target of opportunity.

It was defended by some anti-aircraft and maybe some 100mm from Sam Son, a town close by on the coast. Dillan was convinced that it would be a great target for a couple of air craft going into Hanoi or Thanh Hoa, maybe as a secondary target, but it was one of those assigned to Sea Dragon. At this point there was a lull in strikes northward.[lxv]

The second day on Sea Dragon, cruising at 15 knots around 19 degrees, 30 minutes north, 106 degrees, 10 minutes east. There was a lot of work between the CO, Fred, and the XO on the encrypted voice radio with GLOVER. Then there was an all officer's meeting.

"Good afternoon," from the skipper. "We have our first mission. XO."

"OK, men, we're going to shoot up some fast junks in their lair," pointing to the resurrected chart board.

"We've worked out a technique with GLOVER to run at them, bang away, do a 180 degree turn, and then run back out banging away again. We will use VT frag on the way in and then add a little HE on the way out. We expect to do this quickly and expend roughly 100 rounds per ship, about evenly split."

Two hundred rounds total? My God, that is a lot of ordnance: over 10,000 pounds. That little cove is going to get it big time. If the fast junks are there, it will be a short and violent morning.

"Intel indicates that there may be 100mm available to the enemy. It has a maximum range of 21,000 yards and fires a 30

302

pound projectile. And we'll be inside its range most of the firing run."

"Fred will give you the particulars. Fred."

"Thanks, XO, Captain."

"We will come in line abreast, 1,000 yards apart and will commence fire at a range of 15,000 yards from the target. We will fire about 3 and a half minutes inbound, cease fire, and then after our 180 degree port turn will open up with mount 52 for another 3 and a half minutes."

"Attack speed 17 knots. We will make the turn 13,000 yards from the target. Charted low water depth 40 feet. Chart depth accuracy is not great. This area has a diurnal tide and a range of 10 feet. We will be in some thin water."

"We will come in from the north east to present a small profile to the guns at Sam Son. But we also want to stay 10 miles north of Hon Me island which is said to have 122mm guns. So we will be going southwest in column, and then make a turn to 315 to end up line abreast."

"We do not anticipate taking heavy fire. Sam Son is on the strike approach to Hanoi and has been bombed often. Although the 100mm guns are portable, they are visually sighted and essentially field guns. But we do not want to be unaware of the potential for a lucky shot."

"Questions?"

"When will we be doing this?" from Joe Rederman.

"The OTC has indicated anytime during high to mid tide in the next two days. He wants some significant sun and we will go in near sun rise, probably day after tomorrow, mid tide and rising. The enemy will be looking right into the rising sun at us and it will make us a lot more difficult target. Plus the junks should be there since their action usually happens later in the morning. We want to catch them just waking up or sitting on the pot."

Laughter. *Wow, Fred, humor? Didn't know you had it in you.*

"Forty feet isn't much. Is that why we're staying offshore as much? We could improve accuracy if we were in closer." from Len.

"Old charts and we do not want to drag the sonar dome over a sand bar. So we decided to keep off shore a bit and time the run for mid to high tide. We really need to watch the fathometer, and if it starts shoaling. we will abort and haul out to the right. GLOVER will go left. On the bridge we will have the messenger call out fathometer readings every two minutes."

A few more questions and the meeting was over.

Our first Sea Dragon assignment. Thin water will make it even more exciting. Maybe a little cross current. Do not like the part about shooting back! Unfair! We should get to shoot at them only. Oh, the power of wishful thinking.

Two days later, set general quarters at 0430. At first light, about 0530, GLOVER and LARTER were in column, course 225, speed 10. By 0600, the OTC had increased speed to 17.

"Quicksilver, Tin Man, immediate execute, turn niner, I say again, turn niner, Standby, execute, over," came out of PriTac.

Fred answered, "Quicksilver, roger, out," and nodded to Dillan.

"Right standard rudder, come to new course 315."

"My rudder is right standard, coming to new course 315, sir," from the helmsman.

LARTER healed over. As the two ships swept around the 90 degree turn they ended up in line abreast, 1000 yards apart, headed at shore at 17 knots. Combat was plotting, weapons free.

"Bridge, combat, range to target, 16,500 yards, commencing fire in 2 and one half minutes."

"Fifty two feet," from the messenger.

The fathometer, a narrow beamed small sonar mounted about 1/3 of the way aft, just behind the sonar dome, sent out a pulse to the sea floor. It bounced back and the time it took round trip was measured and converted to distance. Since it read from the keel, about 15 feet below the water line, it was different than the charted water depth.

Then one had to allow for the dome which stuck down another 10 feet or so. If the fathometer ever read 10 feet, crunch. It took awhile to process the data and the fathometer was really telling you what the water depth was 10 yards ago.

The skipper walked over and pushed the button on the 21MC. "Hold your fire, Weaps, until I give you the go ahead."

The second hand swept around. Boom went the forward mount on GLOVER. "Fire," from the skipper on the 21MC.

"Boom, boom ...boom, boom from Mount 51. The skipper had held fire to keep from opening up before GLOVER had. GLOVER's CO was about 100 lineal numbers senior to LARTER's CO. The skipper was deferring to a senior.

Bright orange flashes, like long tongues of flame spitting out of both barrels of mount 51. Grey smoke wisping back to the bridge windows. The windows rattled from the shock waves. Noisy as hell. He could feel the ship vibrate at each shot through the soles of his shoes. Boom boom boom. The bridge ventilation system picked up some of the cordite smell. Its distinctive acid sting tickled the nostrils and added to the adrenalin level in the men. From NGFS and SAR, Dillan knew that this was occurring in combat also.

Starting to sweat in the long sleeve shirt and flack jacket. And the heavy steel helmet on my head doesn't help much. Makes the back of my neck hurt after awhile. The flack jacket is heavy, restrictive, and a pain to wear. And a belt pouch inflatable life vest. If I ever go over the side I'll have to ditch the flack jacket as soon as possible. Its weight'll pull me down like a ton of bricks.

"Forty three feet."

Water getting thin already.

And time passed slowly, only the boom of the guns and the messenger's announcement of water depth. Otherwise the Bridge was eerily silent and bathed in the yellow light of the gun flashes, deck vibrating at each shot.

And 3 minutes and 30 seconds after GLOVER had opened up, "Quicksilver, Tin Man, Immediate execute, 18 turn, I say again 18 turn, Standby, Execute, over."

This was the tricky part. Both ships were doing a 180 degree turn to port. At 17 knots, LARTER would almost end up going through water that GLOVER had just gone through. Not really but with the advance and transfer, LARTER would end up taking GLOVER's old wake just to starboard.

A nod from the skipper and, "Cease fire."

"Left standard rudder."

"Left standard rudder, aye sir," from the helmsman.

"Mount 51 reports 50 rounds expended, bores clear, no causalities."

"My rudder is left standard, no new course given, sir," again from the helmsman.

"Thirty one feet."

Getting even thinner.

"Passing 270, sir."

A little slow, the helmsman is supposed to say passing at each 10 degrees. He missed one plus. Twenty feet of water to the dome.

"Passing 250, sir, no new course given."

"Steady on new course 135."

"Steady on new course 135, aye sir." Now the helmsman did not have to do the passing bit.

But I better watch the compass swing carefully. The helmsman has to ease his rudder and then maybe even add a little right rudder to stop the swing right on the money. BM3 Thomas is our best helmsman and is on the bridge for GQ and unrep. But it would not do to make snakes in the water (a wake that wandered around).

"Steady 135, checking 137, sir."

"Very well."

Once the ships steadied on the new course, GLOVER opened fire with her after mount and LARTER followed. Another 3 and one half minutes of bang bang.

A little excitement when the fathometer got down to 28 feet, 18 feet to the dome. Skipper watched the dial intently until it started back up.

When GLOVER ceased fire, LARTER did also.

"Mount 52 reports 49 rounds expended, bores clear, no causalities." What happened to the other one? Dillan thought. Mount 52 was always a bit mixed up. But Billy's job was to get them in shape.

"Forty eight feet."

Awhile thereafter, "Quicksilver, this is Tin Man, Immedi-ate execute, niner turn, I say again, niner turn, standby, execute, over." Turning left 90 degrees and back into column, now with LARTER in front of GLOVER.

"Quicksilver, roger out,"

"Left standard rudder, come to new course 045," from Dillan.

"Left standard rudder, come to new course 045, aye sir."

"My rudder is left standard, coming to new course 045, sir."

This is interesting. GLOVER is following us, but she is still the guide. We have to keep station on her from 1000 yards ahead of her. Keep one's wits about you and watch the range through the hood on the bridge radar repeater. Go out on the wing, use the pelorus, and give orders to the helm and lee helm through the voice tube.

"Sixty feet."

"Messenger, belay fathometer readings," from the skipper. "Got a little thin there Fred, must be some uncharted bars in this area."

"Yes, sir," Fred said.

I bet the skipper's stomach was churning away. Uncharted sand bars at 17 knots would do that.

Shortly thereafter, the OTC put LARTER 2000 yards behind her: a station changing exercise, from ahead to behind, concurrently slowing ordered speed to 15. One had to do this by keeping roughly 1000 yards from the guide (actually about 750 yards closest point of approach off GLOVER's port bow). Dillan was going to go right, but the skipper said do this one to the left.

When off the GLOVER's port beam at 1000 yards, another left to 185, then finally a sweeping left turn into station dropping to 15 and ending on course 045. Another maneuvering board challenge. Fred did the board, Dillan watched, and Fred told the skipper his plan. With a wave from the skipper, Dillan got on with it.

"Left standard rudder, come to new course 305, all engines ahead full, indicate turns for 20 knots." And off they went to station. Shortly thereafter, tucked in and back to base course.

"Now secure from general quarters, set the regular condition III watch."

The sun was fully up now and the entire evolution had taken a little more than an hour; and no incoming.

The rest of that day and into the next, the Task Unit just milled around smartly in the perpetual haze, making circles in the ocean, 30 miles off shore. Dillan watched the messages for any new targets.

The crew had settled in to normal duties again. Gun crews practiced. Deck division men touched up paint. Engineers did preventative maintenance. Morale had improved with the recent action.

51

For the next week plus, they did 3 more fire missions, mostly suspected radar sites, or AA sites working off Sam Son. They even made a long range attack on a bridge on route 1, at Ngac Tra across the Song Yan River. They were told that the bridge on route 1A had been taken out by a previous air strike, and all the task element was doing was disrupting final repairs.

This mission was only about 100 rounds per ship and all VT frag, done in the mid morning, so Dillan figured the goal was to shoot up the workers on the bridge. It was almost high tide, and another 10,000 pounds of ordnance which would shred workers and equipment alike.

In all cases, they had not taken any return fire. At night, they went out about 40 miles from the coast to somewhat stay away from PT boats and fast junks. The surface picture was always watched closely, and there was one GQ scare, but nothing came close enough to shoot at. Surface contacts would show up at almost maximum radar range, fade in and out, and then disappear.

Dillan figured that the NVA P-6 skippers were not interested in dealing with two destroyers throwing massive amounts of VT frag at them. Many of their peers had had very short careers getting close to US Navy destroyers. But north SAR was vacant; no air strikes going north, so LARTER and GLOVER were the only bait in town.

Pete insured that the radar ET's were busy keeping the surface search radar and its repeaters tuned for maximum sensitivity. And the EW men were on their toes watching for P-6 radars.

Once they were assigned to take up 'targets of opportunity' along route 1A between Hoang Xa and Hao Mon Trung. One could actually see part of the road here about a mile inland. But the southern end was awful close to Hon Me island, so LARTER decided to work the north portion. LARTER was detached for this effort and cruised along the shore 4 miles out in some thin water at GQ.

It was about 3 hours after high tide, so the water was shrinking. It was hazy, and only the director's high power optics could see much. LARTER was going 4 knots and everyone was nervous as hell. They would fire at any good targets they saw from the director's optical sights. Only once did the director officer, Len Ottaway, open fire with VT frag from mount 52, about 20 rounds. Then that exercise was over.

That noon in the wardroom, from the skipper, "OK Len, tell me again what'd you shoot at?"

"As I reported to the bridge, it was suspected NVA traffic, Captain."

"I got that Len, but suspected NVA traffic what?"

"A suspected NVA courier, sir. On a bicycle."

"On a bicycle? And what makes you think it was an NVA courier Mr. Ottaway and not just some poor damn farmer pedaling home?" That was said quite directly. The skipper was not happy.

Silence.

"And what happened to this bike rider, Mr. Ottaway."

"I think we got him, sir."

"No, Mr. Ottaway, you got him. If we get to do targets of opportunity again you will not shoot up people riding a bicycle, got that?

"Yes, sir."

"And there better not be some damn silhouette of a bicycle painted on the director."

"Yes, sir."

Shooting 20 rounds of VT frag at a guy on a bicycle was a little much. Next of kin would find little if any to bury. Maybe bike parts, small burnt bike parts. Len is too trigger happy.

Both ships ran south one day and night and refueled and rearmed from SACREMENTO again. The ram had been fixed and it was a non event although there was not much sleep that night.

It was another day; 1315 and another all officer's meeting called in the ward room. Jim and Len had the watch. The skipper pulled the director officer and CIC evaluator off watch for the meeting. There was the flip chart with a topographic map on it, and a red line with a kink in it showing a course, aimed right at the coast just north of a small island.

The skipper stood up and said,

"We have another mission. The XO will take you through it. XO."

Dillan had seen a message operations order that came in last night. It was long and complex, but he had the gist of what was up.

Into the dragon's mouth!

"Gentlemen, the target is to be at a place where route 1A and the main north south railway lines cross a marshy area. Grid sector whisky golf seven four," pointing to the chart.

"Very close to where we just did the target of opportunity stuff. In this area, the mountains force the road and railroad close to the coast. The rail and road run parallel and next to each other. So this is kind of a two birds with one stone opportunity. The rail road and road have many concrete, and steel, and even some wooden bridges over the marsh. The target is near the small town of Lan Tra. This area is well defended."

"To the west, on an 1100 foot hill, is a major SAM site with anti-aircraft guns. To the south, on a smaller hill near the coast is AA, maybe 100mm gun emplacements and maybe another SAM site. Intel believes that to the southeast, just off shore on Hon Me island, are more AA and possibly 122mm guns. Remember Hon Me from our first mission? The Hon Me guns will be our largest threat since, if they are there, they will have us in range for the longest time. Almost 45 minutes. The NVA's 122s are essentially the equivalent of our 5 inch 38s."

"Air recon has seen activity on this island but as of a week ago, no guns were spotted. Remember that the NVA have refined camouflage to reduce the effectiveness of air recon to a fine art. There may also be 122mm and AA guns near the Mui Bang promontory, but we don't think so," pointing to the chart.

"This area is well protected. Access is from the northeast. To get in close enough to be effective, we'll have to come in from the northeast and then turn west, exposing ourselves to fire from three or even four locations. By the time we get to the turn around point, we will be in 45 feet of water, 4,000 yards from the coast, 7,000 yards from the target, and effectively surrounded by guns on 3 sides. We will be presenting our beam to Hon Me, and be 4,600 yards away at our closest point of approach. That is close. Damn close."

"Previous air strikes have tried to damage the road and railroad. But the area has 2 very effective SAM sites and a number of self propelled Z-SU-23-4 AA radar directed guns which are death to low flying aircraft. They move these around a lot and they camouflage them well. This has been a particularly challenging target for air strikes. Not only is it well defended, but the valley is narrow and the road and rail lines are very close to a steep 700 foot high ridge, which makes bombing runs difficult."

"There are 2,000 foot hills all around. Aircraft have to make their runs on a north south axis, and the enemy knows that and has set up their weapons accordingly. We've lost 2 A-4s in this area over the past month, but all pilots were recovered. BDA[lxvi] indicated that there was only minor damage."

"If we can tear up this section of track and roadway, it will be difficult for them to repair it. Even they will have to approach from both ends and work their way towards the center of any damage. We intend to jointly put 64,000 pounds of ordnance on target, the equivalent of 32 aircraft with 2 each 1,000 pound bombs. This is why we have been assigned."

My God, that is a lot, an enormous amount!.

"We'll make our approach at 20 knots, 1000 yards apart in offset column. We intend to commence fire when the target range is 18,000 yards. The OTC will lead. It will be a 12 minute firing run in, then another 6 minutes after a small turn. Then we'll do a 180, another 6 minutes of firing, and then a small turn to port. Following this a 12 minute firing run out. We should be able to put 600 rounds on target from each ship. That's a major piece of ordnance. This'll be the largest attack ever for Sea Dragon."

"We'll keep a double plot, one minute intervals, on the bridge and in combat, just like a maneuvering team evolution, and feed information to Weapons for input into the computer. There are a few visual points but lots of locations for radar ranges. Study them and have your GQ teams study them. Combat's plot will have priority since visual bearings may be difficult."

"Engineering will have all 4 boilers on line, but no super-heat, so we can bug out if necessary. The damage control teams, Red, need to understand that we will probably be taking some return fire. Although we do not expect to be hit, there is always that possibility. They need to be on their toes. Got that Red?" A nod.

"We'll be firing blind and will have to navigate carefully. Essentially it's another NGFS attack at speed. We'll use mount 51 when we commence fire, HE, fuse long. We want some penetration prior to detonation to maximize damage. Once we make our 180 degree turn to port, we'll use mount 52 reserving 51 for counter battery fire from the director. However, we must hold off on counter battery from 52 until 52 has delivered as many rounds on target as possible."

"We have one gunfire control computer, and it needs to be concentrated on the target. If 51 can visually target gun fire flashes for counter battery, we will allow local control. Mount captains, nodding to Billy and Joe, should bone up on firing locally using visual. When we switch to counter battery, we'll use VT frag. We're a bit short on VT and will shift to AA common if necessary. The AOE last time was short on VT."

ENS Billy Hoffman and LTGJ Joe Reiderman were the mount captains and stood on a platform with their helmeted head just outside in a shielded position on the mounts, centered between the guns and at the top back edge of the mount enclosure at GQ. The mount had a trainer and a pointer and the guns moved together. The trainer and pointer in local control could use their visual sights, through periscope-like windows on the sides of the mount, to aim.

From their mount captain positions, Billy and Joe could direct the 27 man, including the upper handling room crew and mount staff. They had just recently swapped assignments again. Billy was now back in mount 52 for GQ, Joe Rederman in 51. LTJG Len Ottaway manned the director with some FT's. LTJG Jim Kirpatrick was in sonar and wouldn't have much to do. He would help the plotters in combat.

"Gentlemen, we will not be taking evasive action on the way in or out as long as guns are firing on the target. We have to hold a steady course and speed if we hope to be accurate. That is why the approach and withdrawal speed is limited to 20 knots. We want maximum rounds on target and will attempt to spread rounds to cover about 1000 yards along the long axis, roughly 030 to 210 of the target. Our assignment is the northern 500 yards. If some rounds go long, hopefully we can dump some of the hill behind the target on it. If rounds go short, we will just be digging holes in a marsh."

"We have the rest of the day today and all day tomorrow to prepare. Everyone needs to understand their job. By the end of today we want the topographic maps in place so we can practice plotting and getting gun target lines and range data into the computer. We're going to try setting the target points as if they are moving and we're stationary into the computer so it will track. This should improve accuracy. We'll set GQ tomorrow morning for drills."

"This is a serious mission gentlemen. Let's do it the LARTER way. Questions?"

"XO, that island on the chart looks like bad news. We'll be presenting our profile to it for almost 45 minutes. Could we get an air strike first on it?" said Len Ottaway.

"The OTC has requested an air strike. CTF 77 will run one this morning, two A-4s. We would like it closer to our firing run the day after tomorrow but the carrier is a bit busy supporting I Corps right now."

"XO, why aren't we doing it like we did the run at the fast junks, like going in line abreast?" from Ted Brunshall.

"Ops will answer that, Fred."

"In line abreast we give the NVA gunners on Hon Me two targets in range. We all know destroyers are a difficult target because we're so narrow. We do not want to give them another target in range if they overshoot the first." from Fred.

"Isn't there a way to stay more to the north, say come in down the coast, instead of getting so close to Hon Me?" from Red.

"We would love to. It would keep us from being as subject to fire from the island. But there is reported and uncharted shoaling there, and if we hit one and got hung up, we would be a sitting duck. When we were doing the 1A target of opportunity thing we had a shoal water scare in the same area. The charts are not correct – probably old and French from the 20's or 30's."

"XO, why wait another day? Why not tomorrow?" from Tony Carpiceso.

"Well, we don't get to pick, Tony We think our attack is timed to when they expect train traffic. If we could catch a train there, or almost there, we get a major win. Plus we have to watch the tides and want to time the run fairly close to high tide and slack water."

"And what time is it, XO?"

"We will commence our run at 0700."

The enemy is listening up on most UHF frequencies and a strong signal would give them a heads up. "XO, will we be using PriTac?" from Dillan.

"PriTac. If we're taking fire we don't want the signalmen out there playing with the flag bag or flashing light. If radios are out, flashing light or flag hoist is always a back up. However, we have tried to coordinate this attack in a way that requires very little communication. Run essentially right at them, do a 180, run out and shoot hell out of them."

"If we have 4 boilers on line and are doing 20 knots, you must be anticipating the need for 25 or more," from Eric Ebersole.

Surprising, I have not heard more than 10 words from him in a month.

"We want to be ready to get the hell out of Dodge if necessary. If we're taking fire as soon as we get back out to 18,000 yards on our departure course and cease fire at the target, we will commence zig zagging. At that range we'll be 10,000 yards from the island and can use the director and mount 52 for counter battery, so we may choose not to zig zag. But the director can't train all the way aft, so 52 may still have to do visual. But the computer can track. We can also use smoke (smoke screen, make black smoke out of the stacks to hide behind if the wind is right) but we want to be in a position to use directed counter battery by optical sights if we can. Smoke would prevent that."

"Do we know if the enemy guns are aimed visually or with fire control radar," from Dillan.

"We do not know for sure. Their mobile AA guns are radar controlled and are quite effective. They have shot down some A-4's doing their bombing runs and can reach out to 2,000 yards easy. We shouldn't be surprised if we get radar targeted. Mr. Donavan, make sure your EW men are ready and know what signals to expect, especially from the 122mm or 100mm gun radars."

There had been a bit of excitement while on a quiet night watch during Northern SAR when the EWs picked up what was cataloged as a Skory class destroyer surface search radar. But the bearing and weak signal strength indicated that it was coming from land. Fred had advised the watch that the NVA was known for taking whatever extra equipment they could get their hands on and using it to fulfill their needs. It was probably an old unit they set up for coastal defense on land. There were sure no known Soviet Skorys in the area.

"What's the weather supposed to be like, XO?" from Billy Hoffman.

"According to Mr. Finistry's crystal ball (snicker) we get more of what we have today. That's a few clouds, 90 degrees, some haze, and light winds."

"Do we have to worry about the AA guns?" from Sam Blongerinski.

"We don't think so. They are 23mm and 2500 yards is just about max slant range. We don't intend to be that close."

"Are we going to have an aircraft spotter?" from Tony.

"No. We're on our own for this one."

"Why, XO? Seems like it would improve our accuracy and give us a heads up on counter fire."

"We requested a spotter aircraft, but one was not assigned. There are some SAM sites close, and the 23s would be bad news. We think that the admiral decided that a spotter wouldn't last very long."

Questioning went on for awhile longer. Interest level was high. Although there had been other situations where LARTER was at some risk, this would be the first time that she had deliberately stuck her head in the lion's mouth.

Finally the captain stood up.

"Gentlemen, it's been awhile since any US Navy destroyers have attempted shore bombardment at this speed. The XO and Mr. Finistry have done an excellent job preparing for this evolution, working very closely with their counterparts on GLOVER. GLOVER's CO and I have discussed options and we agree that this is our best opportunity to destroy this target. It will not be easy and getting rounds on target and without a spotter will require a very accurate plot and the efforts of all hands."

"We're talking about a lot of rounds and mount crews will be working their collective butts off. They will be doing some serious weight lifting."

The 5 inch gun system was designed to limit weight lifting. Projectiles were presented in a hoist from the upper handling room. The hoist actually set the fuse. Then the powder man would get a cartridge from the scuttle in the deck and drop it into the loading tray, primer down, cork plug up. The projectile man, usually one of 3, would roll the projectile into the tray in front of the casing. The gun captain would hit the ram lever and the ram would shove the projectile and cartridge into the chamber.

The breech block would close, and bang, off the round would go. The breach would open, and an extractor would flip the empty cartridge out to be caught by the hot case man. He would shove it out the back of the mount. Then repeat. With the guns elevated for a ballistic trajectory, the chamber was tilted and there was little actual lifting required. More just grabbing and placing.

But one screw up and a man could get badly hurt or worse. A 5 inch 38 gun was rated at 20 rounds per minute but seldom achieved that. Sustained fire was closer to 15.

"Please brief your troops but don't panic them. When we're at GQ tomorrow, I intend to come around and see how it's going. LARTER has an opportunity to deal a real blow to the enemy, and we will do it! Dismissed."

52

Dillan was going to brief his radiomen and signalmen.

I know the men are nervous. Hell, I am a bit. I won't say things that generate unhealthy fear, just enough to get the men on their toes, but not enough to incapacitate anyone. There is a possibility of taking some hits, maybe not a great possibility, but still there. A lot would depend on how quickly the NVA can get their guns into action, how well trained they are, whether on not they have gunfire control radar available, and just pure luck.

A 390 foot long destroyer only 40 some feet wide going 20 knots (33 feet every second) is not an easy target to hit at 3 to 8 miles away. Bearing change rate will be a problem for them, but range has to be right on due to the narrowness of the ship.

As they walked out of the wardroom, Dillan caught Pete.

"Think the EW guys are up for this?"

"Yes, I think they are. I'm going to insist that they have a crib sheet with all the expected radars, especially the fire control ones. I'll hit the pubs (electronic warfare publications) tonight. I'll have Morgan on the WLR-1. He's young but he seems to have a feel for it."

"Morgan's new, isn't he? He wasn't there when I had OE."

"Came aboard just prior to deployment, fresh out of "C" school and can play that old gear like a piano. Has a real feel for it. And, he's up to speed with the break lock feature on the 6s."

"Great, hope we don't need the 6s. See you later."

When Dillan was EMO, before Pete arrived, he had spent some long days in the tiny EW room when LARTER was testing some new classified gear in the So Cal op area. Hot and crowded. The new gear, the AN/ULQ-6s, allowed for countermeasures, like amplifying an enemy's fire control radar's signal, changing its phase and reradiating it. It was supposed to break lock-on. It worked, somewhat.

Watches were tense. This was the general area where MADDOX and TURNER JOY had been jumped by some P-6's and the "Swallow" ex Chinese patrol craft in 1964. Surface contacts created excitement, like always. One showed up, a big one. They determined it was a freighter, Haiphong bound, Soviet merchant surface search radar. Out to sea and moving north at 12 knots. Nothing like a lull in the bombing to get re-supply flowing again.

Even meals in the wardroom were quiet. The CO continued with the small talk as they ate, but the usual banter in the lounge prior to the CO coming in was muted. They engaged in serious and mostly business discussions.

The next morning the ship went to GQ. The captain insisted everyone be in full battle dress. For the bridge this meant steel helmets, flack jackets, the belted inflatable life jackets in pouches, and pant legs tucked into socks.

This is a little weird, but it supposedly limits flash burns on the lower legs. Men are wearing long sleeve shirts for the same reason.

The sound powered telephone talkers had big steel pots that went on their head over the phone headsets. Heavy. All stations were advised to inspect battle dress on their crews. It was hot as hell in battle dress and the men had gotten used to drifting out of it when they could. Flack jackets were hot and heavy, but only required for exposed stations. The bridge was considered exposed. One did not want to be in them for long.

Each station did drills. The captain, still in full battle dress with "CO" painted in black on the front and back of his grey helmet, checked combat, radio, the director, mount 51 and mount 52. Then he went below and surprised Repair I forward and Repair II aft. Repair I hung out on the main deck in the passageway near the ET compartment. Repair II was in the athwart ships passageway just behind after officer's country, near the ship's store.

Dillan could follow the skipper's progress as the phone talkers reported on it. Each gun crew did some time on the 'loading machine.' Not a super simulation but acceptable for honing skills.

The XO had set up a topographical chart on the plotting table and drilled his bearing takers and quartermasters. Dillan figured they were doing the same in combat. The XO would be in combat for this evolution. And Pete was probably going through the radar identification drill with his people.

Mounts trained, elevated, and practiced. Dillan could see mount 51, two decks down and forward of the bridge, move around. From the phone talkers it was obvious that Red and Sam were really putting the repair parties through their paces with simulated hits and fires to investigate and put out.

Although he wasn't there, he knew that the chief corpsman, his two hospital corpsmen, and the stewards had turned the wardroom into a casualty center. Above the wardroom table were operating lights that could be lowered. Stewards would also be used for transporting causalities in the metal 'stokes' basket stretchers or two pole canvas ones kept in various racks throughout the ship.

And everyone was keyed up.

A last chance to practice before the big game.

The captain kept them at GQ until 1330. Lunch was very late.

It was a relatively quiet 20-24. The task unit was moving slowly west, changing course every so often so it looked to an outside observer like it was just meandering along. But the goal was to be at or near 19 degrees, 30 minutes north latitude, 106 degrees, zero minutes west longitude around 0500 to commence the run.

I am jumpy. Trust in the training and teamwork of the ship to pull us all through. But adrenalin is already flowing a little. Like a college football game. On any given Saturday afternoon - the team who wants a victory more can usually get it – regardless of their ranking.

Dillan slept well for 4 plus hours.

Reveille was at 0430. By 0515 the chow line had been secured.

At 0530, "Bong, bong, bong, bong... General quarters, general quarters, all hands man your battle stations."

Dillan was on his way to the bridge.

Afraid? No. Not even now, just full of anticipation. The difference between courage and cowardice is training and determination.

The ship was manned and ready in under 4 minutes. Most men were already on station when GQ sounded.

And there was Dillan, in battle dress, on the bridge as JOOD. Although one would think that in a battle situation the ODD, Fred Finistry, would have the conn, that was not normal.

Fred needed to watch other things and usually the JOOD had the conn. Then Fred or the skipper could just say "do this" or "do that", without going through all the formality.

And they just meandered around for a long hour and one half. The men were fidgety. Dillan had some butterflies, but a cool calm had started to spread over his body.

LARTER was on station, offset column, 5 degrees to the right and 1000 yards astern of GLOVER.

From the PriTac speaker, "Quicksilver, Rockyroad, Immediate execute, corpen 232, speed 20 standby, execute, over."

Fred answered, "Quicksilver, roger out." GLOVER was using her commander task element call sign.

A nod from the skipper and Dillan said,

"All engines ahead full, indicate turns for 20 knots."

"All engines ahead full, turns for 20 knots, sir," from the lee helm.

"Engine room answers up all ahead full, turns for 20 knots, sir"

"Very well."

Here we go. Let's give it to 'm good.

Since they were in column he would wait until he got to GLOVER's 'knuckle' or flat spot in the wake caused by her turn to turn to the new course. If Dillan turned on the knuckle he would turn where GLOVER had. Reality was he would not turn on the knuckle.

He would turn to the right of it as LARTER was in off set column. If they had been in normal column, one right behind the other, the knuckle was the turn spot. Follow in the wake of the guide.

Looking out the port wing, Dillan could see the bearing taker, swinging the pelorus ring and talking into the quartermasters on his sound powered phone. To keep from having to push the phone talk button every time, it was taped down. He had a big steel helmet on his head.

LARTER was still a bit out, and although Hon Me island was a visible dark hump to the south, the shore of the mainland was just a grey line. Combat, using radar ranges, would have to do the initial set up. The actual gun fire run would not start for another few thousand yards.

Dillan came to the ordered course. Speed was up to 20 on the knot meter. At this speed they covered 2000 yards every 3 minutes.

Time seemed to drag. The shoreline got clearer through the morning haze. The island got a lot clearer.

"Officer of the deck, we will be in range of the guns on Hon Me very soon," from the skipper.

Then he leaned over to the 21MC. "Combat, bridge, make sure the EWs are searching the sector to the south."

"Combat aye."

The skipper is nervous. Of course Pete is keeping them on their toes. CTF 77 had a couple of A-4's make some napalm runs on the island yesterday morning. They reported roads and fire clearings through the scrub but no visible guns. Lots of dirt. Lots of wheel ruts. So what's up there?

"Bridge, combat, Racket one bearing 183, evaluated as enemy surface search radar."

A Racket was an electronic warfare signal intercept. The bad guys had a surface search radar on the island that had escaped the napalm. Most of their radars, surface search and fire control, were truck or van mounted and could be pulled into dugouts and then redeployed after the aircraft had left. Napalm tended to be a better item for use on these because it would burn off camouflage netting and splash around a lot. But equipment in caves wouldn't see much damage.

They must have had it in deep redoubt. The NVA are like moles. They can dig caves and hideouts anywhere. Getting trucks and guns on that island must have been a drill. Gooks have few helos, probably manhandled it all over on barges – and probably at night.

"Well, it's not like they don't know we're here," the skipper said.

"Sixty six feet," said the messenger.

Lots of water, relatively speaking, closing in on the open fire point.

Weapons was advised weapons free.

They will fire without command at the 18,000 yard point.

A few minutes later, the forward gun mount on GLOVER erupted. Dillan could see the flashes before he heard the report.

And a minute and a half later mount 51 opened fire. Bang, flash, and a puff of grey smoke, again, again. The bridge shook. Orange tulips spitting out of the barrels leaving a glowing ring for a moment, elevated 45 degrees. Smoke, and the 20 knot wind blew it back at the bridge windows.

One had to be careful that the flashes did not screw up the eye sight, like watching a welding arc but not as bright. The inside of the bridge lit up with a weird yellow glow. Colors faded to black and white. The radio antenna whip on the top of mount 51 was vibrating to the tune of the shots.

"Sixty feet."

Off to the port side of GLOVER about 500 yards a splash, and a column of water jumped into the air. Then another. Like water cannon at Disneyland. Soon more splashes and water columns. Some were off GLOVER's starboard side. From Dillan's position he couldn't tell if they had the bearing right but they were off on range.

They're shooting back! The bastards are shooting back!

Time started to dilate. There was an awful racket from mount 51. The guns were elevated and the orange flashes continued. The deck vibrated at each detonation. One starboard bridge window rattled. And there were almost continuous flashes from GLOVER's forward guns. Five minutes to the first turn.

Five whole minutes? It seems like an hour already.

"Fifty eight feet."

Combat kept feeding ranges to the turn over the sound powered phones. The skipper was no longer in his chair, standing by the bridge window now, massaging his binoculars.

Whoom, whoosh. A column of water jumped up 100 yards to port of LARTER, 10 seconds later another, roughly in the same relative position. Dillan startled. The water sparkled in the sun, little old faithfuls. Exploding shell generated water geysers.

Then two more, a bit more forward and maybe 200 yards off. Dillan could see columns of water sprouting up around GLOVER but they were either long or short.

From PriTac, "Quicksilver, Rockyroad, immediate execute, corpen 256, standby, execute, over."

"Quicksilver, roger, out," from Fred.

This time LARTER would have to slow a bit since GLOVER had a bit further to go. One and a half minutes after GLOVER turned, so did LARTER.

"Fifty one feet." *Six minutes on this course.*

But there were no more rounds hitting around LARTER that he could see. The turn confused the NVA gunners a little. But then again, he could only see in about a 180 degree arch ahead and to the sides from his position in the center of the bridge by the window.

Mount 52 could be doing visual counter battery. Why not?

Even with smokeless powder and at 20 knots, there was still a light grey smoke haze streaming quickly by the bridge from the guns. Someone's misplaced coffee cup vibrated off the chart table and hit the deck with a crash. Everybody jumped.

The quartermaster yelled, "Damn it, where'd that come from?"

GLOVER was taking a lot of incoming but no hits. And none real close. A splash or two to port of LARTER but not very close.

These guys are not very good marksmen, concentrating on the lead ship.

"Forty eight feet."

From PriTac, "076 corpen, standby, execute, out."

No need to roger that. Just do as told. The GLOVER was making her port turn, maybe a few seconds early. Dillan could see the aspect ratio change. GLOVER had ceased fire during the turn. And the turn caught the enemy gunners by surprise. Splashes were falling around where GLOVER would have been.

Yeah, where we're going to be since we have to make a wider 10 degree rudder turn to end up where we belong. And we will be going directly astern of GLOVER, crossing the "T" so to speak. Bet she holds fire till we get by.

A defective round detonating 800 yards out of a barrel would be above LARTER. Dillan had one and a half minutes from GLOVER's turn. He counted it down on the bridge clock second hand.

53

"All ahead full, turns for 23 knots." LARTER had to make an outer race track and had further to go. Dillan would slow back to 20, about 2/3rds of the way around.

"All ahead full, turns for 23 knots, sir."

"Forty six feet."

"Engine room answers up all ahead full, turns for 23 knots."

"Very well."

"Left 10 degrees rudder, come to new course 076."

"Left 10 degrees rudder, coming to new course 076, sir."

"My rudder is left 10 degrees, coming to new course 076, sir."

LARTER was heeled over and MT 51 had ceased fire. Splashes were all around but not close. GLOVER's after mount opened up. Dillan had to ease the rudder to left 5 to keep from turning inside station. Then boom, whoosh. Close! Spray splashed over the starboard bridge window.

Damn close!

Water droplets were running down the glass.

Dillan had to tweak the rudder angle a bit more, and went back to 20. Then he had to add some turns.

"Steady on course 076 checking 080, sir," in an excited voice.

"Very well," he said calmly.

Don't buy into other's fear. Deal calmly with your own. And hope your perceived calm keeps the helm and lee helm calm.

"Fifty feet."

LARTER was again 1000 yards behind and about 100 yards to the right, headed east with the coast behind now, and Hon Me off the starboard beam. Close, about 800 yards closer than she had been on the approach.

"Mount 51 reports 283 rounds expended, bores clear, no causalities."

"Weapons, bridge switch mount 51 to VT frag and prepare for visual counter battery. Fire when you have a target," the skipper said into the 21MC.

Dillan knew that combat would give mount 51 a bearing and range to the top of the hill on Hon Me. Shortly thereafter, mount 51 opened up again, turned almost into the stops. The deck vibrated from the reports and the bearing taker on the starboard wing was sitting down on the deck behind the shield, a pulsating orange glow behind it. He was keeping out of the close gun flashes. Soon, mount 51 would be unable to fire at Hon Me, since she would be unable to train further right.

Mount 52 erupted. Dillan could see the after mount on GLOVER banging away. The smoke was drifting back to LARTER. Or it was stationary, and LARTER was running through it.

Weird how one thinks of something like that in the middle of all this.

Six minutes to another left turn. Lots of splashes around GLOVER and LARTER, some again close enough to wet LARTER with their spray.

"Fifty one feet."

Mount 51 was trained almost hard to starboard. Trying to spot the flashes and shoot at them. Mount 51 was putting out a lot of rounds. As fast as Dillan had ever heard. Looking out the starboard bridge window through the remaining water droplets one could see some black puffs on the top of Hon Me.

The gun crew should be tired after all that rapid and continuous fire. That's 300 rounds, or 150 each gun, of projectiles that had been loaded by that crew. They should be exhausted and running on pure adrenalin.

"Quicksilver, this is Rockyroad, immediate execute, 052 corpen, I say again, 052 corpen, standby, execute, out."

Shortly thereafter, LARTER followed GLOVER around the turn.

Another long 12 minutes to get the hell out of here and cease fire at the target, Dillan thought. Actually 24 minutes total to get totally out of Hon Me gun's range. Splashes were still occurring, along with a muffled bang, bang, bang from mount 52.

"Mount 51 reports 42 rounds expended on counter battery, bores clear, no casualties." Mount 51 was into the stops and had ceased fire.

On the 21 MC, an excited voice, "Bridge, combat we have Racket two, bearing 173, evaluated as Flap Wheel fire control radar, raster scan."

Fred answered, "Bridge, aye, advise if it goes to conical!"

This was the fire control radar generally associated with 122mm guns. In raster scan, it was searching for a target, in conical, it would be locked on. It had taken the NVA awhile to get this radar up, but it was bad news, very bad news.

"Now we're going to get it," from the skipper.

Relative quiet. No splashes.

By now we should be getting lots of in-coming. We have about 15 minutes to go to be out of range. And another 3 minutes until 52 will be able to switch to counter battery.

Boom, whoosh, and again.

They have opened up on us again. And on this course our bearing rate change is not as fast. Just a little longer to get clear. Just a little longer.

"Bridge, combat, conical scan, conical scan! We have activated the ULQ-6."

Oh shit! Hope the break-lock works.

Everyone got totally quiet. Forty seconds later, there was a boom, whoosh quite close. Then it happened again.

"Mount 52 reports 290 rounds expended, bores clear, no causalities, shifting to counter battery and VT frag."

Shortly, mount 52 took up counter battery fire. The lookout reported that Hon Me island had started to show puffs of black smoke near the top again.

Hope that keeps their f'ing heads down!

"Sixty feet."

"Distance to out of range, Fred," the skipper yelled.

"Four thousand yards, sir."

"Damn." Six more minutes.

The ship shook like it had bumped something.

"Forward boiler room reports close aboard hit, port amidships, auxiliary steam line leaking at flange. Securing steam to the evaps." The NVA had put one close in the water and the concussion popped a flange. No hull penetration. Since it was behind and to his left, Dillan hadn't seen the hit.

They are concentrating on us!

Splashes were all around. Spray on the bridge windows again. Three minutes to go.

GLOVER had mostly ceased fire. Every now and then her mount 52 would erupt on counter battery. Then it ceased. LARTER's mount 52 was still banging away. LARTER was 15,000 yards away from Hon Me.

A very loud Crack! Wham! Flash of orange light reflected off the port bridge wing. The bridge deck actually jumped enough that it was like an elevator jerking. Like the ship had run over a big log. Like a car going fast over a speed bump.

Bright white flash reflected off the bridge wing and a muffled whoomp, then another flash and a louder whoomp. The deck jumped again slightly. LARTER had been hit somewhere back aft.

The continuous rumble of mount 52 had ceased.

"Weapons has lost contact with mount 52."

"DC central reports hit Bravo. Hit Bravo. Hit near mount 52, sending out investigators." Phone talkers were all doing phone checks on their circuits.

Still more boom whooshes, some close but they were falling astern. Another shudder as a round detonated close aboard starboard side aft, in the water, but smaller than the first. Main control acknowledged a close aboard detonation but no apparent damage. After steering noted no electrical power to the lighting, but that was probably from the first hit. The main cables that supplied power for the steering hydraulics were deep in the ship and duplicated.

The captain went through the port hatch onto the bridge wing.

"Quicksilver, Rockyroad, 016 corpen, out." Turning north to move away quicker. LARTER followed.

At the turning point. "Left 10 degrees rudder, steady new course 016."

"Left 10 degrees rudder coming to new course 016, sir."
"My rudder is left 10 degrees, sir."

LARTER heeled to port. Both gun mounts were silent. Eerie. It was the first silence in almost 40 minutes. LARTER was a bit behind station. Dillan added a couple of turns.

"Steady 016 checking 019, sir."

The skipper came in from the bridge wing, ashened faced.

"We took a hit somewhere aft. We have a fire back there, streaming black smoke. Anything from DC central?"

"Not yet, sir," from Fred. It would take time for an investigator from Repair II to get to mount 52, since he had to wear an OBA and get through the black smoke.

I knew it was a hit. Felt it, and saw the flash. Wonder where? We still are showing speed, so it couldn't have done much damage to the stern or props.

"Steady 016, checking 019, sir," doing what he was trained to do, repeat until the conning officer acknowledged.

"Very well."

"Seventy feet."

"Belay fathometer readings."

"Aye, sir."

Two very long minutes later,

"DC central requests the captain come up on the handset."

The captain walked over to the sound powered phone talker for the JA circuit. JA was the captain's command circuit. The talker had a handset mounted on a wire cradle right below the mouthpiece breast plate. The skipper put the handset to his head.

"Captain." Silence, "Oh. Shit, Red. How many? Damn. Can you get help back there? Damn."

He walked back to front of the bridge.

"Fred, are we out of range?"

"Yes, sir, out of effective range. They may try a few long shots, though."

"Dillan, start zig zagging, 20 degrees either side of base course, every two minutes."

"Aye, aye, sir." "Left 10 degrees rudder, come to new course 356."

Then the captain went to the 21MC. "Weapons, anything from mount 52?"

"Nothing, Captain."

Silence on the bridge for awhile.

"Out of range now Captain," from Fred.

"Mr. Dillan, slow to 12 knots and come back to base course."

"Aye, aye, sir." GLOVER was still going 20.

We're abandoning our station.

Dillan did as he was told. The captain was standing next to his chair, hands grabbing the arm rest, knuckles white, head bent forward. He stood like that a while, seemed like full minute.

Finally he turned, "We have taken what appears to be a direct hit on top of mount 52. There were two secondary explosions, probably from cartridges. We have no contact with the mount. We have a class Alpha fire in the crew's berthing aft of the mount's upper handling room. We have a class Alpha fire in the ship's store area."

"We lost the corpsman from Repair II and have some more wounded there. Probably a lot more in the mount. Auxiliary electrical power is out aft on the main deck. We have taken causalities, men. We, undoubtedly, have some men killed, God rest their souls."

A moment of total silence.

Damn. Men killed. Who? The bastards killed someone!

"Fred, take over for me, I'm going into combat and advise GLOVER."

"Yes, sir."

A hit on top of mount 52. There was only maybe ¼ inch of steel. It was not a turret, an armored turret, just a mount shielded from the weather. Billy and 27 other men were in that mount or in the handling room below. Good God. The class Alpha fires were probably started from the flash over.

But the round must have detonated prior to or at contact. If it had penetrated the mount all the way, and into the upper handling room, it would have set off projectiles, maybe blown the magazine, and we would be sinking now, stern almost blown off. A very lucky shot for the little yellow bastards.

Dillan went over to the starboard bridge wing and looked back: lots of black smoke. He couldn't see mount 52, or even the helo deck, well from the wing. Other structures and the whale boat were in the way. He glanced forward. GLOVER was pulling away.

"Bridge, combat, DC central. We have a closed chamber on one gun on mount 52. There are no gunner's mates back there capable of doing anything about it."

A closed chamber was bad news. A projectile and casing were in there. On rapid and continuous fire, the chamber opened automatically, and when tripped, it closed, and the primer was fired electrically. A closed chamber meant that it was loaded and had not fired. That barrel had fired at least 150 rounds over the past minutes. It was hot, very hot. The projectile or cartridge casing could cook off. If the casing went, the projectile would be expelled and could detonate when fired.

If the projectile cooked off in the chamber, there would be even more damage. The barrel would split and shrapnel would fly. A barrel would open up like pealing a banana from the base of the chamber. The chamber would be over-pressured and the cartridge would fire, following the barrel split, with a propellant flash.

"DC central, bridge, weapons, we've dispatched GMG3 Norman from mount 51 to mount 52. Ask Repair II to assist him in getting there and provide a phone talker."

This could easily be a suicide mission. If the projectile cooks off while Norman is there, he is dead for sure, blown to bits and then the bits incinerated.

"Captain's on the Bridge."

54

"Bridge, DC central, we've dispatched Repair I to assist Repair II with causalities. We've lost the Repair II corpsman and only have the chief and two others left."

Dillan knew that the Repair II corpsman was a 3rd class. That left a 2nd class and a striker to help the chief.

"Bridge, DC central, we have established fire boundaries at frame 140 and frame 160. The class Alpha fire in compartment 2-144-0-L is under control. We have jettisoned 3 projectiles from mount 52."

They were getting the unexploded rounds that were in the hoists or trays at detonation over the side. No projectiles were detonated from the hit but the double flashes were cartridge casings detonating. Just lucky that projectiles had not gone off. It did not take much of a shock to set off casing primers when the casings were out of their aluminum shipping tubes. But projectiles were a little more resilient unless their fuse was hit.

Those men went in there and got those rounds, and any live causalities, knowing that they had a potential cook off awaiting them. Brave group.

GLOVER had turned around and had pulled to about 500 yards off the starboard quarter. The wind was blowing the smoke to port. Combat indicated that they were asking on the encrypted voice if they could assist. The skipper told combat to tell them that LARTER needed corpsmen.

"Mr. Dillan, all engines stop, please."

"Yes, sir. All engines stop."

"All engines stop, sir" Ding, ding. "Engine room answers up all engines stop."

LARTER slowed and the knot meter slowly ran down. Here we sit DIW, Dillan thought, 4 boilers on the line and DIW. The skipper wanted to minimize wind feeding the fires.

"Bridge, DC central, the gunners mate is going to try to fire by percussion."

"Bridge, Aye."

"Combat, bridge, advise GLOVER we have a hot round in 52 and intend to clear it. Ask them to move up," the skipper told combat. A moment later GLOVER moved forward.

Boom, and almost instantly there after, another boom as the round was fired and then detonated 100 yards away and above and to the left of the ship's stern. The lookout reported an air burst just above the fantail.

Wow, that projectile was almost well done. The fuse started counting immediately, or almost immediately.

"Bridge, DC central, bores clear on mount 52." Brave gunners mate, Dillan thought.

"Sir, I have lost steerage way."

"Very well, rudder amidships." With no way on the ship the rudders didn't work. The helmsman could not steer the ship.

Dillan anticipated that maybe the captain would secure general quarters once the fires were out, but maybe not. When the crew was at general quarters, no one was wandering around. This was good, since no one would be in the way as the repair parties worked. He walked out on the wing. The smoke was less and wafting up forward and to starboard now as LARTER slowly swung to the southeast. A slight swell and LARTER was starting to move to it, mast top sweeping back and forth. He could smell burning cloth and an awful smell, like burnt bacon.

GLOVER was lowering their motor whale boat. Dillan stepped into the bridge and told Fred and the captain.

"Prepare to receive motor whale boat on the port side amidships." was passed over the 1MC. Dillan expected they would do this with a cargo net, not taking time to fool with the gangway. From the wing he saw a couple of very dirty hatless men swing a cargo net over. Repair party men, he thought. Soon the GLOVER's whale boat was along side and three men scrambled up the net and were pulled onto LARTER.

One was in khaki, two in dungarees. The GLOVER's chief corpsman and a couple of others, Dillan figured. Each had a moderate sized green bag over their shoulders. The whale boat crew passed up 4 stokes stretchers.

The whale boat pulled off and started back to GLOVER who was now making slow circles around LARTER about 1000 yards off.

"Bridge, DC central, please ask the captain to pick up the sound powered hand set."

"Bridge, Aye."

The skipper walked over to the hand set. "Captain." Another long silence, everyone on the bridge was watching his face. It was almost haze grey. Jaw set tight.

Now what?

"I'll ask GLOVER to request medevac. Get the supply officer to clear space in the reefer (refrigerator), Red."

The skipper turned back and looked out at the sea through the front bridge window. Staring at the end of the earth, the 1000 yard stare as it was called, seeing nothing.

Then he turned and said, "We have 17 dead, including Billy Hoffman. We have another 5 who probably will not make it due to severe burns or trauma. The corpsmen are trying to keep them comfortable. We have 4 seriously injured and 5 badly injured. These need care far in excess of what we can provide. We have 8 minor injuries, mostly from Repair II."

"The aft end of the superstructure was penetrated. Mount 52 is out of commission with the top blown off and extensive damage. We have a 3 foot hole in the ship's store and repair locker area. We have a fire, almost out in aft crews berthing by the mount 52 handling room. We have a fire in the ship's store and repair locker."

Then on the 21 MC, "Combat, bridge, XO, call GLOVER. Ask for an immediate medevac for 14 men.

"Yes, sir." A few minutes later he came back.

"Captain, GLOVER already asked for medevac helos from Yankee Station. They estimated 70 minutes with their foot in it. He told 77 about our hit on the 7th fleet HF net. If we can get underway, he wants us to go east at our best speed and he will keep station on us."

"Thanks, XO. Dillan; let's see how fast we can go, try 20 knots to start, 120. Get main control to bring up superheat on two boilers and secure the other two."

There is no way we can go full speed and not run the fuel tanks dry long before we can get to Subic. Even at 20 it will be damn near impossible.

"Yes, sir, Captain. All engines ahead full, indicate turns for 20 knots. Come left, steer 120."

"All ahead full, indicate turns for 20 knots, sir."

"My rudder is left full, coming left to steer 120, sir."

"Engine room answers up, all ahead full, turns for 20 knots, sir.

The quartermaster of the watch said, "Recommend 125 to set a course for Subic and clear Hainan by 20 miles."

"Very well," from Fred.

"Ease your rudder to left 10 degrees, come left to 125."

"Ease my rudder to left 10 degrees, come left to new course 125, sir"

"My rudder is left 10 degrees, sir."

"Very well," from Dillan.

As the speed increased, full rudder for what now was going to be almost a 90 degree turn to port, might heel the ship too much, and Repair parties were still fighting a fire and probably moving causalities, Dillan thought. As soon as the helos were in sight, LARTER would slow to 12 knots and head into the wind, right now 030.

The men would have to be lifted into the helos off the DASH deck in stokes stretchers, one at a time. It would take awhile to get them through the ship from the wardroom, and up and out to the DASH deck. The stern still had a fire and was puffing grey smoke.

Fred came over. "Why such a slow turn, Dillan?"

Dillan told him, "Didn't want to put a heel on while the guys are working below. Until there's sufficient way on, the turn will be very slow, and then speed up."

Fred just nodded.

"Main control, bridge, we want 2 boilers on line, full superheat," Dillan said.

The phone talker repeated, and then added, "Main control, aye."

As GLOVER went by, Dillan could see men on her DASH deck rigging the helo refueling rig.

The skipper went to the 1MC. He repeated most of what he had said earlier about casualties, leaving out the gory details and names. He said that he was going to secure from battle dress for all except the repair parties, and that he probably would not secure general quarters until after the fires were out and over-hauled and the helo transfers made. Then he asked for the supply officer to call the bridge.

Squawk went the growler and the CO picked it up. "Captain."

"Good Tony. Put the body bags in that reefer and lock it. They are well marked?" Silence. "Shit. OK, forensics at Subic will need to deal with that. And Tony, leave space for more if we need it. Thanks."

The skipper walked over to the Combat phone talker, "Combat, bridge, ask Mr. Donovan to come to the bridge."

A minute later, Pete walked on to the bridge with a questioning look on his face.

"Mr. Donovan, good job on those rackets. I guess break-lock didn't work very well."

"Yes, sir. Thanks, and the 6 had a good signal and was trying to get the Flap Wheel off us, but as soon as it flipped back to raster it locked on again. That close, the signal was strong for the 6."

"They need to tweak that, damn it. Wish we had had some of the chaff launchers they're putting on cans now. Anyway, relieve Dillan."

"Aye, aye, sir."

What is going on?

Once they had done the formal transfer of the watch for JOOD and Pete had the conn, the skipper said,

"Dillan, you are hereby designated as qualified officer of the deck underway, fleet steaming, relieve Fred."

"Yes, sir."

Fred had a questioning look. Dillan went through the formal procedure of relieving.

"On the bridge, this is Mr. Finistry, Mr. Dillan has the deck."

"This is Mr. Dillan, I have the deck."

Then they each saluted the captain in turn. "I have been properly relieved by Mr. Dillan, Captain," Fred said.

"I have assumed the watch, sir," Dillan said.

"OK, good, Fred we need to get an immediate OpRep (Operation Report) out to CTF 77, copy the rest. Please draft one for my release. Include dead and wounded count. No names, include damage; indicate we're proceeding in company with GLOVER to Subic, copy appropriate commands, including COMDESRON FIFTEEN. We want to insure they have a heads up in case this leaks to the press before the Navy generates a press release. Families will call them if they hear LARTER was hit. Do it now, Fred."

"Yes, sir." And Fred left the bridge for combat and DC central.

The bridge was quiet, very quiet as men were lost in their own thoughts. They all knew men or had friends in mount 52.

"Bridge, main control, two boilers on line and super heat up, ready to answer all bells."

"Bridge, aye."

Dillan looked at the captain who nodded, then to Pete. Dillan waved his hand upwards.

"All engines ahead full, indicate turns for 25 knots," Pete said.

Dillan grabbed the PriTac handset, "Rockyroad, this is Quicksilver, mike speed 25, over."

"Rockyroad, roger out,"

"Bridge, main control, we have a hot bearing on the starboard shaft, recommend slowing to 20 knots."

"Bridge aye." Then Dillan notified GLOVER, "Mike speed 20."

"All ahead full, indicate turns for 20 knots," from Pete. Answered.

So much for speed. A hot bearing usually meant a bent shaft. Hope not. We'll end up in a dry-dock if the shaft's bent.

"Damn," the captain said. "That last hit must have messed with the shaft."

"Combat, bridge, advise GLOVER on encrypted voice that we have a hot bearing on the starboard shaft and do not want to exceed 20." Dillan said on the 21MC.

"Have the chief engineer come up on the JA," the skipper said walking over to the talker and picking up the hand set.

"Red, what's up with the shaft?" Silence. "OK, we'll have to baby it a bit. Keep me in the loop."

"Bridge, combat we have two air contacts bearing 168 range 32 miles, headed our way, IFF identification SH-3s from the Tyco (TICONDEROGA)."

"Bridge, Aye," Dillan said.

The helos went to GLOVER who had slowed and hauled out to windward. One at a time they were midair refueled above GLOVER's DASH deck, alternately doing plane guard for each other.

The skipper said, "Mr. Dillan, I'm going into combat and then back on the helo deck to look after the transfer. Set flight quarters and head into the wind at 12 knots when the helos finish refueling. Remember, you are the guide now, so keep GLOVER informed. The XO will be with me."

"Aye, aye, sir" and the skipper was gone.

"Captain left the bridge," from the messenger. Dillan and Pete were alone as officers on the bridge.

"That sure was a quick fleet OOD qualification," Pete said.

"Sure was. I kind of figured that he would do it on our transit home, but this was a surprise. And taking the XO and leaving me here alone with you surprised me. Let's do this right."

Then neither said much, all business on the bridge. No banter with the residual sadness all felt.

They went to flight quarters. They used the DASH helo deck. The main deck aft was a mess with fire hoses and all, and although buckled aft, the DASH deck was the best place to handle stretchers. Still a little smoke from a blower outside the aft crew compartment deck hatch as the repair parties tried to extract it. Pete slowed to 12 knots, and turned into the wind. Dillan executed a signal on PriTac asking GLOVER to drop back 2000 yards as plane guard.

Once steady, he hit the 21MC. "Combat, bridge, advise the helos green deck on the DASH deck. Wind 020 at 15. Advise that we have two guns sticking up 45 degrees from mount 52."

Those two barrels, probably bent, would be a hazard for the helos trying to lift stretchers. The SH-3s were bigger than the

Hueys and had to be very careful. The smoke, however, would stream aft and out of the helo's way.

The transfer took awhile. Although LARTER had planned to transfer 14, they only transferred 12. The other two had passed away in the interim. After sending up 12 stokes stretchers, six per helo, the heavily loaded helos were off at best speed for USNS HOPE, steaming off I Corps about 100 miles south. They would not have a lot of fuel when they got there. HOPE would refuel them for their run back to Yankee Station. LARTER's wounded would be in a full service hospital ship in a little over an hour.

Dillan had to assume that he should head for Subic based on what the CO had told Fred for the Oprep after the helo transfer. He got the quartermaster of the watch to plot another course for him. Then he had Pete set the appropriate course. They had been headed almost the wrong way while transferring wounded.

The task unit would need an unrep for fuel to make Subic. LARTER was under 70% already. The skipper, XO, and Fred had not come back to the bridge, so Dillan was the decision maker.

A radio messenger came on to the bridge and walked over.

"Who is the OOD, Mr. Dillan?" looking around.

"I am."

"We have an immediate from CTF 77," the messenger said.

The messenger handed Dillan the board. Essentially CTF 77 had ordered LARTER and GLOVER to proceed at best speed to Subic. Dropping below 60% but no lower than 30% was authorized. An oiler would be waiting about half way if needed for fuel. LARTER to advise if she required more medevac helos. LARTER was guaranteed a priority tender availability. Then the messenger went off to look for the CO, XO, and OPS, WEPS, and CENG.

Finally the CO came back. "Captain's on the bridge."

"Where we headed Mr. Dillan.?"

"One three zero for Subic, Captain, in accordance with the CTF 77 message."

"Good. I'm going to secure from general quarters but don't do it yet." He walked over to the 1MC.

"All hands, this is the captain, as I told you before, we have lost some shipmates, God rest them. Since I last talked about it, we have lost 2 more to their wounds. The remaining severely wounded have been medevacted to the hospital ship. There they will get outstanding care. We have more wounded than I originally thought. Men have been hurt fighting the fires."

"DC central had advised me that the fires are out and overhauled. Consequently, I am going to secure general quarters. All hands, less authorized personnel, must understand that the main deck aft of after officer's country and the helo deck are off limits. There has been damage back there, rails are missing, and we must keep this area clear. Those personnel who were berthed in the aft crew's berthing are to be temporarily berthed in other compartments and the supply officer will be making new berthing assignments, to be posted in the mess decks by 2000."

"We will also be using some spaces for our wounded. We will be doing some creative assignments, so don't be surprised. Hot racking may be required (men taking turns sleeping in the same rack). Officers will subsist out of the general mess since the wardroom is now our expanded sick bay."

"Before I secure general quarters, let us all remember our shipmates who have given their lives for their country with a moment of silence."

A full minute went by.

Seemed like a year. What do I do? Remember Billy and the men of the mount. Say a silent prayer?

From the skipper into the mike, "God, please accept the souls of our brave shipmates into your high abode. Grant them your blessing and comfort their loved ones. Please take pity on our wounded and guide the doctors, nurses, and corpsmen who work toward healing them. Give those of us remaining your strength to bear this sorrow, Amen."

He hung up the mike and turned, "Mr. Dillan, secure from general quarters."

"Yes, sir."

"Now secure from general quarters, set the regular condition III watch."

LTJG Len Ottaway came on the bridge to relieve Dillan. His uniform was dirty and his face was pure white. His hands shook. He was a bit surprised to see Dillan as OOD.

"Dillan, you hear about Billy?"

"Yeah, Len, I did."

"They only found his legs, only his legs! They identified him by his burned khaki trousers, good God."

"He didn't suffer, Len."

"I know. Most didn't. But Chris said 6 survived the inferno of shell casings going off. Four men in the handling room and even two in the mount. But all badly burned. The 2 from the mount didn't make it. It must have been 3000 degrees in that mount. And Chris heard that there is a lot of carnage. It was awful. I can't believe one hit could do so much."

"Are you sure you are ready to take the watch? I'll hang around awhile if you want. You lost some of your division. I understand."

"Thanks Dillan, but I can ... I can do it." He stood there for a moment. Then a tremor swept through him.

"But ... but, maybe I'll go see Chris and see what I can do for the wounded. We don't even know who is who. Who lived or died. We aren't even sure of our count yet."

Len Ottaway stood quiet for another moment and stared out through the window at the sea. Then he turned and left the bridge. The skipper, who was in his chair again, had heard at least some of the conversation. He waved Dillan over.

"Mr. Dillan, you may just make a fine officer yet, I think. Nice touch to let Len help Chris."

"Thanks, Captain."

Dillan went back to the center of the bridge, leaning against the pelorus to get some of the weight off his numb feet.

Not done for recognition, done as what I would expect another to do for me given the same circumstances. Len was a little shaky to take over OOD anyway.

55

Pete did not get relieved. Billy had this watch as JOOD. So they just stood there, ship boring into the mid day haze headed east. Amazing how things returned to almost normal routine. The skipper sat in his chair and stared into the empty sea ahead. The bridge was silent, only the slight vibration from the engines and the wind noise from the open bridge hatch. Nine men lost in their thoughts.

Fred came up with the OpRep draft. The skipper changed a few words. "Send it Op immediate, Fred."

"Yes, sir," and Fred was gone. Walking off the bridge Fred looked at Dillan with a questioning look. Dillan just shrugged.

Dillan and Pete were relieved at 1545. Dillan had been on the bridge since 0530. He had no feeling in his legs from the knees downward. It was like walking in high boots full of water. He almost fell down the ladder. His lower back was screaming. He went into radio. Radio was quiet except for the clatter of teletypes. The rest of the Navy was going on with their war.

"The chief went below, Mr. Dillan. Some of the chiefs are moving to forward officer's country or to crew's berthing to open their bunks for wounded," RM2 Stephy said. "And there is the outgoing OpRep you might want to read."

"We have any equipment casualties?" Dillan asked.

"We lost the HF antenna on the EW platform, so we had to shift to another. I heard that the WLR-1 was down due to shrapnel. But otherwise we're fine, sir."

Stephy switched from one foot to the other. "It's bad Mr. Dillan, isn't it?"

"Stephy, I haven't seen it. We have 19 dead and a bunch more wounded. We sent 12 to the hospital ship. It's bad Stephy. But we're still afloat. If that 122 hit had penetrated the mount all the way before it detonated we would probably be swimming right now. Some very brave men died today, Stephy. Our shipmates."

"Is it worth it, sir? I mean is the war and what we did today worth them getting killed?"

"Hell, I don't know. They died doing their duty and serving their country just like so many others have. We're military men. We do what we're ordered to do. Only history will be able to say if it was worth it. We'll get through our grief and continue to do our duty. It's the families of those who died we should say a prayer for. You a religious man?"

"Not really, raised Baptist. But I'll say a prayer."

"Not religious much myself, but I will too. OK, where is the outgoing message board?"

Stephy stood for a moment like in a trance, then, "Sorry sir," and he reached over to the board rack, pulled one, and handed it to Dillan.

How in God's name can I tell them if it was worth it? All those men and their families? Is it ever worth it? Why must young men die like that? Why can't mankind outlaw war? It seems like the ultimate affront to God. That is heresy for an officer and gentleman by act of congress. But, I am a human by act of God, and I think God has precedence.

Dillan opened the board.

140313Z MAY 68

IMMEDIATE

FM   USS LARTER,

TO   COMSEVENTHFLT

CC a lot of CTGs and CTUs, some that Dillan could not recognize. And copy JCS.

That was the Joint Chiefs of Staff!

Also copy CINCPAC

CINCPACFLT,

COMFIRSTFLT,

COMCRUDESPAC,

COMCRUDESFLOTELEVEN,

COMDESRONFIFTEEN, etc.

God and everybody. This will cause a lot of brass to get midnight phone calls.

SECRET NOFORN (no foreign dissemination - not for NATO, SEATO or other allies).

The message was crisp and in a preset format:

SUBJ OPREP ONE MOUNTAINTOP (C) //3300//

A. CTF SEVEN SEVEN 140203Z MAY 68

1. (S) WHILE CONDUCTING SEA DRAGON OPS SOUTH OF TRANH HOA TONKIN GULF VAC NINE-TEEN PT FIVE NORTH ONE HUNDRED SIX PT ONE WEST ORIG HIT BY ENEMY FIRE AT 0745 LOCAL 14 MAY 68. MOUNT FIVE TWO (52) OUT OF ACTION. FIRES ENSUED AND EXTINGUISHED. DASH DECK AND SUPERSTRUCTURE AFT DAMAGED. DASH DECK DECERTIFIED. MAX SPEED REDUCED TO TWENTY (20) KTS FROM HOT BEARING STBD SHAFT.

2. (S) CASUALITIES THIRTY NINE (39). NINETEEN (19) KIA. TWELVE (12) CRITICAL WOUNDED MEDEVACED USNS HOPE. EIGHT (8) WOUNDED REMAIN ABOARD.

3. (C) SEA DRAGON ABANDONED IAW REF A. ORIG ENR NAVBASE SUBIC ICW USS JEFFERY C. GLOVER.

4. (C) ETA 0800 LOCAL 17 MAY 68.

Other items followed, showing position at the time of the action, target location, rounds expended primary fire, counter fire, counter battery location, assumed enemy ordinance, assumed enemy rounds, etc. It was long.

The Navy would be drafting a press release. But not until LARTER could provide the names and service numbers of those killed in action, and wounded in action. There would be no mention of North Vietnam.

The next of kin of those killed would get a visit. That dreaded black sedan, slow walk to the front door by an officer and a chaplain in uniform, and a knock on the door that Navy families, less carrier pilots or those sent incountry, really did not expect. The severely wounded kin would get a visit also, but only after those who died.

It will leak. Washington is like a sieve. By tomorrow, it will be on the news. "Navy ship hit, many dead, details at 11." Then lots of jabbering newsmen that do not have an idea what was going on supposing this and supposing that. Unless, of course, there is other news of more shock value, or news with movies. Scenes with movie footage or photos always get more press. Then our story will end up on page 3. The media has to fill pages and TV air time.

If one screws up on a slow news day the screw up is going to get front page coverage. Anti-war demonstrators would be grabbing mikes and saying that not only were thousands of army men being killed, the war had escalated to the point where ordinary Sailors were being killed. God, I hope the squadron calls Patty. If she sees LARTER on the nightly news, she'll flip.

Dillan went into crypto and took out a sheet of stationary. "My Dear Patty…," and stopped.

I just don't know where to begin. My mind is numb and hollow. Like a sponge wrung out dry. A deep sadness and anger.

Then from the 1MC, "All hands muster on station, all hands muster on station, submit muster reports to the ship's office." This was normal for inclimate days in port in the morning and on sea days, again in the morning. Dillan checked his watch. 1620.

The XO is doing one more check to see who is missing. From it and an inventory of the wounded, he will have a confirming idea of the names of those who perished. Bet the carnage is not conductive to identification.

All hands had to wear the identification tags, called dog tags, that listed name, rank, serial number, date of birth, blood type, and religious preference. They hung on a chain around one's neck. There were two of them, one on another small chain, and one on the main chain.

Cold and noisy so most men had taped them together with adhesive tape. The Navy Exchange also sold black rubber grooved rings that could be stretched around them to stop the noise and insulate them a little. Most wore these tags between their shirt and "T" shirt.

Collecting the small chain ones, and jamming the large chain one into the deceased man's mouth between the front teeth was the way to get a list of the dead and identify the bodies. But that was very hard to do when there was not a lot left and dog tags were missing.

At 1700, Dillan was in the mess decks for evening 'dinner for the crew.' It was a quiet meal as he went through the chow line, got his tray, and silver, and had meat loaf and mashed potatoes, canned green beans, bug juice (Kool Aid). Pete was there, and they sat together.

"Stephy said the WLR-1 was down," Dillan remarked.

"Yeah, the antenna was damaged by flying debris. When I was up there looking, I could look down on the DASH deck and see mount 52. The back end of the DASH deck is all heaved up, and the back fold down safety nets are twisted like a pretzel. I could just see some of the top of the mount. It looked like a huge can opener had torn the top off. On my way down here from the ET shack, I mistakenly opened the wardroom door, men on the floor on mattresses. One on the table while the two chiefs worked on his burned back. Ugly."

"Poor bastards, flash burns are first degree. I haven't been back to the stateroom yet. After we eat, I'm going back. That's pretty close to the damage."

"I'm bunking in the ET compartment. They're using my rack for wounded. Sam told Fred that some partitions were buckled in the two aft most staterooms but no fire or smoke damage. But the entire athwart ships passageway, ship's store, repair locker and etc. are pretty much trashed from the explosion and fire. So is after crew's berthing."

He went on, "How we didn't have more killed or severely wounded in Repair II was a miracle. I guess when it hit they were all sitting on the deck. The corpsman was standing up getting something out of the locker and caught shrapnel full in the face. Died instantly. They flooded the after magazine once they got the people out of there and the handling rooms."

"Yeah, Pete, those who died instantly, like Billy were the lucky ones. The flash burns on the men who were medevacted were awful, I heard. If they live it's going to be a long painful recovery."

"Are you going to be OOD now?"

"Don't know, I am going to assume that we have reverted to the normal watch bill, unodir (unless otherwise directed), but the 12-16 and 00-04 is short a JOOD. Red is way to busy to be worrying about a watch bill. I'll just go up there at 2000 and assume that I'll be the JOOD like always."

"Guess I'll do the same for my normal watch. See ya later."

"Yeah, later."

56

Dillan went aft towards his stateroom. Red and Sam had gotten the lights back on. The port passageway was roped off. He could see black soot on the far end. Then to his stateroom. Eric was there. Said nothing. At his desk writing. There was no damage he could see. But he could smell burnt something. He went aft to the two staterooms at the end.

The overhead was buckled a bit and partitions were pulled loose and rivets popped. One light fixture had broken loose and was tied to the cables with marline. Otherwise, nothing. No damage to the head or showers. Just smelled of burnt cloth. He stuck his head back into his stateroom.

"Eric, what's up with the shaft?" Dillan asked.

"Close aboard hit must have shocked the aft bearing. It was running hot. Vibrates a bit, feel it?" he said pointing to the deck.

The deck was vibrating indicating that LARTER was up to speed. Dillan guessed that they were at 27 knots but knew they were going slower. Damn bearing.

"Yeah. Think Subic can repair it?"

"Probably. Shaft still runs true. Top bearing casing is cracked and we'll need a new one. Two bolts sheared. Hit must have whipped the shaft and stressed the bearing. We pulled the top casing. Running without an aft bearing top so shaft whips around a little. Decided slower was safer and less wear on the stuffing tube. Lucky it didn't trash the stuffing tube or bend a strut. A trashed tube would leak like a sieve and we would be dealing with flooding and headed for dry dock. A bent strut, and we would be just dragging that shaft."

"Thanks. Sounds like we got lucky with that last one. I'm headed back to radio. Later."

"Later."

Dillan left and went back to radio.

Eric's men sure couldn't work on the shaft bearing out here in the gulf. And they would need parts. Thank God the shaft isn't bent.

An outgoing Confidential message was on the board listing the dead and wounded – a long list.

Fred came in. "Dillan, the skipper wants you to be the OOD on the 20-24 and 08-12. Pete will be your JOOD. The XO made up a new watch bill. It's posted on the bridge. Red and Sam are off for now. Ted will be taking Red's evaluator slot. So you finally got your fleet OD qual, about time."

"Yes, sir."

So, back on the bridge as OOD for the next watch. OK. Made sense for Ted to be evaluator. He knows as much or more about combat as any other JG on the ship. God, my legs are sore and will be even more so by midnight.

Fred picked up the sitrep board. "I bet CTF 77 is going to send an air strike to level that island," he said.

"Hope they make it disappear into the ocean," from Dillan. "Bomb it flat and exterminate the little bastards."

Fred went back to the boards, and Dillan went into crypto, feet up on the desk.

Let's see if I can finish the letter. Or at least start it. Still drawing a blank. Feel old. Feel like maybe 50. Real old.

The 20-24 was basically boring. With LARTER as the formation guide, all they did was go in a straight line towards Subic at 19 and a half knots. All they could muster without tearing up the shaft. The skipper was in his chair for awhile, staring into the dark bridge windows. Then he went to his sea cabin.

The skipper is going to have to write 19 very difficult letters, and another bunch of not so great ones. Then maybe some form of citation for GMG3 Norton for risking his life to get that round out of the hot gun. Hopefully something for the repair boys that cleared the mount.

Bronze Star, combat "V", that's what I would give Norton, but probably just a Navy Commendation Medal with the combat "V". Enlisted seldom get a Bronze Star. Probably some Navy Achievement Medals, also with the "V" for some of the repair party. Achievements were for JO's and enlisted. Washington will do the Purple Hearts for the dead and wounded once the list is final. Billy will get a Purple Heart and maybe a Navy Commendation, posthumously.

Medal distribution at this stage of the Vietnam War, at least in the surface Navy, was sporadic to say the least. Few were given out and usually only lower precedence ones.

Pete and Dillan talked quietly about Billy, remembering little things that he said or did. So young. And Dillan shared his experiences on shore patrol about Seaman Apprentice Morton and Seaman Gates. Morton had died in mount 52. Gates was badly burned and was on the HOPE.

Just kids. Just kids! Damn.

The rest of the bridge watch talked quietly also. There was none of the usual banter with the skipper off the bridge.

Two days later, May 17th, LARTER entered Subic Bay, at 0700, and went alongside the tender. The ships in port were lined with onlookers quietly staring at LARTER's damage as she went by. So, but for the grace of God go we, was probably what they were thinking, Dillan assumed. The XO made a good approach and they were moored, shift colors. One can was pushed in alongside LARTER. LARTER was first can outboard of the tender.

Pete was sporting a silver bar. His LTJG promotion occurred with a DOR of 5/17/68, exactly one year from commissioning. The skipper put off his wet down. There was to be no immediate celebration.

There was a message from CTF 77. Air recon indicated that route 1A and the railroad line were severely damaged and out of commission. The train had retreated northward and was back in Thanh Hoa. An air strike had obliterated the top of Hon Me island. Tranh Hoa was getting it now, also.

As soon as they were tied up, the tender's repair officer and his chief were on the quarterdeck. There was also some photographer's mate with a camera bag. Red and Sam went with them. Lots of photos of the damage and soon working parties from the tender were removing body bags to a truck. Dillan counted bags: twenty six, some small. But the military always used closed caskets, adding sand bags if necessary to bring the weight up.

Then the four wounded in stretchers were put on a truck for transport to the medical center. The truck took the four walking wounded there also.

Dillan got permission to go ashore, shifted to his officer's cap, and headed for the telephone exchange. It was an hour's wait.

It was 6:30 PM the preceding day San Diego time when he got on the line.

"Hi Honey," he said.

"Oh, God, Pat are you alright?"

"I'm fine honey. We lost Billy Hoffman, and a bunch more."

"The staff called last night late and said that LARTER had been hit, and that there were casualties. They wouldn't tell us who or how bad. I waited all day here for the black car to show up but thank God it never did. I went to church late this afternoon and prayed a lot. I think God told me you were alive."

"Did it make the news?"

"Just a side bar about US destroyer hit off Vietnam, men killed, was all on the evening news yesterday. There was a lot about some fire base being attacked with movies and some anti-war demonstration with fire hoses, also, so it didn't get much coverage. You didn't get wounded did you?"

"No, Honey, I was on the bridge and the hit was back aft, a long way from me. I'm fine."

"How many died?"

"We lost 19, and another 12 were badly injured and transferred to the hospital ship. Eight others were wounded."

"Christ, Pat, so many. Billy was just a kid. Are you coming home now, for God's sakes?"

"I don't know for sure, but LARTER is going to need a shipyard. We have a shaft problem we need to get fixed. Hopefully they'll wait until after our stand down for any major work. I expect we'll head east with the next carrier going back, probably in a few days if the shaft is OK for the trip. A carrier is scheduled to return to Alameda and we'll probably go back with her."

"Why don't you just leave now. Right now!"

"Can't do that, Honey. We need a carrier to tote fuel for us. It's a long way. Besides, the starboard shaft is screwed up, and they have to fix that."

"How long? When will you be home?"

"Maybe 30 days, less if we get to go fast and don't stop anywhere. If the shaft is OK. If not it could be longer if we have to go in dry dock to pull it. Eric thinks it's OK. They sure won't let us try a crossing with a screwed up shaft. But Eric thinks it can be fixed in a couple of days by the tender."

"Damn it, a whole month? Where would you go if the shaft thing is broke?"

"Probably Yoko. Only place over here where a shaft can be replaced. But don't worry. If Eric thinks it's OK, it is."

Then they talked about the families of the killed and wounded for awhile. Dillan said that maybe Patty could call Chris's wife, and see if she could help her console the families that were there. Chris' department had taken 80% of the casualties. Dillan said he expected the CO's and XO's wives would also be doing that. Patty said she would.

"Come home to me. Come home to me, now. Will you call me again?"

"I'll try. We'll be here a few days while they make temporary repairs and get the ammo and Westpac stuff off-loaded. If I can't get through before we leave, I'll call you via Ham radio once we cross the date line."

"OK, OK, just a little while longer. Love you and miss you."

"Love you and miss you too, Honey. Bye."

At least the staff had not screwed this one up. Bet more than some JO's made those phone calls, probably LTs or LCDRs.

Ham radio on ships used the MARS or Military Amateur Radio System. Ships could make phone patch calls with the help of Ham radio operators ashore in the USA, but only in Eastpac on returns from deployment. It used HF single sideband. Families were responsible for paying the Ham operators for any long distance telephone calls they incurred with the phone patch. It required one licensed Ham operator on the ship. Many radiomen were licensed.

Dillan knew that all the ammo from the aft magazine had to be offloaded and probably destroyed. It would be suspect. It would be a dirty, messy job since the magazine had been flooded. And cartridges got squirrelly after immersion, if they had leaked.

The ship formally published the names of those killed in action, severely wounded in action and transferred to USNS HOPE, and other wounded in action. ENS William (Billy) Hoffman, USN, was first. ENS forever, Dillan thought. Billy would have made LTJG on June 3rd. There were 19 on the KIA list, 12 on the USNS HOPE list and 8 others. Amazingly all the Sailors transferred to HOPE were still alive, although in critical or serious condition.

Once they had gotten downgraded to serious, HOPE would have them flown via Ton Son Naut or DaNang to the big Naval Hospital in Pearl Harbor on a C141 evacuation flight with doctors and nurses aboard. The same was happening to the more severely wounded put ashore in Subic. The walking wounded were also being transferred to Pearl and then back to the states.

The tender cut the ragged top off mount 52 and welded some temporary patches. They patched the hole in the back of the main deck house. They put a haze grey canvas cover over mount 52 so that it almost looked normal, but was missing the barrels. The tender had removed them. The mount was about a foot or so shorter than 51. The tender cleaned and painted most of the burned areas inside and out with the exception of inside the mount, and provided new bunks and mattresses for aft crew's berthing.

The upper handling room for 52, and the lower and magazine were sealed off and locked. The wardroom was cleaned and reopened. They pulled the damaged shaft bearing and tested the shaft. It ran true. They installed a new bearing. They worked 24/7. To the uninitiated, LARTER looked almost normal. The DASH deck was officially decertified.

LARTER was short one officer and 38 enlisted men for watch standing. About 14% of the crew were causalities. Since most of the lookouts, bosun mates of the watch, and messengers came from WG or 1st division, some storekeepers and even a few designated strikers like RMSA Kilmer were pressed into service. Repair II had to be mostly remanned. Many of the crew would be in 3 watch sections.

The captain eliminated the requirement for condition III watches and LARTER's officers went to 4 sections, OOD, JOOD, CICWO, maybe ENG watch officer, on each watch. The chief engineer, Red was off the watch bill. Chris was going to have to help the CO with the letters. Dillan was one of the OODs along with Fred, Len, and Ted. Pete remained Dillan's JOOD. Sam would come up and stand JOOD for Fred.

Dillan did one last RPS run. He and Pete offloaded the Westpac equipment. The KY-8 encrypted voice device, the Prick

10's, extra 9s, and other stuff went ashore. Troops bought booze from the package store and it was stored under lock and key in the brig.

Dillan bought a set of salad bowls and a string of pearls for Patty. It was a small string, but all he felt that he could afford. Pete had a small "wet down". It only lasted about an hour and everyone was back on the ship early. No one, including Pete, felt much like celebrating.

57

On May 21, 1968, LARTER was underway with a carrier for the states. One other destroyer accompanied them. It was a 27 knot 17 day great circle route passage going well north of Hawaii. It was a fast passage.

Once LARTER crossed the International Date Line, and gained a full day, Dillan had the radiomen set up a high frequency 1000 watt SSB transmitter on the best MARS frequency, and the crew started making phone calls home through Ham radio operator phone patches at night. Dillan talked to Patty. A bit odd since he was standing in tiny Radio II next to the transmitter with others, and they could hear everything said. And one had to transmit and wait, and Patty's voice sounded weird due to the single sideband distortion.

"Hi, Honey, I'm on my way home, over."

"Where are you and you sound weird ... over?"

"Northwest of Hawaii and coming straight home, nonstop, over."

"When will you be home? Over."

"In a few days, the staff will call you, over."

"You have an audience don't you? ... over."

"Yes, Honey, love you and miss you, over."

"Love you and miss you too. I'll be on the pier waiting, over."

"I'll probably be on the bridge wing, wave to me, over."

"Will do, I cut my hair so I hope you recognize me, over."

"I'll be looking hard. Have to go and let some other guys call, bye, over."

"I'll get some reservations in Tahoe, over.

"Wait till the staff calls with an arrival date, then get them for a couple of days later, over."

"OK, bye, over." Technically it should have been, "Bye, out."

Watches were mostly boring. The crew all filled out their customs declarations. LARTER did unreps with the carrier every 3 days. North of Hawaii the task group rendezvoused with an oiler and topped off.

They were also lucky with the weather. The north Pacific was a large area and was well known for storms. But late spring/early summer was not a prime storm time. And it was also out of the typhoon belt. Typhoon season had not yet started. Mostly sea state 3 or less, the ride was not bad.

Dillan was also expecting some preliminary orders. Being in split tour mode, a transfer was in sight. One afternoon a couple of days prior to flying off the carrier's air group, the chief brought him a message.

It was Unclassified from CHNAVPERS (Chief of Naval Personnel). On or about 15 August, and when relieved, proceed and report to COMDESRONTHIRTYSIX, Charleston, South Carolina, for duty as Staff Communications Officer, delrep 15 days.

This is good. East coast squadron staffs deployed to the Mediterranean but seldom went to Westpac. And an afloat staff job for a boot LTJG is a good one. Get to see the bigger picture. Not as much sea time. Being on the east coast means that Patty's home is in driving distance, she'll be pleased. The delrep means that we can take 15 days leave enroute plus travel time if we want. Probably only 10 days since that's about all I'll have on the books after the upcoming leave[lxvii].

The message contained other preliminary orders. The CO, having been in command of LARTER for 2 years, was headed to the Naval War College, Command and Staff, a year's course. Prepping him for his forth stripe, Dillan thought. Chris Harcourt was going to Dam Neck, Virginia to some weapons development billet: a great chance for him and shore duty to boot.

Red Redmond had orders to an east coast LST as XO via Little Creek, for Amphibious Warfare training. That was just about a guarantee of LCDR soon. Sam Blongerinski and Joe Rederman were headed for DLGs, one out of San Diego and one out of Long Beach. But this was typical; rotate the split tour people after a cruise.

The Navy news message told the story of John F. Kennedy's brother Robert Fitzgerald Kennedy's assassination on June 5th. This shocked most of the crew. It sure shocked Dillan.

I am coming back to a country I don't even know. It has changed so much in 8 months. Now two assassinations in 3 months. My God. Maybe I've changed, but so has the USA.

On June 7, 1968, the task unit arrived off San Francisco around 8 AM, and the carrier set flight quarters to fly off the air group. They had one more plane guard assignment. Then, at the golden gate, the destroyers were detached.

LARTER ran south, detaching the other destroyer for Long Beach. Thirty four knots in the dark night between the Channel Islands and the southern California coast. Getting in the high speed run, which was required every quarter. LARTER was at 1SD, the San Diego Harbor outer buoy, just after sun up.

"Now station the special sea and anchor detail."

Out came the pilot boat flying the "Hotel" flag, with the US Customs official aboard. They slowed and picked up the customs official, with a jacob's ladder, who was escorted to the wardroom. He would review and stamp all the crew's customs declarations. But he would not look at anything. After being gone over 6 months, there were no real customs duties. And the ship was full of stereos and china the crew had purchased. The official would leave the ship when it tied up.

Dillan was JOOD. Everyone was in tropical white long. This was a white short sleeved shirt, white pants, and for officers and chiefs, even white shoes. The ice cream salesmen's uniform. They had to do some creative sharing for the men from aft crew's berthing, since most of their clothing was lost and Subic just did not have enough to issue total replacements.

As they started down the channel with Point Loma on the left, everyone was keyed up. Dillan had the 20-24 the night before but maybe slept an hour, maybe less.

All these years in the Navy and I still get 'channel fever' returning from a cruise. But this is my first real deployment and my first as a married guy. God, I miss Patty. Soon boy. Soon.

The men had all kicked into a pot for what was called an 'anchor pool.' One could pick a number from 0 to 60. The exact moment from the quartermaster's log that the first line went over to the pier would be the winning number. All with that number would share the pot. This time the winners would get 25% and the other 75% would go to the deceased next of kin. Maybe $120 each but it was the thought that counted and the crew came up with the idea on their own.

The 1st class signalmen came up to Dillan, "Mr. Dillan, should we tie a broom on the halyard?"

A broom, bristles up, on the periscope was a signal World War II submarines used to use to indicate a 'clean sweep', or that all their torpedoes had been fired when they returned after a war patrol. Some destroyers had used it also when returning from the Vietnam War.

"No. It would look too much like a celebration. Just do the international call sign like normal," Dillan said. All ships used their "November" call sign in flag hoist when entering or leaving harbor.

Dillan had put in for 10 days leave effective upon arrival. They drew straws for this as OODs since the ship needed them to stand CDO in port. But LARTER had 9 qualified now, so half got to go early and half waited. Many of the other officers and crew had leave also.

The captain was going and the XO would be acting CO for 15 days. LARTER was scheduled to just sit tied to the pier for 30 days. Then off for the yards in Long Beach. Those remaining aboard the next 30 days would be in 4 section duty. There would be liberty at noon and all weekend for those who did not have the duty for the duration, a full stand down.

LARTER went down the channel with the men in ranks at quarters. Another perfect morning: warm, sunny, and a light sea breeze.

God, San Diego looks good, all the sailboats at Shelter Island. Downtown and the Star of India to port, couple of cans hanging off mooring buoys – suffering through their own Reftra. We get our own pier, starboard side to, end of the pier. A few days later we'll be moved to a nest with the rest of the destroyers.

The XO made the approach. A couple of pusher boats were standing by to port in case they were needed. The pier was jammed; wives, kids, all in their Sunday best. Line handlers from some other ship on the pier in whites also. A small Navy band. COMDESRONFIFTEEN and even the Admiral himself, COM-CRUDESFLOTELEVEN and some other four stripers were on the pier, a formal welcoming committee.

The first line went over at 0813, June 9[th,] as a bosun on the bow threw a coiled messenger line with a monkey fist on the end to the pier from the bow. The line handlers had to clear some of the civilians back to keep them from getting hit. They had been gone 223 days, just short of 8 months, and in port very few days of that.

"Moored, shift colors." Then other lines went over and were doubled up. Men scrambled ashore to secure the brow and put rat guards on the lines.

Later, shore power cables would be snaked aboard and the ship's boilers would be secured, cold iron, the first time in almost 8 months.

The brass was bonged aboard and taken to the wardroom. The captain and XO would meet and greet. Then some families were let aboard. Dillan stood on the bridge wing and searched through the crowd for Patty. He knew she would not come aboard. It took awhile but he finally spotted her waving. He waved back.

Wow, she had cut her hair! Nice trim dark blue dress. Beautiful woman. Lucky man, Dillan, lucky man.

"Now, secure the special sea and anchor detail. Set the regular in port watch. The officer of the deck is shifting his watch from the bridge to the quarterdeck."

Dillan put his binoculars in their box. Turning to Fred, "Permission to leave the ship, sir."

Fred was putting his own binoculars into their box, fastidiously coiling the neck strap around the hinge in the center.

"Granted. Come back ready to get to work. We have an admin inspection in a couple of months and I expect your division to pass with zero discrepancies. I will be going over the inspection guide in detail the next two weeks."

God, Fred, can't you ever think of anything but Navy?

"Yes, sir," he said.

Then, "Fred, you should get a life."

Fred turned towards Dillan, "I have a life Mr. Dillan, a US Navy life. Plenty of time for me to clutter up my life with a wife and family. For now, I intend to insure my future as a naval officer. You should consider working more diligently on yours, unless you intend to get out."

"Sometimes, Fred, I think I might just do that. Get out and live like a normal human in a couple of years."

A surprised look on Fred's face, like Dillan had just indicated that he thought the moon really was made of green cheese; totally awestruck. Dillan turned and was gone.

He went down the ladders to the brow, had to wait a bit since it was jammed with wives, sweethearts and kids coming onboard. A few were on the pier staring at mount 52 and pointing.

Then Dillan was out across the pier and into Patty's waiting arms. A very long hug; then a kiss.

I never want to let go again. Never.

Slowly they walked up the pier to the parking lot, arms around each other, Dillan matching Patty's stride.

"Lots of wives or mothers wouldn't come to see you return," she said. "They're burying their men or visiting them in the hospital."

"I know; it's a sadness that we'll share forever. But we're lucky, we still have each other."

Silently she tightened her grip around his waist.

"I think that moustache has to go, Mister," from Patty, looking up at his face.

"Yes, Dear."

The best answer to all statements or questions from a wife. Bye bye moustache.

Their war was finally over, at least for now.

Epilog

When leave was over, Dillan was back standing CDO duty every 4 days. Just over two weeks after LARTER returned to San Diego, there was a memorial service at the Naval Recruit Training Command chapel, the largest base chapel in San Diego. Service dress white, the officer's uniform with the choked collar and long sleeves. Patty went with Dillan in a basic black dress. Most of the ship's officers, less those on leave and out of the area, were there. And their wives.

The admiral and a lot of other brass were present. There was a space in the front row for the deceased's wives, children and parents. Only 3 families were present. Behind them were the brass, ship's officers and then the enlisted crew. A few who had been returned to the Naval Hospital in San Diego were still in wheel chairs or bandaged. There were over 300 people.

The service was conducted by the flotilla chaplain, with organ music and the San Diego Navy chanters. There were remarks about the bravery of the deceased by the admiral and CO. The chief gunner's mate sounded a bell slowly, 19 times.

Most of the dead had been buried in small towns and cities across America, one grieving family at a time standing beside a flag draped casket and then listening to taps as the casket was lowered into the ground. Honor guards were provided by the local Naval Reserve centers, sometimes with help from the American Legion, and the mother or wife was presented with the draping, tricorner folded, American flag.

All the deceased were ultimately presented with the Purple Heart Medal. Billy Hoffman's mother received her son's Navy Commendation Medal with a Combat "V" awarded posthumously.

All the wounded also received Purple Hearts. GMG3 Norman got a Navy Commendation with V. Three of the Repair II Sailors got Navy Achievement Medals, also with the "V"s. The rest of Repair II got letters of commendation from the squadron.

But there were a lot of campaign medals passed out. All hands got the Combat Action Ribbon, a campaign medal for Formation Star (Armed Forces Expeditionary), and the Vietnam

Service Medal with two stars for a total of three campaigns. The Tet thing counted as one, then prior to Tet, and after.

The Republic of Vietnam issued first a Vietnam Campaign Medal, and later a Gallantry Cross Unit Citation with palm for the NGFS work during Tet. Three months later, the ship got a Meritorious Unit Commendation from the US Navy. The green with yellow, blue and one red stripe ribbon to be worn by all who had served during the deployment, or any part thereof. The ship could then fly the small pennant from her mast.

The CO and XO both got Bronze Stars. Department heads got Navy Commendation Medals. LTJG Joe Rederman and LTJG Sam Blongerinski got Navy Achievement Medals, both academy graduates. There were no other personal medals issued for officers or crew.

All other officers got fancy certificates of commendation from COMCRUDESFLOTELEVEN. As Dillan said, with that and a quarter, he could get a cup of coffee at the Navy Exchange. But it would make a nice sentence on his next FitRep. Dillan did manage to get letters of commendation for his radioman chief, first class signalman, and RM2 Stephy.

He got Ted (Acting Operations Officer) Red (Acting Executive Officer) and the CO to agree to submit them up the chain of command while Fred was on leave. Dillan figured Fred would be opposed to giving recognition to enlisted people just for doing their job. Some of the other officers had their best people recognized, also. Pete got his chief and Thomas recognized.

Dillan and Patty came down to the ship late the afternoon after arrival and got the stuff he had bought. He signed out on leave. Others were doing the same. They spent a week in Lake Tahoe, and then a few days at home, just learning how to be husband and wife again.

Patty and Dillan both had significant emotional hangovers from the cruise, and it would be a long time until all the issues were addressed between them. They held them inside and didn't want anything to disrupt their time together now.

Exactly 30 days after the return to the states, LARTER went into the shipyard at Long Beach, and all of mount 52 and most of the after end of the DASH deck was replaced. The shaft was checked again. Being in the yard was a real downer for Dillan since Patty was still in San Diego. The ship ran busses down to

San Diego on Friday night and back to Long Beach on Monday morning.

Dillan traded duty whenever he could, so he could come home every weekend. LARTER was in the yard until early August. They were back in San Diego in time for Dillan to get relieved although his formal orders were late.

Dillan's division passed the Administrative Inspection with only 2 minor discrepancies. Fred was angry – but it was one of the best divisions inspected on the ship. And Fred's department was the best department. It reinforced Fred's management style.

Dillan, Sam, Jim, and Joe received orders and were transferred between June and September. Pete went off to comm. school and then took over Dillan's communications officer slot. Dillan's last fitness report was a top 5%. What he expected.

Eric Ebersol left active duty. The captain was relieved in September. Lots of the enlisted got orders. Red and Chris had left, Tony got out. So did Len and Ted. Lots of new officers reported on board.

By January, 1969, LARTER had mostly a new crew. She was a repaired ship and started abbreviated refresher training for her next Westpac deployment. She passed her Operational Readiness Evaluation in early April. In late April, 1969, she headed west again.

Quicksilver, a greyhound at sea, back into harm's way.

About the Author

Jack Wells enlisted in the US Navy in June, 1960. He attended Penn State University, was commissioned Ensign, USN, in 1966, and served aboard destroyers, intelligence ships, and mine sweepers during the Vietnam War. He holds the Vietnam Service Medal with 5 campaign stars in addition to multiple other decorations. After 10 and ½ years service, he left active duty at the end of 1970 as a Lieutenant. A qualified Surface Warfare Officer, he progressed to Commander in the reserve component, serving as Commanding Officer for four different units. At his request, he went on the retired list in 1983 after 23 years service. He also retired as the Technical Director for a major consumer products company, cruised the Caribbean on a sail boat for awhile with his wife Terry, and now lives in Florida.

www.JackWellsAuthor.com

Acknowledgments

There are a wealth of web sites on the internet dedicated to the Vietnam War and the individual units and ships that were involved. Most of these are maintained by veterans or veteran groups who care enough to freely share their knowledge. Some sites cover the entire history of U.S. Navy ships from commissioning to decommissioning. Many of these wonderful sites have links to out of print manuals, topographical maps and technical information which are unavailable elsewhere. Visit these if you want more information on the Vietnam War in general and the sea war in particular. There are hundreds of sites; way too many to acknowledge each individual one, so thanks to all.

Credits and End Notes

Credits

<u>Photographs</u>:

1. Front Cover: Official US Navy photograph, from the collections of the Naval Historic Center, public domain photo, 1967, USS GURKE (DD-783), SoCal Operations area, annotated by the author.

2. Inside: page iii, Official US Navy photograph, from the collections of the Naval Historic Center, public domain photo, aerial view, 1965, USS GURKE (DD 783), San Diego, CA, annotated by the author.

3. Inside: page ix, USS J.P. KENNEDY (DD 850) CIC. Photo by author.

4. Inside: page ix, USS J.P. KENNEDY (DD 850) Bridge. Photo by author.

5. Back Cover: same as item 2. above.

<u>Drawings</u>:

Excerpt, page iv, U.S. Naval Shipyard, Philadelphia, PA, drawing # 425, Warship Drawing, USS J.P. KENNEDY (DD-850), 1965, public domain drawing, Naval Historic Center, annotated by the author.

Page v, 5 inch 38 Caliber Mk 38 twin gun mount. Drawing by author.

<u>Maps</u>:

1. Page vii, Indochina Military Regions, #57923, 12:68, www.vietvet.org, annotated by the author. Permission to use reprint and publish, www.vietvet.org, 17 Mar 2007.

2. Page viii, East Asia, Corel Draw 6, generic, modified and annotated by the author. Permission to use reprint and publish Corel Corporation 1995.

3. Page viii, Formation Star – Sea of Japan, Corel Draw 6, generic, modified and annotated by the author. Permission to use reprint and publish Corel Corporation 1995.

End Notes

[i] Navy (and Coast Guard) officer ranks corresponded with other services as follows:

Navy & Coast Guard	Army, Marines, Airforce	Insignia
I Ensign	Second Lieutenant	One gold bar
II Lieutenant Junior Grade	First Lieutenant	One silver bar
II Lieutenant	Captain	Two silver bars

III Lieutenant Commander	Major	Gold oak leaf
III Commander	Lieutenant Colonel	Silver oak leaf
IIII Captain	Colonel	Silver eagle

The Armed Services also had Warrant Officer ranks that fit between officers and enlisted. Generally for technical experts, these went from W-1 through W-4. Today there is also a W-5. Warrants were few in the late 60's, and seldom if ever were assigned to FRAM destroyers.

[ii] OTC: Officer in Tactical Command. The senior officer and boss of a Navy task organization.

[iii] Corpen: signal flag and radio telephone term for set course or direction of movement. Many tactical signals used modified words to preclude confusion. Examples: "corpen" for "course", "niner" for "nine", "zero" never "oh." Letters always used the phonetic alphabet.

[iv] Speeds were set by setting propeller RPM. One Third was 1-6 knots; Two Thirds 3-12 knots, Standard 11-17 knots, Full 18-23 knots and Flank 23 - 34 knots. Max RPM was 280 per shaft. On LARTER 280 RPM was 34.1 knots, essentially flat out. This required all 4 boilers, full super heat, and the maximum authorized boiler fuel sprayer plate nozzles. Max speed on two boilers, full superheat, was 27 knots and was seldom exceeded. But speed was also related to sea state, and rough seas would slow the ship significantly. Unless twisting the ship in tight maneuvering situations, shaft RPM was kept the same for both shafts.

[v] Magnetic declination (variation) was different for different parts of the world. And it changed slightly over time, adding or subtracting tenths of a degree each year. The magnetic north pole was somewhere NW of Greenland. The South China Sea was close to zero or 1 or 2 degrees negative variation. Off San Diego it was plus 14 degrees. In the southern Indian Ocean almost minus 50. Once needed these corrections to determine true north. Then every magnetic compass had some of its own deviation. So to get true north from a magnetic compass one had to correct the compass reading for both variation and deviation.

[vi] Traditionally, any officer in command of a ship was always called "Captain" regardless of his actual rank. Any officer in administrative command of a group of ships, like a division, squadron or flotilla was always called "Commodore", again, regardless of actual rank.

[vii]A pelorus was a compass repeater. Receiving a signal from the master ship's gyrocompass, it was a rotating compass rose and showed the ship's heading. Mounted horizontal on a pedestal with a bearing ring on top, it could be used for sighting the true bearing of other ships or objects at sea. On the bridge there were three horizontal units, one on the centerline and one on each bridge

wing. There was another on the front of the signal bridge. There were also compass repeaters mounted vertically through out the bridge, and in other spaces throughout the ship.

[viii] Military time was stated in 4 numbers starting at 0000 for midnight, and continuing until 2400 for the next mid night. So in the morning 0400 was 4AM. But after noon, which was 1200, 1PM was 1300. To convert from military time in the PM, just subtract 12: 1300 = 1PM, 1700 = 5PM, 2100 = 9PM, etc.

[ix] From the Quartermasters pencil log the formal, highly abbreviated, pen and ink deck log would be prepared by the OODs for approval by the Captain and submittal to Washington. Writing these formal log entries was a big pain. A day's log sheet would be passed from OOD to OOD and each had to do theirs. The XO kept track and would require completion prior to going ashore. These formal deck log pages were bound and kept in the Naval Archives for ever.

[x] The Navy had a rate or job type structure for enlisted. Rates had a two letter code. In most cases the rate name made sense – really identified the job function. But not always. Men wore a rate emblem on their uniform, above their Seaman's rank insignia or between petty officer chevrons and the eagle on their sleeve. Most rates had schools, attended after boot camp. Highly technical rates had schools that lasted up to 48 weeks. But most schools were in the 12 to 24 week range. There were literally hundreds of rates, and some even had sub specialty rates. In the Navy enlisted "rating" and enlisted rank were synonymous. Examples:

RD	Radarman	Operated the radars and equip. in CIC.
RM	Radioman	Operated the ship's radios and teletypes.
SM	Signalman	Handled visual communications.
ET(R)	Electronic Tech.	Maintained electronic equipment, radars.
ET(C)	Electronic Tech.	Maintained electronic equip, comm.
QM	Quartermaster	Helped with navigation, charts and log.
MM	Machinist Mate	Operated and maintained main engines.
BT	Boiler Tender	Operated and maintained the boilers.
BM	Bosun's Mate	Op. and maint. deck equipment, boats.
FT(M)	Fire Control Tech.	Op. and maint: FC for missile weapons.
FT(G)	Fire Control Tech.	Op. and maint: FC for guns.
TM	Torpedoman	Op. and maint: torpedoes and launchers.
GM	Gunners Mate	Operated and maintained gun systems.
DC	Damage Control Man	Maint: DC equipment, & ship's structure.
SK	Storekeeper	Handled supplies. maintained inventory
MS	Mess Service Man	Managed the galley, the cooks.
YN	Yeoman	Ship's secretaries.

PN	Personnel Man	Maintained crew's records.
PC	Postal Clerk	Handled the mail.
EM	Electricians Mate	Repaired shipboard electrical equipment.

Enlisted ranks:

Enlisted ranks went from E-1, Seaman Recruit through E-9, Master Chief Petty Officer. Each of the other services had other designations for the enlisted ranks, some more than one. Few men could look at another service's sleeve stripes and equate it to their own service's enlisted ranks. The Airforce titles for E-5 and E-7 were one rank junior from the Army and Marines. And the Army started with "Specialist" ranks from E-4 and up also for technical fields. This caused mass confusion at joint commands sometimes.

PayGrade	Navy/CG	Marines	Army	Air Force
E-1	Seaman Recruit	Private	Private	Airman B.
E-2	Seaman App.	PFC	Private 2nd class	Airman
E-3	Seaman	LanceCpl	Private 1st class	Airman1st
E-4	Petty Officer 3c	Corporal	CPL/Spec4	Sr.Airman
E-5	Petty Officer 2c	Sergeant	Sergeant/Spec5	StaffSGT
E-6	Petty Officer 1c	StaffSGT	StaffSGT/Spec6	TechSGT
E-7	Chief Petty Officer	GunnerySGT	SGT1stClass/Sp7	MasterSGT
E-8	SeniorCPO	MasterSGT	MasterSGT	SrMastSGT
E-9	MasterCPO	SGTMajor	SGTMajor	ChfMSGT

Although "Seaman" is noted above for E-1 through E-3, engineering department rates were "Firemen," aviation rates "Airman," and construction (Seabee) rates "Constructionman."

[xi] You will note that Sailor is always capitalized when it refers to a US Navy member per SECNAV May 19, 1994. Also Navy is always capitalized unless referring to a foreign navy.

[xii] Hospital Corpsman. This was an enlisted rate that performed as the US Navy's version of health care providers. Well trained in medical procedures, these people provided front line medical care to Sailors and Marines. Smaller ships and units had corpsmen only – no actual doctors or nurses.

[xiii] Most navy communications, from the mundane through the serious, were transmitted in the blind by Naval Communication Stations located around the world on high frequency radio. This was called the broadcast, was electronically encrypted, and could send anything from UNCLASSIFIED through SECRET. TOP SECRET and above were also off line encrypted, and then the 5 letter/number coded groups were sent on the broadcast.

All navy ships had to copy at least one broadcast. The Seventh Fleet Net, and Seventh Fleet Cruiser and Destroyer Anti Submarine Warfare Net were copied by destroyers on Westpac deployment. You were not just watching for your ship's name. You were a member of multiple administrative and task organizations so you had to watch for them all. The list of these was called the ship's "Guard List."

And, each message on each broadcast was sequentially numbered. Ships were to scan the broadcast and pull off the messages addressed to them or addressed, shot gun fashion, to one of the organizations she was a member of. If you missed numbers you may have missed a message for you. Not good. Atmospheric conditions affected the transmissions so, depending on your location, you could miss numbers.

You had to find out if the missed numbers contained messages for you. If you were lucky, the carrier, with better antennas, would have not missed those numbers and could check their skeds (the continuous rolls of teletype paper printed with all the broadcast messages) and let you know if the missed numbers were for you. If they were, they could send them to you via the task group teletype net on ultra high frequency, short range, radio.

[xiv] Being a steward was a job few Americans wanted but for Filipinos it paid like middle management in their country. Some only did it for four years, sending money home. Some stayed for a full career. A retired chief steward lived very well back in the Philippines. But once they had completed their 20 year tour, they could also become US citizens and stay. Many did. Quite a few of the chefs at nice restaurants in Navy ports were retired Filipino stewards.

[xv] If there was a strike going out, a lot more CAP were required to escort the strike and provide protection for the task group. And there were specialized CAP for barrier patrol, search and rescue, etc. The carrier also kept an Air Early Warning (AEW) aircraft up most of the time. This was a propeller driven aircraft with a big radar that looked like a flying saucer on top and could spot air contacts over 250 miles away.

[xvi] Seaway: Navy term for an ocean with a sea running or some waves high enough to make a ship roll or pitch.

[xvii] NROTC officers were either commissioned in the Naval Reserve, or if selected, in the Regular Navy upon graduation. OCS was mostly USNR. Regular officers had a promotion and duty station advantage. They served at the discretion of the President, and had no official date of release from active duty, although no less than 4 years from graduation/commissioning was required. If a USN officer wanted to get out, he/she had to formally resign. And resignations were usually accepted – but many times with 6 months or longer extensions.

USNR officers had a set date of release, usually 4 years from commissioning – and typically ROTC commissioning occurred at college graduation. During force reductions, USNR officers could get an "early out." A USNR officer could also apply for augmentation to USN. Not all were selected. NROTC officers got scholarships during their college years, partial for USNR, full for USN. OCS officers got no scholarship unless they were in the NESEP program.

Today there is no specific differentiation between USN and USNR. All are USN although reserve officers are sometimes noted as USN (RC) if specific status information is essential. The RC is for Reserve Component. This change is recent and was done to make all feel part of one US Navy with no second class members, i.e.: a total force. Most USNR officers have dropped the R.

Many reserve component members have been recalled to active duty one or more times for the War on Terror.

[xviii] Perfection was the National Guard or Reserve but one needed a little pull. The Guard/Reserve could get all it needed and then some. After serving six months active duty, mostly training, one would be in the reserve for another 5 and one half years. No Vietnam. Without a draft deferment, the reserve was the next best bet – and so everyone wanted it. The reserve was being held back for recall in case of a wider war or an altercation with the Soviets or Red China: a strategic reserve.

Blacks were poorer, a lower percentage went off to college, and they sure had little pull. Most young black men didn't marry even if they had kids. They got drafted. So the net effect was that the Army had a much higher proportion of black soldiers. A percentage well above what the general population had. Consequently, the black population provided more of their members to the draft pool, more front line soldiers, and sustained a much higher proportion of the causalities in the Vietnam War.

[xix] Most announcements were preceded with a call on a bosun's pipe. The pipe was a small curved chrome metal tube with a small metal sphere on the end. The sphere had a slit. It sounded like a whistle. Most of the bosun's mates wore the pipe on a white braided lanyard around their neck and had filled the sphere part way with wax, since it took a lot of wind to blow a pipe properly.

One could change the pitch by partially closing the hand over the slit. There was a short call for 'attention' and other longer ones for other evolutions. The call to chow was the longest and included a long warbling phrase. It took experience to do the chow call correctly. Bosun's pipe calls were traditional and went back to the days of sail.

[xx] The Soviet Union almost always sent out a long range Tupolev 4 engine, turbo prop, reconnaissance aircraft, the Bear C. These aircraft would leave Siberia and fly over a carrier task group just to show that they could. They would then turn around and start the long flight back. An over flight was expected, watched for, and the goal was to have a US fighter escort for the Soviet bomber well prior to him getting within weapons release range. It was a game.

The Soviet aircraft could find the task group by intercepting the carrier's radar or radio signals and then homing on them. Sometimes carrier task groups set Emcon (emission control) and emitted no electronic radiation at all. This made it very difficult for the Bears, but it also made it difficult for the task group. By 1967, Emcon was normally not used. Not worth the effort.

[xxi] There was a policy that any north/south US Navy transit in the western Pacific went through the Taiwan straits between Formosa and mainland China. It was done to continually establish the right of free passage while concurrently showing support for the Nationalist Chinese government on Taiwan. The Taiwan straits were notoriously bad weather areas and a strong wind opposing the current could whip it up significantly. Seas were not high, but steep and confused. Large ships hardly noticed. Small ships took a pounding.

[xxii] Thousands of American POWs had been shipped out of Subic to the home islands as slave labor in 1942 - 1945. Some who had miraculously survived the Batan death march ended up in Subic enroute to Japan. Subic was just north of the Batan peninsula. The US Navy expanded the base significantly in the 1960s. The bay was large, had a narrow opening, was extremely well protected, and surrounded by high terrain.

[xxiii] In the early years of the war, especially 1964, and 1965, there was a second carrier station to the south called Dixie Station. But it had been abandoned when more ground based aircraft were deployed. Yankee station tended to provide air support to the northern Corps areas, and strikes at North Vietnam itself.

South Vietnam was broken up into four Corps areas, starting at the Demilitarized Zone at the border with North Vietnam with I Corps, and continuing south to the Cambodian border or IV Corps. The northern most corps area, I Corps, was under the US Marines area of responsibility with headquarters in DaNang.

[xxiv] The Tonkin Gulf Yacht Club was an unofficial name for the ships and crews who were or had been assigned to the combat zone and sailed in the waters of the South China Sea and the Tonkin Gulf. Sailors could purchase a patch with a yellow background, 3 red stripes, and a black sailing junk on it. It was not a real yacht club or even a real club.

[xxv] Crowectamy was a created word for getting busted – having a stripe taken away by the captain. Petty officer's insignia was an eagle with chevrons below it and their job function or rate symbol in the middle. These insignias were called "crows" and there was one red chevron (blue uniform) for 3rd class, two for 2nd class, 3 for 1st class and 4 for Chief. The Chief's was the same as 1st but with a rocker over the top. Senior Chiefs had a star above the badge, Master Chiefs had two stars.

[xxvi] Evolutions were things like General Quarters (Battle Stations), where the ship was fully prepared for battle with all weapons manned. Then there was the Special Sea and Anchor Detail, used for entering and leaving port, Underway Replenishment Detail, Flight Quarters for working with helicopters, etc. There were some special teams, like the maneuvering team for close to shore navigation, the Anti-submarine Warfare team for plotting submarines in the Combat Information Center, and etc.

371

The Watch, Quarter and Station Bill also listed watch stations. Many of the men on the ship stood watches. Although watches were required in port to protect the ship, watches were primarily for controlling the ship when at sea. The Bridge, Combat, Radio, Signal Bridge, Main Engine Control and boiler spaces were manned. Normal underway watches were 4 hours on and 12 hours off, or 1 in 4. But wartime steaming in a war zone was different. Condition III was set and watches were 1 in 3, or 4 hours on and 8 hours off.

In this condition, the gun director and one gun mount was also manned 24/7. The idea was that if attacked, the ship could respond immediately. It took time to get everyone to battle stations. Time that a ship may not have if under fire.

Officers stood watches as follows:

BRIDGE

Officer of the Deck. OOD. The man who directly controlled the ship. The Captain's representative.

Junior Officer of the Deck. JOOD. The OOD's helper and in training to become an OOD. Usually the conning officer.

COMBAT INFORMATION CENTER.

CIC Watch Officer, responsible for the collection and dissemination of information on friendly and enemy movements external to the ship.

MAIN CONTROL

Engineering Watch Officer. Responsible for the operation of the ship's boilers, engines, and auxiliary equipment. Sometimes not an officer but a Chief Petty Officer.

When a ship was at Condition III, the following were added:

COMBAT INFORMATION CENTER

CIC Evaluator. Normally a relatively senior officer, on LARTER a Lieutenant. The Evaluator had the right, as the Captain's representative, to fight the ship.

GUN DIRECTOR

Director Officer. Under the direction of the Evaluator, this officer could direct the ship's gun fire on surface or air targets. Sometimes this was not an officer, also, and was manned by a Chief Gunner's Mate or Chief Fire Control Technician.

[xxvii] Mostly AGIs just watched and stayed out of the carrier's way, and mostly they had a US Navy destroyer or even a Navy fleet tug as a shadow. But if there were major strikes north going on, they would transmit. It was a known fact that they were radioing the number of aircraft and make up of the strike to the North Vietnamese. They undoubtedly copied and recorded all the radio transmissions that were not encrypted, and probably some that were.

Sometimes they would even try to move into the carrier's intended path. But they were slow and were kept away by having a US Navy ship between them and the carrier at all times. So they couldn't disrupt much.

xxviii It was the Navy's policy to neither confirm nor deny that any of its warships carried nuclear weapons. Some Japanese would get up tight, also the Australians and the Kiwis. If the word got out in a foreign port, the Greenpeace group would make a big deal about it. So the Navy kept silent. Generally, carriers, cruisers, and destroyers carried nukes.

In the late 1960's there were only four US Navy surface ships that were nuclear powered: USS ENTERPRISE (CVN 65), USS LONG BEACH (CGN 9), USS BAINBRIDGE (DLGN 25), and USS TRUXTUN (DLGN 35). These ships would also get a hassle if they tried a port visit to some locations. It was 1971, before TRUXTON could be the first surface nuke to visit Yokosuka, Japan. Most US Submarines were nuclear powered and they suffered from the same situation, but with their hull numbers painted out they were not obvious, and came and went undetected.

xxix There was an experimental program in the Westpac to equip DASH with a TV camera and a jungle penetrator for use in finding and retrieving downed pilots in areas subject to heavy enemy ground fire. It was called "snoopy" and the idea was to drop the penetrator from the DASH on a wire, into the jungle, so the pilot could unfold it, climb aboard and ride it back up. Then the DASH would take the pilot out over the sea where he would be lowered into the water to wait for a real manned helicopter pickup. "Snoopy" worked a couple of times and it also did some recon, but mostly it was ineffective.

For a pilot to climb on that penetrator hanging from what looked like a very large and angry dragonfly, and then let it reel him up and take off with him dangling below it took a lot of intestinal fortitude. Only in extremis – you have 3 choices, get dead, spend years in the Hanoi Hilton or a tiger cage, or ride that thing, would a pilot choose to ride.

xxxi The only other electronically generated alarms in the 1MC system were the Collision Alarm, and the Chemical Alarm. Collision was a warbling sound and the Chemical Attack Alarm was a constant tone. Alarms were tested every day at 0800 in the morning, so all hands knew what they sounded like.

xxxii An officer had to have sufficient time in grade and between LTJG and LT this was 30 months. This was called being in the zone for promotion. Promotion to LT occurred normally after 4 years of commissioned service. This was new. Previously it had been after 5.

Then, once annually, the selection board would meet and review the Fitness Reports and career experience of officers in the zone. Officers selected for promotion were then promoted when the needs of the service and the congressionally mandated officer rank limitations allowed.

Not a big deal at the lower ranks, but by LCDR and above, restrictions applied. The Navy dodged this a little with "temporary" promotions. Then the permanent (congressional mandate) rank was one grade down. However, in the Navy, "temporary" promotions were never rescinded unless an officer really screwed up.

Almost all LTJGs were promoted to LT unless they had done something really stupid like running a ship aground, committing a crime under the UCMJ, or getting a letter of reprimand. But after LT, promotions were tougher. An officer could expect to spend many years time in grade as a LT. And then everyone did not get promoted to LCDR. Get passed over for promotion twice and your Navy career was over.

[xxxiii] Unless a ship was in an officially designated stand down, destroyers had to be able to get underway under their own power with the duty section only in 4 hours or less. In Eastpac, COMCRUDESPAC would require such a demonstration on weekends every so often. Although the skipper was allowed aboard for such a test, he was not permitted to coach the CDO. This made destroyer skippers prematurely grey.

[xxxiv] Mail was hit or miss, mostly miss. Mail addressed to someone on a ship got forwarded from the states to a Fleet Post Office in San Francisco, then flown to Subic by circuitous routes, then flown out to the carrier on a daily COD flight – weather and operations permitting. Then it would be transferred to the destroyers by helo, or high line when the destroyer was alongside for unrep. Outgoing mail followed the reverse path. One could go two weeks without mail, and then get 10 letters. If a ship was assigned to things like NGFS or Sea Dragon, where there weren't helos coming and going, there was no mail service.

[xxxv] Each compartment number was like 2-65-1-L. Two was for the second deck down from the main deck (1). Above the main deck, decks were numbered 01, 02, etc. going up. On the carrier the hanger bay was the main deck so the flight deck was really the 04 level, there being 2 decks between to starboard.

The second number was the frame number, counted from the first frame at the bow sequentially back to the last frame at the stern. The "1" was first compartment off the center line to starboard (odd number), the letter was for compartment use and "L" stood for living compartment. So theoretically one could find a compartment by using this system: 2-65-1-L = Second deck down from main deck, 65 frames back from bow, 1st compartment on starboard side from center line, used for living space.

[xxxvi] Carrier flight deck crews all wore different colored jerseys based on their jobs: purple for fuel handlers, blue for plane handlers, green for cat and arresting gear operators, yellow for cat and arresting gear officers, red for ordinance men, brown for plane captains (enlisted in charge of aircraft maintenance), and white for safety, medical, and landing system officers.

[xxxvii] Air intercept control was primarily used for vectoring fighters against incoming enemy bombers using the information available from the powerful ship mounted air search radar. AIC certified men, achieved through attendance at a 4 week course, could also do other vectoring. An aircraft was

vectored in on the incoming bogey, usually trying for a lead – pursuit position so the aircraft did not encounter each other head on.

Head on the two aircraft could have closing speeds of over 1,000 miles per hour, with no time to react. The idea was to get the fighter into a good position to acquire the enemy on his own nose mounted radar and then be able to launch air to air missiles.

Missiles would run out and acquire the enemy aircraft's heat signature, then close for the kill. Many times this was done with out the pilot ever having a visual on the target.

^{xxxviii} Although the biggest overall danger to a ship from battle damage was sinking, flooding could be controlled by keeping it from spreading compartment to compartment. And each hatch or scuttle door had a designation X (X-ray), Y (Yoke), Z (Zebra) or W (William). X meant normally closed, even in port. Used for voids and tanks. Y was for ones that were normally closed at sea. Z was for buttoning the ship up tight. W was for making the ship air tight: essential in the case of nuclear, biological or chemical attack.

Condition Zebra was set when general quarters was set. Some designations had circles around them which meant that they could be opened for passage providing that they were immediately closed again. The ship could be closed up so that it was a honeycomb of separate water tight compartments.

A fire at sea was a major peril. Although the ship was steel or aluminum, almost everything aboard was flammable. Fuel, ammunition and aviation gasoline yes. But also all the paperwork, bedding, clothing, and even the tile on the passageway decks, insulation on the electrical cables, and paint on the bulkheads and overhead would burn. And burn hot. Many internal fires were of the dark grey smoke, smoldering type. Killers due to the toxic oxygen deprived smoke.

And with all that jet fuel, ordnance, and pyrotechnics aboard there was always a significant fire risk as the crew of USS ORISKANY (CVA 34) knew from 1966. Forty four officers and men perished in a fire started by a flare going off in a flare locker on the starboard side. Then in July 1967 a fire broke out on the flight deck of USS FORESTAL (CVA 59).

Aircraft already armed with ordnance got involved. The flight deck fire crews were blown away as they tried to fight the fire and more ordnance detonated. It got worse when untrained men were called upon to fight fires after the trained ones were killed or injured. Lots of mistakes were made which turned a major disaster into a conflagration. When the smoke cleared, 134 were dead, 2 were missing, and 62 were injured. It was a carrier out of action for months.

The FORESTAL fire had provoked a reassessment of damage control and fire fighting training across the navy. All hands were to be trained instead of just repair parties.

^{xxxix} A "dead horse" was a navy term for a pay advance. One could get up to a month's pay in advance in special circumstances.

[xl] Gator navy Sailors had a lot of different things to learn, like making amphibious landings and such. But they knew little about ASW, or other destroyer operations. It was almost two separate navies with their own schools and training evolutions. Cruiser and destroyer officers, LT and below, were seldom assigned to the gator navy and gator navy officers were seldom assigned to the cruiser and destroyer force. LCDR and above, after some intensive courses, were cross assigned to build knowledge.

Amphibious ships performed important and often unsung services during the Viet Nam War. They executed some amphibious landings, hauled a significant amount of war material and troops, and some of their small fire support vessels delivered ordnance to targets ashore. And they took some hits and had some KIA – in DaNang from enemy frogmen, and in the Delta.

[xli] A fire at sea could ruin one's entire day. And every ship had a small fire about once a month. Usually smoking or electrical overload related. Every now and then the deep fat fryer flashed over. They were dealt with quickly. To insure this, fire drills were an almost daily occurrence underway and a daily occurrence in port. Keep the crew on their toes. Stop small fires before they got big.

[xlii] When in port at 0730 each morning, all hands were ordered to "Quarters for muster, instruction, and inspection". Each department and division in that department had a set chunk of weather deck to form up in ranks on. The idea was that division officers would take muster, then look over their troops to insure that they were in clean uniforms, and report such to their department heads.

In a place like Subic, the working uniform of the day was basically wash khaki for officers and chiefs, and dungarees for the troops. And some of the troop's dungarees could get pretty ratty. The ship's laundry washed them but did not press them like they did the khaki uniforms.

Some enlisted would iron their own uniforms but this was the exception rather than the rule and it was done less and less as the cruise went on. People were too tired for the niceties. But amazingly, many of the supply department's petty officers had starched and pressed dungarees. It was nice to be an insider.

After division officers reported to department heads, they would then report to the XO. Sometimes the XO would have information to share and this got disseminated back down the chain of command.

Following this all hands were smartly turned to face aft for colors. At exactly 0800, "On deck, attention to colors" was passed. The National Anthem was played from Subic's base loud speakers while division officers stood in front of their troops and saluted the ensign (flag) being raised on the stern flagpole.

Concurrently the union jack was raised on the bow. It was all very formal like. Then "carry on" and normally troops were dismissed to "Carry out the Plan of the Day" and "Turn to, commence ship's work."

xliii Here one put 5 dice in a cigar box with its hinged top. The first guy shook it, peeked in and said something like, "two threes", closed the lid, and passed it to the next guy. The next guy had a choice. Believe it and then better it without shaking, shake and still better it, or refuse to believe. If one refused and the stated score or higher was in the box, you lose. If it wasn't there the passer lost. Only after you believed or challenged could you peek in. If you believed you had to better it, like "two fours." Then you could pass it on. Now the next guy had the same choice. When it got up to things like "four sixes" it got very tough. If you lost, buy a round.

xliv At the time the Navy's biggest worry was Soviet submarines. And more destroyer types were needed to counter the threat. But congress was not in the mood to appropriate funds for "big" destroyers as escort ships. So the Navy sold them on destroyer escorts and a cheaper solution. Enter the BRADLEY class DEs. They were longer and wider than FRAM destroyers, 3900 tons. These ships only carried two single barrel 5 inch 38 caliber gun mounts, one forward, one amidships, but lots of sonar and ASW gear. Although sometimes used for gunfire support, they had only one half the available gun barrels that FRAM destroyers had.

And to save money, they were single screw steam plant ships. With two unreliable high pressure boilers, they were dangerous to take into restricted combat waters. A boiler or turbine problem and they were dead in the water. Most were stationed on the east coast of the USA in place for protecting convoy routes to Europe. By 1968, some were deployed to Westpac – an indication of how stretched the US Navy was filling requirements for destroyers in Westpac. By the 1970s, most class ships had their boilers replaced with more reliable ones. Redesignated as FF (Fast Frigate) they served the US Navy for many years, were great as ASW platforms, and were later sold to foreign navies.

xlv The Whiskey class was the most numerous class of submarines in the world. It was conventional: not nuclear powered. Better than the WW II submarines that the Germans, Italians, Japanese and the US and her allies had then, it still was restricted to a finite battery capacity and the need to surface and recharge. The US Navy had recorded the sound signature of Whiskeys for years. They were almost to the point where they could tell one pennant number (hull number) from another.

xlvi A destroyer could launch an older Mk 44 or Mk 46 Mod 0, relatively new, ASW ADCAP (ADvanced CAPability) torpedo using ASROC and put one right on top of the sub's geographic position. The torpedo, boosted with a small rocket motor, would pop out of the launcher and arch towards the target. The spent rocket motor would fall away and the torpedo would continue.

Once it hit the water, slowed by a small parachute, it would ditch the chute, light off its electric motor and go into spiral mode, circling downward to a preset floor and then back up to a preset ceiling, hunting for a contact with its own tiny sonar.

There was also a snake search mode where it would zig zag either side of base course. Snake search was used in the torpedoes fired from the ship mounted tubes, after they completed their initial run out. Once a torpedo acquired, it would home on the target. Bad news for a submarine, especially a conventional one that couldn't try to out run the 40+ knot speed of a MK 46 on final.

Not that a conventional sub could not get away if he was good. Dropping a noisemaker in the water astern might confuse the not so intelligent torpedo and make it home on the noisemaker. A hard turn at full speed might force the torpedo into search mode again if it lost active contact. And the torpedoes were battery powered and had a limited life. When the battery ran out they opened a small port on their side and sank to the bottom.

A destroyer could also launch a small nuclear depth charge. These would be shot out about 6 to 8 miles using ASROC as close to the sub as possible and were instant death for any sub remotely near the detonation point. This was a weapon for use against fast nuclear submarines which could easily out run a Mark 46 at its slower 28 knot search speed. But they required special permission from the President to launch, and never, ever, were.

[xlvii] A snorkel was really just a big air tube that would allow combustion air into the sub's diesel engines. But it had to be raised enough above the sea surface to keep most waves from splashing into it. And the tube had a flapper valve to close if one did. One did not want water getting into the diesels.

When the flapper closed, combustion air had to come out of the boat itself. This would drop air pressure inside the boat significantly making the crew's ears pop. A snorkeling submarine was no place for a man with a chronic sinus condition.

[xlviii] One could not just send a Sturgeon a UHF message. The nukes seldom surfaced. One would send it via the normal navy message system. It would then be re-transmitted, in very low frequency, from one or more of the special sub broadcast stations. The subs would trail a wire and could receive these broadcasts while still submerged.

But very low frequency was slow and messages had to be coded to minimize characters. Many times the low freq message just said pop up to receive a real HF message. Then the sub would come to periscope depth, run up a radio mast, grab their message off another special HF broadcast, and then dive again.

One could also talk to submerged submarines on "Gertrude." This was using the ship's and sub's active sonar at low power and modulating the signal with audio data. Range was short, shorter than regular sonar. And it sounded like the operator was gargling while he was talking. But it was at least a way to communicate at very short range.

[xlix] With the PUEBLO captured, the Navy had a problem. PUEBLO had lots of crypto material aboard. The rule of thumb was that you drew it for 3 months, always keeping at least a 2 months advance supply aboard. So the Navy had to assume that the North Koreans, and undoubtedly their Chinese and Soviet friends, not only had the crypto material but the equipment it ran on.

They were reading our mail, and could go back and read everything they had recorded over the past few days. This was one of the largest security "awh shits" in US Navy history.

After a review at the National Security Agency, who had a record of what PUEBLO had aboard from the Registered Publications System, it was determined that the main Navy broadcast could only carry UNCLASS. Lots of other encrypted communication was also downgraded to UNCLASS. Classified traffic for 7th fleet was shifted to the ASW net and some other nets that PUEBLO did not copy.

Other equipment modifications and special codes were instituted. And all the compromised material was scheduled for replacement – a huge worldwide logistical nightmare. It would be months before things were totally secure again. Some items, like CONFIDENTIAL and even SECRET tactical publications and contingency operations orders would take years to fix.

[i] Although the Soviets had no carriers, they had some serious ships, all bristling with missiles – many of them surface to surface. The Soviets had deployed almost their entire Pacific Fleet. And the US task force was well within easy range of the Soviet naval air arm from Vladivostok running Tupelov TU-20 Bear and Tupelov TU-16 Badger bombers with AS-3 and AS-1 standoff air to surface missiles.

[ii] Once the NVA or VC were aware that an area was subject to NGFS, and if they couldn't find and eliminate the spotters quickly, they tended to depart for safer ground. For the NVA, air strikes were bad news, as were the armed helo runs they called "muttering death." But NGFS was long term bad news since they would be targeted for extended periods instead of a short period, and lots of ordnance would be thrown at them, just like being in range of an artillery fire base.

In dealing with the NVA or VC, there were few wounded to locate. They dragged them off as they melted back into the brush. If they had time they took the dead also. Never let the other side know that they had been hurt.

[iii] A dream sheet was a standard form indicating where one wanted to go for duty assignment. Officially a 'duty preference card' – usually meant nothing. Officer assignments were done by 'Detailers', a duty assignment for other officers to the Bureau of Naval Personnel in Washington. Any shore duty was good but these detailers took a lot of heat from those they were assigned to detail. Since 'needs of the service' took precedence, followed by the Navy's predefined career patterns, an officer's dream sheet was last to be considered.

[iiii] Theoretically, empty shell casings were to be put back in their aluminum canisters or "tanks" and turned back in for refilling. Many went to Davy Jones' locker. Reality was that only about half really got recycled. The AE's were not happy getting empties casings back anyway, although they normally got the empty canisters back. And it was a known fact that the Navy had tons and tons of 5 inch 38 ammo left over from WW II and Korea.

liv Messages were kept in radio in their original, torn off the teletype, format. Messages that needed duplication and distribution to many locations on the ship were mimeographed on to an appropriate color paper. White for Unclassified, green for Confidential, yellow for Secret.

Red was used for Top Secret but destroyers got few of them and the Comm. Officer, or the Supply Officer, who was also qualified to do off line decryption, typed those on red paper or glued the offline decrypt tape on to red paper, and almost never made copies. Every copy of Top Secret and Secret messages had to be accounted for and logged.

Secret were routed by radio's messenger on a special board to the appropriate officers who initialed them after reading. They were then kept either in radio or in combat. Obsolete Confidential, and above, were shredded into brown paper 'burn' bags. When weather and operations conditions allowed they were burned and the burning witnessed by radiomen in a 'burn barrel' stowed back aft and pulled out for the occasion. Sometimes radio was full of these brown burn bags.

All hands had a Confidential Security Clearance. All officers, radiomen, CIC radarmen, most electronic technicians, fire control techs, sonarmen and a few others had Secret. Only the CO, XO, department heads, comm. officer and a limited few others, had Top Secret. Above Top Secret were 'compartmentized' classifications – and destroyers never received anything like this and were not cleared for it.

All but Top Secret messages were kept by general subject on 2 hole clip boards and hung on a rack in secure TTY, the teletype room in the back of radio central. Seventh Fleet Secret Intel summaries were long and many times had to be cut into two or three sheets or were sent as multiple part messages. Top Secret were kept locked up in crypto.

Intel came from a lot of sources. The cardinal rule of intelligence was to never divulge the source, only the 'analyses'.

lv Time was on the North Vietnamese side. And they knew only to well that POWs, and higher causality numbers, played poorly in the USA. Already more protests had started back in America: protests over the draft and protests over the number of troops incountry, protests over any incursion into supposedly neutral Laos or Cambodia – sanctuaries that the NVA and VC hid behind and used to smuggle supplies south.

The NVA had lost the Tet offensive. But they had surprised the world on just how much pressure they could exert. So Washington was increasing troop numbers again. Vietnam was the first of the 'evening news' wars and Americans were watching daily footage at dinner. It made it real, or even more than real, since good news tended to be given little press while bad news got major and graphic coverage.

The only real way to get North Vietnam to sit at the negotiation table and start talking was to bomb them until it started to hurt. Then they would talk – but threaten to stop talking if the bombing did not stop. This meant that the US Navy saw orders for bombing designated targets in North Vietnam come and go, off and on, and then off again, all the time with little understanding of why and why some targets were selected and some were hands off.

lvi For years lots of Hanoi and its sea port of Haiphong, were off limits. Hanoi had embassies from most iron curtain and some third world countries. Trashing their embassies did not enamor you to them. And Soviet ships routinely made port calls in Haiphong. They were one of their major suppliers, trains from China being the other. Bombing and sinking a Soviet merchant ship, especially since their merchant marine was really a part of their navy, didn't make a lot of friends. So the Washington crowd took a dim view of unrestricted bombing.

Finally the Geneva Convention, and any other international agreements signed by any government that was not friendly to the North Vietnamese, were considered irrelevant. They painted Red Crosses on the roof of their ammunition factories. Stored fuel for the NVA in schools and announced the locations of their schools to the world. They established orphanages on the top floor of troop barracks. Put a 55 gallon drum of gasoline in every homeowner's back yard. They paraded sympathetic foreign journalists through bombed stage shows and wounded children's wards. They were good at playing world public opinion.

Ho Chi Minh had been fighting someone since 1931. First there were the British in China, then the French in Indochina, then the Japanese, then the French again, then the South Vietnamese and Americans. By 1968 it had only been 35 years. He was in it for the long term. He didn't live to see victory. He died in September 1969. But his legacy lived on.

lvii This was another of the Navy traditions that went back to the days of sail. The noon reports. Keeping very accurate time was essential for celestial navigation, hence the chronometers. Accurate time was required for star sights and was the only good way for mariners to tell their longitude. Latitude could be told from the sun at local apparent noon without a clock, and longitude guessed at by the time of the sun's apogee. The invention of accurate sea going timepieces was the most important development for navigators since the sextant.

Chronometers were 3, very accurate, mechanical, key wound, clocks kept in wooden boxes in the Chart House: on FRAM destroyers a tiny room just aft of the bridge. They were checked with a radio time tick transmitted worldwide from WWV on high frequency radio, based on Naval observatory master atomic clocks. Each clock's variance in seconds from standard was logged. Then accurate time was available for celestial navigation.

Eight bells was also old. Prior to everyone having a wrist or pocket watch, it was how they told time at sea. On each 4 hour watch bells were struck on the half hour. One for the first, adding one each 30 minutes up to 8 for the last, for 4 hours total. An hour glass was used to time the intervals.

lviii Two block: make the blocks on the line touch, all the way up.

lix PMS stood for the Preventative Maintenance System. All shipboard equipment had preventative maintenance checks that had to be performed every so often to insure that the equipment was working and available for use, if needed. I was a big task, requiring thousands of man hours. This PMS work kept the crew busy every day.

^{lx} Another form of non radio communication was by directional flashing light. This was used a lot since any enemy or AGI could tune their receivers to the proper radio frequency and hear what was going on. At night, flashing light could be done using infra red so it did not light up the world. There were infrared lights on the ends of the small yard arm on the mast. This was called 'Nancy.'

In the day time, a directional flashing light could be seen and copied 3 or 4 miles away. If you were not on or near the same bearing, you couldn't see it. When a signalman on watch received a signal, either by flag hoist or flashing light they would notify the Bridge and Combat. If it was a formal naval message, the signalmen would route it on a board like radio did, and then give it to radio for the message log.

^{lxi} PCO = Prospective Commanding Officer's course. Required of all officers ordered to command at sea. Officers had to screen for command – be selected by a Washington selection board. Today it is PCO/XO, and Executive officers have to attend also. Then they can fleet up (move up) to CO without attending again. Command at sea was as close to being an emperor as was possible in the USA. Ship's COs had almost unlimited power over their crews and total responsibility for them and their ship.

^{lxii} In the Navy in 1968, the first flag rank was Rear Admiral lower half, two stars, then Rear Admiral upper half, still two stars. Both wore one broad and one regular gold band around their sleeves. In the Army, Marines, and Air Force the first flag rank was one star: Brigadier General. This was sold as essential since the official Navy one star rank was Commodore and only activated in a declared war for convoy commanders. It really pissed the other services off. One sure couldn't tell an upper half from a lower by his rank insignia. Today this has been fixed and RADM (LH) wears one star and one broad sleeve stripe.

1968 Flag ranks in the Navy corresponding to other services were:

Sleeve	Navy & C. Guard	Marines, Army, Airforce
II	(Commodore) Rear Admiral (LH) **	Brigadier General *
II	Rear Admiral (UH) **	Major General **
III	Vice Admiral ***	LieutenantGeneral ***
IIII	Admiral ****	General ****
IIIII	Fleet Admiral *****	General of the Army *****

(Five stars were only activated in WW II to make top US flag officers equivalent rank to allied Field Marshals).

^{lxiii}Mast (the name came from the sailing ship days where the Captain doled out discipline before the main mast of the ship) was non judicial punishment. Offenders were brought before the Captain and their case heard. There was no trial or defense counsel. Although the punishments the Captain could impose

were relatively small, they were sufficient to make an offender think twice the next time.

[lxiv] The Navy provided for two movies each day on ships, both shown at 2000. One was shown in the wardroom and one in the crew's mess. The movies were generally old, and in 16 millimeter format on three reels. Many were black and white. Ships would get up to 30 movies in large green boxes with black straps. Called sea prints.

Then a ship could swap movies with other ships by high line, helo, etc. In Subic, there was a movie exchange that had hundreds of movies. After six months in the war zone, most ships had seen most movies more than once and some many times. To make up for the fact that Hollywood had not made enough to go around, some movies were really old TV shows, two per movie, without commercials. Like Gunsmoke, the Rifleman, etc.

Movies with partial nudity or steamy sections were the favorites. On some ships, some enterprising enlisted would cut these scenes and then splice them together for a stag film – to be shown in secure locations. The original movie was missing the scene. One did not want to get caught doing this. Punishments were severe. When a movie that promised skin jumped around the missing skin scene, there was major disappointment and grumbling from officers and crew alike.

[lxv] Strike target selection, timing, and intensity were micromanaged in DC, not in theater like they should have been. So it took days to formulate target plans as messages flew between the Far East and the pentagon. Targeting was not very dynamic.

[lxvi] Bomb Damage Assessment. After each strike, air recon tried to evaluate the effectiveness. But in well defended areas BDA was hit or miss. Air recon couldn't get in close enough for the photos to be clear enough for detailed assessments. And there were no fancy high resolution spy satellites.

[lxvii] Leave was not to be confused with liberty which was authorized time off the ship of 72 hours or less, usually only 48 maximum. And the distance one could go when on liberty was restricted to a relatively short distance from the ship and men on liberty were subject to recall. Leave was like vacation. Everyone accrued 30 days leave a year at the rate of 2 ½ days per month. But leave included weekends and holidays, counted day for day. And leave could not be combined with liberty.